If you'd like to keep track of the
titles you've read,
please don't mark up our books
– mark this paper instead.

THE HIGH DIVIDE

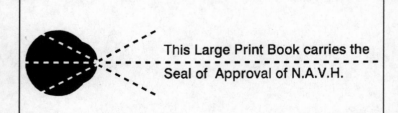
This Large Print Book carries the
Seal of Approval of N.A.V.H.

THE HIGH DIVIDE

LIN ENGER

THORNDIKE PRESS
A part of Gale, Cengage Learning

GALE
CENGAGE Learning®

Farmington Hills, Mich • San Francisco • New York • Waterville, Maine
Meriden, Conn • Mason, Ohio • Chicago

GALE
CENGAGE Learning·

LIBRARY OF CONGRESS CATALOGING-IN-PUBLICATION DATA

Enger, Lin.
  The high divide / Lin Enger. — Large print edition.
    pages cm. — (Thorndike Press large print historical fiction)
  ISBN 978-1-4104-7488-9 (hardback) — ISBN 1-4104-7488-7 (hardcover)
  1. Large type books. I. Title.
  PS3555.N4224H54 2014b
  813'.6—dc23   2014034295

Published in 2014 by arrangement with Algonquin Books of Chapel Hill, a division of Workman Publishing Co., Inc.

Printed in Mexico
1 2 3 4 5 6 7 18 17 16 15 14

— *for Gus*

DOMINION of

MONTANA
TERRITORY

Missouri River

Missouri River

THE HIGH DIVIDE

Yellowstone River

BAD LANDS

BISMARCK

DICKINSON

Yellowstone River

MILES CITY

Tongue River

CROW
RESERVATION

NORTHERN
CHEYENNE
RES.

Little Big Horn R.

Missouri River

DAKOTA

CIRCA 1886,
showing the routes of the POPE FAMILY's
travels, taken in that year by way of the
NORTHERN PACIFIC LINE,
and likewise the
Expedition Route of the autumn
HORNADAY BISON HUNT,
carried out on behalf of the
SMITHSONIAN INSTITUTION,
Washington, D.C.

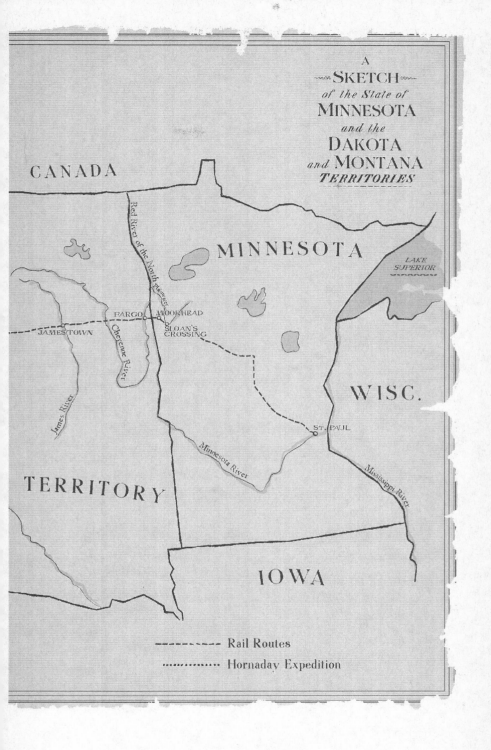

WALKING OFF

That summer was cool and windless, the clouds unrelenting, as if God had reached out his hand one day and nudged the sun from its rightful place.

Way out on the lip of the northern plains the small town lay hidden in fog, the few moving about at this hour ghostlike, not quite solid: the shopkeepers, the man driving his water-wagon, the dressmaker with her quick, smooth strides. In a clapboard house a stone's throw from the river, a lean, square-shouldered man knelt before an old flattop trunk. He closed the lid, locked it, then stood and moved across the room and set the key on top of a window casing. On his way through the kitchen he stopped and looked to his right, at the door closed to him, then turned left instead and climbed a ladder that led to a sleeping loft.

"Anybody awake up here?" he asked.

"Yup." His son's voice was high, a couple

years short of changing. He still gave off that clean child-smell, like carrots pulled from the garden.

"I'm taking old Rufus to the chicken man today, then helping put up a brooder house there. You got a squeeze for me?"

The boy rose from his straw tick, came over sleepily, and put his head on his father's chest, wrapped his arms around him. "Are you and Mom still mad?" he asked.

"No, we're fine."

"I want to go along."

The man shook his head and pulled away. He brushed his son's soft cheek with a finger before moving back down the ladder. In the kitchen he made straight for the back porch, where he grabbed the leg hook and walked with it toward the cowshed, unaware as the hens scattered before him that his wife had emerged from the bedroom and stood watching through the kitchen window as he shooed off the new rooster, then flung out an arm and hooked the old one, a rusty-feathered stud cock, by a gristly leg. She watched him tuck the bird beneath an elbow and cup one hand on its head to keep its beak in check. The shirt he wore, which she'd sewn from a set of old drapes, hung too loosely on his shoulders, and she had a mind to call him back, make him sit down and eat some eggs and fried potatoes, some side-pork, before he left. But then he turned, sharp-boned face heaving into view, and she ducked back into the bedroom and closed herself in again.

Outside in the cowshed he found the wooden hoop cage, shoved the old rooster inside of it, and threw the latch. Ten feet away his older boy sat leaning into the dusty flank of their big Guernsey, strong fists pumping, streams of milk hissing into the pail, barely glancing at his father, who spoke the boy's name — "Eli," he said — and lifted a hand for him to stop.

"What?" The boy only half turned. He'd gotten so tall that his knees angled sharply up from the stool. The first shadow of coming whiskers darkened his lip and chin. Eli was barely sixteen.

"You might want to fix the fence, down by that corner where it keeps giving way. We don't want her getting out again."

"Why don't you fix it? You're the carpenter."

In the yard the hens bickered and flapped, provoking from the caged rooster a strangled crowing.

"Take the bucksaw and cut down one of those five-inch aspens down by the river.

That'll give you good posts." He reached out to squeeze his son's shoulder, which felt hard and grown up and very tight, then turned and picked up the cage and walked across the yard, pausing at the edge of it to look back before moving off into a fog so heavy it washed away the ground beneath him, the trees above him, and the houses on either side, even as he remained somehow visible to his son, who had risen from the stool and stood now at the door of the shed, watching him go.

I
PURSUIT

1
His Father's Son

Six weeks later there had been no word at all. Nothing. No reassuring telegraph from St. Paul or Minneapolis, or some other city, saying, THINGS ARE WELL, DON'T WORRY. No letter describing the work he'd found and promising money to follow. The note he'd left was cryptic, cruelly brief: "A chance for work, hard cash" was all it said, and Eli had managed to convince himself that was a reasonable explanation, a fair accounting. His anger had dissolved. He'd decided the loan his father took against their house, which caused such a stir between his parents, must have been necessary, and would not bring himself even to consider that his father might be gone for good — never mind how people talked and despite the fears his mother couldn't hide. After all, who could say what kinds of trials and odd contingencies might come against a traveling man?

When Eli was small he'd often day-
dreamed his father's life, imagining the
childhood spent on a farm at the edge of
St. Paul or the moment in the war that cost
him his ear — a Rebel cannonball, Eli
fancied, or a bayonet. This labor of invention was necessary, since Ulysses never
spoke of such things himself. But now with
his father not merely distant but gone, Eli
had been making up stories again. He could
see him standing at the wheel of a Mississippi riverboat or perched on scaffolding
high above the city, trowel in hand as a
building rose brick by brick into the sky. Or
loading a freight car, sacks of potatoes
riding both shoulders. Other times, though,
at first light or late at night under the stars,
no image whatsoever came to mind — only
the sound of his father's voice, audible, close
by:

I could use your help.

On a September afternoon in the back
room of the mercantile, Eli removed his
cowhide apron, hung it on the peg behind
the door, and poked his head back inside to
make certain the old man was still occupied
at the counter, which he was, face bent close
to the ledger and squinting through the gray
thicket of his eyebrows. Eli withdrew and
pulled the door closed, though not all the

16

way. From the front pocket of his trousers he took out the envelope he'd intercepted from the fill-in postman. It was of good stock, ivory-colored, and still sealed. He flattened it against one palm and examined the looping, graceful script that spelled out the name of his father, Ulysses Pope, and beneath it his address — *their* address — Sloan's Crossing, Minnesota. He lifted the envelope and smelled French perfume of the sort Goldman bought from the wholesaler and sold to the local men for their wives. Eli's hands shook. His mouth was dry. It smelled like flowers — but like something else, too, that reminded him of his mother's baths on Saturday nights.

When his boss called out for him, Eli flinched and dropped the envelope, then scrambled under the packing table to pluck it up. Back on his feet, he jammed it into the pocket of his trousers and poked his head into the store.

"Yes, Mr. Goldman."

"Aren't you walking Danny home?"

"Just going."

"Stop in at Russell's on your way back, tell him those hinges haven't come in yet."

Outside, Eli had to grab his hat to keep it from blowing off his head. With the letter crinkling against his thigh, he passed the

17

barber shop, Merchants National Bank, Ben's Tailor Shop, and of course the rooming house where Mead Fogarty no doubt stood watching through his leaded-glass window, thumbs notched around his wide suspenders. In the grassy lot beside the schoolhouse Miss Waterson gripped her dress in a knot against the wind and offered a parsimonious smile to the circle of boys surrounding her. Eli climbed the stairs but stopped when he heard from inside a croaking, familiar voice:

"You're shittin' me, Danny. Know what I think? I think you ain't heard a word from your old man. Not a word."

Eli moved light-footed into the cloakroom, slid along the inside wall, and drew up just short of the doorway to the classroom. His little brother had always been frail, but recently the headaches had started coming so often that last week when school started their mother insisted to Mr. Goldman that Eli be allowed to leave work each day long enough to pick up Danny from school and walk him home.

"And he ain't coming back," the boy continued, "because he found some other woman. A better-lookin' one. And everybody knows it."

No response from Danny — but the slosh

of water meant that he'd pulled chalkboard duty again. Eli drew himself up to full height and stepped around the corner where he found himself eye-to-knobby-throat with the only sixteen-year-old boy in town still attending school: Herman Stroud, son of the banker. At the end of the chalkboard, dripping rag in hand, Danny stood hunched and still in his bib overalls, large bug-eyes staring up at Eli with a bald need.

My brother, Eli thought.

The tall boy took a step back. "I was only joshin' around," he said. "Right, Danny?"

Eli's hands ached at the prospect of making Herman Stroud feel more pain than he'd ever imagined in his velvet life.

"No harm meant," Herman said. "You know me." Standing there in his cream-colored shirt with red piping around the collar and cuffs, he tried to smile.

Since July when their father left, Eli had been in three fights, each time as payback for what some foolish, mean, or stupid kid had said to his brother. Herman, of course, couldn't know that Eli's violence in each case had been calculated, that he'd never knocked out anybody's teeth or kicked anybody's glands without thinking to himself, *Do I want to do this?* and then deciding, *Yes I do.* He couldn't know, either, that

Eli had promised his mother he was done with fighting.

"How come Danny's doing the work and you're only watching?" Eli asked him.

"Teacher told *him* to do it. Not me."

Danny was moving inside his clothes now, as if he had an unscratchable itch, the first sign of a headache coming on.

"Is that how it is?" Eli asked his brother, and when Danny shook his head, Eli turned to Herman. "Take your shirt off," he said. "You'll need it to wipe the board."

"There's another rag in the bucket," Herman said, and bent down for it — but Eli laid a hand on his shoulder and straightened him back up. He put his face two inches from the taller boy's neck where a patch of skin, like a handprint, was turning bright pink, fingers snaking down toward his chest. When Eli reached for Herman's collar to tear it away, the boy jerked backward, knocking his head against the slate behind him. "All right, all right," he said, and started on the buttons.

Danny stood with his forehead bunched in a hard frown, wet rag still dangling from his fingers and dripping water on the floor as Herman finished the buttons and then paused, his shirt hanging open, his belly as white and glossy as well-kneaded dough.

"Get at it," Eli told him.

The boy shrugged off the shirt, balled it up, and plunged it down into the bucket. The chalkboard was filled with neat rows of long division, and Herman, starting at the top, made a long, wet swipe. Eli took his brother by the hand and led him out of the school and down the street toward home, the dusty wind cool in their faces, Danny's feet dragging, his steps slow and arrhythmic.

"How does your head feel?" Eli asked him.

"I want Mother."

"Here, you better hop on." He crouched in the dirt so that Danny could climb up on his back, and then he carried him that way, Danny resting a hot cheek against the back of his neck, Eli gripping his brother's legs, which felt as skinny and light as candlesticks.

The headaches came hand in hand with strange dreams — of talking beasts and far-off lands, or sometimes, of things to come. A week before the flood of eighty-four, Danny had dreamed it, right down to the family of mud hens swimming in and out through the front window and the long-tailed rat perched on the brass lamp their father had ordered from Chicago. If their mother got to him early enough, before the real pain came on, she could often save him from the worst of it — by singing, stroking his face, applying to his forehead a poultice she'd learned from her grandmother in Copenhagen who'd used it on her husband, himself a headache sufferer. Other times there was nothing to do but let him lie there in bed, elbows gripping his ears, and wait for the pain to work its way through him, a day or two in most cases, sometimes three.

At home their mother was hanging the wash, her face suspended like a dull moon above the flapping clothes and sheets. Her eyes quickened with fear and she ducked beneath the line and rushed forward, saying, "Give him to me." Eli turned and leaned backward, allowing Danny — all legs and skinny arms — to wrap himself around his mother, who pumped her knees to get a better hold and headed for the house, humming in Danny's ear, his face wobbling on her shoulder as they went.

In the kitchen Eli peeled and grated three large potatoes into a bowl, added a palmful of mustard seeds, a heavy pinch of dried dandelion, a tablespoon of ground pepper, and just enough water and flour to make a sticky ball. His hands worked on their own, his mind given over to the letter in his pocket, the sweet smell it carried, and the new fears he had now because of it. He was lucky it arrived today, though — he knew that. The regular postman, Smith, was down with a fever, and a man from Moorhead had come out to handle the mail. Smith, of course, would have noted the feminine hand on the envelope and made sure to deliver it in person to their house.

By the time Eli started back to the store, Danny had been tucked into bed, their mother's, and all the shades had been drawn. The poultice covered his forehead and eyes. Eli took the long way back, stopping to climb the half-dead cottonwood that leaned out over the river, its wide trunk offering a saddlelike seat that Eli leaned back against, trying to calm himself. His heart was beating inside his ears and pulsing in his neck. His hands were weak. He forced himself to take long breaths, and when his heart slowed, he took out his jackknife and sliced open the envelope, careful not to damage the letter inside, which was written in the same hand, though the ink was a different color, not black but a shade of purple that made Eli think of the veins on the tender side of a woman's wrist. In the upper left-hand-corner was the return address — 1020 5th Avenue North, Bismarck, Dakota — and in the upper right, the date:

September 10th, 1886.

Dear Ulysses,
   I trust this letter finds you healthy and
rested from what must have been a difficult journey. It would have meant so
very much to Jim that you came, and for
me your visit, I hope you know, was a
burst of sun in a long gray season. I've
been fine and busy since you left . . .

Eli scanned down the page, registering her
mention of a garden — ripening pumpkins
and late tomatoes — house painters, a new
pastor at church, pleasant weather. Then,
toward the bottom of the page, her words
caught him up again:

   Although I wouldn't wish upon you or
anyone else the loneliness I know, at
least I can say now that my heart is
capable of human feeling again. Thank
you. And if future travels bring you this
way, you would be more than welcome.
But you know as much already.
                                    Yours,
                              Laura Powers

For half a minute the interior of Eli's skull
was sparkly and white, like his mother's

kitchen on baking days when the air was full of flour, the sun pouring in through the window. Then his head cleared. Above the river a mallard set its wings, tilted in a fast drop to the water, and skated into the calm pool inside the river's bend. Eli's stomach twisted inside him. His parents had always been happy together, hadn't they — except for that fight over the promissory note? Hadn't they made a habit of taking walks in the evening, holding hands? Hadn't he spied them kissing sometimes, early mornings down by the outhouse, or after dark beneath the drooping branches of the old birch? Or was that long ago now? He thought about last winter, not even a year past, when his father managed to offend the entire congregation of Our Savior's and, soon after lose most of his carpentry jobs, notably the schoolhouse contract. He remembered, too, watching his father pummel a man at the train depot and lose that job also — justified though he had been. All of this leading to their money problems, and finally his leaving. Something had happened with his father, that was certain, something Eli didn't understand. Yet he was just as certain — or at least determined to be — that one day everything would be set straight.

But who was this Laura Powers from

Bismarck, and how had his father come to know her? Why would he go and visit her? What did she have to do with anything related to their family? And what did that mean: *a burst of sun in a long gray season*?

Eli supposed the right thing to do was to take the letter home and show it to his mother, yet he dismissed the notion out of hand, because he knew this about women, or thought he did — that jealousy could make them incautious and at times irrational. If he showed her the letter, she'd likely decide that Ulysses was lost to her and give up on him, and then, when he *did* come home, confront him in a way that would drive him off for good.

In the first days of his father's absence, Eli had decided he was obliged, on behalf of his mother, to go off and find him. Each week he'd put aside from his wages a dollar and a half and had hidden it in the loft where he and Danny slept, behind a loose board in the wall. The money was still there, more of it now. He checked on it every day, counted it to make sure his brother hadn't stumbled across it. He'd also squirreled away a loaf of his mother's bread and half a dozen eggs that he boiled up one day while she weeded the garden. Then late one night in the middle of August — it was the same

26

night the summer's long pattern of windless days and thick fogs finally broke — he'd stolen outside and sneaked through town to the depot, where he waited behind the water tank for the eastbound night freight. Partly it was the weather — rain, lightning, a terrific wind — and partly the fear of leaving his mother and brother behind, but mostly it was the image of himself in a rattling boxcar, alone and hurtling east toward St. Paul, a city he'd never visited, that made him turn around and walk back home in the driving rain. There was no evidence, after all, beyond his mother's hunch, that St. Paul was the place to start looking. In fact next time he'd be heading west when he left, not east, his destination certain — at least the first leg of it would be — and nothing was going to stop him.

2
GREEN TURTLE

Tonight, a similar night with rain and wind, Gretta lay in bed remembering her first time with Ulysses, their wedding night, and the fine-linked brass chain he'd worn around his neck, and how it dangled above her as they made love, and how the small green tin turtle, strung like a pendant on that chain, dipped to touch her breastbone again and again, a cool, light tapping she would come to know so well. The chain had been his grandmother's, he explained, telling her this so seriously, and the tin tag, no larger than a dime, a plug-marker from the brand of tobacco he favored during his service years. Gretta remembered, too, the day before he left, in July — more than six weeks ago — and the bitter argument they had in front of the boys, something they'd never done before, and the way she shouted in his face, saying things she didn't mean. And then that night, turning him out of their bed, angry.

She still couldn't understand him, though. It was one thing to sign a note that put their home at risk, making an arrangement with Mead Fogarty of all people, and then keeping that loan a secret for months, but something else again to leave as he had without warning or explanation, and allowing her with every day that passed to wonder where he'd gone and whether he meant to come back, or whether he was even alive — although she believed he was, she could feel it, just as she believed he still loved her. There was some relief in allowing herself to picture him coming through the door some afternoon, just walking in and laying out on the kitchen table the cash he'd earned, then wrapping his long arms around her and pulling her close. But she tried to keep from doing that, it was too dangerous. Time and again, she told herself that his leaving had to do with their money problems — because there were things harder to fix than money.

At dusk this evening a storm had moved in, a sudden hard blow followed by an unholy rain, and now the streets were all mud, the town littered with yellow leaves and tree limbs. She was listening to Danny's uneven breathing and wishing for sleep herself when she heard the rapping at the

29

door. She eased closer to her son, curled like an infant beside her, and prayed whoever it was would go away.

The knocking came again, louder. *Where's Eli?* she thought. *Why doesn't he go answer it?*

She started sliding toward the edge of the bed, then heard her son's feet on the ladder, descending. He landed easy, a soft thud, and then moved quickly to the front door, which gave a shriek on its hinges. Gathering her flannel nightdress close around her neck, Gretta heard the male voice, pitched a few notes higher than Eli's, its tone abrupt and self-assured. *Fogarty, damn him.* She knew what he wanted, and in fact had gone out of her way to avoid him since the first of the month. Yesterday when he'd come by with his laundry, she'd hidden in the small dirt cellar beneath the trapdoor in the kitchen, holding her breath as he traipsed all through the house, finally leaving his bag of soiled clothes on the kitchen table, of all places.

Her bedroom door cracked open, and Eli spoke without coming in, his voice controlled as it nearly always was now, a man's voice. "It's him," Eli said. "I told him you were sleeping."

She bent to put on her deerskin slippers,

then lifted her robe from the hook on the wall. Behind her Danny groaned and curled up tighter.

Eli had lit the oil lamp, and within its circle of light Mead Fogarty stood just inside the house, squinting through his thick, rain-spotted glasses. He was a short, wide man — wide face, wide red nose, wide chest and hips, widely spaced eyes. Gretta thought of him as measuring his life according to what he could gather: food, money, property, the good graces of the towns-people — all of which he possessed in abundance. He wasn't lucky, though. A year ago his tiny, barren wife had died of pneumonia, and since then he'd neglected himself, going about unshaven and carrying a smell so strong that Gretta wondered if he'd given up entirely on bathing. When she started doing his laundry, as partial payment of their rent, she'd expected an improvement in his smell at least, but it hadn't seemed to make a difference.

"May I?" Fogarty asked, looking past her toward the kitchen. He offered a mechanical smile, revealing a set of stained teeth.

Eli, standing apart, pointed down at the man's wide-toed boots, encased in mud from the street.

"It is a mess out there, isn't it," Fogarty

31

said. "Might freeze too."

"It's late," Gretta said.

"For which I apologize, Mrs. Pope. But you've been difficult to find, and I do have a subject to broach with you." He turned to Eli and regarded him coolly over the tops of his misty lenses.

With a pang in her chest, Gretta turned. "You can let us talk now, Eli."

Her son regarded her a moment too long and then left. Fogarty shoved a plump hand into the front pocket of his trousers, moved it about down there, brought out a piece of rock candy and held it up to the light with his thumb and forefinger. Popped it in his mouth. A sharp lemon scent cut through the reek of his breath, and he sucked and clicked on the candy with relish. When he took a step forward, Gretta found herself backing up.

"Your boots," she managed to say, putting up the flat of her hand.

"Ah, forgive me." He bent over, grunting, to remove them.

"No, no, here," she said, and guided him back to the hemp mat by the door. "Danny's sick and I don't want to wake him. Please, I just need a few more days."

Fogarty cracked down on his lemon candy, shattering it with a violence that sent a spike

32

of pain through Gretta's stomach. "Mrs. Pope, believe me when I say it's not the rent that concerns me. You need to consider your future, not to mention the well-being of your two boys."

"He'll be home soon," Gretta said. "By the end of the month."

Fogerty shook his head. "I spoke with Smith a couple days back, and he's seen no letter from your husband. And Percy tells the same story." Percy was the telegraph man.

"I know where my husband is, Mr. Fogarty," Gretta said. "I know where he is and what he's doing, and you can be sure that when he returns you'll have every penny you're owed, with interest. According to agreement."

Fogarty touched a stubby finger to his chin. His eyes — magnified by the glasses — widened, then narrowed to slits. "I admire you, Mrs. Pope. Loyalty is a solid quality in a woman. Understand, though, I'm a man of business, and I'm better than you are at seeing the world for what it is."

"You don't know him," she said.

He shrugged. "I know there's nothing left for him in *this* town. His bridges, you might say, have burned to ash and scattered to the winds. Don't be naïve." He propped an elbow on a bookshelf against the wall and stared at her.

She couldn't help thinking of the day last spring when Ulysses, all by himself, had spoken up in favor of Mary Bond's request to bury one of her girls in the churchyard. It was humiliating enough for Gretta that her husband would take up publicly for that woman — but then, right there in the sanctuary, Ulysses raised his arm and pointed at the pastor, at the banker Stroud, at the mayor and several of the town's prominent businessmen, most of them sitting with their wives. He said, "If those girls of Mary's haven't done you boys any harm lying next to you in bed, I don't see the danger in letting one of them lie out there under our grass."

Fogarty filled his lungs and exhaled dramatically, as if for her sake he was going far beyond his obligations. "I have a proposal to make," he said, "one you would be wise to consider. There are currently fourteen men in my establishment renting by the month, and I'm in need of a cook and housekeeper. If you come to work for me, you will have rooms of your own, you and your boys, at no charge to you, and free board as well, in exchange for cleaning and cooking. I can arrange also for a small salary."

Gretta tried to read his face, the curl of his heavy lips, the pricks of light sparking from his eyes. *Does he pity me? Is he pleased with himself?* She couldn't help but wonder whether any woman had ever loved him, whether his dead wife ever looked at him and felt what she herself felt now, the pressure at the back of her throat as the taste of her last meal — pork hocks and boiled cabbage — rose into her mouth.

From her bedroom came the small sound of Danny crying out from his dreams.

"Eli," she called, "please check on your brother."

"Aside from my churchgoing, I'm not partial to religion," Fogarty said, "and no doubt at times I've advanced my own case at the expense of other men. But your husband — my God, what he's done to you makes my sins look like virtues."

He turned in his muddy boots toward the door, and when he opened it a bitter draft rushed in and parted Gretta's robe, exposing her knees to the air and also to Fogarty, who glanced backward, as if sensing an opportunity. She snapped the robe back in place. He made his exit at once, leaving the door open behind him so that she had to shut it herself, heaving with her shoulder until it latched against the wind.

In the kitchen she heated water for tea and sat down with her grandmother's blue teapot in front of her, hands wrapped around a small cup for warmth, her feet and legs folded beneath her on the ladder-back chair. She hadn't worked up the courage to look inside her husband's locked trunk until the day after he left, after going to see the chicken farmer, Bulwick, who told her Ulysses had been there indeed and put up a brooder house as promised — "See for yourself," he'd said, pointing. Ulysses had left the rusty-feathered rooster, too, for which Bulwick claimed to have paid him two bits, a generous sum, considering the bird's age and disposition. "And here's a dollar for your husband's labor," he added, producing a silver coin for Gretta. "He told me you'd be around for it." The man could tell her nothing else of any use. Ulysses had finished his work at sundown then walked off, apparently toward home.

When Gretta had finally searched the trunk — its key resting in the usual spot — she'd found their savings intact, all twelve dollars. The only items missing had been his mouth harp and the beaded tobacco pouch. His other treasures — canteen, compass, beaver hat, things mostly from his years in the service — all were still there. She'd also found in the flattop trunk his brief farewell note, such as it was.

Although her husband's leaving was something Gretta had not anticipated, his behavior had grown strange over the past year, ever since his river baptism by an itinerant preacher whom Gretta did not care for. She'd noticed in Ulysses a growing distractedness, his eyes often roaming the distance. Also an almost volatile impatience with people's weaknesses, and a tendency to judge them according to his newfound piety. Was he trying to make up for his own sins? Had he been a visitor himself at Mary Bond's house north of town? Gretta didn't think so. But he had stopped playing whist on Saturday evenings, and stopped visiting the Old Vine Tavern with his friends, and he'd taken to sitting alone in the kitchen, late into the night, reading his Bible and muttering, his head in his hands. As for the tobacco pouch, the fact that he'd taken it with him worried her, object of beauty that it was — a piece of woman's work, clearly. When she'd asked him about it years before, the explanation he'd given was too simple: a gift from a fellow soldier, an Indian from northern Minnesota, and she'd always believed there must be more to the story.

She lifted the teapot and poured hot water, set it back down. Gretta had been twelve when she bought it for her mother in a shop down by the canal, eighteen when she left Denmark and begged her mother to let her take it with her. For years after, the little blue pot provided comfort, a bit of home and childhood. Now as she drank the tea it reminded her of how alone she was. She finished the cup, got up and checked once more on Danny, whose breathing was steady, then moved across the floor to the ladder that rose to the sleeping loft, climbing until her face was on a level with Eli's. It was too dark to see, but she could smell the down in his pillow, which she had sewn and filled after the hunt on Silver Lake when Ulysses and the boys had come back with fifty-six fat mallards in the back of the wagon.

"Are you sleeping?" she asked.

He didn't answer, but the way he exhaled through his nose told her that he was awake.

"Are you?" she repeated.

"You can't do it, Mother. We can't live there. When Dad comes back, what are we going to tell him?"

"So you think he's coming back," she said. "Don't you?"

"I'm not sure. Well, yes."

"Why do you say it that way? What do you mean?"

"A person gets tired, I suppose."

"You cannot be considering moving us there," Eli said.

"I have to look out for us, can't you see? For Danny, more than for you. I have to make certain he is safe."

"He's safe *here.*"

"Mr. Fogarty owns this house, more or less, you know that. He holds the deed now. If we don't pay him what we owe, he has every right to move us out."

"Dad left money behind," Eli said, and the edge in his voice cut her deeply. "Where's that?"

"It takes money to pay the doctor, Eli. It takes money to buy flour and sugar, to buy pencils and paper for school. Everything takes money, don't you see? And God knows there was not much to begin with."

"How much is there? Fogarty needs fifteen dollars, doesn't he? Or twelve, since you're washing his filthy clothes."

"I have seven dollars," Gretta said, regretting the sweets she'd bought for Danny last week and the cotton for sewing a new slip, which she'd needed badly. *We have to live, don't we?* she thought. She was already

39

cleaning at the Star Hotel, Fogarty's competition, and taking in sewing from the dress shop, trying to do right by her sons. Working herself to dust. What more could she do? "And I'll have two dollars more tomorrow," she said. "Which makes nine."

"What if *I* had three dollars for you?" Eli asked.

"You don't. Or if you do, I will be angry."

The agreement, when he'd gone to work for Goldman, was for him to bring home the two dollars he made each week and put it in the family pot. When he needed money for himself, he'd asked his mother for it.

"I've done some extra jobs for him lately — deliveries. That's why I've been late sometimes. Tomorrow's payday, and I should be getting it. Then we'll have Fogarty's money for him. We cannot go over there, Mother."

Gretta reached out in the dark and found her son's face and placed the palm of her hand on his cheek. For days she'd been haunted by a fear she couldn't hold on to any longer. "Promise me something," she said.

Eli pulled away from her.

"Please," she said. "That you won't go off looking for him. That you'll stay here and help me. I need you here, and so does your

40

brother." She reached out for his face again, but it wasn't there.

"Elijah? Do you hear me? Your brother needs you too."

When her son spoke next, it was in a hoarse whisper from a point farther away in the darkness, saying words she had no choice but to settle for: "I'll do what I can to help," he said, "I promise you that."

3
NORTHERN PACIFIC

The rifle was a Spencer carbine, .50-caliber, an old army issue his father brought home from the war. It was kept in the mud room off the kitchen, tucked behind the winter coats in a tall chifforobe, and the next day after work while his mother and Danny helped their neighbor dress some geese, he brought it over to the shop off Railroad Street where Two Blood bought, sold, and fixed guns, but mostly fixed them.

"He wouldn't mind you selling this?"

Two Blood's eyes were the color of a sky in winter, a shocking light blue against his dark skin, and they had a way of making Eli wonder if the old man could read minds. His face and movements were smooth and young, but his fingers curled like tree roots. He wore his yellow-white hair in two braids to his shoulders. Ulysses had often come here to sit and smoke with him, and during the past weeks Eli and Danny had found themselves stopping in to look at the old man's guns and his stuffed buffalo head, and to drink the cool milk he drew from a cistern beneath the floorboards. He was the only person in town whose questions about their father didn't sound like accusations or gossip.

"Do you want it?" Eli asked him.

Two Blood lifted and dropped his skinny shoulders. "Does your mother know you're here?"

Eli handed him the rifle. "Have a look."

The old man took a rag and ran it up and down along the barrel, put it to his shoulder and drew a bead through the window. He lowered it and tested the action, pulling back the large hammer until it caught and clicked, then releasing it with a squeeze of the trigger, his thumb easing the hammer forward. His hands roved, fingers touching every joint and nick. He patted the scarred stock. Eli walked down along the counter and peered into a felt-lined box of revolvers, most of them well worn, their wooden grips stained and scratched, barrels shiny from use. He picked up the one he'd kept an eye on, a .32-caliber Smoot's with a bone grip, small enough to fit in the pocket of his coat, and he pictured himself on a dusty street, coat flapping in the wind, one hand hovering close to where the Smoot's lay hidden, the men of the town stepping clear to give him a wide berth. Until now, going off to find his father had seemed like an obligation, but he was aware at this moment of how badly he wanted to leave this town behind, along with the crushing weight of his mother's fear and the burden of his brother's ill health.

"Will this be a trade?" Two Blood asked.

"That depends."

"Ah, Goldman hasn't wasted his time on you." Two Blood sighed and let his head fall to one side. He leaned the rifle against the counter, removed a tablet and piece of lead pencil from a drawer, and started to figure, pausing to scratch the side of his face with the tip of the lead.

"The Smoot's and three dollars for the Spencer," he said. "People want the newer repeaters, you know. Not these old models." He smiled.

"Four dollars," Eli said, "and a box of shells."

"Done."

They shook hands, Eli mustering the strength to meet the old man's grip, but Two Blood didn't let go. "Are things well in your house?" he asked.

Eli nodded.

"All right, then," Two Blood said, still not letting go, still squeezing. "All right then."

At supper, when Eli reached into his pocket and brought out three silver dollars and pushed them across the table toward his mother, he expected questions but they didn't come. She looked at him, her eyes searching his, slid the heavy coins off the edge of the table into her hand, then got up and dropped them into the coffee can on the shelf above the cook stove.

Deep in the night, Eli's bladder woke him. He'd planned it this way, forcing himself to drink four glasses of water before going to bed, and now he lay still in the dark, listening, hoping his brother was asleep. Danny had come through his recent struggle unscathed, the pain passing over him, and tonight he was breathing easy and slow. Eli rose fully dressed from his straw-filled tick and put on his blanket-lined coat, which he'd tucked last night beneath the covers. Quietly he rolled up the quilt his grandmother had made for him and which he'd slept beneath for as long as he could remember. He tied it up with a shoelace. He crept to the wall and from the space behind the loose board removed the letter, the Smoot's, and four dollars — one left over from his trade with Two Blood and three from his

45

wages at the store.

Downstairs in the kitchen he held his pocket watch up to the window. Three-fifteen, plenty of time. The Northern Pacific eastbound, with both freight and passenger cars, stopped for water at four-thirty.

As he crossed through the kitchen to the back door, avoiding the planks that moaned, his mother called out from her bedroom: "What is it, Eli?"

Damn it. He set down his bedroll.

She was lying on her side, up on one elbow, her face pale in the starlight filtering through her curtained window. "Where do you think you're going?" she asked.

"I didn't want to wake you. Fargo, remember? A shipment of rugs came in from New York," he said. "Mr. Goldman wants to pick them over before, you know, everybody else gets there. We're leaving at four."

"Who has the rugs?"

"Michaelson."

"You didn't tell me."

"Yes, I did."

"You said that he wanted you early, not in the middle of the night."

Eli shrugged.

"When are you getting home?"

"I don't know. Six or seven, I guess. No earlier, with that team he's got. The one

46

mule's blind, you know."

She was quiet for a few moments. "You're not going to eat anything?" she asked.

"He said he'd have rolls for me — those hard, flaky ones his wife makes. With the chocolate inside."

"Well go on then. But give me a kiss first."

When he bent down, she took hold of his head, a palm on each ear, and pulled his cheek hard against her lips. "You be careful now," she told him.

You, too, he thought, and turned away, the muscles twitching in his back and legs.

The night was clear and still, the stars a chalky whitewash across the sky, no weather this time to make him give up and turn back home. The town was quiet, every window black, and at first he walked along the dirt street, right down the middle of it. Then, out front of the tailor shop, a kitten darted in front of him, making him cut over into the alley where there was less chance he might be seen. A block later, at the back of Fogarty's rooming house, he heard a faint cough and dived behind a brittle lilac bush. For a minute or so he kept still, watching. There was nothing astir in front of him and nothing behind, not that he could see, but then it came again, the same cough, and he was able to track the sound to its source:

the third floor of Fogarty's, an open window there, and the orange glow at the end of a cigar. It was Harry McLaughlin, former baseballer with the Cincinnati Red Stockings, former town alderman, former proprietor of a water-hauling business he lost to gambling. The man was blind now, and rumor had it he was dying.

In a rush, an idea came to Eli — a bold picture that rose up and danced in his mind's eye. He couldn't turn away from it. Two months ago he'd delivered a new porcelain chamber pot to McLaughlin. It was eighty-thirty or nine in the morning when Eli arrived, and he found Fogarty in the lobby, wiping down the maple woodwork with a vinegar rag. When Eli announced his purpose, Fogarty reached beneath the counter and came up with the ring of keys he liked to flaunt, a couple dozen or so large brass skeleton keys on a steel ring and chain. Fogarty led Eli up two flights of steep stairs to the third floor and down the dark hallway to McLaughlin's small room, all the while playing with the keys, tossing them forward and snapping them back into his hand, forward and back, up and around. At McLaughlin's door he knocked. No answer came from inside.

"He's paid for it already," Eli said. "You

can give it to him later, he's probably still sleeping."

"Sleeping? Nah," Fogarty had said, and then selected a key from his ring, slipped it in the lock, and pushed open the door, all in a motion.

McLaughlin managed to throw his legs free of the dirty bedclothes, and he sat in his yellowing shorts half in and half out of bed, shaking his head back and forth, arms crossed in front of his pendulous breasts, empty mouth moving soundlessly, knees pressed together like a child's. His eyes blinked and fluttered in their sockets. Fogarty took the porcelain chamber pot from Eli's hands and set it on the floor. Then he reached out and clapped the old man's bony shoulder. "Rise and shine," he told him.

Overcome by the ammoniac smell, Eli had backpedaled into the hall, then followed Fogarty all the way back downstairs to the lobby, having to listen as the man chuckled to himself.

Now, though, crawling out from behind the lilac bush in the alley, it was Eli who couldn't help chuckling. He knew the basement entrance of the rooming house was always left unlocked for coal drops, and so he lifted the big trapdoor and descended the stairs, pulling the door back down behind him. He lit a match and located the steps leading to the main floor, and then upstairs he tiptoed across the wide lobby to the counter, went around to the back of it and reached underneath, where, sure enough, his fingers touched the cool brass fan of Fogarty's beloved room keys. Eli didn't know what he was going to do with them, only that he wanted them. He wanted Fogarty to wake up in the morning and not have them. He imagined the man searching, panicked, then racing to the sheriff's office, imagined him blaming his renters, or better yet, Herman Stroud, who sometimes ran errands for him after school. The keys felt pleasantly heavy as he tucked them into the pocket of his coat, then he returned to the basement and left by way of the coal door.

In the alley back of Harlow's barber shop, as Eli passed by the outhouse, another idea occured to him and he made no effort to resist this one either. He opened the outhouse door, stepped inside, and dropped the heavy ring of keys down the black, smelly hole, laughing at the soft clanking sound it made when it landed.

He crossed the tracks fifty yards short of the depot, climbed onto the platform of the grain elevator nearest the station, and tucked himself behind a pile of feed sacks. From there he had a clear view of the depot and, beyond it, the water tank next to which the engine would rest while its reservoir filled. Depot agent Wheatfield made a habit of ambling the train's length, front to back along its north side then back to front along its south, and striking each empty car with his hickory walking stick — though he'd never been known to confront a free-rider. If it was a mixed-use run, the passengers who weren't sleeping might venture outside to stretch their legs. In any case there would be plenty of time for Eli to find a car and get himself settled.

The eastern clouds were starting to purple at the edges when Eli heard it — a far-off, steady thunder that rose in volume until he could feel it through the soles of his boots. Then the engine came around the last curve, cone of light sweeping before it, whistle blowing, and the air shaking with noise as the first cars howled past. He waited until the clanking stopped and the train was still, until the big cylinders were panting like tired dogs and Wheatfield had carried out his ritual tour. Then Eli climbed down from the platform and found an empty car toward the rear of the train, a lumber car from the smell of the redwood wafting out of it. He tossed his bedroll inside and climbed up after it and pulled the big sliding door three quarters closed.

As good as gone, he thought. No one was going to catch him now.

The steam cylinders huffed and cleared their throats, and the long steel spine started snapping and clanging. The car jerked beneath him. He crouched low and set his hands on either side for balance. Then as he rolled past the grain elevator, he blinked and jammed his knuckles into his eyes to push the nonsense out: materializing like some droll spirit from behind a heap of crates, and dwarfed by the giant coat he wore that flapped and billowed around him, his brother Danny came running, arms pumping, knees lifting and falling, head jabbing forward chickenlike — all this motion, and yet there was a dreamlike sluggishness about him, too.

Danny's arm stretched forward. "It's me, it's me," he yelled.

Eli jumped up and grabbed hold of the doorframe with his left hand and leaned out, reaching. Danny's hand felt small and damp. Stretching farther, Eli clamped hold of his brother's narrow wrist then pulled back hard against the doorframe, leveraging his weight and hauling Danny up like a catfish out of the river until they both fell back. Side by side they lay on the rough plank flooring of the boxcar, breathing hard.

"What in the hell," Eli said.

Danny turned on his side, his roll of blankets caught beneath him. His eyes were huge. Besides the coat, which reached to his ankles, he wore a big, wavy-brimmed hat that made his ears stick out even more than usual. Both the coat and hat were their father's. Danny's dog-eared book — *Buffalo Bill, King of the Border Men* — had come free of his bedroll and lay open on the planking.

"Where are we going?" he asked.

How in God's name? Eli thought. What would their mother do when she found Danny gone in the morning? He was tempted to grab his brother by his ears and toss him back out. Picking up speed, the train blew its whistle at the crossing west of town. Eli sat down, legs crossed Indian-style, on the rocking floor of the car, and Danny did the same, facing him.

"How did you figure it out?" Eli asked.

The boy shrugged, matter-of-fact. He said, "That money you've been putting in the wall."

"You think this is going to be easy? You think it'll be fun? Well, it won't — sleeping outside, nobody watching out for us. I've

53

got to send you home, you know."

But Danny didn't seem to hear. He shook his head, smiling. "I didn't know if I was going to make it there, for a minute."

"And no one cooking for us, either," Eli said.

Danny reached into the pocket of his big coat and pulled out a tube of sausage and a brick of cheese that smelled so good Eli's jaw began to sting.

"Where'd you get that?"

"Fogarty," Danny said, grinning.

"His smokehouse?"

Danny nodded. "While you were inside the hotel. What were you doing in there, anyway?"

"Doesn't matter," Eli said. The mischief he'd pulled with the ring of keys seemed pointless now, foolish, not to mention dangerous and stupid.

"So where's Dad? Did he send for you?"

Eli took the letter from his pocket and gave it a shake. "All that snooping around you were doing and you didn't see this?"

"You must've just put it in there," Danny said.

"A couple days ago."

"Let me see." Danny snatched the letter from Eli's hand. There was a flash of orange, and then Danny's matchlit, grinning face.

"Here." He handed the wooden match to Eli, reached into his big coat for the stub of a candle, and set its wick to the flame.

Danny flattened the letter on the splintery floor, then moved the candle back and forth across the lines. Eli sat and watched, recalling the sick turning of his stomach when he read it himself the first time — also the relief at having something real in hand, the testimony of someone who'd actually seen his father. Danny finished reading and folded it up and slipped it back into the envelope, which he handed to Eli, along with the burning candle. He rolled over onto one side, facing away, and drew his knees up close to his chest.

In Moorhead the lamps still burned yellow inside the ramshackle saloons, and two white steeples rose like pointing fingers through the fading dark. Eli stood in the door of the car as they passed over the Red River of the North, the silty, vegetable smell rising, two paddleboats at rest down there beside the big wooden pier. With the bridge behind them and the train slowing for its Fargo stop, he pulled the heavy door closed, worried about the yard bulls. He needn't have been. The car barely came to rest in front of the depot before it jerked back into motion and accelerated to the pace of a horse's trot. As they rolled through down-town, Eli cracked the door to watch the hulking shape of the Headquarters Hotel slip away behind them.

The air on this side of the Red wasn't the same as back home. It was drier and dustier, not as ripe or settled. He'd always had the feeling, the few times he'd come to Fargo, that anything might happen here, that the men he saw in the noisy streets with their rawboned faces and hard hands would just as soon kill you as tell you the time. Even the women looked tough, as if the prairie wind had blown the softness out of them. As they passed by the stockyards west of the city and the slaughterhouse with its sour, bloody smell, Danny said, "Aren't we going pretty slow?"

"Not for long."

But the train shuddered then, the engine powering down, and soon they'd come to a full stop. In the silence the boys sat, wait-ing. After a minute or two, men's voices sang out from the west, and then boots crunched on gravel, the steps coming closer. The men stopped a few cars ahead, banging and knocking on something, steel on steel. Eli tried to peek out through the slit between the door and frame but couldn't see any-thing — and when the big pistons started going again, building up to the pull, there was something missing. The floor beneath them was still, no pulse or tremble, not even when the long line of couplings ahead started to snap and clang.

Eli got up and pushed the door wide and jumped down to the gravel alongside the tracks. Empty cars were all around them. He counted three ahead of their own, four behind — eight altogether in the abandoned string. Half a mile or so to the east were the lights of Fargo.

Danny jumped down from the car. "Now what?" he asked.

"Walk back to town, I guess. Figure it out."

"You think they'll catch us and send us home?"

"No, but I'm sending *you* home. There's an eastbound coming through at ten."

"If you're not going back, I'm not either."

"It's only fifty cents, and you'll be home in time for lunch. It'd be the best thing, Danny. What if you get sick out here?"

"No," Danny said.

"You've got to think about Mother, too."

"If you make me go back, I'll tell her everything. I'll tell her where you're going. I'll tell her about the letter."

Eli walked back to the car, climbed up

57

and sat down in the doorway, legs dangling. After a minute, Danny clambered up to sit down next to him, and together they watched the morning colors, pink and orange and red, the clouds above Fargo like a range of hills where there were no hills, and the dark line of trees along the river.

"I had a dream about him," Danny said. "Night before last. His beard was grown out, it was long and gray, and he looked skinny."

"Was he all right?" Eli asked.

"There was a lot of smoke and a lot of people. And they were running around, screaming. And I heard a band playing. There were tinkling horns and a drum. It was cold outside, and snow on the ground."

"What happened?"

"That's all," Danny said. "That's it." He took off his big, floppy hat and set it on the floor beside him. He said, "Do you think that woman is the reason he left? That's what Herman Stroud told me. That he left Mother for another woman."

"No," Eli said.

"Do you think he still loves Mom?" Danny asked.

"Yes," Eli said.

"We're going out there to Bismarck, though, aren't we? To her place — that

Laura Powers? Even though he's not there?"

"What else can we do? At least she's seen him. She has to know *something.*"

"Maybe she sent the letter right after he left, maybe he's already home," Danny said, his large eyes gleaming. "Have you thought of that?"

"Nope," Eli said, "but I like the idea. I really like it."

"But you don't believe it."

"No, do you?"

Danny shook his head. "Where is he then?" he asked, his thin face knotted up by the question. He looked like an old man suddenly. "Where *is* he?"

4
PLAINWATER

For all the worry he'd caused in the home
he walked away from, all the justifiable tears
and anger, his movements across the coun-
tryside by rail and by foot had attracted
little in the way of attention from those who
may have seen him. A tall man, eyes drawn
to the ground, carrying no bag or rifle, and
sleeping in barns, ditches, and a house or
two. By appearance, a man stripped of luck,
cuffs frayed and cheeks unshaved, stopping
finally in this river town where for several
weeks he'd hired himself out to a merchant
who was building a warehouse down along
the shore. Nights, he'd been sleeping in a
small, unpainted church. He rose now from
the maple pew he'd been using for a bed,
rolled his blanket, gathered his few pos-
sibles, and walked up the aisle. He passed
by the altar and knocked at the door of the
room where the parson prayed in the morning, early, before the sun.

The old man was sitting next to a book-case, oil lamp burning on the table beside him.

"I wanted to thank you for letting me sleep here. It's been comfortable."

"You're no burden to me," the parson said. "Are you moving on, then?"

"I am."

"You never said where you're from."

"It's been my opinion that people don't harbor what you'd call any real concern for those not kin to them."

"Where are you from?" the parson asked. "If you don't mind."

"Nowhere that you would know about."

The parson smiled, a hundred wrinkles claiming his face. "Is the idea to be gone from there? Or to go someplace?"

"I like to think I'm going someplace."

"It would seem, then, you're looking for something."

"Or somebody, yes."

The parson turned down the flame of his lamp as the sky outside the window lightened. He cleared his throat. "As pastors go, I likely haven't been a good one. The words people need to hear have been hard for me to come by." He gestured toward the sanctuary. "It's my fear that those who sit out there on Sunday mornings often leave unsatisfied — unless they've fallen asleep, in which case they go off rested at least. But I will say this. I have a clear notion that my prayers reach heaven, and in that respect I am fortunate. More to the point, of late I have found myself praying for you."

Ulysses laughed. "I'll take all the prayers you've got, though I ask that you spare me your sacraments."

A rooster crowed in the distance. "I can hardly give you Communion against your will, can I?" the parson said.

"Nor baptize me all over again, thank God for that. Another dunking might just be enough to do me in."

The parson rubbed a palm over his bald skull. "I have to say that's an odd complaint. Afterwards, one normally feels purged. Lighter on the feet."

"It had the opposite effect on me, no offense intended. Sent me searching for a remedy, is what it did."

The old man drummed his fingers on the side table. He frowned. "Remedy? Forgiveness is free, of course. You know that, surely. God is no merchant selling his wares."

"I understand. Tell me, though — are the sins we commit against God alone?"

The parson shook his head. "No, but it's to God that we answer for our mortal souls."

"With respect, sir," Ulysses said, "I believe we have more to answer for than just our mortal souls."

Frowning, the parson leaned back and stared off into the corner. He lifted a hand as the other took his leave.

5
GOODWILL

In town she asked first at the depot, trying hard to look unconcerned, as if she meant only to round up her sons for some chore they'd ducked out of. She put on a smile and cocked her head and set her hands on her hips.

"They ain't been around here," Wheatfield said. "And if they was, I would of put them right to work."

"Send them straight home if they show up," Gretta told him, then turned away to avoid his eyes. It was a temptation to give in, to go back to the house and cry until she couldn't cry any longer, and then go to sleep, only to wake in a few hours to find her boys returned, home from some adventure — like their expedition upriver last summer in a neighbor's leaky rowboat. Instead she walked to the mercantile, where she hovered in one of the side aisles, telling herself that Eli may in fact have gone off to

Fargo with Mr. Goldman this morning. And who was to say Danny hadn't chased after him and ended up going along? That wasn't such a stretch, was it? As she feigned interest in a display of serving bowls, leaning close to inspect them, she felt herself being watched. Sure enough, when she glanced up at the counter Mrs. Goldman was there, watching her, lips pursed. A tiny woman with stingy, birdlike features.

"You tell your son that Anton left without him, that he waited fifteen minutes past leaving time. It's a long drive, you know, and he got a late start."

Gretta nodded. "I'll tell him."

"Was there something else?"

"No, no. I was only looking at this bowl."

"That's from England, of course. Real bronze, hand-hammered. And the price you see is firm."

"Thank you," Gretta said.

She stopped next at the barber shop, then at the pharmacy, and finally on a whim at Two Blood's gun store, where he opened the door and stepped aside to let her in. She knew how much her sons liked this place — the guns, of course, and the tobacco smell, and the old, dusty buffalo head presiding from the wall above the counter. He offered her a chair next to his worktable, but she said no, she had to be getting home.

"I only stopped to ask if you'd seen the boys," she told him.

His face was so furrowed she couldn't imagine he'd ever been young. He said, "I don't sleep so good anymore. I was sitting here this morning, early. Smoking. Saw your boys walking past on the street." He pointed out the window.

Gretta's hands went cold. Her throat tightened. "What time?"

"Eli came first, and then the small one a minute later. This was before the first light. They carried blanket rolls, both of them."

"They didn't say anything?"

"They didn't see me. I had no lamp burning."

"You must have wondered what they were doing."

Two Blood smiled. "Boys have their reasons."

"Do you think they were heading for the depot?" Gretta asked.

"That might be so."

"You could have stopped them, talked to them, asked them where they were going," she said, knowing he would have done no such a thing.

The old man shrugged, a fluid roll of his shoulders.

At home Gretta thought to look in the chifforobe, and when she found her husband's rifle missing, also his winter coat and hat, she realized there was no choice but to go looking — and that meant a trip to St. Paul, where Ulysses still had a sister living, and a brother-in-law. Or did as recently as a two years ago, when they'd last heard from them at Christmastime. In July Gretta had written to Florence, asking if she'd seen Ulysses, but so far had heard nothing back.

Panic twisted in Gretta's stomach, and she sat down at the dining-room table to calm herself, making fists to keep her fingers from shaking. Her lungs had risen into her throat, and though she needed air, she couldn't seem to take any more in.

"Think!" she said aloud, then pushed away from the table, went into the kitchen, and drew a tall glass of cold water from the pump and forced herself to drink it all down. She took a breath and blew it out. At the China hutch she took out the silver candlestick-holders her mother had received as a wedding gift, and she set them on the table. They were fashioned in a plain, heavy style, and whenever Gretta polished them — at Christmas and Easter — their weight in her hands summoned to mind her mother's silvery blonde hair, always pulled back in a tight bun on holidays, and her father's eyes, which even at family gatherings seemed to search out windows and doors, a route of escape. There were other things, too, that she could sell — her lace handkerchiefs, the blue pitcher painted in the royal Danish pattern, her grandfather's brass letter opener. The local undertaker, Burlingame, had a pawn exchange at the alley entrance to his store, and though Gretta had never sold him anything, she'd heard that he was more generous now that a new funeral man had set up shop in the town five miles east. She gathered her things on the table and wrapped each up in dishtowels, then put on her best coat and regarded herself in the mirror that hung in the front room. With the panic rising in her belly it was hard to stand up straight, but that's what she did — pushed her shoulders back and stepped up close to examine her face. She brought her lips together in a line and pushed the bottom one out in a way that suggested confidence. She studied her brow, which was neither too thin nor too thick, and then her nose, which she had often been told was well formed. She collected a fallen lock from her forehead, tucked it behind an ear, and took a step back for a full view. Her black wool coat was smooth, with no obvious creases or wrinkles, and tailored well to her shape. Her hands looked chapped, though, and so she went to her room for the balm that Ulysses used on his fingers in the winter.

She was sitting on the edge of her bed when a knock at the door brought her to her feet. She dried her hands on the bedspread, moved quickly across the house, and opened the door a crack, blocking it with the toe of her shoe. Mead Fogarty stood on the front stoop with his derby hat in his chubby hands.

"I hear that your sons are missing," he said. "I might be in a position to help you."

Gretta pulled back. The man wanted his money, that was all — unless he'd come to observe her pain, and to gloat.

"Let me inside, please."

With no other choice, Gretta withdrew her toe from the door. Fogarty pushed forward, snagging the shoulder of his jacket on a nail jutting from the doorframe.

"Damn it!" he said.

"What do you know about my boys?" Gretta asked him.

He gave his chin a careless toss. "They've gone in search of their father, I imagine."

"Have you seen them?"

"I haven't."

"You said you knew something."

"No, I said I might be able to help you. Listen." He lifted both hands, palms out. "We have to sit down and talk."

She led him to the kitchen, where they sat across from each other at the table. Fogarty planted his elbows and grasped his hands together in an oddly formal gesture. He tipped back his head and looked at her along the uneven line of his nose. "I've lost my ring of keys," he announced. "The ones to all the rooms in my building. And I'm afraid it's your fault."

God help me, Gretta thought. Fogarty's red face was composed and serious, his plump lips neither smiling nor pursed. He coughed and swallowed, then reached into the pocket of his jacket for a tin flask, which he held aloft and squinted at.

"It's been a trying day," he said, and took a drink, eyes rolling back in his head. "I don't often indulge myself — my wife would have vouched for me on that. But there are times a man requires help in what he needs to do." He offered the flask to Gretta, who made a face.

"You were saying about your keys," she said, aware of the clock ticking on the secretary and the growing number of miles separating her from her sons.

"Mrs. Pope, you so upset me the other night that I haven't been thinking straight since. Owing me rent as you do, and then taking my generous offer so lightly. Last night, in fact, I was so distracted that I must have lost my keys while I was up at Lowman's Bend, fishing."

Gretta could not respond. The man's mind and motivations were unknowable, absurd.

"I'm on my way to find them now, and I insist that you come along with me."

She almost laughed, out of confusion. "I don't have time," she said. "Can't you see that? I have to figure out what to do."

Fogarty narrowed his eyes. His gaze fell on Gretta's lips and then her neck, which Gretta moved to cover with her hand. "If you help me find my keys," he said, "I will give you money for the trip you're planning."

"What trip?"

He took another swallow from his flask and offered it to her again. This time she accepted, wincing as the whiskey burned its way down her throat. Fogarty smiled, head cocked like a bird dog.

Be careful, Gretta thought, *there's no one looking out for you.*

"When I heard your boys were gone, I

71

knew right off I had to help out, it's the honorable thing to do. On the other hand, one good deed deserves another, doesn't it?" He smiled again, only for a moment. "I may be a homely man," he said, "but I'm no fool. And I won't be mocked like some rube. You've been telling me you know where your husband is, that he's coming home soon. That is not the case, is it?"

"Not exactly," Gretta said.

"So you've been lying to me."

"I am trying to be optimistic."

"An admirable trait." Fogarty pressed his hands together palm to palm beneath his chin. "But if your husband has taken a permanent leave, which I believe he has, it's to your benefit — and mine — to reach that conclusion sooner, not later."

"I don't understand," she said.

"Because," Mead Fogarty said, "I mean to take his place."

Gretta stood up so fast the room went black, and she reached out to steady herself against the table. She wanted to run to her bedroom and shut and lock the door.

"I don't expect this comes as a welcome surprise, anxious as you are right now. But I am a decent man, offering help you happen to need. I urge you to give it serious thought." He got up from the table and gestured toward the door. "In the meantime, I need to find my keys. My rig is out front."

"I can't go with you — it wouldn't look right," she said.

Fogarty laughed. "It doesn't look right either when a woman's husband leaves her and stays away for months on end. Now take my arm, hold your head up, and come along. It's only a mile north, and we'll be there in no time. If folks happen to see you, fine. I'm good people."

She refused his arm, but the tremor in the man's bottom lip gave her courage, and she consented to follow him out of the house and into the street where he helped her onto the buckboard of his spring wagon, which was covered in a fresh coat of white paint. He tipped his flask for another swallow, then took up the driving lines. Gretta kept her eyes trained ahead as they drove north toward the edge of town, looking to the side just once, when a man's voice called her name — "Gretta?" — a voice she knew and could not ignore: Otis Bending, an old carpenter who often helped Ulysses with his larger projects, the houses and barns. She lifted a hand and offered a flat smile she hoped he could see through, a smile that said, *It isn't what you think.* Otis only scowled, his enormous hands hanging like spades beside him. Gretta felt cold suddenly. The sun had gone behind a bank of clouds, the dead scent of autumn in the air, dust and woodsmoke and dead grass. She imagined her sons walking along some strange road or hunched in a woods, sharing a loaf of her bread — or the pair of them in a train car, wrapped in their blankets and lying close together for warmth. Tears welled in her eyes, but she squeezed them back and dried her face with her sleeve. She couldn't help thinking of the nights she'd climbed into the loft and touched their hair as they slept — Danny's silken curls and Eli's full, heavy ones, cool in her fingers.

Fogarty yanked on the driving lines and the young gelding veered left, plunging off the road onto a dirt trail. Gretta had to grasp the seat with both hands to keep from pitching off the wagon. "Whoa, easy there," Fogarty said, flicking the lines and driving on, the wagon jouncing and squeaking in the ruts. They wound through a stand of cottonwoods, the blue stripe of the river glistening as they headed toward a place Gretta knew from years ago when she and Ulysses still fished together. Once he'd caught a catfish the size of a piglet and staked it over a wood fire, and she still remembered the tangy flavor of its gray meat.

"Where is he?" Fogarty asked.

"I don't know."

"If you want my help, I need to know where you're going."

"He might be in St. Paul, where he grew up," Gretta said, unable to look at the man. She despised him for the power he had to question her like this. "I don't know where else he'd go."

"But he hasn't contacted you?"

"No."

Fogarty removed his flask again and drank, though it wasn't easy, his hand bobbing at every jerk of the wagon. There was the dull ping of teeth striking tin, but he managed to fasten on with his lips and take a long pull. Thirty feet from the water he hauled back on the lines and yanked the hand brake. The gelding snorted and shook itself. Fogarty turned and raised a finger to Gretta's face. He licked his bright lips. "I was faithful to my wife while she lived," he said, "and I've been faithful to her memory since she died. I try to be a good man." His cheeks were blotchy and his breath sour.

Gretta couldn't speak.

"No doubt you've been holding out on me, keeping a tight grip on that rent money.

But I'll add to that." He tapped an index finger against the chestpocket of his tight-fitting vest. "I have five dollars here. For you. I have to know, however, that my generosity will be met with a mutual feeling."

Gretta's hair prickled at the base of her neck. "Mutual feeling?" she said.

"A reciprocal goodwill."

"Do you mean will I take your money?"

He reached out and placed his cool fingers against her forearms where she'd crossed them in front of her breasts. "That's *not* what I mean," he said. "Let's find my damned keys."

They searched without success along the tight bend of the river where water eddied in a deep pool favored by the oldest of the bottom-feeding cats. On the opposite bank stood the charred ruins of a barn where nineteen horses had perished along with their owner, Bill Grandin, who went to sleep drunk one night in a straw-pile, smoking. Or so the story went. They squeezed through a thicket of red willow and they crept on all fours, parting the dead grass with their hands. They found no keys. After a quarter of an hour, Fogarty straightened up on his knees like a bear on its hind legs. He'd been nipping at the flask and now rose unsteadily to his feet and pointed at the ground beneath him. Looming above was a giant cottonwood, its bark coarse and green-tinted.

"Here's where I had them last," he said. "Or I think I did. Now where are they?"

Gretta got up and walked over to where he stood sweating and wiping his brow in the shade of the tree. She almost pitied him.

Fogarty said, "It's unbecoming for a woman to chase after a man the way you're doing." Then he reached out and took her shoulders and pulled her close, locked her to his chest, his mouth grazing her ear and his breath hot against her neck as she tried to escape from his grasp. He slid his hands down the length of her back and took hold of her buttocks, squeezing hard. She tried to get a knee into his groin, but he anticipated this and lifted his knee between her legs and pushed up hard. And so she threw her weight forward, toppling him backward to the ground, she on top of him. The shock of their fall loosened his hold on her, and Gretta kicked free, the hard toe of her shoe connecting with his shin. She rolled away and got to her feet.

Fogarty was curled on his side, clutching his leg and whimpering, his face as flushed as a rooster's comb. The flask of whiskey was lying in the grass beside him, and she picked it up and handed it to him. After a while he quieted and opened one eye, then the other. He uncapped the flask and put it to his mouth, tipped it up. "You've pushed me to my limit," he said, squinting, as if he could read his own words in the air. "And you probably think you should still have your train money."

Gretta stood above him. His thin brown hair had fallen all to one side and hung past his ear toward his shoulder. On his chin was a mud stain in the shape of a question mark.

"You owe me nothing," she said.

"But you'd take it if I offered."

"I have to find Eli and Danny," she said, immediately hating herself for not adding her husband's name — or maybe for realizing how close she was to giving up on him.

Fogarty cranked his neck a couple of times, blinked, and sat up. He fished out the bill from his vest pocket and showed it to her, fingers trembling. A five-dollar silver certificate, crisp and new and bearing the likeness of Grant. He waved it in the air. "Come here," he said.

This time she was ready when he reached for her, prepared for what he wanted and resolved to take what she needed. As she had done now for weeks, she pushed her fear away like an unwanted memory. It was a trick of the mind, turning the feared thing into something else entirely — in this case, turning Fogarty into a little boy, stamping his feet against the ground and demanding a stick of peppermint. Trying to stand up, he slipped in the grass, then struggled up again and wrapped an arm around her, not groping this time but holding on for balance.

"Here, let's sit down together," she told him. "Maybe I could have a drink, too."

He handed her the flask and she pretended to swallow, jogging her throat for effect. Then they sat down and passed the whiskey back and forth until it was empty. It didn't take long.

"Let's go over there," she said, pointing to the edge of the river where the grass was less trodden. He stood up, stumbling, and she had to help him, allowing him to lean on her until he went to his knees and then laid himself down.

"There," she said, forcing herself to pat his shoulder.

"Yes," he sighed.

She sat down next to him and listened as he started talking — first about his lost keys and then about his hotel, and how the people who stayed there didn't know a good place when they saw one. The sun was high, straight above them, and sitting out of the wind as they were, the day felt almost warm.

"Let's just rest for a minute, I need to relax," Gretta said.

Fogarty shifted his hips against the earth, spread his legs and smiled, his eyes closed. Five minutes later he was snoring, drawing air through his mouth in long rasps, as if breathing underwater. Gretta reached into his vest pocket for the five-dollar note, which she pushed deep into the side pocket of her coat. Then she set off for the walk back to town.

6
THE DARK MUCK OF YOUR HEART

During his father's short time at the depot, Eli had often gone to work with him, sensing he might be needed, and in fact he was there on the night his father got into the fight that caused him to lose his job. He was sweeping the floor when a passenger on a westbound got off during a watering stop, came inside for a cup of coffee, and began shouting, "What kind of place are you running? What are these savages doing here?" He was a big man, tall and round-bellied, and he pointed toward the lobby, where a family sat waiting for their train, a mother, father, and three small children. They had shining black hair and brown faces.

"Same thing you're doing," Ulysses said, coming out from behind the counter.

"Well get 'em out of here. Get 'em out of my sight." As he'd marched to the coffee table, one of the little boys, scuttling to avoid him, tripped and fell headlong to the floor. The man kicked the boy's sprawled legs away with the side of his boot, carelessly, and the boy's father stood up fast. Ulysses was faster, coming straight at the man and putting a fist in his big stomach. The man went to one knee, gasping.

"Go back to your car," Ulysses told him, but the man stood up, pulling a knife from his coat. Ulysses swept it away and hit him square in the mouth, bursting his lips, which began spewing blood, then he went about beating on the man's body until the porter and telegraph operator pulled him off. Eli had never seen his father like that before, had never seen him lose control of himself, had rarely seen him angry. It was like watching the calm surface of a lake erupt beneath a sudden storm, and ever since, he'd been dreaming about it — not about the fight itself but his father afterward, and the excited state of his breathing, which was fast and hard, like a dog that has scented another dog, its entire being caught up in a blood rage.

It was early afternoon, and Eli was sitting on hard ground in the shade of a towering cottonwood, watching his brother sleep. Twenty feet away the muddy Red slipped by. They had spent the morning trying to jump a westbound — first in the big switching lot where they'd been stranded, and then at the Northern Pacific depot in town. But there was too much yard help, too many watching eyes, and they finally retreated downhill to Fargo's quiet, overgrown river shore. The plan was to let Danny catch up on the sleep he missed last night and wait until after sundown to give it another try.

Behind Eli a branch snapped, and he turned and stood. Approaching from uphill was a man walking briskly, thirty paces and closing. Eli stepped back and to the side, thinking to hide himself behind the cottonwood, but the man lifted a hand in greeting.

"Eli? Eli Pope?"

Eli crouched to shake his brother awake, and stood up again. The man was tall and straight, with bristly white hair an inch long. His nose was tilted so far to one side that it seemed to rest against the hollow of his cheek, and his light, frozen-green eyes put Eli in mind of a wolf. He wore a frayed black coat that reached past his knees.

"Reverend Pearl," Eli said. He hadn't seen the man since he'd dunked his father in the Plainwater River more than a year ago.

"And Danny too," Reverend Pearl said in his low, nasal voice, watching as the boy got to his feet. "You two have come a distance."

"Not so far," Eli said.

"On your way somewhere?"

Eli gave his brother's arm a squeeze, which meant *Keep your mouth closed.*

Reverend Pearl blinked. His smile loosened a bit. "I was up at the creamery for a brick of butter —" From his coat pocket he pulled a square of it, wrapped in white paper. "Got some catfish waiting for the pan. Come along." He pointed north, past where the railroad bridge spanned the Red.

The boys hadn't eaten since last night except for a hard-boiled egg apiece, mid-morning. Danny glanced up at his brother, just the slightest movement of his eyes, but Eli said, "We ate already."

"Please. It's plain to see, Danny's hungry." The reverend turned on his heel and headed north, not so much as glancing back to see if they were following.

He's a hard man to say no to, their father had said more than once, and Eli found himself falling into step behind him, pulling Danny along. During the week of Reverend Pearl's revival, he had stayed in a barn Ulysses was building at the edge of town, and by week's end, he was taking his meals at their home, though their mother didn't take to the man and didn't attend his meetings.

A walk of five minutes brought them well past the bridge, high above on its timber struts, and down along the water to a thicket of young poplars growing like weeds. They passed through it, bending the slender trunks aside, and then through a dense stand of red willows, coming finally into a small glade, at the center of which stood a gnarled cottonwood tree. There were two men, one crouched before a campfire, another, with flame-red hair, wrapped in a blanket and lying in the dead grass. Around the edge of the clearing was an assortment of crude huts made of crates and weathered planks, battered sheets of rusty tin.

"Have a seat." Reverend Pearl pointed at a log lying next to the fire, then stepped over the sleeping man and plucked a pair of tin cups from nails in the cottonwood. He poured coffee and handed a cup each to Eli and Danny, then glided away through a gap in the willows, heading for the river.

The coffee tasted like boiled earth, bitter yet dull, and Eli washed it around in his mouth before letting himself swallow, the coarse grounds scraping at the sides of his throat. His stomach burned and clenched. A pulse started up at the back of his eyes. A second swallow tweaked his vision — widening the world, everything seeming larger than it was a moment before.

The red-haired man on the ground rolled onto his back and draped his long arms over his face, elbows jutting straight up. The one sitting at the fire smiled across at them, then stood and moved off to a lean-to of twisted boards, where he sat down on a kitchen chair and commenced cleaning his nails with a knife. Reverend Pearl reappeared, pushing aside the springy branches of red willow. He was laden with catfish, a chain stringer hoisted in his right fist, three fish — no, four — their heavy bodies rolling against each other, long whiskers juddering. "You boys better be hungry," Reverend Pearl said, laying out the catch on the dry grass.

He made quick work of the catfish, gutting them, tossing away viscera, and skinning and deboning the fillets. Then he pushed a pair of logs together at the edge of the fire, set a big iron frypan on top of them, and tossed in a chunk of the fresh yellow butter from the creamery. As soon as the butter started sizzling and pooling, he laid in the eight gray fillets, setting them down with care, side by side by side.

"Praise be to God for the fish of the sea — Amen, Elmer?" He poked a booted toe into the ribs of the red-haired man, still supine in the grass, who raised a finger beside his head and wagged it in the air. Reverend Pearl stirred at the fire, leaned down and blew on a smoldering ember. Flames jumped up and licked at the pan. "Here we go," he said, grinding pepper on the humming fillets with a mill he pulled magically from a pocket.

By the time the fish was ready, its buttery, sharp scent rising in the air and filling the clearing, the men had dragged themselves to the fire circle and waited with plates on laps, their eyes fastened to the sputtering pan. Eli and Danny had plates, too, chipped ones from a makeshift cupboard in one of the huts. Eli's was pink china, clean except for a smear of dried egg yolk, which he tried to avoid looking at. They all applied themselves to their food, handling the hot fish gingerly with their fingers and washing it down with swallows of lukewarm coffee.

"Meet your approval?" Reverend Pearl asked, inclining his head toward Eli.

"Good," Eli said through a mouthful. Next to him, Danny nodded.

"You haven't yet told me where you're heading," Reverend Pearl said. The smile he offered was more interrogatory than friendly, and his light-colored irises twinkled.

Eli didn't answer. It seemed unlikely that the man would feel compelled to go out of his way to report back to their mother. On the other hand, wasn't it possible he might know something about their father? Eli searched his mind for what to say.

In his flat, guileless voice Danny said, "Mother claims it's your fault that he left us."

"I see. And would you like to say more on the subject?" Reverend Pearl asked.

Danny shook his head. "Nope."

The reverend leaned forward and hooked the coffeepot with a finger, then brought it around to Eli and refilled his cup. Danny's words were flat-out true. Their mother *had* laid on Reverend Pearl the blame for their father's leaving, saying more than once, "A man like that can afford to spread those principles of his, all that guilt. Traveling place to place and expounding as if from on high, too haughty to settle down with other folks. Of course he wasn't too proud to accept my hospitality."

The reverend moved now from man to man, boy to boy, collecting their dirty plates, then set out toward the river, turning around at the line of red willows. "Your mother came and found me at the meetings I led in Moorhead last month. Gave me a piece of her mind, she did. I told her what I knew and what I know — which is nothing — and told her also that I am sorry for anything I might have contributed to what's happened. Now I must wash these dishes." He turned and disappeared through the willows.

The red-haired man and the other one, too, wandered away, and Eli and Danny conferred about their next move. It was Eli's opinion they ought to find another place to hide until dark, that avoiding everyone who knew them — the reverend included — was the prudent thing to do. They were just getting up to leave when he emerged from behind the big cottonwood.

"You can't sneak off without dessert," he said.

"We ain't sneaking," Danny said.

"Then why've you got your tails tucked between your legs? Come on, sit back down."

Reverend Pearl reached into his pocket yet again, his hand returning this time with a bright foil package, a flat rectangle that he flourished in the air before presenting it to Danny. "Man that sold it to me said it comes from South America. You have tasted nothing like it." Danny kept his hands on his lap, and Reverend Pearl said, "You don't

89

think I feel badly about your father?"

Danny glanced at Eli, who reached out for the packet. His fingers stripped away the foil and he took a small bite from the corner of the chocolate bar, eyeing Reverend Pearl as he did so. He took another, larger bite — half the bar — before handing the rest to Danny, who broke off a corner of it. It was dark, more bitter than he was used to, but good. Nothing like the bland ones that Goldman sold.

Reverend Pearl laughed. "What did I tell you? Makes me want to make a trip down there some day, hold some meetings." He sat down again across from the boys and poured himself another cup of coffee, took a swallow, and sighed. "I grew up in Ohio, in a nice brick house where my mother would never have served fish without an accompanying dish or two. A baked potato, creamed beans and corn. Now there was a woman who could put a home in order. She told me, 'Charles, if you're going to preach the Word, you need to get yourself a well-built church in a respectable town.' " Reverend Pearl looked up through the branches of the big cottonwood, straight up into the blue sky. "And here we are. Tell me, what did your mother think about you boys leaving her?"

Eli watched the man's eyes for the self-conscious flicker people had when they were after something. He didn't find it.

Reverend Pearl said, "Boys have a right to find out what it is that's got its teeth in their father's spleen. I'm not against you."

"He went to Bismarck," Eli said.

"How do you know?"

Eli shrugged.

"Do you know what he's doing out there?"

"He's not there anymore, but he was. We're not sure what he's doing."

Reverend Pearl pressed his lips together as if making up his mind about something, then smiled, his teeth and the empty places between them forming what looked like a broken puzzle in his mouth. He tried again. "How did you boys get here?"

"The westbound, this morning."

"First-class tickets?" Reverend Pearl lifted his brow and winked.

"Our car got dropped on a siding," Eli said, pointing west. "It wasn't how we planned things."

"No doubt you'll be jumping back on."

Eli nodded.

"I'm heading that way too, as it happens, and my situation being what it is, I might be riding steerage — then again, one's fortunes can change, God willing. You boys can trail along if you like, as far as Jamestown. That's my next stop."

Eli asked him when he was leaving.

"Tomorrow or the next day. Depending on how things go tonight. I'm preaching in the city park." He pointed along the river, to the south.

"We're leaving tonight," Eli says.

"That would be your prerogative. You may want to think on it, though. I do know trains. Been riding them since the tracks were laid, and I can make sure you find your way to Bismarck. No more cars stranded on the siding."

That afternoon they tagged along with Reverend Pearl as he broadcast word of his meeting. At the brick hospital he spoke to the ill and lame in a high-ceilinged room with polished floors, as Eli and Danny stood in the hallway listening through the door. Through the window Eli saw the people's heads inclined toward Reverend Pearl, their faces open and their eyes as bright as new coins. At the First National Bank, the reverend simply walked in and began speaking, his voice low and gravelly, a human sound against the monied tension of the place. A ceiling fan spun lazily above his head, and if anybody noticed the smell of him in that brass-appointed room, they didn't let on. After several more stops — the cattleyards, the big mercantile on Front Street, and a couple of hotels — the barkeep at the Senate Saloon served them a sit-down meal of liver, onions, and mashed potatoes, with a glass of warm ale for Reverend Pearl and milk for Eli and Danny.

At a quarter to seven folks started drifting down the hill from town in ones or twos, and in small clusters. They gathered on the east side of the oak-strewn park next to the river. The day had warmed. It felt more like summer than fall, with a damp heat that made Eli's shirt cling to his shoulders and back. Using tumblers from the barkeep, he and Danny ran back and forth between the hand pump at the center of the park and the gathered assembly, which by seven o'clock was settled and waiting, many of the people middle-aged or gray-haired, though several young families had turned out as well, their children playing tag or somersaulting in the grass.

Eli, pausing in his work, counted a congregation of thirty-eight.

As the sun descended into the oak trees behind them, and the windowed buildings of Fargo turned orange and pink to the north, Reverend Pearl stepped to the front, no pulpit or lectern to shield him, no white

robe or surplice either, no clerical collar —
only the plain dark suit he'd been wearing
all day, its shoulders faded to gray, and a
pair of square-toed shoes he'd polished
earlier with shoeblack and a horse brush.
He made no attempt at rhetorical flourish
but simply introduced himself and thanked
the people for coming.

"I believe we ought to sing for a while,"
he told them.

He led with no instrumentation beyond
his own voice, which sounded like a man
calling through a steel pipe, and soon the
congregation had begun to relax and sing
along, the children quieting and falling in
next to their mothers. It wasn't long before
an old woman brought out a harmonica,
and then a young woman with startling
blonde hair produced a fiddle from a cloth
bag and started sawing with energy, missing
a few notes at first and losing others in
screeches and high shrieks, but soon enough
finding her way. For half an hour this went
on, nearly all on their feet, some clapping,
some with folded hands and bowed heads,
the boys carrying water the whole time,
until finally Reverend Pearl lifted his arms
and motioned for everybody to sit down in
the grass. He bent over to pick up his Bible.

Eli and Danny moved to the side of the

hill and sat leaning against a double-trunked oak tree, catching their breath. They exchanged a commiserating look. It was one thing to get some help in catching the right train but quite another to spend half a day as the Reverend Pearl's personal servants. Eli would have sworn he wasn't interested in hearing what the man had to say, and yet it wasn't long before he found himself leaning forward and straining to make out the quietly uttered words, same as everybody else was doing. Some held cupped hands behind their ears, while others turned to the side, heads cocked. It seemed no one dared move for fear they might miss out on something. The harder they listened, though, the quieter he spoke, until he might as well have been whispering.

"I don't care about your holy thoughts or the earnest plea of your prayers. There is no true belief that is not marked by humility. Seek forgiveness from God, by all means. But remember, any coward can do as much. I'm here to tell you to bring yourselves low, brothers and sisters, to sink down into the dark muck of your hearts and look hard at what you find there — and then go and make things right."

Eli thought of his mother back home and how she must have felt, waking that morning to find herself alone, how her face must have looked, squashed and fallen. He thought of the day his father left with the rooster in its cage and couldn't help feeling remorse now at refusing even to speak to him, angry as he had been. He thought of Mr. Goldman, from whom he'd stolen tobacco on occasion and, once, a pocket-knife he wasn't able to carry with him or even use for fear Goldman might see it, and how he ended up just tossing the thing away into the river. Head bowed and eyes closed, the record of his transgressions unfurling inside his mind, Eli became aware that all was quiet, that Reverend Pearl had stopped speaking. Looking up, he saw a line of people forming out of the crowd to approach Reverend Pearl where he stood at the bottom of the slow rise of ground, watched as the man prayed for each briefly, whispering into their ears, long-fingered hands wrapped around their heads, before releasing them to return to their grassy seats on the hillside. Some smiled as they left him, some cried, some moved haltingly as if through a world they had never seen before. Eli got up from the tree and came closer to see if he could hear the man's prayers, make out what he was saying, but all that came to him were soft murmurs and the occasional sucking in of breath, whispers of assent. Sweat ran down the preacher's arms, dripped from his hair, and by the time he was finished and standing by himself in the near dark, slumped and diminished, the sap gone out of him, Eli was disturbed to notice his eyes alternately widening and narrowing as if he wasn't able to bring them into focus.

The reverend cleared his throat, licked his lips. "We'll pass the satchel now," he said. "I don't ask for what you can ill afford. If you have enough for your needs and nothing more, hold on to it. I require little."

Eli and Danny carried the leather satchel between them, holding it open as they moved among the gathering, coins spilling out from purses and wallets, and from the pockets of trousers that were patched and frayed. Finished, they closed up the satchel and retreated to the double-trunked oak tree to wait for Reverend Pearl's benediction and the gradual dispersal of the small crowd uphill toward town. The amount collected was fourteen dollars and eleven cents, which Danny counted out slowly under the eye of Reverend Pearl, who then led the boys back to the river camp, where he handed a silver dollar to each of the men there — four now, including the two from earlier — all of whom jumped right up and headed for town.

"Thirsty, I fear," Reverend Pearl said. He sighed and let his body sag down to rest on an old chair with twisted legs.

"Are we leaving in the morning?" Eli asked.

Reverend Pearl was quiet for a few moments, absolutely still, as if he didn't hear the question. Then he shook himself all over, like a large animal waking, and wagged a long finger. "For everything there is a season, boys. This morning you rode into town on a boxcar, today we cooked fresh-caught fish on a fire, and tomorrow I hold one more meeting for the edification of the good people of Fargo. But the *next* morning," he added, a smile widening his face — "the next morning, we three sojourners after truth will be eating from silver spoons on a Pullman car, heading west."

7
St. Paul

The stall in momentum tugged her body forward, waking her. Then she fell back against the seat as the car rocked to a stop, brakes hissing. It was dark, the dead middle of the night, and through the window a small depot stood beneath a single street-lamp. Beyond, through a fringe of trees, lay a glimmering lake. She pressed her hand against the glass before leaning back and taking a long breath. Not only had the train been stopping at every small town on its eastward course, but an engine breakdown earlier had caused a three-hour delay. Now they were far behind schedule.

Gretta closed her eyes, wishing herself back inside the dream she'd been having, in which her husband came strolling up the street in front of their house, his hair cleanly barbered and beard trimmed, wearing a starched white shirt that smelled of soap. He walked up to where she stood in the yard, his eyes sparkling like river stones, and said, "It looks like you made out fine without me." But Gretta couldn't sleep again. She was thinking of the day he left and the strange feeling she had that night as she sat down with her boys for a late supper, the urgency in Eli's face, the flat resignation on Danny's. "What's keeping him?" she'd asked, trying to keep control of her voice, in answer to which Danny said, "He won't be coming back, and you know it," his words so true to what she feared that she reached across the table and slapped his cheek. Gretta did not slap her children. Danny had pushed his plate of food away and blinked, accepting the offense as nothing compared to the cause of it. Then came that long, terrible night, waiting in front of the fireplace for hours before finally going to sleep on the floor, all three of them together. At first light she'd woken to find both boys gone — same as she would six weeks later. She ran outside and started for town, her stomach loose and bowels threatening, but hadn't gone a block before she met them coming back toward her, Eli carrying his brother, who was shaking his head, flailing his arms, trying to break free. "No," Danny was crying, "I want to go too, I want to go too."

Eli had always taken care of Danny like

that, anticipating his spells, doing his chores, standing up for him when other boys pushed him around. Yesterday, though, during her panicked search through town and then her ride out to the river with Fogarty, Gretta had failed to see what she *could* see now in the clarity following the hard sleep of dreams: Eli, whose instinct was to ease his brother's passage through the world, would never have taken him along on his search for Ulysses. Never. He wouldn't risk Danny's health in that way. Which meant, Gretta realized, that Ulysses must have come back for the boys, either that or he'd sent for them. It was the only explanation that made any sense. The problem was, it forced Gretta to look at something else, too, something she hadn't been willing to confront, at least nakedly and straight on — the likelihood of another woman. Why else would Ulysses have failed to write even a single letter home or send a telegram to explain his absence? And why else would he have taken with him the beautifully beaded tobacco pouch, which he'd claimed was a gift from a fellow trooper in the Minnesota Ninth, a man from the Chippewa tribe? Wasn't it an odd gift for a man to give another man? Of course it was, and Gretta knew it was high time she accept what might well be the truth: that after stealing her love and her trust — as worthless as they must have seemed to him — and trampling them under his boots, now Ulysses must want their sons, too.

Behind her the door latch rattled, and she turned to see a lantern-bearing porter striding to the middle of the car where he stood with his chest thrown forward and chin lifted. "The conductor wishes to inform you that we will be laying over here for three hours, due to unforeseen mechanical problems."

From several rows ahead, a man shouted, "The damn engine quit again?"

"Everything is under control. Stretch your legs, if you like. The depot's open, and the station manager has coffee and tea." He clapped his boots together and continued on to the next car.

The old woman across from Gretta shook her head, snorted, and turned aside to sleep. Gretta stood and looped her handbag over her shoulder. Outside, the air was still and she drew the collar of her sweater high against the chill. She needed to think, and the motion of walking, especially at night, allowed her to see her life in ways she couldn't see it otherwise. She walked down past a grain elevator to the lake, where a pair of mallards glided off toward the moon's reflection. At the shoreline she crouched to touch the water with her fingers. She cupped her hands and took a drink. The tang of vegetation was strong, and she spat it out. A fish turned itself over in the shallows. She walked back up the dirt street toward the depot, around the last car of the train, and then out of the rail yard toward the empty commercial district. The small town was silent except for occasional animal sounds, and Gretta thought of her mother's night walks in Copenhagen, especially during the year that her husband was gone, how she'd walked north from their place near Tivoli Gardens, crossed the canal bridge, and strolled the grounds behind the library. Gretta, sixteen then, followed her mother many times, wondering if she was going off to meet someone, suspecting it might even be her husband, Gretta's father, who'd gone to live in the Nyhavn district with a woman he'd known during his sailing years. But in fact her mother never rendezvoused with anyone, never went to fetch her husband either, but waited for him to come home of his own accord. And when he did, she took him back, commencing to feed him as she'd always done, launder his clothes, and even receive him in her bed,

103

though Gretta always sensed her mother's bitterness toward him. It wasn't long after, when he died, that Gretta left for America, unable to bear the thought of living any longer with someone who by turns was either angry or sad.

She came round a corner that brought the depot back into sight. *I won't come begging on my knees, and I won't play the fool,* she thought. *I have my dignity, after all. And damn it, I won't let you just come back and take my boys away.*

The repair took longer than the porter's estimate, but at least Gretta was able to sleep again, and by the time she woke, morning had arrived and the train was curving through the hills of St. Paul, the city larger and louder and richer than she remembered, nearly unrecognizable after so many years gone — the long views of the Mississippi blocked now by grand structures of brick or limestone, the sparsely settled streets filled in with two- and three-story homes beneath canopies of elm and linden and maple. Back here in the place where they met, Gretta felt certain that Ulysses was close by, that she was going to find him. But she also dreaded more than ever the humiliation of discovering what he'd been unwilling to tell her when he left — that he had no intention of returning to her.

Her plan was to visit her sister-in-law, who lived on a little side street off Summit Avenue with her husband. Or at least she hoped they still lived there. It seemed unlikely Ulysses would return to St. Paul without enlisting their help, though it was also possible that shame might keep him away. He'd always been given to brooding over mistakes others would shrug off as nothing. Once during their first year together, when he was in the habit of making breakfast and bringing it to her in bed, he gave her a hard-boiled egg which, when cracked open, revealed a shriveled, bug-eyed chick. Gretta shrieked, but she wasn't nearly as horrified as Ulysses had been. For months he berated himself, and he never made her breakfast again.

At the Union Depot she splashed water on her face and brushed out her hair and moistened a handkerchief to freshen herself beneath the arms. She sprinkled herself with the rose water she kept in her handbag, but still she felt dingy and rough, too coarse for the city. And so she kept her face lifted and her back straight, her eyes busily engaged, trying at least to present an air of knowing her business. On the brick street outside the depot she caught a horsecar and rode out toward Summit Hill beneath a sky marred only by high puffs of cloud. She meant to go straight to her sister-in-law's, but the approach of an old landmark — a Romanesque church on a corner — caused her to ask the driver to please stop.

She gathered up her skirt, took up her bag and her valise, and climbed down from the car, which rolled on without her, leaving Gretta standing at the top of a narrow, dead-end street that descended past the church into a grove of red maples, their leaves fast approaching their deepest coloration. It was the street on which her aunt and uncle had lived and where she lived with them for just less than a year, until she married and moved away. They'd died within a few months of each other a decade after Gretta left, and she still regretted never going back to visit. In truth, though, she hadn't been close to them, or at least that's what she told herself. They had an old-country reserve and seemed to resent her presence in their house: the food she ate, the popular songs she played on their piano, the language she took to so naturally. Yet for all that, she had longed to see them during her first years in Sloan's Crossing, if only to hear their consonant-thick speech and remember her childhood, and the country she feared she would never visit again.

The houses grew smaller and simpler as the ground descended, brick and stone two-stories giving way to wood-frame bunga-lows. Near the end of the street, though, standing higher and wider than the homes above it, was a bright Queen Anne. Appar-ently her aunt and uncle's little place had been torn down, she thought, replaced with this one — though another few paces brought her directly to the front of the house, and she could see that crouched in its shadow was the original cottage, its sid-ing flaked away to bare wood, its front stoop gone, most of the windowpanes missing or broken. A section of roof had caved in. Gretta walked carefully toward it, skirt knot-ted in her hand, stiff weeds snapping under-foot and slapping against her stockings. The front door stood ajar. A tuft of flowers — geraniums and daisies, still blooming some-how — sprouted from the window box that her aunt had been so proud of. Gretta stepped close and put her face to one of the unbroken panes, where she saw her reflec-tion.

That's me, she thought, staring. It was hard to believe, though, with the deep creases at the sides of her mouth and the sunken cheeks, the tight, straight line where she used to have lips, the jutting cords in her neck. Disgusted, she stepped to the side, took hold of the doorframe and pulled herself up and over the rotting threshold to stand where the welcome mat used to be, the one that said VELKOMMEN. She waited for her eyes to adjust. Then she moved toward the corner of the big room where Aunt Matty had kept her single extravagance, the piano with the lift-top that she'd insisted be shipped from Copenhagen, no matter the fee — *Or I won't cross over with you,* she'd always bragged of telling her husband. But there was a gaping hole in the floor, boards splintered and broken at the edges, and above this a corresponding hole in the roof, where a small dark cloud was passing across the sky. She slid her feet ahead, one foot-length at a time, until she stood at the very edge, leaning over the lip. The piano sat tilted on the cellar floor, lid slammed shut, its once well-oiled surface as dull as dirt.

"I'm sorry," she said, as much to the piano as to her aunt, who she hoped couldn't see this from wherever she might be.

Other things also remained. The round, claw-footed table where they'd taken their meals. A painting on the wall of a city street in Denmark, all the vivid colors gone out of

108

it. And lying on the floor, its glass missing and face cracked, the clock whose hollow ticking used to keep her awake at night, wondering if she'd made a mistake in leaving her mother to come here. Gretta left everything where it was, didn't venture into the bedrooms or kitchen, the pain too great, all these cherished things meaning nothing to the people who'd bought the place and built their house beside it. And yet she couldn't help feeling that she was the culpable one, ignoring her aunt and uncle in their last years.

She went back uphill and waited at the church until a horsecar pulled up in the same spot she used to catch it every day. The driver was young, his straight body tense with confidence, and his eyes took her in whole before glancing past her, frowning, as if she'd left some kind of trouble behind. During the months Gretta had lived here, the driver of the car had been Ulysses, who each morning gave her a ride west to the grand house on Summit where she cleaned and cooked for a shrunken, aging merchant who sat all day in a massive chair before the fire, filling journals with his cribbed hand. Then in the evening Ulysses would come by and carry her home again. He'd never talked much — predictions of the weather, his dream of leaving the city — but he was a patient listener, and Gretta admired his military bearing and his masculine certainty, not to mention the cleft in his chin and his pale eyes, which seemed to harbor some hidden pain. She'd been so young then, eighteen, and she saw in him everything she needed to see in a man: hardness enough to protect her from the world and kindness enough to make him a pleasant companion — an able guide through the perils of this new country. She had not pressed to learn how he had gained these qualities, although she knew he had been in the war. Nor had she considered that he might have seen in her the cure for his own needs and fears, and now she mused on her youthful selfishness.

At the intersection of Summit and Dale — another familiar stop — she got off and walked two blocks north. The house appeared unchanged, a two-story clapboard that looked like it belonged in a farmyard. The buildings on either side were recently built, three stories high, brown brick, modern and shiny. For a few minutes she stood in the street, summoning her courage. She'd never been comfortable with Florence and Charles, and in fact had spent little time with them, even though Ulysses, when she met him, was living in a small room at the back of their house. Florence was twenty years older than her brother, and by the time Ulysses stayed with her, she and Charles had already raised their children. It had always seemed to Gretta that her husband had avoided his sister, and once he and Gretta had moved to Sloan's Crossing, the annual letter at Christmastime was the only contact they had had with St. Paul.

She knocked on the door and a boy appeared, twelve or thirteen years old, with a cleft in his chin that she couldn't help smiling at, and familiar hands, long and thick-knuckled. Despite herself, she imagined taking those hands and pressing them to her face. She stepped back, nearly stumbling.

"Can I help you, Ma'am?"

"I'm wondering, are your parents at home? Or your grandparents, I mean."

He turned and called back into the house, "Grandma, there's a woman here to see you," then turned back again. "She don't move so quick these days."

"Or your grandpa, I could talk with him too," Gretta said. "That would be fine."

"Grampa ain't well," the boy said, matter of fact. "Got seized up good, which is the reason I am here. My folks left me to stay on and help take care of him." He aimed a thumb over his shoulder as he spoke, the act of doing so seeming to produce the woman herself, Florence, who was bent over double and leaning on a cane. Her face was thinner and grayer, though still wide through the jaw, and her eyes were as pale as her brother's. She came up close behind her grandson, took him by the shoulders, and looked up at Gretta.

"Hello, Florence," Gretta said. Standing on the wooden step, she studied her sister-in-law's eyes, watching for recognition. They blinked but remained neutral.

"How is my brother?" Florence asked.

All at once the valise suspended from Gretta's fist felt impossibly heavy, and she leaned to the side to let it fall on the step. Her first glimpse of the house had caused her to think Ulysses was close by, but that feeling passed now like a sparrow from a room.

"Didn't you get my letter?" Gretta asked.

Florence nodded. "We've had troubles here. I figured you would write again if he didn't show up. Louie?" — she pushed her grandson forward and pointed him toward Gretta's valise — "bring that grip inside for her." Then she backstepped into the house, waving Gretta forward. The sitting room was unchanged: dark wainscoting halfway up the walls, a painting of ships on a stormy sea, the pine stairway rising to the dark second floor. Florence pointed her to a cane rocker with a leather seat, and Louie set her valise on the floor next to her. Florence took a high-backed chair upholstered in rose velour. Louie pulled up a stool.

"Recognized you right off," Florence said. "You look mostly the same."

Gretta was not able to respond in kind, but tried to smile. "I'm sorry about Charles," she said. "What happened?"

Florence swatted the air, as if Gretta's condolences meant nothing.

"Gramma don't like talking about it," Louie said.

"He had a spell in early July. Can't move anything on his left side. Can't even get out of bed for his private business."

"I'm sorry."

A voice floated down from upstairs. "Louie? Louie?"

Florence said, "I never did understand my brother. 'Course I was out of the house by the time he was born, and then after the wars when he lived here with Charlie and me, he stayed to himself. Preferred his own company, such as it was. Never seemed interested in talking or spending time. We weren't like family, somehow." She cleared her throat and leveled her face at Gretta. She narrowed her pale eyes. "We haven't seen him," she said. "He has not been here, I assure you. Wish I could tell you that he had."

From upstairs the voice came again, more urgent this time. "Louie, Florence. I'm going to need somebody now."

"Go ahead, please," Gretta said. "I'm fine here."

Florence rolled her eyes, then nodded at her grandson and pushed herself up from her chair. As she moved toward the stairway, leaning on her cane, Louie cut a line around her and mounted the stairs two at a time.

Gretta crossed to the kitchen, where the pine floor was still painted red and the big Glenwood stove dominated the north wall. She pushed open the door to the back room where Ulysses had slept. The narrow bed was gone, and in its place stood an open cabinet crammed full of canned goods, sacks of flour and sugar, spice jars. The desk he'd used was still here, in the same corner, but instead of the neat row of sharpened pencils Gretta remembered, and the half-drawn building plans, its top was covered with haphazard piles of yellowing newspapers. The floor, too, was a shambles, unnavigable, littered with broken chairs, cardboard boxes, empty bottles, stacks of magazines, the whole mess reinforcing Gretta's sense that Florence was telling the truth, that Ulysses had not been here — and that Florence wasn't going to be of any help in finding him, either.

Should I be surprised? Gretta thought.

The only other place she'd thought to go was the Minneapolis headquarters of the Grand Army of the Republic, in the Loan and Trust building. Ulysses used to receive their letters in fine, official-looking envelopes, and it was Gretta's notion that she might discover in their offices lists of the men with whom he'd served, along with their addresses. Then again, she might return home empty-handed, with nothing more than she already knew. What frightened her most, however, was that her search might lead in some roundabout way to a place she wished she hadn't found.

Florence and Louie returned from upstairs, and Gretta, trying to exhibit a concern she didn't feel, asked if Charles was all right.

"If all right means your face hasn't got any color in it and your fingers can't hold a fork, then yes, he's fine and dandy. We've been trying to feed him cow liver, for the iron, but he's not fond of it. Seems to bleed straight through him." Florence offered a humorless laugh. "Not that Charlie's any concern of yours, Gretta. Now about my little brother — you gave me the impression he left without saying anything."

"Well, there was a note — to the effect that he had found work. But he didn't say where."

"Work that he needed, as I recall. Your letter said as much. He was always a hard worker, Ulysses. Hired himself out from the time he was big enough to handle a shovel or lift a hammer. And if there was nothing for him in Sloan's Crossing, then I suppose he had to go someplace else."

"Of course. But wouldn't you think he'd have said where?"

"Yes." Florence rolled her eyes again. Another unexplainable phenomenon, like her husband's illness.

"Tell me," Gretta said. "Were there ever any women that you remember? Before *me*?"

"No. No. I used to tell him he needed one, though, I remember that."

"He has a buckskin tobacco pouch, about this big" — Gretta indicated its size with her hands — "with a lovely beaded pattern, yellow and blue, a mountain beneath a sun.

116

I've always wondered who made it."

"I wouldn't know, because I never snooped in his things. But I will say I'm surprised he walked off like he did. He was always so dependable." Florence looked up at Gretta, and for a moment her eyes looked darker and softer. "And I know he loves you," she said. "Of course my brother is a loner — at least before you came along, he was. Hardly came out of his room at night, especially after he got back the second time. He used to take his plate of supper back there and eat all by himself."

"What do you mean, the second time?" Gretta asked.

"After his second enlistment."

"I don't understand."

"You don't understand what?"

The feeling in Gretta's stomach was the same as what came when you were walking at night and stepped forward onto ground an inch or two lower than expected — that brief sensation of falling then catching yourself. "He enlisted twice?" she said.

Florence looked off in a corner, frowning. She blinked and turned to Louie, who had been sitting quietly on his stool. "You know that chest of drawers in the north bedroom? Run up and yank the bottom one, right side, and bring it down here. The right side,

Louie. Go on." As the boy headed for the stairs, Florence turned back to Gretta. "He was discharged in sixty-five, after the Rebs surrendered, and came back here that summer. He didn't stay in the service between campaigns."

Gretta waited, not sure what question to ask.

"He stayed around for about a year, I suppose it was. Worked for a builder by the name of Sirkel, putting up houses all over this part of the city. I thought he was doing pretty good. But then the next summer he reenlisted. Sixty-six, it would've been. No, maybe he was here two years. Might have been sixty-seven he went back in. He went down to Kansas, anyway, and joined up with the Cavalry."

"Kansas?"

"That's what I said. Kansas."

Gretta was light-headed suddenly, her fingers tingling. She had never heard Ulysses mention reenlisting. Not once. She had never heard him mention Kansas or, for that matter, the Cavalry. He had never spoken of a Mr. Sirkel, or of building houses after coming home from the war. As far as Gretta knew, he came back to St. Paul in sixty-five, started driving horsecars, and stayed at it until she came along.

"It was the second time he came home —
this would have been in sixty-nine — that
he started driving the horses, working the
route. Not so long before you met him."

Louie was back from upstairs now with
the drawer, which was wide and shallow,
glass-knobbed, and when Florence nodded
at him, he dropped it unceremoniously on
Gretta's lap. There was little in it — some
of Ulysses's old drawings and building plans
scattered across the top of whatever else
there might be.

"He was never one to talk about his time
out there," Florence said, "and I never saw
any of his service papers. But I think there
might be a few letters from a fellow he
served with." She nodded at the drawer.
"Been a long time since the last one came.
A dozen years probably."

"Why didn't you send them on?"

"I sent the first one, soon's I got it.
Ulysses wrote me back and said if any more
showed up, I should toss them out, he
didn't want them. I didn't have the heart,
though. Figured he might change his mind
one day. Anyway, there's only a few, three
altogether I believe, and I didn't open any
but the first."

Gretta's impulse was to get up and carry
the drawer out of the house and go off to a

place where she could sort through its contents alone. She clenched her stomach as she lifted out her husband's old drawings one by one, half a dozen of them, and set them on the floor next to her, pencil sketches of houses, barns, granaries, along with hand-drawn floor plans and lists of building materials. Beneath these were a couple of stories cut from newspapers — nothing that caught Gretta's eye — then finally a small packet of letters, tied in string. She slipped the top one out, a faded white envelope from the U.S. Army. She held it up to read the address, then read it again for good measure before looking sharply at Florence.

"This one isn't his," Gretta said.

Florence scowled and blinked. She pointed a finger at the letters still lying in the drawer.

Gretta set aside the one she was holding and picked up the next, sent by a Jim Powers from Fort Riley, Kansas. A brown envelope. This one, same as the first, was addressed not to *Ulysses Pope,* but to *Ulysses Popovich,* 416 Dale Street East, St. Paul, Minnesota. She put it down and reached for the next two, both unopened, both bearing the same address and return address. Gretta had become so accustomed to masking what she felt that her face remained composed, even though her neck and back were suddenly flushed and slick. The beat of her heart was so heavy that she put a hand on her breast to calm it.

"Popovich," she said.

Florence turned to give Gretta a sideways look, frowning at her. "You didn't know?"

"How would I know if he didn't tell me?"

"Pope, Popovich — I suppose it doesn't matter."

Although she hadn't taken a breath, Gretta's lungs were full to bursting. She coughed hard, expelling what she could, then managed to suck in a thimbleful of air, enough to say, "It doesn't matter that I don't know my husband's name?"

"Well he changed it before he met you, obviously."

She concentrated on her breathing. Closed her eyes and saw Ulysses on the day of their wedding, standing tall and straight at the altar where they exchanged their vows. Looked into his pale eyes and tried to find in them a place to rest, some bit of green earth or brown soil, anything at all to lean against or fall down upon.

"Are you all right?" Florence bent forward and touched Gretta's wrist with surprising sympathy. "Louie, go fetch a glass of water."

121

Gretta gathered her wits and picked up the first envelope from the floor, the one from the U.S. Army. Inside were the discharge papers, dated February 18, 1869 — six months before she met him — of Ulysses Popovich. *My husband,* she thought. She picked up the next one, the already opened envelope from Jim Powers, from Fort Riley, Kansas, slipped out the single sheet, and read. In a scrawling hand, the man complained of the heat and the terrible food, bemoaned a lost but well-deserved promotion, and boasted of his upcoming marriage to a woman from nearby Junction City, a widow with three young children. Gretta returned it to its envelope and then the other letters to the drawer, along with the drawings and the newspaper cuttings. She accepted the glass of water from Louie and took a long drink. Then looked at Florence.

"Why?" she asked her sister-in-law.

Florence shook her head. "I'm not sure I know. Or I should say, I'm not sure I understand. He did it when he got back in sixty-nine, the second time. He said our name made him sound like our family just stepped off the boat, instead of going all the way back to the last century, which we do. We had people here before the War of the Revolution, for pity's sake. But he said the men in the service made jokes. Popovich, Papa bitch, popinjay, I don't know. Said he wanted his children, if he ever had any, to have an American name. Now, Charlie and I didn't think much of the idea, I'll tell you that. Pope? Sounded awful high and mighty to our ears. Not to mention we aren't Catholic. But of course Dad was the one who would have cared, and by then he and mother were long gone."

"But why wouldn't he say anything to *me*?"

Florence laughed. "Does my brother ever say anything he doesn't need to say?"

Gretta couldn't muster a response, only shook her head before asking Florence if she could take the letters with her.

"I don't need them, God knows. Louie, go and get her a paper sack," she said.

"Aren't you going to take her upstairs, Gramma, before she leaves?" Louie asked.

"Oh." Florence raised a hand dismissively. "Charlie said he wanted to see you, as long as you're here." She pointed up toward the second floor and managed a thin smile. "He always thought Ulysses did well by himself — with you, I mean."

"He did? Well, thank you," Gretta said.

Upstairs, Charlie was propped against the headboard, chin on his chest, the bony knobs of his shoulders jutting beneath the filthy cotton bedshirt he wore. When Gretta touched her lips to his sunken cheek, he cried from one eye. He reached up with his good arm and pulled her close. The smell of him took her back to Denmark, standing as a girl next to the bed of her dying grandfather.

"Sorry," he whispered into her ear. "I'm so sorry."

She pulled away and looked into his eyes, their blue irises swimming in yellow. "Do you have any idea where he might have gone?" she asked him.

Charlie licked his lips, which were skewed to one side and colorless. He shook his head. His voice when he spoke was wet and shallow. "Only that he came back different — from out west. Only that. He came back different." He lifted his hand again and opened it wide, palm out, and Gretta recalled the day she and Ulysses left St. Paul for Sloan's Crossing, Florence and Charlie standing on the platform as the train moved off, Charlie's hand lifted just like this as he waved good-bye.

Ten minutes later she was back on the car, heading toward Minneapolis and the offices of the Grand Army of the Republic, where she hoped to find names and addresses of men with whom Ulysses had served. Possibly Jim Powers, whose remaining two letters she had already opened and read. They were not interesting, full of masculine banalities, but written nonetheless by a man who likely knew more about her husband's past than she knew herself.

As she watched the city move by, she leaned back and tried to relax. The place may have changed more than she had expected, but the rhythm of the horse's shoes against the brick street could hardly be more familiar. The smells, too. The dying leaves of the sycamores, oaks, and elms, the leather padding on the seats, the sweating horse, and the scent of the people themselves. What brought her back more than anything, though, was the driver, sitting right there in front of her, straight and broad-shouldered, and wearing a canvas jacket. He might as well have been her husband all those years ago, and she half expected him to turn around and give her that long look, his pale eyes cutting into her.

Where are you? she thought. *Who are you?*

8
ALONG THE TONGUE

Down next to the stream the air was filled with ice crystals, and the ragged blanket of clouds, no higher than the tops of the cottonwoods, dipped and swelled before a small breeze. Last night this valley had been a naked cleft beneath the dome of sharp stars. Now it was a small gray room, cut off from the world beyond it. As Ulysses pounded his feet into the cold-stiffened boots, the ox, attached by its lead to a cottonwood branch, swung its ugly head and made a low, guttural sound, like an old man huffing in his sleep.

"Yes, yes. Give a man the chance to piss, will you?"

He'd leased the animal from Miles City's liveryman, named Church, and so far he was unimpressed. Two days out, and they'd covered thirty miles at most. The ox had a tendency to wander off trail, though the ruts were well established, and come to a full stop every time Ulysses set down the switch for more than a minute. "A good puller" is what Church had said, "not an ornery bone in its body."

Ulysses buttoned his pants and walked up to the beast. He scratched its hard head. "That doesn't look good," he said. "Not good at all." Its right eye, which appeared rheumy yesterday, was covered this morning with a greenish, viscous matter. Ulysses wiped it away as best he could. "I'll be wanting my deposit back on you," he told the animal, and led it down to the water, where it drank long and patiently, lifting its head a couple times and swinging around to have a look at Ulysses, as if it didn't quite trust a man who used the switch so freely.

"Still here," Ulysses said, kneeling upstream and bending to drink. The water had a bitter, almost licorice flavor. No color to it, though, and no visible particles afloat — better water, in any case, than much of what passed for drinkable during his time in the wars. After retying the ox to the cottonwood, he went searching for dry windfall, finding what he needed in an aging stand of cedars on the hillside above camp. He set the kindling sticks to flame and put on a pot of water for coffee. Using a small keg of molasses for his chair, he sat chewing on a strap of jerky, waiting for the water to boil and adding branches to the fire. Early moments like these were the dangerous part of the day, when dreams still occupied the mind, and it didn't help being out here alone, no sounds but the small breeze in the dead leaves, the moving water, the crackle of burning wood. He reached out and set the middle knuckle of his fist against the pot. It was getting warm.

As he took his morning pipe, he turned in his Bible to the book of the prophet Isaiah, his eyes falling on words from its first chapter: "Though your sins be as scarlet, they shall be as white as snow; though they be red like crimson, they shall be as wool. If ye be willing and obedient, ye shall eat the good of the land: But if ye refuse and rebel, ye shall be devoured with the sword." Above him the sky hovered thick and low, like a clever lid fashioned for the sake of keeping his prayers on earth. He prayed anyway, for the past to stay where it was until he could find his way back to it, and for the chance to make good. Then the water was ready, and he drank his morning coffee, which had the effect as always of lightening his mood and improving the look of his prospects. It might be possible yet that all would be fine.

When the sky had cleared enough to show

the tops of the hills, he kicked out the fire, rolled up the dusty robe, and packed his gear and the keg of molasses, too. He put the half-blind ox in its traces and set out in the wagon for the Cheyenne agency. It was a long, steep climb, Ulysses urging the ox to the top, but once they had achieved the trail again, their wheels fell into the double-rutted path and they rolled on, squeaking, the Tongue River a mere curving twinkle beneath them. The late September sun had burned off every trace of fog.

By midmorning the back and flanks of the yellow ox were dark with sweat. Ulysses drove with his sleeves rolled to his elbows and shirt collar open to catch the small southwesterly breeze, which kept the dust they raised behind them. From time to time, he took out his mouth harp and blew a few tunes, hymns mostly, with the occasional Army song tossed in for good measure, and long about noon he approached a small cluster of unpainted wooden buildings, a dozen or so, set out on the brown plain. Off to the north on a low rise, he saw a scattering of white tipis. Spitting distance to the south, a group of skinny boys played with sticks and a ball of hide, yelling and spinning and swatting each other. They caught sight of Ulysses on his wagon, and they set off in a run toward him.

All but one of them stopped well short of the wagon. The smallest boy came closer. He reminded Ulysses of Danny, his eyes too large for his head and seeming to take in the entire compass of space around him. He had a crippled leg but managed even so to skitter like a bug around to the back of the wagon, ducking as he went, and then pull himself up by his hands and peek over the backboard. There was not much to see, everything covered with tarpaulin, but the boy's nose twitched at the scent of edible goods.

Ulysses crooked a finger at him and the boy dropped out of sight, then reappeared, moving in a wary arc, circling like a sly mutt around the wagon's starboard side. The other boys — five of them — hung back in a tight knot.

"Bet you're hungry," Ulysses said. He set the handbrake and crawled back into the wagon's bed, where he peeled away a corner of the canvas, exposing large bags of potatoes. He shook out half a dozen cloth sacks, one after another, sliced open one of the big burlap bags, and put together a bundle of potatoes for each boy, now and then glancing at the little one, who had come up close to watch. He lifted the first sack of spuds and dropped it with a wink into the boy's waiting arms. The boy staggered to one side from the sudden weight of it, then righted himself and trotted back to his friends. One by one the rest of the boys came forward.

"You boys got mamas?" he asked them.

They looked first at each other, then off to the north at the tipis white beneath the noon sun.

"That's good," he said.

Their faces were wind-burned and gaunt, their cheeks hollow. They stole glances at the sacks full of potatoes, which rested on the buckboard next to Ulysses.

"One more question. Where do I find Adams?"

The five biggest boys turned as one to the small one, their spokesman now, who raised his arm and pointed a narrow finger west toward a long, squat building with a green door.

"Thank you." He tossed down the sacks of potatoes one by one, then watched the boys run off toward the north and the tipis. He released the handbrake, whistled, and snapped his switch at the ox, which bellowed and swung its head before pulling forward. At the building with the green door, he hauled in and climbed down. A

131

crude sign hung from the eave: TONGUE RIVER AGENCY. He knocked and waited, knocked again, and stepped back into the street, such as it was. Except for the boys, he seemed to have attracted no interest. A hundred feet away a pair of old women sat in the scant shade of a stunted poplar, bent at some kind of handiwork. Ulysses started toward them but hadn't gone a dozen steps before the sound of a dry hinge stopped him. He turned.

A man with a lumpy, turnip face leaned out from the green door, just his head and shoulders visible. "You're wantin' *me*?" he asked.

"I am if you're Adams."

He emerged from the doorway. He was round like a turnip, too, and stood with his fingers tucked into the front of his dirty pants, thumbs on the waistband, stomach thrown forward.

Ulysses put out his hand, which Adams regarded for a moment before meeting it with a soft, damp grip.

"I'm Pope," Ulysses said.

"What kind of freight you got?"

"I'll give you a look."

At the back of the wagon Ulysses pulled back the canvas to reveal the potatoes in their burlap bags, a dozen fifty-pound sacks

132

of flour, a few bolts of cotton in bright colors, and the keg of molasses he'd found on the side of the trail his first day out of Miles City. A few other odds and ends.

"I ain't seen you before, have I?" Adams asked.

"No. But I heard in Miles City that you had need of provisions down here. Heard the government shipments are running behind."

"Heard from who?"

"Church, at the livery. Also from the bone-man, Slovin."

"There's a pair of thieving bastards for you."

"They told me wrong?"

Adams pulled one small hand from the front of his pants and rested it on the top of his belly. He lifted his eyes to the empty sky as if searching for something there.

"They said considerably more than that, truth be told," Ulysses said. "About hungry people and the cold weather coming on, nothing in the storerooms. They said there's been talk of men getting restless and going off the reserve to hunt for game that's already hunted out."

"You got an earful then."

"I did."

Adams turned south, in the direction of a

cluster of men who had gathered across the dirt road and stood between a pair of squat log buildings, watching. The old women beneath the poplar tree watched now, too. Adams hawked and spat.

"You're not interested in what I've got?" Ulysses asked him.

"That ain't what I said. It gravels me, though, when a fellow I don't know from Judas comes rolling in on a Sunday morning, over-estimating the value of his load."

"We haven't talked about the value of my load. And what does Sunday morning have to do with it?"

"Day of rest and all — shit, not a thing," Adams said, breaking a smile. "Remember, though — I'm a Indian agent, not a banker. And the federal sons of bitches have me drawing from a well that's near to dry."

The men from across the road were coming forward, their feet raising little puffs of dust in the air. Seven of them. The pair of old women got up from beneath their tree and followed after. They all passed close enough to have a look at the cargo before they went to stand in the shade of the agency building. Ulysses reached into the bed, right behind the buckboard, and shoved a couple bags of potatoes toward the back, exposing a woolen blanket, which he tossed aside. On the wagon's plank bed was a layer of oilcloth packages, each a foot and a half in length and as big around as a man's arm. He lifted one out and covered up the rest with the blanket, then walked past Adams, unwrapping the package as he went. The men were old, most of them, or getting there, gray hair to their shoulders, faces lean and wrinkled. A couple had wide-brimmed hats, pulled down low. The old women were thin, too, and just as wrinkled. They were barefooted. Ulysses stepped toward the women first and offered the opened package of jerked beef, each strap of it as thick as cinch leather. The smell of grease, pepper, and smoke was sharp. The women reached out, nodding their thanks. Ulysses moved toward the men.

From the wagon, Adams said, "Hey, What's-your-name — you don't just *give* the shit away!"

"Well I don't plan on hauling it back to Miles City."

"Here now, let's talk." Adams lifted his hands in the air like a preacher inviting his congregation to stand. "I believe you and I can work something out. Strike a reasonable deal. Come on now."

Ulysses distributed the entire package of the beef, the women securing several lengths each, and then he bunched up the oilcloth and tossed it back in the wagon.

Adams pointed at the buckboard. "Jump up there now, man, you hear me? And pull it around back."

The old men were tugging at the beef with their teeth, chewing and swallowing, their eyes steady on Adams. The women meanwhile headed north toward the tipis. Taking his sweet time, Ulysses climbed up on the buckboard and picked up the driving lines, snapped them against the animal's back, and clicked his tongue. The ox didn't budge. When he touched the switch to its rump, though, it bellowed and stamped, then grudgingly stepped forward. Adams ran ahead, rounding the corner of the building and pointing the way toward a door that opened at the back. "Right over here," he said.

The ox, catching the smells of tobacco, gunpowder, and lard, put its big nose in the air and pulled the wagon right up close along the wall, next to the door. Adams angled a pair of two-by-ten planks to stretch between the back of the wagon and the threshold of the doorway then put his body in motion. Ulysses wouldn't have guessed the man could move so fast or work so hard — grabbing the large bags of potatoes, one under each arm, and bouncing along the planks into the storeroom. Each time he re-appeared from inside, he blinked against the bright sun and rubbed his hands together like a fly. In ten minutes the wagon was empty. Sweat ran in dirty streaks down the fat man's face. His shirt was soaked through.

"You'll load it all back on if I don't like your price," Ulysses told him.

Adams tipped his head straight back and squinted at the sun. "Let's go in and sit down," he said. "I'm thirsty as a mule in hell."

He led the way, ducking into a sunnier room at the front, where he lifted a jug from a cupboard and set it down upon the table. He pointed Ulysses toward a hoop-backed chair, then grabbed a pair of cloudy drinking glasses from the windowsill, pinching them together with his thumb and first two fingers. Pouring from the jug, he filled both to the top, handed one to Ulysses, and drank off his own like it was water.

"Whuff," he said and smacked himself on the chest.

"You all right there?"

"Oh God, that's good. That's so good. Give it a go."

"Looks dangerous," Ulysses said. But he

lifted his glass anyway. The whiskey tasted the way turpentine smelled, strong enough to curdle a man's liver. He set it down and looked at it. Specks of black, like pepper, floated in the dark brown liquid.

"She's got a kick, don't she," Adams said.

Ulysses could feel a slight pressure, like oozing oil, settle across the crown of his head and begin seeping down into the roots of his hair. He blinked a couple times and pushed the glass to the middle of the table.

"Twenty-five dollars for the load," he said. "Not one penny less."

"I'll give you fifteen." Adams poured himself another whiskey.

"Thirty, then, or you start reloading my wagon. Or listen" — he pointed out the rippled window at the front, where the men were still gathered, chewing on the jerked beef — "I'll call your friends over to help. Thirty."

"Twenty-five then," Adams said.

"Now it's thirty. You lost your chance at twenty-five."

"Piss on you." Adams sighed and poured himself a third big glassful and put it to his red lips. After a long swallow he set it down, lifted a finger as if to say *Give me a minute,* then stood wearily and hauled himself grumbling into the back room.

Without thinking, Ulysses reached into his pocket where his fingers grazed the small agate Eli had found along the riverbank when he was three. It was red, with three white spots on it, two large and one small. "Look — it's Mother, and you, and me," Eli had said that day, pointing at each spot in turn. Ulysses had drilled a hole through it, strung it on a small circle of buckskin lacing, and had carried it with him ever since, devoted as he was to tokens and keepsakes — like the broken watch he carried, and the green tin turtle, given to him by a priest at Fort Dodge. Drawing the agate from his pocket and holding it up to the window light, he experienced a paralyzing clutch in his chest at the thought of his wife and sons back home. It was going to be hard to explain everything, he knew that. And especially to himself.

Twice in Bismarck — before the widow, then after — he'd walked into the telegraph office meaning to send a message home. On both occasions he failed to do it. In Miles City he made one more attempt, but he might as well have been trying to speak in Chinese for what it cost him to stand like a fool before the telegraph man, shaking his head, lips frozen, paralyzed by competing aches: shame for who he was, and a palpable love for his wife. It wasn't so different from what happened when he'd tried telling Gretta that he needed to leave, that there was something he had to do. Several times during the months leading up to that last day, he stood up from the supper table, kissed her good-bye, and walked off toward Fargo with no intention of coming back. Once he'd made it ten miles down the road, clear to Glyndon, not returning home till long after midnight and with no explanation for Gretta, who didn't ask for one. She could be timid like that, afraid to confront him — likely aware that the truth, if she let him tell it, would complicate her life in ways she wasn't ready to cope with. And so her habit had been to accept him back wordlessly, finding a place for his body against hers and insisting in this manner that all was forgiven. Of course she could be a whirlwind, too, like when she'd learned about the note he'd arranged with Fogarty, letting him have it good, telling him that a man as stupid as he was couldn't be of any possible use to her.

Adams returned from the backroom and dropped into the chair opposite Ulysses, a clutch of bills in one hand, silver dollars in the other. "You're a bloody gypsy," he said, laying out the money on the table. "I hope you're satisfied."

"I'm not."

Adams let out a groan.

"I'm looking for somebody."

"Ah. Who's the lucky bastard?"

"His name's Magpie."

"A Indian. What do you want with a Indian?"

"Do you know him?"

Adams leaned back and frowned at the ceiling. Folded his hands and rested them on his belly. Closed his eyes. "This Magpie, is he Cheyenne or Crow?"

"Cheyenne. Southern Cheyenne."

"This here's the northern reserve. You know that." He looked at Ulysses straight on. "Don't you?"

"I do. And I've got reason to believe he's up here someplace."

"Reason to believe."

"I've been told."

The fat man shrugged. "A few southern bucks come up this way in seventy-six for that little party Sitting Bull had. Got themselves a few scalps, too. Some stayed on. Of those that went back a few hightailed it up here again a few years later, complaining about the heat down there in the territories. I reckon your Magpie could be one of them."

"So, what can you tell me?"

Adams, sighing, poured himself more whiskey. He took a swallow then made a show of thinking for a while before he said, "I don't make it my business to know every Indian on the reservation, is what I can tell you. My advice is, ask around."

Ulysses tidied up the pile of bills and coins on the table and tucked them into his money pouch, which he returned to the inner pocket of his jacket. "All right then, I thank you for your time."

Adams lifted his glass the full length of his short right arm, as if in a toast, and smiled bleary-eyed. Ulysses took out the red agate again, held it up to what little light the dirty window allowed, and he stroked his finger along its spots, trying to bring their faces to mind.

9
A PAIR OF GHOSTS

After helping Reverend Pearl with another service in the oak-strewn park, they'd slept once more in the river camp. This morning, waking with frost in their hair, they'd tied up their bedrolls and followed the reverend to the depot, where he bought a ticket to Jamestown for himself and tickets to Bismarck for the two of them. Then he'd led them straight to the dining car, where he showed them how to rap the side of a boiled egg with a single swat of his table knife, remove the top, and spoon out the tender whites and runny yolk.

"I'm happy in a boxcar," he told them, dabbing his lips with a pressed, white napkin. "But happier in first class."

The prairie was brown, flat, and mostly treeless, the sun cool and white as it climbed toward the west. In every direction, endless, wavering Vs of geese aloft. Sentinel hawks on telegraph poles. Reverend Pearl had gotten off at Jamestown, bedroll under his arm, a pair of socks poking out from his coat pocket. He had smiled as the train pulled away, walking along the platform beneath the boys' window. "Say hello to your father when you see him, won't you? And tell him I said God is there waiting for him, wherever he's going."

Now it was late afternoon and the boys were standing in the dirt street, in front of a big four-square house, white with green shutters. To find the place, they'd walked about half a mile north from the rail station. Before they could go up and knock, the door swung open and a woman appeared, carrying a watering can. Seeing her made Eli's heart sink. She was both prettier and younger than he'd allowed himself to think she might be, maple-colored hair falling in waves past her shoulders, good color in her face, a full mouth, and a jawline that ended in a fine, pointed chin, which lifted now as she tried to make out who these boys were, standing in the street, watching her. She was tall and slim like their mother, wearing a yellow dress tailored close to her body. She tipped the can to sprinkle a pot of red flowers on the stoop.

Danny gripped Eli's arm, pulled down, and whispered into his brother's ear: "You think he's here?" It was the question Eli had tried to push out of his head all day long.

"Course not. Quiet."

"Hello," she said.

"Ma'am."

"Is there something I can do for you boys?" She was still smiling, but Eli could see her lips tighten, he was sure of it.

He put a hand at the center of his brother's back and together they moved forward, Eli at the same time retrieving the letter from the inner pocket of his coat and holding it out to her. She blinked at it for a moment, then took it and scanned down the page. Eli could tell that she wasn't as young as he'd first thought. She had worry lines on her forehead and crow's feet at the corners of her eyes, which were large and light green and tired. She took a breath and handed the letter back. "Well I guess you know who I am," she said. "You boys had better come in."

Eli steeled himself, half-expecting to see his father at her kitchen table — but there was no one here, and the tightness in his belly eased. She pointed them into chairs and poured out glasses of milk from a pitcher she took from the icebox. Although Eli was thirsty, he paced himself, unwilling to seem too grateful. He looked straight at her as he sipped the cool milk, asking her in his mind, *Where is he? What lies are you going to tell us?*

Danny quickly emptied his glass.

"More?" she asked him, then refilled his glass and watched him drink that down as fast as he did the first. He didn't even pause to breathe.

"You've been traveling hard."

Danny nodded, wiping his mouth. Eli said nothing. Her gentle elegance and comforting voice made him nervous. She seemed like a woman able to accomplish whatever she set her mind to.

"I'd imagined he was home by now," she said, and pushed the letter across the table.

"He never came home," Eli said. "We haven't seen him since he left in July. He hasn't sent a letter or a telegram, nothing. We thought you might be able to help us."

Arms crossed in front of her, Mrs. Powers lowered herself into one of the ladder-back kitchen chairs and leaned forward. She looked briefly at Danny then back at Eli. "He never received it then," she said, nodding at the letter still open on the table.

"That's right."

"My brother got it straight from the postman," Danny said.

146

She waited, her head moving in a subtle nod.

"Didn't see any reason to show it to our mother," Eli said.

She leaned back in her chair, laid her hands in her lap, and looked out the window that faced east, where the afternoon light was fading. "Does she know where you are?"

"Yes," Eli said. "Of course."

Beside him, Danny nodded emphatically. They'd talked about the questions she might ask, rehearsing the answers.

"Because if she doesn't know, first thing I have to do is walk downtown and have a telegram sent."

"She asked us to go," Eli said.

"But you told me she didn't see the letter."

"She didn't see it, Ma'am. But all the same, we knew he was coming out this way. He talked about it."

"He *told* you he was leaving?" She was still gazing out the window, the lines in her forehead sharpening.

"He talked about finding work, yes. On a rail crew. Or in the silver mines. Something anyway." Eli was surprised at how easy it was, lying to her, and watched her face to see how she took it, how it jibed with her own account of things.

"We needed the money," Danny said.

"I see." She turned and looked at them now, her eyes bright and hard, and Eli knew there were two conversations going on here, one with words and the other inside their heads.

"Do you know where he is?" he asked her.

"No, I don't," she responded, just that quick. "You have to understand, I never laid eyes on your father until he stopped by that day, the end of July, I believe it was. I knew *of* him, of course, from my husband — they served in the army together. Jim died a year ago, but your father hadn't heard about it. He didn't know until he got here."

"I'm sorry, Ma'am."

"He mentioned Jim, surely. Didn't he? He must have told you stories."

Eli shook his head. "He never talks about the war."

There was an awkward silence. Then Mrs. Powers smiled. "Men can be funny that way, can't they — what they say and don't say about things. Of course, your being men, it might not seem funny to you." She stood abruptly from the table and put her palms together. She said, "What am I thinking? You must be starving, and I don't have supper even started yet. Let's get you situated. Come on, now" — and she gestured them up from the table. "I'll go out back and dress a nice big chicken, dig some red potatoes from the garden. Here —" and she ushered them into the sitting room and a pair of high-backed, upholstered chairs. "There's some books on the shelf there — Jim loved to read. Or maybe you want to just rest awhile. I won't be more than half an hour. We can talk once I've got supper going."

As soon as she was gone, Eli and Danny climbed the stairs to the second floor and began searching, hunting through the dressers and closets of all three rooms, sifting fast through letters and papers, catalogs, magazines, books, men's shirts and trousers, women's dresses, blouses, stockings and even undergarments, some of these light and silky — lifting them up and then laying them back with care, so that nothing would appear disturbed. Yet they didn't find a thing to suggest that he'd been here, the men's clothes all smaller by far than what their father could wear. Back on the main floor, they searched the kitchen cupboard, the china hutch in the dining room, every nook and cranny, working as fast as they were able, and going at last through the massive oak secretary that took up the whole north wall of the sitting room. Every

149

minute or so, Eli glanced out a window to check on Mrs. Powers — chopping off the head of a flapping bird, talking with a gray-haired neighbor lady at the far side of the yard, kneeling in a row of wilted potato plants, a spade lying beside her.

"What do you think she's going to tell us?" Danny asked.

"Less than she knows," Eli said. "Keep your eyes open."

By the time she came inside, the boys were back in their chairs, and through the archway they watched her move about the kitchen, peeling potatoes and putting the hen on to boil. Setting the table. Eli felt himself giving way to exhaustion, his arms and legs tingling, sand-filled. Danny's head hung forward and to one side, and he was blinking to stay awake.

"You look like a pair of ghosts," Mrs. Powers said, joining them. Her face was flushed from her work. She pulled out an ottoman from between their two chairs and sat down, crossing her knees. "You've put me in a tight place, haven't you. Either I decide to believe what you've said about telling your mother, in which case I'm obligated to help you. Or else I *don't* believe you — and then I have little choice but to send you home."

Eli says, "You can believe us, Ma'am —"

She lifted her hand, stopping him. "But whether I should or not, I have decided I will." She smiled. "It must be those honest faces of yours. Now, you asked me where he is, and I told you the truth — I don't know. But I do know that when he left here, he was heading to Miles City, Montana Territory, to see if he could make some money in bones. Buffalo bones. Hearing him talk, there must be good profits in that. From there I expected he would be going back home."

Eli kept his eyes on her, willing her to say more, holding her gaze with a hardness he feared might be impolite.

"He thought he could persuade Jim to go along with him, though I would never have allowed such a thing — I preferred to keep my husband close by. The way I saw it, Jim had gotten more than his fill of wandering by the time we married. Not to mention, I lost a husband when I was young and had no intention of losing another, not if I could help it. You see, I had three young children when I met Jimmy."

"They're grown up?" Danny asked.

"One's in Denver, yes, and I'm lucky if I see her every other year. She's my oldest. Another's in Seattle, the older of the two boys. The third one's gone." She swept a strand of hair from her forehead and stood to light an oil sconce on the wall behind them. She said, "I have something you boys should have a look at, just so you know I'm not making up stories here." At the front of the oak secretary she opened a door Eli hadn't noticed in their search and lifted something out. It was a tintype in a gilt frame, and when she sat back down on the ottoman she tipped it up on her lap for the boys to see.

They leaned close, Eli feeling a sudden loose warmth in his chest, Danny reaching out to touch the image but catching himself and drawing his hand back. Eli had never seen a picture of their father as a young man, never seen what he looked like before his hair turned gray, before his eyes had retreated into the sockets of his skull. There was only the wedding picture their mother kept on the bureau in their bedroom, taken when he was past thirty, already old. Here, though, was someone else entirely: dark hair and eyebrows, a face without shadows or lines, both ears intact, and wide, sparkling eyes. And yet it was him: the same high forehead, long nose, and square-set shoulders. He looked like the sort of father Eli had often wished for, one who smiled for no reason and whistled when nobody was listening. He was in uniform and standing with another soldier, who was shorter, the two of them posing in front of a painted backdrop of Roman columns. In a show of casual deportment, they held their rifles propped on their shoulders, fists gripping the barrels, stocks sticking up behind them. The shorter one was blond-haired, with a square jaw and wide shoulders. He wore spectacles.

"Jimmy always told me how much fun they had, how your father was always playing pranks," Mrs. Powers told them.

"He was?" Danny asked.

Eli looked more closely at the image. He touched the cool surface with his fingertips, trying to decide if it was a trick of some kind, or if the woman had confused their father with someone else, if the man her husband knew was another Ulysses Pope, not their father at all. Yet this was proof, wasn't it, right here?

"One time, Jimmy told me, they were marching through some godforsaken place in the heat of summer, men fainting right and left, and their C.O. wouldn't halt the march, not even when the trail brought them alongside this nice blue lake. And so your father, he got up close to one of the cannons and yanked the linchpin from the

153

wheel. It spun off the axle and rolled down the hill, and that was that. The men got their rest and had themselves a swim in the lake besides."

Eli tapped the top edge of the gilt frame. "Where was this made, do you know?"

"I'm not sure Jimmy ever told me. Likely some traveling man did it for them. Could have been anywhere, I suppose. I know they served together for quite a while."

"Did they write letters back and forth? Afterwards?"

"No. Well, yes. In the early years they did, when Jimmy and I were first married. But I don't have them anymore. This would've been after your father left the army and Jimmy was still with the Seventh, at Fort Riley."

"The Seventh?" Eli asked. He remembered the newspaper article in his father's lockbox that told about the Minnesota Ninth and its southern campaign — Tupelo, Brice's Crossing, the Battle of Nashville. The Ninth had been a regiment famous for having Chippewa Indians among its regulars.

Mrs. Powers got up and went again to the big secretary, opened the same door, and reached inside. "Here," she said, extending a yellowed envelope. The letter was on

Seventh Cavalry letterhead and written in a sloppy, forward-tilting hand. It was dated June 23, 1869.

Dear Jimmy and Laura,
Please accept the congratulations of Libby and myself on the joyous occasion of your wedding. We would have been there if we could, as you know, but have kept you much in mind and wish you every future happiness.

Yours,
GA Custer

Eli handed it to Danny, who brought it close to his face, his lips moving silently as he read. "G. A. Custer," he said, finishing. "Custer," he said again.

"Our father was in the *Ninth* Regiment," Eli told her.

Mrs. Powers frowned. "The Ninth?"

"The Minnesota Ninth, yes."

"During the Rebellion, you mean. That may be so. But afterwards he served in Custer's Seventh, down in the Indian Territories. He and Jimmy both. Your father was mustered out in sixty-nine, early that year."

"The Little Bighorn Custer?" Danny asked.

"Well, yes. But we're talking about an earlier time. The Custer battle didn't happen till seventy-six."

"The year after I was born," Danny said.

She nodded, but her face was serious, eyes cutting back and forth between the brothers. "He never said *any*thing about the Seventh or General Custer?"

"I don't think so," Eli said. "Not to us he didn't."

"It could be that he didn't think there was much to tell," she said. She picked up the tintype and carried it back to the secretary.

Eli was aware of being at fault somehow, unworthy of his father's history. The room had darkened, and he could hear the wind rising in the eaves and specks of rain or ice spattering against the windows, but these sounds were far off, unimportant. He looked at his brother, who was chewing his bottom lip, waiting for a signal from Eli that would let him know what to think, how to react. At school a couple of years back, Miss Waterson taught them about Custer's Last Stand, her voice quavering as she described the man's long yellow hair and buckskin jacket, and the way he and his men had fought against impossible odds, thousands of warriors swirling about them on that hill, told the class how afterward the Indians had stripped and butchered their bodies, all except for the young general's, out of respect for his courage. She showed them a painting of the battle — Custer at the center of a whirling, hellish scene, revolvers ablaze — and read to them from stories cut from newspapers. At one point Danny had raised his hand and asked, "Why did he want to attack that big village of Indians, anyway?" to which Miss Waterson said, "They had it coming."

"Well," Mrs. Powers said, standing above them, palms pressed together. "Chicken's done, I can smell it. Let's put it to good use, shall we?"

As usual, Eli took the breast meat, Danny the wings and legs, and though the bird was large and tender, the boys ate with little relish. They left their plates half full then barely touched the apple pie she laid out for dessert.

"Is there something wrong, aren't you hungry?" Mrs. Powers asked.

Eli was tempted to say something cruel — about the food, her home, her person — anything to punish her for what she knew about their father and he did not. And when she said, "I suppose you'll be leaving in the morning," he told her there was a westbound scheduled to leave at ten, careful not to explain that he and Danny, with any luck, would be on the seven o'clock freight-hauler, the first train leaving in the morning, squirreled away in one of its boxcars.

She took them upstairs to a bedroom overlooking the street, the room her sons used to sleep in, she told them, with a bed that had real springs. She pressed on it to show them how comfortable it was.

"Bacon and eggs at seven sharp," she said. "That should give you time to catch your train. Good night now."

They crawled into bed, exhausted but not sleepy, Eli's eyes scraping like sandpaper every time he blinked, and Danny's narrow face drooping. Outside, the wind had let up, but a cold light drizzle was tapping the window glass.

"Do you believe her?" Danny asked. "You think he fought in the Indian Wars?"

"She didn't say anything about fighting."

"Custer, though."

"Yeah."

"Do you think he'd lie to us?" Danny asked.

"He never lied. He just didn't tell things."

"Why, though?"

"It's probably like she said, because nothing much was going on. Nothing to tell about." Eli didn't believe this, but in fact he had no idea what was going on during those years, down in the territories.

"Do you think Mother knows about it? You think he told *her*?"

"I do."

"No, you don't."

"Truth is, we don't know, do we," Eli said.

"I know one thing — if it was me, I would've told *my* boys. Wouldn't you?"

"I guess I would, yeah. Unless it was something I didn't want to remember myself."

"You think he doesn't?"

"It might remind him of men he knew that got killed. Friends of his. He probably doesn't want to have to think about them anymore."

Danny was quiet for a little while. "When we get back home," he said, "I'm going to tell everybody that my dad rode with Custer. Everybody. Herman Stroud, too. He will leave me alone then, won't he."

Eli held his breath, lines of heat burning through the veins in his arms and pulsing in his neck. Sometimes his brother made him crazy, saying things out loud that needed to be held on to. Some things required silence and thought — not talk — and Eli hated it when people didn't understand that.

"Won't he?" Danny asked. "Herman?"

159

"Listen," Eli said, "I can take care of Herman Stroud and anybody else. Now be quiet and go to sleep."

Danny had been lying on his back, but now he flipped around. "Are you mad at me?" he asked. "Why are you mad?"

"I'm not mad, I'm only tired. Now leave me alone, will you? Please."

"I was only saying —"

"I know what you're saying, Danny. As far as I'm concerned, you can tell everybody, Herman, too. But we have to go to sleep now, all right? We have to get up early, like I told you."

Danny sighed and shifted around the other way and retreated to the far edge of the bed. He fidgeted for a while, turning from one side to the other, but soon he was sleeping, his breath coming slow and rhythmic.

Eli was exhausted, but his mind wouldn't stop spinning, his thoughts leading him into corners he couldn't find his way out of. If Mrs. Powers was telling the truth, and their father had gone out to Miles City after bones, why hadn't he explained that before he left? If it wasn't Mrs. Powers he'd come out here to see, but her husband instead, what had there been to hide? He remembered the words of her letter — *a burst of sun in a long dry season* — and tried to imagine his own mother widowed, and the loneliness she would feel. Possibly the letter carried less meaning than Eli had given to it. Or a different meaning. But whatever had brought his father out here, and wherever he was now, and whyever he'd chosen to leave without an explanation, there was now also the matter of the Seventh Cavalry and a whole secret chapter in his father's life.

Why would he do that? Eli thought, lying in the dark room. *Why would he do that to us?*

On the dresser beneath the gable window a loud clock tapped away the minutes like an impatient finger, and several times Eli climbed out of bed and tiptoed across the floor and put his face up close to the clock's face to check the time. At ten-thirty he heard Mrs. Powers move lightly down the hall and climb into a squeaky bed. Then around midnight he heard what sounded like a quiet knock on the front door. Instantly Mrs. Powers was out of bed and padding quietly along the hall and down the stairs. A door latch sounded below. Then the melodic tone of her voice floated up in the stillness, though Eli couldn't make out what she said. He climbed out of bed, crept into the hall, and paused at the top of the stairs, one hand on the rail. Below, in the kitchen, heavy bootsteps sounded across the floor, then stopped. In the same instant, a square of light rose out of the hallway floor. Eli bent down and knelt at the heat grate, put his face right into it and saw the kitchen table below, its oak surface gleaming in the lamplight. At the far edge of his view he could see a man's knee and booted foot. A dark hat rested at the center of the table. Eli wondered for a moment if it was the one his father had worn on the foggy morning he walked away, but no, the brim wasn't wide enough.

"You're pretty sure about about this," the man said, his tone low and pinched, a voice Eli didn't recognize.

A large hand moved across the tabletop, and its fingers drummed against it for a few moments before the hand retreated. Mrs. Powers spoke softly. Eli couldn't make out her words.

"They might be telling you God's own truth," the man said, "and if they are, it wouldn't be right to stand in their way. Least the way I see it."

For half a dozen breaths Eli heard nothing. Then it was Mrs. Powers again, but with more volume: "I take it you couldn't get a telegram through," she said.

"I had Weldon give it a try. Had him try the depot there. But nothing doing. He'll have to give it another go in the morning."

"The boys are leaving, though, right away," Mrs. Powers said. "They plan to be on the ten o'clock, or so they say."

The man's hand came back into view and his fingers drummed again. "Safe thing, if we go with your woman-feeling on this, is have them stay another day. Give us a chance to get that telegram through."

Mrs. Powers said something Eli couldn't hear.

"Or we just let them go. Seems they can take pretty good care of themselves, least the way you're telling it."

A slim hand appeared, and it pushed the man's hat toward him. Mrs. Powers said, "You have sons, Sheriff. Think if you woke up some morning and they were gone. Think how your wife would feel. And imagine someone had it within their power to give them back to you."

The sheriff reached out and picked up his hat, one long finger riding the middle crease. He said, "I can go upstairs now and wake them if you want, take them over to the office for the night, make sure they don't run."

"No, no, we'll let them sleep, they're so

163

tired. If you come back in the morning, early, that would be best."

"Are you sure?"

"I'm sure."

"All right then."

Chair legs scraped and bootsteps moved across the floor. Then the click of the latch, the moan of hinges, and a few moments passed before the lamp went dark. Eli got up and tiptoed back into the room and slipped into bed next to his brother. He didn't wake him up, though, not yet, there was no point. Danny needed his rest, and Eli needed to think, figure things out, decide on a different way out of here — because when the sheriff returned in the morning and found them gone, he'd go straight to the depot and search the train. Which meant they needed to leave town on foot and try to catch up to the train someplace west of here. How far could they walk before six o'clock, if they left, say, at two? Ten miles? A dozen? How far was the next town, the next stop? And how persistent would the sheriff be in hunting them? Eli couldn't imagine a pair of runaways causing the law in Bismarck to beat the bushes too hard or for too long, not once it was clear they'd gotten free of town. In any case, that's what Eli had to count on.

He checked the clock again — twenty minutes past midnight — and dragged himself back into bed, heavy-limbed, exhausted at the prospect of staying up all night and having to keep his brother on the move until daybreak. He hoped the squall had passed through. His head hurt, right at the top, like it did whenever sleep wouldn't come, and his eyes ached — but he knew it was important that he rest awhile. *Ten minutes,* he told himself. *I'll rest for ten minutes.* He rehearsed in his mind how he'd wake his brother, whispering in his ear, and then lead him downstairs and through the kitchen, how they'd move quietly in their stocking feet, holding their shoes, and slip outside, bedrolls under their arms. Then the cry of an owl, close by, took Eli back to a morning last fall when he was checking his muskrat traps in the marsh outside of town, poling his flat-bottom skiff through heavy fog and coming face-to-face with a pair of glaring yellow eyes that hung in the mist above a giant lodge on which Eli had made an open set. A pair of wings lifted and flapped, and the owl rose into the air — but only a foot or so, because the trap chain grew taut and yanked the bird back to its perch. Eli had gone to fetch his father, and together they brought the owl back home, draping it first in burlap to protect themselves from its beak and talons. It seemed confused, stunned, like a man waking from a nightmare only to find that his dream has solidified around him. They opened the spring-loaded jaws that held the bird by just two talons and then pulled away the burlap and stepped back. The bird blinked but made no move to leave. For two days it remained in their backyard, standing immobile in the shade of the willow and ignoring the offered chunks of beef and chicken. Finally on the third morning — early, before sunup — Eli heard its cry. Through the small window of the sleeping loft he'd seen it lift away from the high branch of a cottonwood and flap eastward toward pinkening clouds.

He woke in a sweat, hair matted on his neck and forehead, shirt soaked through at the chest and under his arms. For several moments all he could do was lie there, trying to locate himself, Danny breathing in his ear. Then he pushed off the quilt and swung out of bed and moved lightly across the floor to the dresser. It was dark outside, darker than before, and he had to put his eyes right up close to make out the narrow hands. Five o'clock sharp.

Damnation.

When he touched his brother's shoulder, Danny twisted away, pulling the quilt close around himself. Eli crawled on top of him and took a grip on his small shoulders. "Listen to me," he whispered, "we have to leave. He's coming over to get us and send us home — the sheriff, do you hear?"

They dressed silently, grabbed their bed-rolls, and holding their shoes in their hands crept out of the room and down the hallway in their socks, the floorboards soundless beneath them — *a well-built house,* Eli thought — Danny holding to the back of his coat as they crossed into the kitchen and moved past the table to the front door, which Eli opened as gently as he could, the hinges muttering only a quiet complaint. Then they were outside in the cold air, putting on their shoes and running down the dirt street. Low, gray clouds moving above them. Needles of ice stabbing at their faces.

"Here," Eli said, and grabbed hold of the back of Danny's collar as they went.

The wind was bitter, hard from the northeast, and the sleet was coming stronger even as morning started to show through the ragged clouds that tumbled and pitched through the uppermost branches of the trees and along the rooftops. Eli's shoulders and back were already damp, the icy rain penetrating his coat and shirt, and his feet, too, from splashing through puddles. He stopped beneath the canopy of an old boxelder tree that still had its leaves and pulled his brother close. There was a high fence beside them, and behind it a horse flapped its lips and bumped against the boards.

"Where are we going? I'm cold," Danny said.

"Just let me think."

"The depot? We're gonna catch the train?"

"No."

The horse nosed the fence again, snorting, and a gust of wind almost knocked them over. It was too late to go anywhere tonight. They needed someplace to hide for a day at least, until it was safe to jump a train or walk out of town. When the horse bumped against the boards once more, Eli looked behind them at the pitched roof of a barn. "Here we go," he said, "come on now," and he started his brother climbing. The fence was six feet high but easy enough to scale, and they dropped down on the other side and scrambled through the muddy lot and let themselves into the barn, where the smell of hay was so sharp that Eli sneezed. He couldn't see a thing, but going up on his toes, he was able to touch the ceiling.

"The haymow," he said. "That's where we need to be."

"We do?"

A cow bellowed at them right up close, and from a far corner a sheep bleated irritably. "This is perfect," Eli said, "you'll see. We'll go up and make ourselves a little hay-fort."

As their eyes adjusted to the dark, they stepped past the reaching nose of the milk cow and past a stall that held a colossal sow with her rooting brood. Against the west wall they found a ladder of boards that rose into the mow. "Wait," he told Danny, and he went up the ladder into the high, round-roofed space, dull slices of morning light squeezing in through the siding boards of the east pediment. The rich, dying smell of hay was so strong Eli could feel it between his teeth. The back half of the mow was filled nearly to the rafters.

"Come on," he said, pulling his brother up through the hole in the floor. "Come on." He pushed Danny toward the pile of hay, and together they climbed, sinking in up to their knees and then deeper as they struggled upward. The hay was well packed, though, and they were able to reach the top of the pile and then tumble and roll down the other side, up against the barn wall.

They took off their pants, coats and shirts and spread them out to dry, and unrolled their blankets and wrapped themselves up.

They were barely settled before a man's voice rang out from below: "There, you old devil, hold still a minute." A pail clanked. Then the whacking thud of a man's hand against the solid flank of a cow. "What's wrong with you, anyway?" the man shouted. "Hold still now."

In the silence that followed, Danny whispered, "I don't feel right."

"What do you mean?"

"I'm itchy."

"It's the hay."

"But my head too, like my skull's getting brittle."

"Does it hurt yet?"

"No."

"Look at me," Eli told him.

Danny turned to him listlessly, his face screwed up tight and his eyes clamped shut. Eli imagined the two of them stuck up here for days, his brother groaning and crying. "You're going to be fine," he said. "There's not going to be any pain — not this time, do you hear?"

Below, the man wrapped up his morning milking. His boots shuffled against the barn's plank floor, the hinges creaked, and the door slammed against its frame. Eli let out his breath. "What are the songs Mom sings to you?" he asked.

Danny was quiet, thinking. "Sometimes she just tells me stories," he whispered.

"What stories?"

"Do you know the one about the day I was born?" He smiled, despite himself.

"The warmest day we'd had all spring, I know that. May twentieth."

"He wanted to take Mom fishing," Danny said, "remember?"

"Yeah, but he took me too. He drove us south of town, across that pasture and down along the river to Silver Lake, where he borrowed a rowboat from Jebson Mills." The old bachelor, dead now, had lived for decades in a sod dugout above the water. Ulysses had rowed them across the bay — Eli five years old and Gretta very pregnant — pausing to catch walleyes as they went, four fat ones. Then on Mills Island they'd built a fire on the shore and fried the fish in lard. After, as they lay on the grassy bank in the sun, half asleep, Gretta sat up fast, set her hands on her belly, and said, "Here he comes."

"Because she knew I was going to be a boy," Danny said.

"That's right. And Dad had to deliver you

himself. I remember climbing up in a burr-oak and covering my ears to block out the sound of her screams. I remember Dad saying, 'Gretta, I love you.' And when I came back down, he was crouched next to Mom and holding you in both hands. You were squirming like a puppy but still covered with the caul, head to toe. We looked right through it and saw you. Dad used his knife to cut it off."

"Julius Caesar was born with a caul," Danny said.

That night when they'd rowed back across the lake, there were four in the boat, not three, and Jebson Mills had counted them a couple of times, pointing with his finger and shaking his head.

"I'm lucky," Danny said. He was uncurled now and lying on his back, one arm flung out in the hay as he stared up into the rafters of the barn, his eyes unfocused, mouth lax, his breath coming easily. Eli described to him how he'd looked after their father removed the slick membrane — wet hair matted, one eye stuck closed as though in a permanent wink.

"Like a pirate, right?" Danny said.

"Well you sounded like one too. Like a mad one, the way you kept howling."

"I'm hungry," Danny said, yawning.

"How is your head?"

Danny had to ponder on this for a time. He touched an ear to one shoulder and then tipped his head the other way. "I'm not sure. I'm tired, though, I know that. I'm real tired."

"Get some rest then," Eli said. "That's about all there is to do up here anyway. Sleep for a while. Then we'll see about getting you something to eat."

10
BUFFALO BILL

Danny was aware of his brother leaving, rising from beside him and rustling off through the hay — and though he meant to call him back, he couldn't resist the sleep coming on, so sweet in its promise, like a bright fall day that smelled of old grass. All he had to do was walk into it, the sky clear with a big yellow sun and ahead of him a soft dirt path leading to a high plain where the ground moved beneath him.

Mountains rose like purple clouds in the west, and between here and there was a herd of grazing buffalo, thousands of acres of them, black and brown and smelling like dust. In the middle of this mass of life Danny saw a high, pointed tent. He was thinking on how to cross this lake of creatures, how to reach that tent, when a voice came from behind him. He turned. It was Two Blood, wearing a straw hat pulled low on his forehead and peering at Danny through his light-blue eyes. He said, "Aren't you going over there to see him?"

"He's there?" Danny asked.

Two Blood nodded.

"Does he want to see me?"

"Let's go." Two Blood led the way, the two of them reaching out to touch heads and horns and nappy sides as they went, the animals making room for them to pass.

At the high gray tent, Two Blood drew back a canvas flap. There was a large congregation inside, rapt, heads craning forward, and though Danny expected to see his father at the front, along with Reverend Pearl, instead it was Buffalo Bill with his pointed beard and fringed jacket, standing on a wooden stage. He lifted his rifle and fired into the air at two white doves, which burst into puffs of feathers, one then the other, *bam, bam*. Everybody clapped and cheered. Danny's eyes were drawn to the edge of the stage where a man — his father — lifted two more doves into view, a bird in each hand. He was old-looking, tired, his shoulders thinner than Danny remembered — and when Buffalo Bill shouted *Pull*, Ulysses released the birds, which rose above the stage only to explode, one-two, as the rifle jumped in Bill's hands. Danny ran up through the crowd to the stage, right up close, and waited for his father to spot him. When he did, Danny lifted a hand. His father's eyes were full of tears.

"I didn't want you to see this," his father said, and reached out to lay a finger alongside his son's cheek.

"It's all right," Danny told him. Then the tent began to wobble on account of the press of animals outside, and Danny could feel beneath him the heavy movement of their million hooves — and then he was awake, his eyes coming into focus on the boots of his brother, standing above him in the hay.

"Went out and found you some breakfast," Eli said. "You still hungry?"

11
ALL ONE THING

Home was something that should compass about you like the wind, Gretta thought — you shouldn't have to think about it. And you certainly shouldn't have to build it out of nothing at all, with only love and your bare hands, the way she'd had to do.

Today, though, for all its hard-won familiarity, Sloan's Crossing was strange and cold, the air so thin she found herself taking big lungfuls of it to ward off lightheadedness. She walked with her satchel down Railroad Avenue, feeling more alone than she had on the afternoon her boat landed in New York and she found no one waiting to meet her in that city of peculiar smells and odd-sounding talk — though at least then she'd known herself for a stranger and hadn't been reminded by every tree and lamppost of those she'd lost, or in that case, left behind. For the past two days, in St. Paul and in Minneapolis, she had followed after leads, none of them fruitful. At the office of the Grand Army of the Republic she'd found her husband's name, or former name, and verified his part in the Indian campaigns and his service with Custer's Seventh. She'd also found the name of Ulysses's friend and correspondent, Jim Powers, only to learn the man had been dead for a year, and also several other names, including one she managed to track down, an Indian who had served in Minnesota's Ninth during the Great Rebellion and lived in a rowhouse on Washington Avenue, above the flour mills. He had answered her questions patiently but had no memory of Ulysses. When Gretta described the beaded tobacco pouch, he'd shaken his head and called into the backroom for his wife, who came out and gently escorted Gretta from their home.

The first person she saw after leaving the depot was Mrs. Rolfe, the pastor's wife, walking with an arm around her daughter's shoulder. Gretta slowed her pace to greet her friend, whose eyes brightened before bending away.

"Afternoon," Gretta said.

The pastor's wife pulled her daughter close and glided on by. Gretta turned to watch their progress down the boardwalk,

178

humiliated though not surprised, the snubbing a corroboration of the shame that had been growing inside her through the night and morning as the train carried her here. At the pharmacy she stopped for ointment. Two women stood just inside the door, heads bent close together, the lawyer's wife, whom Gretta knew only by way of saying hello in the street, and Emma Carlsen, the mother of Danny's friend Peter.

"Hello," Gretta said.

The two women glanced at one another, then down at the floor.

"I've been gone," Gretta added.

"So we've heard." This from Emma, who managed a half smile.

The lawyer's wife muttered something about a pie to bake and headed out the door. Emma hurried to catch up with her.

The druggist prepared the ointment and accepted the fifty-cent payment, cordial as always, though Gretta was aware of his eyes regarding her differently than before, moving to her neck and then farther down as he asked if there was anything else he could do. He was short and slight with a closely trimmed mustache, a man known for his prudent way with money. Evenings, he drove his wife about town in a surrey with flowered draperies.

The way home wasn't long, five blocks, and Gretta walked fast, hoping to get there before she saw anyone else she knew. As she rounded the last corner, something caused her to stop mid-stride. In front of their house, in the place beneath their kitchen window where she always kept a large urn of geraniums, there was nothing, only a bare circle in the grass. The welcome sign above the door that Ulysses had fashioned from a cedar shingle was gone. She hurried forward. Bolted to the doorframe was a new hasp, and hanging from it an iron padlock of the sort Ulysses had clamped onto the trunks they'd shipped from St. Paul after the wedding. Gretta felt the blood drain from her face and reached out to steady herself, laying the flat of her hand against the door. Tears pricked at her eyes, but she didn't allow them to come. For a few moments she stood there, gathering her strength, then she turned on her heel and headed straight back downtown, to Fogarty's office at the rooming house, and knocked on the door.

He opened immediately, as if expecting her, but feigned astonishment all the same, lifting a hand to his mouth. She couldn't help but notice his bare feet, which were pale, glossy, and purple-veined, like tulip bulbs.

"Come in, come in," he said, his hand spinning like a little wheel.

She stood in place, arms crossed in front of herself. "Are you going to unlock my door for me?"

"Your door?"

"My door, yes."

"*My* door, you mean to say. And of course I will, as soon as I receive my overdue payment. And additionally, the five dollars you stole from me."

"You gave me the money of your own free will."

He laughed. "I did?"

"You said it was mine if I helped you find your keys."

"But we didn't find them, did we. I had to hire a locksmith and pay him a fortune, in case you're interested. And furthermore, I thought we had an agreement about the rent. Unless my memory fails me, your intention was to go and fetch your errant husband, the assumption being that he would come back with you and present me with said payment."

She watched him. He rubbed a finger on his lips, thoughtfully, and blinked at her.

He drew a handkerchief, white and neatly

pressed, from the inner pocket of his jacket and offered it to her. "You're perspiring," he said.

"I would like to able to go home, Mr. Fogarty."

He returned the handkerchief to his jacket. "It's not your home, Mrs. Pope. It's not even your house. And I'm not sure what you'd gain from going inside, since your possessions aren't there. I've had them removed."

"I'll call Mr. David," Gretta said, although her spirits were flagging. Lionel David was the local sheriff, whose paycheck came from the town council, on which Mead Fogarty sat.

"Please do. Tell him that you haven't kept up on the note your husband signed. And tell him also, for me, that it's not my inclination to store your possessions free of charge. Best not mention the five dollars you stole, however — he may not have heard about that yet."

"Where is everything?" Gretta said.

"Oh, it's quite safe. No cause for worry. I moved it all into the building right back there." He aimed a thumb behind himself. "That old hog shed in the alley. It's dry and locked up tight. You may collect your things now, if you would like to. I'll open it up for you. I can even find someone to help you move it. Then again, if you're still making arrangements and need only a few items to tide you over, that's fine too. You see, I've never been one to hold grudges. And certainly not against you."

Gretta's impulse was to say, *Yes, open it,* just to exercise a bit of control, but the naked bulge of Fogarty's eyes and the appearance of his bright tongue at the corner of his mouth caused her to change her mind. She turned and walked down the hallway, not stopping at the sound of his voice.

"Please don't underestimate the appeal you hold for me," he said to her back. "I am not a handsome man, of course, but I can offer you a life. Which is more than you have at the moment."

She continued down the hall and out the door and back into the street, where the shadows were stretching east and the air was cool on her face. She had a mind to return to her house and break a window to get inside where she might feel safe, at least for a while. Then the knot in her stomach bent her forward to expel the ham sandwich she'd eaten on the train — except it wouldn't come up. Nothing would, although a jabbing pain in her jawbone brought a rush of saliva. Once again she remembered getting off the boat in New York all those years ago and listening to the nonsense of languages as she walked the harbor district, waiting for the man her aunt and uncle had promised would be there to meet her. By the time he finally arrived, it was nearly dark, and she had been approached by two rough boys who told her they'd be glad to help her find a place for the night. One of them she still saw in her dreams, his face like the blade of an ax, his eyes eating her up. A stale, rotten smell clung to him, and he talked with his hands, which looked heavy and purposeful, as if they were meant for prying into and breaking things, each finger a separate threat. She tried to get free of the boys, pretending to know where she was going, stepping aside when they blocked her path, and explaining that she had a friend on the way, but it was only when her uncle's cousin arrived and showed them his pistol that they finally turned and drifted off in the dark.

Now, though, there was no one to save her, no one to go to for help, no one, it seemed, even willing to speak with her in the place she had lived for nearly seventeen years. It was as if she had left Sloan's Crossing as Gretta Pope and returned as somebody else. When she tried to think of who in town was least in Fogarty's debt, Mrs. Peterson came to mind, the dressmaker, a woman who had managed to hold her own among the merchants on Main Street, in part because of the mystery surrounding her husband. Depending on who you listened to, the man was serving time in federal prison, acting in Broadway plays, or piloting a steamship on the Missouri — though people also said he was an invention useful for keeping interested men at arm's length. Several years ago Mrs. Peterson had donated money to the courthouse for a mural commemorating General Stephen Sloan, the town's founder. She was neither a friend nor a peer, it was true, but nonetheless she often hired Gretta for tailoring and hemming jobs. Maybe she would see the similarity in their plights? Gretta approached Mrs. Peterson's Main Street shop and climbed the stairs to the apartment above it.

"I need to see you," Gretta called, after knocking.

The latch twisted and the door swung in, the woman standing tall and well-arranged in a pleated skirt and tailored jacket, hair pulled back in a tight bun. Her face was large, its individual features — nose, mouth, eyes, and cheeks — generous and symmetrical.

"I suppose you're entitled to your side of the story," she said.

"It would help if I knew what the story was."

"Spare me your self-righteousness. You bear some responsibility too."

Gretta summoned her courage. "Responsibility for what? You'd think I'm a criminal."

"Here." Mrs. Peterson moved Gretta brusquely toward a hard chair at the kitchen table and then took one across from her. She sat straight, her mouth severe. She said, "With a man like Fogarty, it's a grave mistake to put yourself in the position of having to tell him no, and then tell him no. As I suspect you did. Don't you understand that?"

Gretta resented the woman's tone.

"He's got you in his vest pocket, to put it tactfully."

"What has he been saying?"

"That you offered yourself to him. That you got him drunk, and that before he woke up you had taken his money and fled. He's ashamed, of course — but in a way that lays all the guilt on you. He's getting it both ways, can't you see? He's taken your honor

186

and then doubled his pleasure by confessing himself to a town flattered to be given the privilege of forgiving him. And there's not one thing you can do about it. There's nothing *I* can do about it, for that matter — he owns half the buildings on this street, including the ones on either side of mine. He means to drive you out of town, Gretta. Or else into his arms."

"I did nothing wrong," Gretta said.

Mrs. Peterson rolled her eyes then looked away, as if the conversation were over. "You've let Mead Fogarty's manhood become the most interesting subject in town, and that's a fine thing for any man, as long as he's the one telling the story."

Gretta put her hands on both sides of her head as if to keep her brain from exploding. "Where do I go?" she asked. "What do I do?"

Mrs. Peterson smoothed her dress against her thighs. She lifted her nose and sniffed, as if detecting something unpleasant in the air. When she stood from the table, Gretta stood too, automatically, and then allowed herself to be led to the door and dismissed.

Numbly, bag slung from her shoulder and valise at her side, she walked down the stairs and outside, where the sun was dropping into a bank of orange and purple clouds, pulling with it any warmth it may have lent the day. A shiver passed from the top of her neck to the backs of her knees. With two dollars left in her purse and not a single blood relative in all the North American continent — aside from her own two sons, whose whereabouts were unknown to her — she walked toward the town's least savory hotel, the one favored by railmen and seasonal farm workers. Last year a man had been murdered there, killed for his new suit of clothes by a drifter who was then arrested at the depot, dressed in those clothes. Gretta wasn't thinking about that crime, though. She thought only of a room with four walls to block the view she presented to the town, a room where she could find a way to collect her wits and plan the next hours of the life Mead Fogarty said she didn't have.

But then at the alley beside the newspaper office, she caught a hint of tobacco in the air, and her eyes fell on the yellow window of a converted rail car tucked away between the photography studio and bookkeeping office. It was the home of Two Blood and his wife, Agnes, who had claimed the silver Pullman after the big derailment of seventy-eight and moved it to this small lot sold to them by Fogarty. He'd considered the land unbuildable on account of its dampness. In fact, there was a natural spring here that Two Blood had tapped with a pipe, and now he sold water to residents of the town's east side, where all the wells tasted like rotten eggs.

"Ho," Two Blood said, appearing in his doorway. He had to stoop in order to fit beneath the metal casing. Beside him, under his raised arm, his wife's face came into view, unlined and fresh despite her long white hair. Agnes had attended Eli's birth and would have helped with Danny's as well, if he hadn't decided to show up early that day on Mills Island. Until the arrival of Dr. Harris from Minneapolis, Agnes had been the town midwife, requiring only tobacco and eggs as payment. She was known for her gentle confidence and for the balm she made that smelled like rancid cheese but worked like nothing else to smooth the way. Dr. Harris had rough hands and made a habit of using steel forceps.

"I thought we might see you," Two Blood said.

Agnes stepped out from behind him. "He keeps asking me," she said, " 'where has that Pope woman taken herself?' "

Gretta was unable to muster a smile for them, but the nervous pain in her stomach was already fading.

"You didn't find your men," Two Blood said.

She dropped her satchel to the ground and let her tired arms hang. Two Blood leaned over and picked it up, then ducked through his doorway. Agnes nodded at Gretta to follow him. The long, single room was like a cave, but dry and warm nonetheless with a slow fire burning in the barrel stove. Agnes sat Gretta at their tiny kitchen table, and Two Blood sat down across from her. He turned sideways to face the fire.

"I don't want to be a bother," Gretta said.

With a flip of her hand, Agnes shooed away the words. "We saw him moving your things," she said.

"Bastard," Two Blood muttered.

Gretta didn't allow herself to make a sound, but sitting at their table her shoulders shook and her tears streamed as Agnes and Two Blood looked down at their hands. When she was done crying, Agnes fried slabs of side pork then mixed a bowl of thick cornmeal batter and set it sizzling in the pork fat. She put it out on plates, and then watched as Gretta ate like she hadn't eaten since Ulysses left in July, leaning into it and drinking cup after cup of the cold spring water that Two Blood replenished from a large brown crock in the corner.

"I don't know what to do," she said when she'd finished.

Two Blood looked at her, chewing his food. "Where did you go off to?"

She explained about seeing her husband's sister in St. Paul but said nothing about the discoveries she made, the secrets he'd kept for so long about the Seventh Cavalry and his name change, revelations so personal she couldn't imagine putting them into words. The humiliation would be too much to bear. And what would Two Blood and Agnes think of her if they knew Ulysses had been in Custer's regiment?

Agnes, who hadn't eaten yet, sat down with her own plate of food. She said, "He believes Ulysses went that way," and pointed a finger at the west wall.

"Why?" Gretta asked him. "Why do you think that?"

Two Blood filled his pipe and went over to the stove where he took a long twig and poked it in the coals and used it to light up before coming back and sitting down again. "He and I smoked together sometimes, in my shop. He liked to ask questions about when I was young, about hunting the black-horns and stealing horses from the Crows. He wanted to hear about the wars I knew and what I remembered."

"Please, if you know where he went —"

He shook his head.

"Did he ever talk about his own wars?" she asked.

Two Blood drew on the pipe and blew out a long stream with its sharp, burnt-apple scent. "No," he said.

Gretta thought of how little her pride was worth — how little it mattered what anybody might think about her husband and his secrets. And considering how people in this town treated Indians, weren't Agnes and Two Blood likely able to bear most any injury? She summoned her courage and said, "In St. Paul I learned from his sister that he served out west" — she looked at Agnes then turned to her husband — "with the Seventh Cavalry."

Agnes glanced over, but Two Blood only lowered his pipe to the table and scratched his long nose. In the distance, a train whistle heralded the arrival of an eastbound.

"I knew about his time in the Union Army, during the Rebellion," Gretta continued. "But now I learn that he signed up again after the war and stayed till sixty-nine. I met him later in the year he mustered out, and he never told me anything about it. He led me to think he'd been out of the service for years."

"Sixty-nine?" Two Blood asked, his eyes on her.

"That's right."

He looked off through the small window, and doing likewise Gretta could see the quarter-moon balanced on the very tip of the Our Savior's steeple. Agnes moved to the corner behind the stove and laid out a heavy robe and on top of this a gray wool blanket. "You can lie here tonight," she said to Gretta. "You'll stay warm."

But Gretta wasn't ready to sleep, not even close. She wasn't the least bit tired, and had a feeling Two Blood might have something more to say. Leaning toward him across the table, she asked, "Didn't he talk about himself at all? Didn't he tell you anything about what's happened over the last year? About losing his contracts? Losing his job at the depot? Anything?"

The old man seemed not to hear Gretta's voice. In the silence she listened to his breathing, and to the soft whistling in his nose every time he exhaled. His pipe had gone cold and lay untouched on the table. Then he turned to her, his eyes as dark as rifle holes. "My father died when I was small," he said, "but I had two uncles, both good men. They taught me what I needed to learn. My mother's brother, he was a man of words. He told me where we came from, and about the land. He told me about the birds and animals, the weather. He knew how to fight also. He had stories about raids into Crow country and the times he had counted coup. He liked to show his scars, could talk all night about each one. Later, though, after the battles, when they started moving us to the reservations, he understood what was happening and he urged everybody to save themselves, make the change. He said, 'Put down your guns.' "

Two Blood lifted a hand in front of his face and held it there, as if to divide his head in half, an eye on either side as he stared at Gretta. "Do you hear me?" he asked. When she nodded, he lowered his hand to the table.

"Now my father's brother, he was different. He wasn't one to say things, but showed me how to ride and shoot, and how to stay warm in the cold. And when they tried to make him farm the land, he laughed and rode away — north, over the medicine line. He wouldn't let his shadow fall anyplace near the land they pushed us onto. He was killed at Slim Buttes, along with American Horse. I never heard this uncle talk about battles or raids. I would not call him a man of war. But you see, he wasn't able to live in two worlds, because he was all one thing. That might be the kind of man your husband is."

Two Blood reached for his pipe and got up from his chair. Agnes called out to Gretta from the darkness. "There's a bowl of water on the cupboard to wash. Privy is out back, up against the fence. The door sticks. You have to push your shoulder into it."

"Thank you," Gretta said.

"Get some rest now," Agnes said. "You need it."

Gretta didn't sleep, though, not for hours. It was comfortable and warm, lying on the heavy, furred robe and wrapped in the wool blanket, but her mind was working so hard that her brain hurt. Two Blood might well be right about her husband — that he was all one thing. But knowing that didn't tell her where he was. The old man might be right, too, about Ulysses going west. But how was she supposed to find him out there? Her comprehension of that territory was vague, mountains and hard-flowing rivers and vast deserts of buffalo grass and sagebrush, a brown and dull-green world with cruel, empty skies. Gretta had never traveled west of Fargo, which was set down

195

in a land so flat and treeless that the first settlers built their homes out of sod. But now she had to imagine going off into the emptiness beyond it, far beyond it, and going alone — although if she couldn't find some kind of evidence that pointed to where he'd gone to, what was the use in even starting out?

At first it had been hard not to think he'd gone to another woman. That would explain why he left without telling her. And when she'd set out for St. Paul three days ago, she did so bearing the dead feeling in her stomach that she was about to discover a shameful truth. Of course she might still have to swallow that pill, but the nature of her dread had changed in the past few days, shifting inside of her, moving higher somehow, and now it seemed to be centered in her lungs and heart instead of in her belly.

Not that it mattered, because when morning came she'd simply have to continue her search. And wherever it took her, even if she came up with nothing, she would have choices to make: how to start life over again, with or without him — and if without him, whether to take advantage of Mead Fogarty's selfish offer, or do what she'd thought of many times since Ulysses left in July: return to Copenhagen.

What must it be like, she wondered, in the city she'd left at seventeen? How much had changed there? Did her childhood friends still fill their days with talk and with trips to the harbor? Did they still act out their favorite stories in the gardens at Tivoli? Spend their afternoons boating in the canals? Did they ever wish they'd done as she had and gone off to America to start new lives? No doubt they had families of their own by now, husbands and children and houses to keep, their own worries and disappointments, their own regrets. As Gretta slipped finally toward sleep, she thought of how things used to be — recalling her summers there, with the beach at Havnebad brooding in the near distance, she and her mother walking out along its sandy, blue-green shores and swimming in the cool water, naked, on those long evenings when dusk lingered past midnight.

12
Cottonwood Blowdown

Out here, though, all these years later, her husband moved through a harder country, a place he would never look back on with longing, no wind to speak of today and no sounds either, except for the ox's hooves against the hard ground and the creaking of the wheels. Powdery dirt lingered in the air, filling his mouth and eyes with grit. The day had warmed enough that he'd taken off his coat and rolled up his shirtsleeves again. Before him, to the north and east, an endless series of gray-brown hills — some rolling, some broken — shimmered beneath a blue sky so bright it made his eyes ache. Behind him, though, in the west, purple clouds were massing, and he figured by late afternoon the weather was going to catch up to him. An autumn thunderstorm, a good hard one, too, by the look of it. And so he kept a sharp eye out for a place to take cover, a shelf of rock or a stand of cedars. Every so often he stung the ox's bony rump with his willow whip, but the animal only flipped its tail and sauntered on.

Two days he'd spent on the reservation, stopping at every lodge and speaking with every man, woman, and child he saw, passing out the jerked beef as he went and sometimes offering other gifts as well: colored hand scarves, glass beads, and the tumblers he had made from wine and whiskey bottles he found back of the First Chance Saloon in Miles City then sawed off with a fine-tooth crosscut. No one had heard of anybody named Magpie, or at least so they claimed. Nor did anyone ask Ulysses what he wanted with the man. It made him wonder if they knew more than they were willing to let on. Of course if somebody had said, "What does this Magpie have that *you* want?" Ulysses had been ready with an answer. He would have explained about a recent newspaper story on the Custer fiasco, written for the ten-year anniversary — an article for which the writer had interviewed a Cheyenne battle veteran who'd later joined the Buffalo Bill Show and toured all through the Eastern states. "Here's how it is," Ulysses would have said. "My brother died at the Little Bighorn, and I think the man might have some answers to the questions I've got."

In fact, there had been such a news story. It was published in the *St. Paul Daily Globe* in June, and when he'd come across the name Magpie, he read it three times. Ulysses didn't have a brother, of course. Nor had he been close to the battle himself, having mustered out years before Custer led his paltry troop against Sitting Bull's confederacy of nations. But this remained: on the worst day of his life Ulysses had, in a fashion, crossed paths with the man whose beaded tobacco pouch he kept hidden beneath his coat, the pouch he'd never been able to rid himself of, as much as he would have liked to.

"God forgive me," Ulysses said, and stung the ox's bony rump with his willow switch.

The storm, as it happened, came on slow, allowing him to reach a cottonwood blowdown where years ago a twister must have come through and yanked out a grove of trees and laid them down in knots. Some were locked together like the antlers of rutting elk. Others were piled like matchsticks, their trunks smooth and white. The downed trees formed a curving palisade, seven, eight feet high, a natural protection from the north, and Ulysses pulled the wagon close to allow a network of dead branches to form a roof above him. He unhitched the ox, which he picketed nearby, then cut boughs from a cedar tree and laced them into the branches that overhung the wagon.

His plan was to wait out the rain and get an early start for Miles City in the morning, picking bones along the way — ten dollars' worth, he figured, more than enough to defray the cost of leasing the ox and rig. After wiring home twenty-five, two months' worth of payments on the note, he would still have something left to stake his trip to the southern agency, the only other place he knew to look. Luckily, he understood the country down there from serving in the campaigns of sixty-seven and sixty-eight, riding as courier for the Seventh, sometimes as far as a hundred miles in a day. Forts Leavenworth, Harker, Hays, Larned, and Dodge, and south into Indian Territory. Empty plains and sand hills, high plateaus, magnificent bluffs. The tribes had still been on the move then, if nearly impossible to find, and the large herds had yet to be annihilated by the money hunters. Once, between the Cimarron and Arkansas Rivers, he was forced to lead his mare into a high tumble of limestone to keep from getting trampled. He'd been watching the herd come on for an hour, their dust rising purple in the east, and as they poured past him on either side, their great heads and humped backs plunging and surging, the earth shook so hard he'd felt like his flesh would come loose from his bones.

Late afternoon, the storm arrived. In minutes a false green night eclipsed daylight, then a hard wind blew in from the east, driving an icy rain left to right across his vision. Wrapped in a canvas tarpaulin and hunched in the wagon's bed, he stayed more or less dry, thanks to the breastwork of woven branches. He was thinking about lying down and trying to sleep out the storm when a mortar-blast of thunder boomed. The ox tossed its head and kicked its hind legs as if fighting off a pack of wolves. Then lightning struck close, casting in its silver glow three men on ponies, side by side by side, thirty feet away and straight ahead. Ulysses waited, the outlines of the men burned in yellow on his retinas. He put his right hand on the .476 Enfield revolver he'd picked up in Miles City and which he wore inside his jacket on a sling. The rain turned to sleet and rattled against the dead wood. When Ulysses could see again, the men were still there, sitting their mounts, watching him. Rifles in their scabbards.

The one in the center was wide-shouldered and sat tall on his pony. Ulysses waved him forward out of the rain, and the man swung to the ground and tied off the pony on a cottonwood limb. Without speaking, he climbed into the wagon across from Ulysses — the knees of the two men separated by less than a foot — then glanced over his shoulder at the others, still waiting on their ponies. They came in, too, now, one taking his place in the wagon next to the first, across from Ulysses, the other climbing up on the buckboard. No one spoke. Beyond their small world, the rain obliterated everything.

The first man, the tall one, wore a campaign hat faded to purple and a cavalry coat with herringbone piping across the chest, epaulets on the shoulders. His dark braids were wrapped in strips of white weasel fur. There was an old single-action Colt tucked in the waist of his buckskin pants. He looked forty or forty-five, hard and fit, the lids of his eyes hooded like a snapping turtle's, his nose hawklike. The one beside him in the wagon was small, no bigger than a boy, though his old face was rough like the bark of an elm tree. He had on a crumpled cowboy hat, faded cavalry pants, moccasins with beadwork. The bone handle of an ancient revolver stuck out from the holster at his side. The third, perched on the buckboard, was barrel-chested with massive hands and long, graying hair. A pistol tied to a leather string hung from his neck like a chunk of jewelry. They were likely Cheyenne or Crow — Cheyenne, Ulysses decided — off the reservation in either case and armed for hunting. Their booted rifles looked like Henry repeaters.

Ulysses shrugged himself free of the canvas, and making sure to let his sidearm show, leaned toward the front of the wagon to grab a quart jar of pickled eggs from underneath a blanket. He removed the lid and handed the jar across to the tall man, who took it and sniffed, his slitted eyes watching Ulysses carefully. He reached in with his long fingers and lifted one out, brought it up to his nose, and then took half the egg in his teeth and bit it off. Frowning, he chewed and swallowed. Then he popped the rest of the egg in his mouth and this time swallowed without chewing.

Minutes later the dozen or so eggs were gone. The sleet had passed but the rain continued, pounding the ground and drumming on their makeshift roof and beating against the surface of the river behind them. Finally, though, the sky began to lighten west to east like a day doubling back on itself, and the rain slowed until the only sound was the light ticking of water from the cottonwood deadfall.

"You've gotten some use out of our camp," the tall man said, raising a hand and touching the roof of cedar boughs. "Good of you to share it." A smile twitched at the corner of his mouth.

"My pleasure."

"I was a boy when the wind came," the man continued. "My father and I watched from there." He pointed southeast, where a light-colored butte rose from a forested line of hills. "It came down out of a black sky like a finger. The trees jumped and they flew."

Ulysses nodded.

"We expect travelers who stay here to pay a fair price. A rent, you call it."

"Yes? And what's a fair price?"

"Whatever the man carries. If he carries a dollar, he pays a dollar."

"I see."

"And what do *you* carry?" The man glanced around at his friends, who sat watching but seemed less than interested. The big one, up on the buckboard, had drawn a loop of plug tobacco from his chest pocket, and he sliced off a piece of it with his knife.

"I carry more than a dollar," Ulysses said.

The second man, the small one with the corrugated face, leaned forward, the vinegar from the pickled eggs strong on his breath. He said something in his own tongue, Cheyenne it sounded like, but Ulysses could not be sure. His teeth were the color of weak coffee, and his eyes watched the place beneath Ulysses's jacket where the Enfield was slung.

"My friend wants to know how much more," the tall one said.

There was nothing in Ulysses that wanted a fight. He wanted nothing to do with killing men over a sum of money, although if it meant protecting his life, he believed he could take them — all three. His double-action revolver gave him the edge over the two in the wagon bed, with their older weapons. They would be dead before the third man, busy on the buckboard with his plug of tobacco, had a chance to marshal his pistol, which hung too high on his neck for easy use.

"How much more?" the tall one asked.

The money was in a pocket sewn to the inside of his coat, and Ulysses reached for it now, wishing he'd tucked the notes and silver into a sock, or hidden them someplace

206

on the wagon. On the other hand, it was better to keep things simple, to do whatever was required to avoid trouble. He opened his coat and removed the money, all of it, and then turned the pocket inside out to prove it was empty. He laid out the money in front of him, on the floor of the wagon.

The men glanced around at each other, as if trying to understand this man's lack of compunction about letting them see his wealth. The tall one reached forward and with his index finger counted and sorted. Then he said, "Thirty?"

Ulysses agreed.

"Or is there more someplace?"

"No, that's all I have."

The man's turtle eyes widened enough to show bright black pupils. "Our rent this time is thirty dollars. And we let you keep the ox and wagon. Is that a fair price?"

"It's fair if you say it is. Of course I will have to charge you for the meal of eggs. And I suppose you have wives at the agency." He aimed a thumb in the direction from which he came. "I gave them some of the best jerked beef you'll find, after your friend Adams tried to steal my potatoes from me. How about this. I'll give you these" — he separated a dozen silver dollars from the pile and pushed them forward — "and I'll keep the rest for myself. Then we part as friends."

"Adams," the big man grunted from his perch on the buckboard. Then he spoke for a moment in his own tongue.

"He says you should have done like the women do when Adam tries stealing from them," the tall one declared. "Kick him in the seeds."

"I'll remember that next time."

"We'll take these, too," the man said, sweeping the rest of the coins — seven silver dollars — back into his pile. He yanked the brim of the campaign cap down over the dark slits of his eyes and added, "You keep the paper ones." He gathered up the coins and put them into the side pocket of his coat, then pushed to his feet and swung over the edge of the wagon to the ground.

"Time to let our wealthy friend go his way," he said. "He must have bones to gather."

The other two followed his lead and climbed down off the wagon. They all watched as Ulysses hitched up the ox and prepared to leave, filling his canteens with drinking water from the rain bucket, folding up the tarpaulins, and taking his time to squeeze some grease into the wagon's wheel housings, just to show the men he was not in a hurry to leave on their account. Finally he climbed up on the buckboard and released the hand brake. The air smelled good after the rain. And it was cooling fast as evening came on.

"You'll need a fire," he said to the tall one, who'd taken a cottonwood stump and sat there with his rifle on his lap. "Dry out those wet clothes."

The man looked up at him, squinting.

"I was wondering," Ulysses said, watching the man's eyes. "Have you ever heard of a Magpie?"

The man sighed and looked away. "Sometimes they're mistaken for crows, but they're not the same bird. The magpie has white shoulders and a white belly. And is smaller than a crow." His mouth turned down at the corners, as if the idea of mistaking one bird for another disturbed him.

"No, I'm saying Magpie as the name of a man. He's Cheyenne."

"I've heard that name, yes." He leaned forward, elbows dropping to his knees. Then he raised his head and called out, "Bull Bear, Leather Top, do you hear this?" and spoke for a few moments, rapidly, a fast stream of words, Magpie being the only one Ulysses recognized.

The big man with graying hair, standing

behind the wagon now, brushing out his wet pony, grunted and nodded. He answered in a low voice.

"Bull Bear said Magpie is part of the southern tribe, that he knew him in better days, but can't say where he might be found. Down in the territories, probably. Or up north in the breaks. He wonders what you want him for."

"I'd like to talk with him. I have some questions."

"Questions."

"Yes."

The man shook his head. He looked tired suddenly, face hanging down between his wide shoulders. "Where do you come from?" he asked.

Ulysses pointed east. "Minnesota."

"And why are you looking for him?"

"I read about him in a newspaper piece on the Custer fight. The writer claimed to have spoken with him."

"Ah." The man tilted his head to the side and blinked. His eyes were neutral, and his hands had begun to clean the Henry rifle with a soft red cloth, moving with speed and grace as if all on their own. His face was hard but serene, his jaw sharp in the slanting light.

"My brother was there," Ulysses said. "He

was killed there."

"Many were killed."

"In the newspaper story, he told about a watch he picked up off the ground when the fight was over. It had a name engraved on the inside. Peter, my brother's name." Ulysses started to reach for his own watch, to make the point, but remembered that he gave it to the liveryman in Miles City, for collateral.

"You want your brother's watch back?"

"I want it for his wife, who gave it to him. Of course, it might not be my brother's at all. Peter is a common name."

"How will you tell?"

"I remember what it looks like."

"I don't understand. You said you came out here with questions. Now I hear you talking about your brother's watch. Which is it?"

"Both, I suppose. We got nothing of my brother afterwards — no remains, of course, because he was buried out here. None of his personal things, either, and a watch is *something.* But it's more than that too. I want to speak with somebody who was there, who can tell me how things went that day."

The man's hands had stopped moving, and his gaze was steady on Ulysses, his eyes narrowing as if to say, *Of what use would that be?* He straightened a little on the cottonwood stump and asked, "Why should he talk with *you*?"

"Why shouldn't he? He didn't seem to mind talking with the newspaperman. And who knows, he might want to sell me the watch, make a few dollars."

The tall man stared at Ulysses for another moment or two then looked away and laughed. "If we run across him, we will tell him to shine it up good. We will tell him you're a man of great wealth and he should make you pay."

Ulysses took up the driving lines and whistled for the ox to start out. The ox did no such thing.

"Tell me," said the man from his stump. "Did this brother of yours have a son?"

"He didn't. Why?"

"No reason," the man said, and lifted a hand to let Ulysses go.

A snap of the willow switch produced an effect whistling could not, and the ox stepped forward with surprising liveliness, pulling northeast toward Miles City. In falling dusk the trail ahead looked unwelcoming, even treacherous. It was easy to imagine washout gullies, hills breaking off into scree, steep declines with hidden rocks to snap his axles. Ulysses wondered what he ought to believe — whether there was any reason at all to think these men had been honest with him. And he wondered if he'd already had his chance, if he'd already found his man and lost him, and if so, how he might have handled things differently.

"Damn," he said.

As night deepened and the cold settled around him, Ulysses drove on, looking for a place to pull off and sleep, telling himself he was not going to fail in this search, trying to persuade himself that he was doing exactly what he must do. And before long the tightness across his shoulders had loosened a bit, and he started working out tunes with his mouth harp, indulging himself meanwhile with memories of the years when his sons were young and liked to hear him play — insisting on it before bed, in fact, as if his poor rendering of "Oh! Susanna" or "Amazing Grace" was a prerequisite to sleep.

13
THE SMOOT'S

It wasn't easy, getting out of Bismarck. They had to wait and be sure that Danny had dodged the headache. And of course they had no interest in being caught and sent home by the sheriff, either. On that first afternoon Eli had stolen into town for something to tide them over — apples, bread, and Danny's favorite, honeycomb. Then after waiting all through the next morning and afternoon, they walked west out of town in darkness, found a skiff along the riverbank, and used it to cross the Missouri. The rail tracks led them to the depot in Mandan, where they waited till sunup in a shack at the back of an overgrown weedlot. At seven o'clock, after a westbound had screeched and ground to a stop, the boys made claim to a vacant car, whose jouncing floor had rattled their teeth all the way to Dickinson, and here, as in Bismarck, they'd found a place to hide until they were ready to try the rails again, after dark. By Eli's calculation they had been gone four days and four nights, not counting the night they left, and time was starting to blur.

The abandoned livery stable, out back of a brick hotel, had a dry dirt floor, a tack room with old harness leather, a box of rotting oats, and piles of hardened lime in burlap bags. Settling in, they lunched on biscuits scavenged from the hotel's rubbish bin and played a two-hand faro of their own invention, using for chips the copper rivets they found in a cobwebbed drawer. Finally, around suppertime, they gave in to exhaustion. Danny had been dead to the world for hours, but Eli was only half asleep, not quite willing to let go. All evening he'd been listening to the murmur of distant voices — men carousing in the saloon — the occasional shout or laugh rising above the drone, and now he heard the crunch of boots. He came fully awake and sat up to peek out through a splintered siding board. He could make out a compact man wearing a neat white hat, an open coat that came to his thighs, and a white shirt with a stiff collar. The man strode forward and stopped a yard or so away from the wall. Eli was able to see only his boots now, which shone in the moonlight. Then came the rustle of

215

cloth, and before Eli could turn away, a stream of urine splashed into the dirt not a foot from his face and splattered against the outside of the wall. A hot bead of it caught him in the corner of one eye, and Eli swore beneath his breath.

The man pissed for a long time, sighing. Then as he finished, a coarse voice cut through the silence: "Take your time there," it said. "Finish up nice and proper. Then put it away and turn around, slow."

Through the crack in the wall, Eli watched the boots pivot as the man turned. "What do you need, friend?" the man said.

"Whatever you can give me in the way of cash money. You'll need to pull your wallet from that fancy coat of yours and toss it over. And you'll want to be nice and smooth about it to show me what a cooperative sort of fellow you are."

"Maybe you should put that away first."

Eli lowered his face close to the dirt floor and was able to see the men from the waist down. At thigh level the second man held a knife with a long blade, curved just a bit, a skinning knife. The other man's hands were empty, his fingers not clenched but open and loose next to his thighs.

The man with the knife said, "You came in this afternoon on the train. Saw you in

216

the hotel. You got a nice room there, and you bought yourself a nice meal. Tell me, where'd you get that pretty hat you're wearing? New York City?"

"Washington, D.C."

"The capitol. No shit."

"No shit."

The voice of the first man, the one with the hat, reminded Eli of his father's voice at times: careless, to the devil with the consequences. He remembered the night the banker came to visit, not long after the meeting in which Ulysses spoke up in favor of the girl from the whorehouse being buried behind the church. The banker, who claimed to speak as a friend, told Ulysses that he ought to start keeping his opinions to himself. That if he didn't, it might get hard to find people in town who wanted to pay him for his work. To which Ulysses had replied, "I'll say what I think when it pleases me, and I guess folks will do with their money whatever they like."

The .32-caliber Smoot's was loaded — all but the firing chamber — and Eli needed only to reach inside his coat, rotate the cylinder one click, and pull back the hammer. Then he crawled along the dirt, careful not to drag the toes of his boots, stood up, and placed a hand on the door. He recalled how badly it was warped and how tightly it fit in the old frame and told himself not to get stuck halfway out. The advantage of surprise was something he needed. He laid his shoulder against it and shoved with the force he used on the milk cow back home when she stepped on his foot. The door sprang wide and Eli nearly went down, catching himself as he stumbled and then leveling the Smoot's at the man with the knife. The man leapt backward and crouched, blade held low before him. He was younger than Eli had thought he was, a boy in fact: his face in the moonlight thin and pitted with scars, his hair lank on his shoulders, his body frail inside a coat and pants too large for him.

Arm extended, Eli sighted along the top of the small barrel, drawing a fine bead at the center of the boy's chest. No one moved or spoke. With a rush of pleasure and fear, Eli thought, *They're all waiting on me.* He wanted to tell the boy to drop the knife, but he didn't trust his voice. Or he could shoot the boy down and be done with it. He lowered his aim so as to take him in the leg, up toward the top where there might be some meat. And then the man from Washington broke the spell, his voice quiet and self-assured.

"Now, Sir, is the time to leave," he said, and plucked off his hat and leaped forward, sweeping the air with it. The boy stumbled backward in his oversize boots, went down on all fours, then got up and ran away down the alley.

The man brushed his hat with his fingers, then set it back on his head. Eli lowered his gun and released the hammer. As he put the little weapon back in his coat pocket, Danny's voice called from inside the livery, uncharacteristically pinched. "Eli? Eli?"

"I'm here, it's all right. Come on out."

Danny's white face peeked around from behind the door. Eli motioned to him, and his brother came forward cautiously, as if he were moving on river ice and afraid of falling through.

"Hey." Eli put an arm around him. "Sorry that had to happen."

The man put out his hand to shake and Eli took it.

"Who are you?" Danny asked him.

"William Hornaday," he said. "And your brother here just saved my bacon. Or I'm guessing it's your brother." He patted the front of his coat and reached inside for a cigar, which he planted in his mouth. When he struck a match to light it, the flame shook in his hand and went out. "Lord, I hate knives," he said. "Are you boys hungry?"

Probably on account of the gnawing ache in his stomach, Eli did not think to question this man's intentions. Nor did he pause to consider what sort of help he might be in a position to offer. He and Danny ran back into the livery for their bedrolls then followed Hornaday up the alley, cutting through between the saloon and hotel, and climbing the steps to the lobby.

It was a fine building, with a bronze bust of Lincoln on a marble pedestal and a high receiving desk. Red carpets were scattered across the glistening oak floorboards. They followed Hornaday all the way up to the third floor, to a quiet, high-ceilinged room that was lit with oil lamps in every corner. There were two beds, each with a night-stand and a china washbasin.

"Leave your bedrolls here and we'll find out if there's anything left for dinner."

In the dining room Hornaday ordered a meal for the boys: game hens, boiled potatoes, yams, late-season cob corn, glasses of milk. "And make sure they're generous portions," he instructed the waiter. "Make certain the cook understands."

"Yes, sir. Can I get anything for you?"

"Whiskey, straight up. An Irish blend, if you have it."

"Yes, sir."

Eli tried to be polite when the food arrived. For a minute or so he resisted picking up his fork, but soon he bent close to his plate and went to work, Danny likewise. They made fast work of the hens, stripping the wings and thighs and neck to get every last fiber of the greasy meat, then turned to the corn and potatoes before finishing up with the yams, which were cooked in brown-sugar syrup so sweet it made Eli's eyes water. He was aware of Mr. Hornaday across the table, sipping his whiskey and stroking his black beard, eyes glittering behind his spectacles.

"Why don't you boys tell me what brings you out here, all on your own, to this god-forsaken end of the world," Hornaday said after the waiter had taken their plates. "Then I'll tell you what brings me. I'm guessing your parents don't know what's become of you."

Eli's stomach went cold, and he glanced at his brother.

Hornaday tapped the table with his fingers.

"They know where we are," Eli said. "But you don't have to believe me."

The man lifted a hand, his signal to the waiter, who spun on his heel and came

221

nearly on the run, weaving through tables, his hair shining with oil, a curving wet loop of it falling in his eyes.

"Is there any dessert in the kitchen?" Hornaday said.

The young man rattled off a list as he stared at the upper corner of the room, as if the menu were printed there. Pumpkin cake, pumpkin pie, apple cobbler, baked custard, bread pudding.

"What strikes your fancy?" Hornaday asked the boys.

Eli glanced at Danny, who looked almost sick, his eyes bulging from everything he had stuffed into himself. There was a smile playing at the corner of his mouth.

"Well?"

"Pumpkin pie," Eli said, knowing his brother's taste for it. "For both of us, if it's not too much trouble."

"Danny?" Hornaday asked.

"Yes, thank you," Danny said, nodding.

"Very good then — two pieces. And I'll have the custard," he added, shooing off the waiter. He took a jackknife from his pocket and began trimming his nails. Eli expected the questions to start in again, but Hornaday only smiled, his white teeth shining behind his drooping mustache. "I didn't mean to pry," he said.

222

"What do you do out there in Washington, D.C.?" Eli ventured.

"I'm a museum curator. Also a taxidermist."

"What kind of museum?" Danny asked.

"The one I'm at is called the Smithsonian, and you could say we've got a sampling of everything, a lot of some things. Art, of course. Paintings from Europe. Sculptures that go back to ancient Egypt. Old vases. I can't even begin to tell you. But we have ordinary things too. Old clothes, old furniture, old machines, anything people don't keep any longer, or make use of. And animals of all kinds. Stuffed, naturally. No live ones. We're not a zoo."

The waiter arrived with their desserts, and Hornaday took a spoonful of the yellow custard, closed his eyes for the first swallow, and nodded approvingly. His eyes snapped open. "Perfect," he said.

"What for?" Danny asked.

"What for?"

"I mean, why do you keep all those things?"

Hornaday frowned, tugging on his long mustache. "For you," he said. "We keep them for you, and for your children and grandchildren, so they can see what the world was like before their time. Did you

know that millions of years ago giant creatures roamed the earth? Have they taught
you this in school?"

"Dinosaurs," Eli said.

"Have you seen pictures of their bones?"

Eli nodded. Danny was already well into
his pie and gave a half shrug, one shoulder
lifting almost to his ear.

"Someday you'll come and visit me, and
I'll show them to you," Hornaday said.
"Bones as large as a wagon tongue, teeth
longer than my hand. Lizards, if you can
imagine it, taller than a barn. We have
them."

"But they're all gone now," Danny said, as
if to reassure himself.

"You mean the animals themselves. Yes of
course, they're extinct." Hornaday dipped
his spoon into the custard, lifted it halfway
to his mouth, but returned it to the bowl.
His eyes were dark behind his spectacles.
He said, "That's what I'm talking about,
you see. That's the purpose of a museum
like ours, to keep the memory of things alive
— because things themselves don't last. It's
not just the dinosaurs. Look at what's happening now, here on this continent. There
wasn't a creature in North America as
plentiful as the bison, the buffalo. Now
there's but a handful left. It's terrible,

unforgivable. It's a shame and a crime. And listen to this. We don't have a single specimen of the American bison in our collection — at the Smithsonian, I mean. Can you believe it? Not one of the thirty million animals that covered the land."

"So you're out collecting bones?" Eli asked. He thought of his father and imagined a big cart, piled high.

The tension melted in Hornaday's face, and he let out a small laugh. "Oh no," he said. "I'm going hunting."

Eli tried to picture this man, dressed as he was now in a well-brushed coat and shiny vest, mounted on a horse and chasing a herd of buffalo across some dusty plain.

"I thought they were all gone," Danny said, as he finished with his pie.

"Nearly all."

"But you're going to shoot one and stuff it?" Danny asked.

"More than one, I hope. A dozen, two dozen, however many I can find. It sounds terrible, of course. But I don't see what I else I can do. What if they should all disappear, as they likely will, and we have no record of them?"

"It doesn't seem right," Danny said.

"What seems right isn't always right, though, is it? I expect you boys have discovered that truth yourselves by now."

Eli thought for the hundredth time of his mother waking up that morning and finding them gone, and he wondered if she would ever forgive him. "Are you hunting alone?" he asked.

"By no means. I'll have an Army escort from Fort Keogh, and I've hired a few cowboys, one of whom I'm meeting tonight, right here. A Mr. Sully. Tomorrow he and I will be going on to Miles City, northwest of which, I have reason to believe, there is small herd of bison still intact. Up near Big Dry Creek. Wild, empty country. Buttes and badlands and high plains."

"That's where our dad is, Miles City," Danny said.

Eli gave his brother a sharp look but could not deny his own wish to level with this man, whose posture and careful way of speaking somehow inspired trust.

Hornaday pushed back in his chair and with an index finger adjusted the spectacles on his nose. "And tell me, what is it your father is doing out there?"

"He might be gathering bones," Eli said, "but we don't rightly know. We're not even sure he's there."

"That's where Mrs. Powers told us he was heading," Danny added. "And we've got to find him so Fogarty doesn't take our house away."

Hornaday pulled a watch from his vest pocket and flicked it open. "It's just after ten," he said, "and Mr. Sully is supposed to be here at ten forty-five. Until then I'm yours. I believe it might be best if you start from the beginning and just lay things out for me. Who knows, maybe I can be of some help to you. How about it?"

Eli omitted a good share of what led to their father's leaving, though he briefly described the family's money troubles and Fogarty's move against them. He told about that last morning and how their father had left with the rooster and never come back, and about the vague note they found the next day. He told about their own departure, by train, and the visit with Mrs. Powers in Bismarck. Hornaday sat straight in his chair across the table, eyes wandering the room as he listened. When Eli finished, the man remained quiet for a minute, staring into the middle distance.

"I would be inclined to take his old friend's widow at her word," he said, finally. "Your father's likely pursuing some kind of venture out here — bones or otherwise — and I bet he means to return home and settle his accounts. But there is something

227

we don't know, isn't there. Some reason he didn't tell you he was leaving and has not contacted you since. Was there any trouble with the law that you haven't mentioned?"

"He spent a night in jail for throttling a man," Danny said. "Busted his mouth and a couple of ribs."

Hornaday lifted a brow and turned to Eli.

"He was working at the train depot and one of the passengers started pushing some folks around," Eli said, but didn't explain further, not sure whether Hornaday would share his father's sense of justice.

"You said he was a carpenter, a housebuilder."

"He was . . . before that. Before he went to work at the depot."

Hornaday waited.

"Before he said some things at a church meeting that made folks upset. Last winter. That's when he lost the contract for the new schoolhouse."

"All right." Hornaday shook his head, raising a hand for silence. He closed his eyes and scratched his beard, then folded his hands together under his chin. "Now please, the gospel truth here. Did you leave home with or without your mother's permission?"

They both sat up a bit taller, unable to

look away, the man's eyes holding them in place.

"I see. And now I don't have any choice but to help you, I suppose. Which makes me an accessory in this crime against your poor mother."

"We're doing it for her," Eli said. "And you don't have to help us."

Hornaday laughed. "Don't be a fool, son. Of course I do — I owe you that much at least." He snapped up his spoon and in a matter of moments polished off the rest of the custard. Then he said, "Here's a lesson for you boys. Whenever you've got something over on a man, like you have on me — when he owes you something, I mean — you've got to make damn sure that you get everything out of him that you can. Because how else are things going to be accomplished in this selfish world?"

They slept that night on the floor of the room Hornaday was sharing with the cowboy Sully, whose outfit had finished a drive that day. Sully was a large man with a face like a baked apple, riven and dark, who spent the better part of an hour cleaning his teeth with a length of horsehair and then his toenails with a Bowie knife. Finally he put on a long cotton nightshirt before turning out the lamp and climbing into his

corner bed. In a low, scraping voice that de-
fied argument, he said, "I trust you boys
won't be keeping me awake tonight."

He snored like an engine, naturally, and
for hours Eli couldn't sleep, trying to see in
his mind what his father would be like after
so long, more than two months now. He
would look older, probably, and harder, the
bones of his face sharper than before, his
restless eyes even less at home in his skull.
Not for a moment had Eli believed that
something dire had happened to his father,
that a calamity or mishap was responsible
for keeping him away. But he did go back
and forth between thinking his father would
be happy to see his sons and fearing he
might be grieved by their coming. It could
be that he had found a life that looked better to him than the one he had. Or that he'd
just gotten tired, taking care of a wife and
two boys. Maybe he liked the peacefulness
of being alone — unless he'd found somebody else, like Herman Stroud said he had.
The image of Mrs. Powers came to mind,
her yellow dress and her fine-boned, pretty
face, and he couldn't help wondering how
much of what she'd said — about their
father, about herself — was true, and how
much was contrived to cover truths she
couldn't bring herself to tell them.

Eli thought of his father's brooding ways, the nights he'd sat at the kitchen table long after everyone else turned in, and how Eli had often sneaked down from the loft to watch him there as he blew on his mouth harp or simply studied his hands, turning them over in the lamplight as if trying to decide if they were capable of the work he needed from them. Or sometimes reading his Bible, elbows on either side of it, the heels of his hands working his temples. Other nights he went off someplace, out through the back door, and didn't come home for hours. Eli would get up from bed and go down to the porch to wait for him, listening for his step in the dark, sniffing the air for the smell of the pipe he smoked at night — and at the first sign of him, slip back inside and scramble up into the loft next to Danny. He wished that his father had talked to him more, explaining things, and he liked to think that Ulysses felt eyes on his back on those nights he sat late at the table, that he must have seen a shadow waiting on the dark porch when he came walking home late. And it was that yearning of Eli's that stopped him from believing that his father intended to stay gone, from believing that he did not want to be found.

14
SCRATCHINGS IN THE SAND

She had a compelling face, a glorious face, and the first time Ulysses saw it — the first time he saw *her* — he'd known he would either marry her or suffer miserably. She was standing out front of the stone church on Summit Avenue that morning, waiting, thank God, for him. He stopped, offering a hand as she stepped up into the horse-powered streetcar he drove, and caught her eye. She looked away, her fair skin coloring, and he turned to watch as she moved past him toward an empty seat, not taking his eyes from her until she had settled there and glanced up, this time meeting his stare. Did she smile? He still believed she did, though she'd sworn he imagined it. Her cheekbones were prominent and her lips as ripe as plums. Wheat-yellow hair. Dark eyes. Dark eyebrows. He took her all in but said nothing that day, nothing the next day either, afraid she might disappoint him, afraid she might not be the girl her face and eyes told him she was: innocent and yet fully conscious of the soiled world.

After letting her off and watching her walk away down the street, head high and hips oscillating subtly beneath her blue skirt, an image had come to him that he'd long forgotten, a memory from five years before, during his time with Minnesota's Ninth Regiment, the Battle of Nashville. Not from the battle itself but the day after. As he'd moved through a shattered settlement on the southern fringe of the city, he came across a large house, seemingly untouched and standing up straight amidst the ruin, its unbroken windows reflecting the devastation surrounding it. That was what he'd seen in this girl, a beauty that allowed him to perceive the waste and blight infecting the world, himself included. It was as if she'd experienced life's hardnesses and cruelties, yet had remained somehow untarnished by them. How was it possible?

In the years to follow, seventeen of them, what he'd learned about his wife had mostly supported that early judgment. She had lost much in her first eighteen years — her family, her country, her city — everything familiar to her. And yet that hadn't broken her. She was strong-willed, adaptable, capable. And beautiful, yes. But her survival had to do also with a ruthless capacity for self-protection. As far as Ulysses could tell, she refused even to think about her losses, and didn't commit her sympathies beyond the point at which they might cause her damage, this marshaling of herself extending to him as well. There were times he'd resented her for this. But now, gone for so long and able to see her in a softer light, Ulysses understood, as he couldn't before, the weakness beneath her strength.

The sun was low, dusk approaching, and his stomach had shriveled to what felt like the size of a buckeye. He hadn't eaten since last night. Earlier he'd missed an easy shot at a goose floating on the river, and before that a mule deer bounded away before he could lay a hand on his rifle. There were times, no matter if you followed every impulse you thought was right and sacrificed the very things that gave meaning to your world, it still felt as if the hand of God was turned against you.

At least my cart is full, he thought — and after just a single day's worth of gathering.

Skulls and femurs and chains of vertebrae, curved ribs the size of hay-rake tines, bones of every sort, most of them sun-bleached, though some with clinging patches of hide.

He'd fitted them into the wagon with care, like a puzzle, so as to make the heaviest load possible. The more he sold them for, the more he would be able to offset the money stolen from him. What had him worried now, though, was the ox — he wasn't at all sure the creature had a day and a half's worth of pulling left in its lungs and legs. The coughing had worsened, the animal stopping every quarter-mile or so to arch its back and extend its neck forward to blow air and phlegm. The skin along its back and belly was turning yellow, scurfy. And now *both* eyes were leaking a viscous fluid, pinkish and foul-smelling. Yet the beast still responded to the switch, and Ulysses had hopes for at least a partial recovery. From his days growing up on the farm in St. Paul, he remembered animals with a similar malady, and there were some that had struggled through the illness and lived on. These, his father explained, suffered infection in only one of their lungs.

It was full dusk when the smell of roasting meat stabbed Ulysses in the jawbone, just below the ear, and made him pull up, yanking on the handbrake, his mouth filling with water. For a long minute he couldn't see it, but then a thin line of smoke gave it away: a hut made of vertical logs, down beneath the trail, dug into the side of the riverbank and well hidden in a stand of snarly hackberry trees.

The door was made of buffalo hide, dusty and mud-stained. "Hello," he said. "Anybody home?" He was off the wagon now, walking right up to it, the smell so strong — venison or antelope, he wasn't sure which — that it clouded his vision. He imagined entering his own kitchen and finding his wife at the cook stove in her green apron, putting his arms around her waist as she tended to the cast iron pot.

A hand appeared at the edge of the hide door and drew it aside to show an eye, dark and deeply set in a brown, lined face, a steady eye that regarded Ulysses without fear or curiosity, as if he were an animal common to these parts, a hare or a fox. She pushed the door farther aside to show him the rest of her. She was tiny, not more than four-and-a-half feet tall, and dressed neck to ankle in darkly aged buckskin. On her small feet she wore coyote-fur boots. White braids no thicker than strands of twine lay slack against the front of her shoulders and followed her flat chest and belly to her waist. She held back the door and stepped aside, indicating with a nod and a crooked hand that Ulysses should come in. Which he did, stooping low.

The room was warm. A kerosene lamp burning some kind of pungent fat hung from a hook in the middle of the ceiling, and in one corner stood a crude stove, a barrel with an iron box set into its top, above which, fixed to a skewer, was the thigh and rump of what looked like an antelope, hissing softly, its surface shining and golden above the fire. The smell of greasy meat was nearly overwhelming. The old woman pointed to a straight-back kitchen chair next to the stove. Sitting down, he was still taller than she was, standing. The width of her shoulders was hardly more than the span of a man's outspread fingers.

"I'm sorry to bother you," he said, "but I smelled your supper. Hard not to come and have a look."

She was at the stove, leaning into the skewered meat and breathing in its smell. She seemed neither comfortable nor uncomfortable about Ulysses being here.

"I'd best unhitch my ox," he said, rising from the chair.

She moved her head enough that he could tell she heard him but not enough to let him know she understood what he said.

When he came back in, she lifted from a

low shelf against the wall a turquoise plate, elegant with gold filigree around the edge, and handed it to him. Then with a knife from the back of the stove top, she made a quick flourish at the roasting leg, her blade flashing in the lamplight. Leaning forward, she dropped a long strip of meat indecorously onto his turquoise plate.

"Thank you," Ulysses said, but didn't touch it until she cut a piece for herself and sat down on the small bench against the wall. The antelope meat was spiced with a bitter herb that cut the grease, and he was surprised by its tenderness. He ate quickly, and when he was finished and licking his fingers, she hopped up and cut him another, this one longer and thicker than the first.

"It's good, very good," he told her.

She shrugged a tiny shoulder.

Afterward she took a pottery bowl from her shelf and with both hands carried it to the hide door. Ulysses followed and held the door aside for her, watching in the fading light as she nimbly ascended three wooden stumps of increasing height that formed a stairway to the rain barrel at the corner of the hut. She filled the bowl, trotted back down, and handed it to him.

The water was sweet and cool, and it tingled through his arms and pricked at the tips of his fingers. He drained it without taking a breath.

"And I have something for you," he said.

In the back of the wagon he rummaged through what was left of his stash of gifts and came up with a green drinking glass and a red bandanna. He brought them inside, where she smiled her thanks, showing four teeth left in her gums — one on the top, three on the bottom. She held the glass above her head, peering through it at the hanging lamp, turning it this way and that before setting it carefully on her shelf. She returned to her little bench, where she set about wrapping the bandanna around her neck and making an elaborate knot at the front of her throat.

Then they sat for a while, a few feet apart, Ulysses on the chair, she on her bench. Her eyes closed, and her chin fell against her chest and remained there.

"If you don't mind," he said, "I think I'll go outside and try for a little shut-eye. First light, I'll be moving along."

She didn't respond, but when he cleared his throat one of her eyes fluttered open.

"I do have a question for you," he said. "I was wondering if you know of a man called Magpie." He repeated the name, "Mag Pie," as if it were two words.

Her second eye snapped open.

"Magpie," Ulysses said again.

In a scratchy, unused voice — it was the first time he'd heard her use it — she said, "Magpie," lifting an eyebrow and pointing a crooked finger at Ulysses and shaking her head, as if to say, *That's not your name.*

He touched his chest. "*I'm* not Magpie, no," he said.

The old woman closed her eyes again.

Outside it was cold, heading toward a good frost. He climbed into the bed of the wagon and pulled his big quilt around himself and the heavy canvas tarpaulin on top of that. He lay on his back, looking straight up at stars so thick some giant hand might have skimmed cream from the pail and tossed it up against the firmament. He could make out Orion and both dippers, big and small. Also Pegasus, Cassiopeia, and Gemini.

He closed his eyes, turned on his side, and curled up tight, pulling his covers close around himself. Fifteen yards away the ox was breathing with less difficulty than before, and Ulysses dared to hope it might have turned a corner, that tomorrow would be better, or at least no worse. From downriver a goose called. Seconds later a coyote answered with three long howls, but Ulysses didn't hear it — he was already sleeping.

In the morning he woke with the sun in his face and knew it was past his usual time to rise. His feet tingled as they did whenever he slept hard and well, but the strap of the beaded tobacco pouch was biting into the skin of his neck, and so he threw off the canvas and the quilt too, and he pulled the strap from where it was binding and settled the pouch at the center of his chest. He breathed in the smell of the dry grass and of the river that sighed and muttered just yards away. For a minute he lay there with his eyes closed, not willing just yet to let his day begin. He might have allowed himself a bit more rest except that he sensed a presence. When he opened his eyes, what he saw — no more than a foot above his face — was the old woman staring at him, her face upside down, her wrinkled mouth pursed and disapproving. She was perched on the buckboard of the wagon, her hands gripping the back of it, and she was looking down squarely at the beaded pouch that rested on Ulysses's chest.

Instinctively, he brought a hand up to cover it, and no sooner did he move than she pulled her face away and scrambled down off the wagon to the ground. Ulysses sat up and watched her move quickly through the grass and sage to the sand along the edge of the river, where she turned around and looked back at him, setting her fists on her waist and tilting her head. She lifted a long willow stick and waved it in the air, motioning for him to join her.

"All right," he said, and pushed himself up from his hard bed, every joint creaking. It felt as if his bones were detaching from each other. He climbed down from the wagon and joined her in his stocking feet on the cold sand.

"What is it?" he said.

She pointed at the river with her stick and then at the sand in front of her and made a line in it, about a foot long and parallel to the river's flow. Then as if to say, *Hear me now,* she pointed once more at the river and again at the line she had drawn in the sand.

"I see. So that's the Tongue," he said, gesturing toward the line she had made.

She drew a second line, this one perpendicular to the other, making what looked like a capital T, though the horizontal top line was longer than the vertical one she'd drawn first. She performed her work carefully, bent over double at the waist, and when she was finished, she looked up at Ulysses, her eyes bright and snapping.

He said, "If your first line, there" — he

pointed to it — "is the Tongue, which flows north, then that one" — he pointed again — "has got to be the Yellowstone, which the Tongue feeds into. Am I right? The Yellowstone?"

She stepped back from her scratching and blinked for a few moments, as if thinking hard. Then she bent over and started in again with her willow stick, this time drawing a series of small lines — tributaries, Ulysses had to assume — all of which led into the Yellowstone from the north. From time to time she glanced up to be sure he was paying attention.

"Yes, yes," he said.

When she was done, she tossed the stick aside and stepped forward to the ground on which she had drawn her map and crouched there, making herself so small that from a distance she might have been mistaken for a child. With her tiny fingers she began to construct mounds of sand like small soup bowls turned upside down. She worked quickly, not glancing up at all, intent on her excavations, and when she had created half a dozen of these mounds, which were scattered among the tributaries beyond the Yellowstone, she finally looked up, her face cocked and waiting.

Ulysses nodded. "Those would be the hills

and buttes of the Divide, the high country north of the Yellowstone and south of the Missouri."

She smiled, apparently satisfied that he understood — though whether she recognized the words he uttered, he couldn't tell. She stood up from the sand, retrieved her willow stick, and aimed it straight at the tobacco pouch hanging from Ulysses's neck, the tip of her stick touching the colored beads. Then she reached out and tapped several times on the hills she'd fashioned in the sand before speaking clearly in her squawky, unpracticed voice.

"Magpie," she said.

15
THE COST OF HELP

For days she'd been lying sick on the heavy
robe, unable to rest even in sleep, unable to
throw off the dead weight that was pushing
her down beneath the surface where the
dream was always the same one. She was
riding in one of the canal boats in her old
neighborhood, sitting in the prow as the
boatman poled her along. For no good
reason, he refused to dock at Holmen's
Street, her stop, and despite her pleas kept
poling on, all the way around the circular
route — past the castle, past the old brew-
ery, past the library and the stock exchange,
and then past Holmen's again, refusing to
come alongside and let her out. Even worse,
each time they floated by the Gammel
Street bazaar, she could see Ulysses sitting
at a table near the beer stand. He was naked
and shameless, his long limbs splayed out in
the sun as he drank dark, foamy ale from a
glass mug. And though she called to him

and waved at him, begged him to help her, he ignored her completely.

On the third afternoon of her fever, she rose through brightening fathoms into the close air of the Two Blood home, Agnes sitting right beside her. Against the old woman's gentle arguments, Gretta dressed herself and went outside into the blinding sun and walked north toward the house she had never visited but only heard stories of — the house she'd questioned her husband about just once.

"Of course I haven't been there," he said, and laughed at her.

At the time, she thought he might be embarrassed by her lack of faith in him. Now she wondered if he was laughing at her for how incompletely she knew him, for thinking the distance between them had something to do with a girl, when in fact his secrets were so much deeper. In any case, she would be a fool at this point if she hadn't seen a pattern — first, the meeting in church about the burial of the girl, likely an Indian, and then his fight at the depot over the Indian family. It was true that her husband's sense of fairness had been oddly heightened by the experience of baptism, but he might have chosen other battles besides those two. And so she needed to see this woman face-to-face, no matter what people might think — as if it mattered what they thought. For all she knew, they'd think she was going to Mary for a job!

The house stood just past the town line, behind a wall of pine trees interspersed with young aspens, the trees so thick there was no seeing through them, and then beyond the trees a high board fence besides. Gretta unlatched the gate and walked up to the door, which was opened to her by a girl who looked fourteen or fifteen, with red hair and gray eyes.

"Are you here to see Mary?"

Gretta nodded.

She was led into the house and through the parlor to a side porch, where the girl pointed her to a rattan chair. Until today Gretta had seen Mary only from a distance. But now, entering the room, she looked tidy, more like a schoolmarm than a madam, with a tailored dress that was buttoned to the neck and graying hair pulled into a neat pile on top of her head. Her fingernails were clean and manicured, her posture was straight and her chin proud.

"I was surprised when you didn't come by earlier, after the meeting last winter," Mary said. "But now after so long, I have to say I didn't expect you." She spoke precisely, enunciating each word, her voice full and melodic.

"So you know who I am."

"It's a small town."

Now that she was here, Gretta wasn't sure what to say — or maybe she didn't know how to say it. She hadn't expected to feel shoddy in the woman's presence, nor underdressed and awkward. "I should have come earlier," she blurted out. "I wanted to."

"Were you afraid?"

"I think I wanted to believe him, but I wasn't quite sure if I could."

"You were afraid."

"Yes."

"What did he tell you when you asked? After the meeting at the church, I mean."

"He said he'd never been here. He said he did what he did because it was the right thing — what God would have told him to do, he said, if God made a habit of coming down and telling us things to our face. He said it wasn't Christian to deny somebody a proper burial, only on account of their sins."

Mary looked off at the sky, which today happened to be the same color as her eyes, a dull blue-green. "He said that?"

"Yes."

"Well, it sounds awfully nice." She took

out a lace handkerchief and dabbed at her nose with it. "But you didn't believe him when he said he hadn't been here."

"I told myself I should," Gretta said.

"And you were right to do so. He has never been here — unlike some of those men in your church, I won't say most. When your sexton, Mr. Peach, came by and reported to me about the meeting, gave me the council's decision and told me who said what, I had to think for a minute to figure out who your husband was. But then Mr. Peach told me he was a carpenter, and I remembered when he put up the barn back there, for Smith." She gestured toward her nearest neighbor to the west, a small farm on the other side of a lilac hedge. "That's years ago now," she added.

"You're not saying this out of respect for my feelings?" Gretta asked. "To cover things over? Avoid further problems?"

Mary laughed. "I don't cover things over, Mrs. Pope. As for problems, I take them as they come."

Gretta reached out and laid a hand on the woman's forearm. "Thank you," she said. "Thank you."

Mary smoothed her dress against her legs and shifted on her seat. "Well, then." She stood up and without further courtesies led

Gretta off the porch, back inside the house — which was neat, quiet, and smelled of soap — and through the parlor to the front door.

Gretta, tired suddenly, was aware of a weight she'd been carrying that was gone now. "Is it true," she asked before leaving, "that the girl who died was an Indian? The one you wanted to bury at Our Savior's?"

"Oh, I didn't want to bury her there — it's what *she* wanted. And no, she was Swedish. I think in all these years I've had one Indian girl, and she didn't stay on long. Of course, people like to think my girls are different from themselves. Black, Irish — or Indian. It helps explain things, I suppose."

"My husband told me she was Indian."

Mary Bond shrugged. "How would he know?" she asked.

Walking back through town Gretta felt lighter on her feet, less constricted in her chest, though in fact she was no wiser in regard to the whereabouts of her men. Not that she'd expected to be, she realized. She was passing by Fogarty's place, staying well to the other side of the street, when the banker's son exited the hotel lobby and made a beeline toward her, half running and half walking.

Gretta didn't slow her pace.

"Mrs. Pope, I have something for you," he called out.

She glanced back at him. It was a bag he was carrying, and Gretta recognized it — a large canvas bag that she'd sewn herself and always used for shopping at the grocer's — and now he held it up for her to see as he came on. She stopped to wait for him.

Herman Stroud was a tall boy with a face that reminded Gretta of a muskrat, his nose flat against his face and a mouth perennially ajar, as if he lacked the energy to close it. He was grinning widely, but she didn't trust him — not after the way he'd picked on Danny at school. "I work for Mr. Fogarty now," the boy announced, "and he said for me to give you this. He said it's got some things in it you might be needing."

She took the bag and looked inside. Her boar-bristle hairbrush was there, a sun-bonnet, and several pairs of cotton bloomers. To make up for the blush spreading across her face, she said, "Aren't you supposed to be in school, Herman?"

"It's Saturday, Mrs. Pope."

"So it is." She turned with the bag and started walking again.

"Excuse me," Herman said, following. "Mr. Fogarty wanted me to ask if your boys are back yet. If that sheriff finally got busy and sent them."

Gretta spun around so fast that Herman almost ran into her. "What do you mean? What sheriff?"

Herman's smile had widened into a foolish grin. "*I* don't know," he said. "The sheriff that sent the telegram, I suppose. Whoever he is. You'd have to ask Mr. Fogarty."

"What telegram?" Gretta asked, looking past Herman toward the hotel, where she imagined Fogerty watching her now, enjoying this. *The bastard, the fat bastard!* How many ways could he think of to ruin her life?

"You'll have to ask Mr. Fogarty, like I said. But he's gone right now — he'll be back from Fargo tomorrow." The boy turned and jumped down from the boardwalk and ran flat-footed across the street, calling back over his shoulder as he went: "He said to tell you he'd be happy for a visit. That he'd love to tell you everything he knows."

Gretta turned immediately, gathering her skirt in her fist, and headed straight for the depot, aware even in the sudden fog of anger that nobody would have anything to tell her. Not the telegraph operator, not the sheriff, not anyone. That as long she stayed here in Sloan's Crossing, there was only one man, apart from Two Blood, who was willing to help her, and that *his* help wasn't the sort she needed — though for all that, she still had to decide whether she would take advantage of it, whether it was worth the cost to her, whether there was another way forward that didn't involve Mead Fogarty.

16
U.S.P.

Hornaday took the cigar from his mouth and cleared his throat. "You know what they say about the Badlands, don't you?" Next to him the cowboy Sully was sleeping again, his stubbled chin resting on his chest. The boys, side by side, were sitting across from the two men.

"Nope," Eli said.

Beyond the window of their car, the earth had fallen away into ancient, cavernous riverbeds, a dream of towers and grotesque castles as far as they could see, a cemetery of fantastic rock in striations of pink and red. Yellow, purple, orange.

"The devil's backyard. Get turned around down there and you never get out. Bottomless gorges and pits of burning lava. I'm just glad we're up here, floating across."

Cracking an eye, Sully said, "Myself, I had to go after some curly-sided yearlings that wandered down a dry creek. Heard 'em bellering someplace ahead of me. Never found 'em, but I'm telling you, you could smell roast beef coming out of that smoking brimstone."

Danny glanced at his brother and then across at Hornaday. "You think they have many derailments along this stretch?" he asked.

Sully laughed through his teeth, but Hornaday said, "I asked the conductor that same question, and he reassured me we'll be just fine."

By late afternoon as they rattled into Miles City — which was laid out south of the Yellowstone — the horizon had regathered itself beneath a pale sky, the reach between here and there an expanse of rolling, gray-brown prairie in all directions. To the west a long, high butte stretched out beneath the sun like a sleeping cougar. The river was blue and wide, its choppy waters dotted with fishing skiffs. There was also a ferry docked at a crooked pier and a big red paddleboat steaming against the current. The dusty town itself was busy with wagons and carts and horses. Down the middle of its rutted central street a herd of a dozen sheep advanced almost formally, neither rushing nor lagging, driven by a mangy dog and a boy carrying an ancient double-barrel shotgun. Eli had never stepped foot on Montana Territory, but there was something here he could feel on his skin, dry and electric, something he could see in the faces, too, with their strong cheekbones and eyes that managed to hold a fair bit of the country's impressive distances — men mostly, all wearing hats and pointed boots, their pants hanging low in the crotch, but women as well, bare legs flashing in their windblown skirts, and hips aroll as if mounted on hidden wheels.

"Here we are," Hornaday said, drawing up in front of a three-story hotel. "Same place I stayed when I came out here this spring. Best in town."

The sign above the double door said DROVER HOUSE, and on its wide front porch a squat woman in canvas trousers stood talking with a pair of men who leaned forward as if putting each word she uttered to memory. "Say," she said now, "there's a good-looking boy, ain't you," and pointed her finger at Danny. Then she turned to Hornaday, mounting the porch steps. "You didn't tell me you had sons."

"Hello, May. In fact, I don't. These aren't mine." He went past her to the front door and opened it for her.

She walked straight for the front desk,

where she flipped up a hinged section of counter and took her position in front of the mail slots, her short, fat hands splayed out on the countertop. It came nearly to her chin. "Your room is ready," she said, nodding at Hornaday and Sully, "but what about these boys here?"

"They can stay with us tonight. They've got their own bedrolls."

"They ain't part of the expedition, I wouldn't think."

"No." And without embellishing, Hornaday explained how they were searching for their father, who might have passed through town, or even spent time here.

"When?"

"Last six weeks or so, as I understand it."

"What's your father's name?" May asked, turning her round face toward Eli.

"Ulysses."

"That's a mouthful," May said, "but I've got no recollection of it, and me a person with a knack for names. How would I know if I seen him?"

Eli described their father. Tall, with straight-up-and-down posture and wide shoulders. No extra weight on his bones. Gray hair.

"That sounds like about a quarter of the boys I see in a given span of time." May lifted a hand to indicate the townful of men just beyond her front door, but then Danny piped up.

"And this here is gone," he said, reaching up and taking hold of his own right ear.

"What — he's got no ear on that side?"

"The war," Danny explained. "He's only got a scar there."

"Well that helps a little. Though now I can tell you I *ain't* seen him. Did he come in on the train?"

The boys nodded. They figured he did, yes.

May tipped her head to one side then the other, as if to shift her memories around, make them retrievable. "Tell you what. Either he came through on the rails and kept on going, or else he needed a horse, maybe a rig, and lit out in that manner. In which case you'd want to go and talk to Church at the livery."

"We think he might be out here collecting bones," Eli said.

"All the more reason to see Church."

The big front door squealed open, and a young man wearing a filthy, ankle-length coat glided in, boot heels echoing on the wood floor. He walked right up to Hornaday and put out his hand. "McNaney," he said, looking Hornaday up and down. "And

258

I'm guessing you're the fellow that hired me."

Hornaday introduced McNaney, the hunter who knew his way around the wild country up north, the buffalo expert, but the man wasn't interested in courtesies, barely managing a curt nod to May and Sully. He said, "Fact is, Sir, Lieutenant Smith needs to see you a couple of days ago. He's got a six-mule team and an escort of troops all shined and polished, but he's got to know what else you're wanting. Mounts, wagons, commissary stuffs. I think we best get you over there to the Fort and get things started. With all due respect."

"I sent word I'd be late," Hornaday said.

"Yes, and he got that word. But there's other things pressing, and Smith needs to get you situated and off."

"All right, then." Hornaday turned to May. "You'll take care of our bags?"

She lifted her hands and chased the men toward the door — "Get going," she said, "hurry up," then snapped her fingers at a big stoop-shouldered boy by the window, working at a ledger book. "Stuart, these young men and myself, we'll be gone for a bit. Be sure you tell Dot to finish off the corner rooms upstairs. Hear me?"

"Yes, Ma'am," the boy drawled.

259

May led Eli and Danny south past a barbershop that smelled of talc and lye, then past a butcher shop with hams and pullets and ripe-smelling beef rolls, jars of pigs' feet, baskets of brown, white, and speckled eggs. They turned right on Main and headed west. There was a land shop, a dry goods, and a sturdy bank on whose portico sat a man with blond hair, shoulder length, asleep in a rocking chair, rifle on his lap. And then finally the livery, with a big sign that said CHURCH AND JOHNSON, an unpainted, slat-sided barn that emitted a rank smell Eli found comforting somehow. Just inside the wide door, a man stood leaning on his pitchfork next to a handcart piled with soiled straw.

"Hello, May. You got helpers?"

"Boys, meet Mr. Church. They're here looking for their old man," she told him.

He removed his hat, a brimless bowl of grimy leather, and used it to wave the three of them out the door and back into the street. "Let's talk in the air, shall we?" he said. "Now tell me, who's your father?" His eyes were cloudy, and he squinted as if he couldn't quite bring the world into focus.

Eli described his father once more, not forgetting the missing ear this time.

"You'd remember a man like that,

wouldn't you?" May asked.

"I would, and I do. Truth is, I'd remember him if he had a pair of ears like a normal fellow. On account of his eyes, the way they looked at me. Burning, kind of. Like he thought I did something to him. Or might."

"That's him," Eli said, remembering the times he'd felt that way himself, wondering what it was he'd done wrong.

"Well?" May asked.

"A week, week and a half ago. He came in out of the rain one day, mud to his knees, that storm we had. Lightning took the steeple off that little chapel down south that day. Remember? Said he wanted an ox and a cart. Well, it was mules he actually wanted, but I had none to let. He settled for the ox."

"For what purpose?" May asked.

"He was after bones. Said he was heading down toward the Tongue River Agency, wanted to know about the trail that goes that way. He didn't seem to know his way around here that much."

"You sure it wasn't earlier — say, in August?" Eli asked.

"Like I said, the day of that storm." Church squeezed the leather cap on his head and pushed long strands of greasy hair behind his ears. "Am I right on that, May? About the storm?"

"Yes, middle of the week, not this last but the one before, like you say. A week and a half back."

Eli said, "And you haven't seen him since."

"I ain't, no. And now he's in it for seven dollars and fifty cents for the rig. I'd like to be seeing that money. And my property too, for that matter."

"What did you get for collateral?" May asked him.

"Egad." Church lifted a fist and knocked on the side of his own head with it. "Hear that? He gave me something, when you see it, you'll think less of me as a man of business." He led them all back inside and into his corner office. There was a battered desk, a straight chair, and a window looking out on the alley. From a drawer he took the tarnished watch Eli had known his entire life, the watch his mother gave Ulysses as a wedding gift, not gold but steel, and which hadn't kept time since it went over the side of the fishing boat one day on Silver Lake and had to be rescued. The sight of it was like a stab in Eli's belly. It was almost as if his father's face had appeared before him in the flesh.

"That's his all right," Danny said. "My dad's."

"Yeah, and it don't work neither. Not so much as a tick. And it won't wind. I didn't make sure to check it when he gave it over to me, dammit." The liveryman wrapped his big fingers around the watch and held it up in front of his face and scowled at it before putting it back in the drawer.

"It just needs a new spring," Danny said, repeating what their father had been saying for years, while carrying it around nonetheless. Until now, Eli had never questioned the strangeness of that.

"How long do the bone fellows generally stay out?" May asked.

"A couple of days, a week. Doesn't take long to fill a cart the size of the one I let to him. Though it's hard to say. He might've come back and gone out a couple of times since then, dropping the bones off at Slovin's. Of course the country's full of renegades and highwaymen, so it makes you wonder." He stretched, arching his back and rotating his head all around on his shoulders. "Sorry I couldn't be of more help."

"What do you mean, renegades and highwaymen?" Danny said.

Church put a thumb to his mouth and closed an eye, thinking on it. He ignored the warning Eli couldn't help but notice in May's face. "Men that'll put a gun in your nose and take your wallet and your shirt too," Church said. "Or even just kill you for the sport of it. Men who don't like working. And don't like to be told what's what or where to wipe their dirty feet either."

"My dad was in the war, and you can be sure he killed people," Danny said.

"Ah." The liveryman nodded, then leaned his head toward the battered desk. "I don't figure you boys like candy, do you? Me, I favor the horehounds." He reached into a drawer and pulled out a paper sack and held it out, smiling in a way that wouldn't fool anyone.

"I don't care for 'em, no," Danny said, and jammed his hands in his pocket.

"How about you?"

Eli couldn't resist. He took one of the translucent little rocks and slipped it in his mouth.

"You best go and visit with Slovin," Church said. "Though you won't find him at his shop right now. I just seen him on his horse, half an hour back. He likes to take the evening meal at his mother's place, you know, up north."

"I wish she'd poison him and be done with it," May said, and ushered the boys out of the barn and into the street.

Behind them, Church laughed. "He ain't

264

that bad," he said.

A herd of longhorn steers had passed by, and alkaline dust hung in the air. It sent Danny into a sneezing fit. Looking at him, Eli saw that his face looked drawn and gray, and that there was yellow in the whites of his eyes.

"You all right?" Eli asked him.

"Only tired."

He threw an arm around his brother's shoulders and pulled him forward to catch up with May, who was ten paces ahead and moving fast. "We'll go and talk to that bone-man, right?" Eli called to her. "When he gets back from supper?"

May turned around. She shook her head. "I'll have no truck with the man. But Mr. Hornaday will take you over there tonight, I'll see to it. Come on now."

"What have you got against him?" Eli asked.

"Let's go, boys — I have to get dinner on," she said, turning and heading off again down the boardwalk. They had to run to keep up with her, Eli half dragging his brother, whose feet didn't want to keep up with his legs.

May fed them that evening in the kitchen, then set them to work clearing off the tables in the dining room and finally washing dishes at a big porcelain sink with a hand pump. By the time she installed them in Hornaday's room, it was past nine o'clock and the sun had been down for an hour.

"Now see here," she said. "The man has a lot to get ready for, but he'll take you over first thing in the morning, I'll make certain of it. Meantime, you boys stay put. This here is a nice enough town, but come nightfall a good place to stay inside. I'll be at the main desk, in case you need me."

As soon as May had left, Danny coughed. "We ain't just going to wait up here, are we?" he said.

"Depends on how're you doing," Eli said. He'd been watching his brother fighting it off, rolling his shoulders and making little chicken jerks with his elbows, squeezing his big eyes shut and then popping them wide, as if trying to surprise himself into feeling better.

"I'll be all right."

"You don't look it."

"I'm thinking, what if he's here tonight. Here in town. What if he's got a mind to leave in the morning?"

"I was thinking the same," Eli said.

"Let's go then."

"You've got to *promise* me you won't get sick," Eli said, hating himself for saying it,

266

but not able to keep the words in his throat.
"I promise."

And so they went down the back stairs that led to the the kitchen and then crawled on their hands and knees through the hall that passed an open door behind the big counter where May was perched on a high stool, facing away, toward the front. As they left by the alley door, the grandfather clock in the lobby marked the quarter-hour with a single chiming note, and Eli's stomach clamped up, scared. The night was cool and getting toward cold. A full moon, yellow as rendered fat, hung low and large in the east, glistening with a sheen that made Eli wonder if it was raining off that way. No rain here, though, and no wind either as the boys headed south toward the railroad tracks. They hadn't gone ten paces before they nearly fell into an old cistern with a low rock lip around its edge.

"Judas Priest!" Eli said, stumbling, but managing to steer his brother clear of the thing. They passed behind the buildings whose fronts they walked by earlier, including the livery where the rear window offered a profile of Church, elbows propped on his desk. He was gazing up in thought like a professor or a parson. Behind the saloon the air shook with the beating of hands on

267

piano keys, and then a door swung open, a man and woman falling out of it, clinging together, the woman squealing in fright or pleasure, Eli couldn't tell, the man's arms around her from behind, his face buried in her mass of hair as he carried and pushed her to a stunted tree in the lee of the building where he spun her toward him and pressed her against its trunk with the whole length of himself — all this as the boys slid past, Eli urging his brother, "Come on, come on," and pulling him along.

Outside the depot an old man, white beard to his waist and reeking of whiskey, sat hunched against a luggage cart, chewing on a leg of turkey. Asked about the bone-man's whereabouts, he lifted the turkey leg and aimed it down along the track, east.

"His name's Slovin," the old man said. "You'll be lookin for a round-roofed building, a barn really, north of the rails. That'd be his bone-house. Might find him there, but I wouldn't put money on it."

"Where, then?"

The man leaned back and yawned, his mouth a gaping hole. A sharp, wet laugh barked out of it, the spray striking Eli's face. "That other house he's got back there, which he'll be keepin' tabs on." The old man laughed again, but this time Eli backed off to a safe distance and stayed dry.

The line of the building's roof was like a giant wagon wheel half buried in the ground, a big sliding door taking up most of its high front wall and next to it a smaller door, on which Eli knocked. He knocked again, louder, this time raising what sounded like a voice from inside.

"He's in there," Danny said, and lifted both fists and pounded on the plank door like it was the single thing standing between himself and his father. He stepped back and nearly collapsed, his shoulders crumpling, arms crossing in front of his chest. Eli grabbed hold of him to keep him on his feet.

"We've got to get you back," he said.

Danny shook him off.

Then the door opened before them, and the boys found themselves staring at a bald man whose face was smooth and white, nearly featureless, his eyes mere holes, his mouth a straight cut above his soft chin. A man-sized garden slug was what he looked like.

"I hope your visit is propitious," he said in a voice deeper than Eli would have guessed. "I'm occupied tonight."

"Slovin?"

"I am."

"We're looking for our father, who might

be a client of yours."

"Of what variety?"

"Bones," Eli said.

"Ah." Slovin turned and cast a look inside.

Eli, looking too, saw a lamplit desk and beyond it the star-salted sky — for the back wall of the barn was gone. The bone pile was eight or ten feet high and extended for at least thirty paces beyond the shelter of the building. There had to be enough to fill two or three boxcars, probably more.

"I have numerous clients," Slovin said, and he turned and shuffled back inside, signaling for the boys to follow. He dropped himself into the chair behind his desk.

"Who is your father?" he asked.

Eli started describing him, but Slovin slapped the air.

"Give me his name!"

"Ulysses Pope," Eli said.

"Pope, Pope." Slovin's doughy hands formed a knot in front of his face, and it was hard to tell if his small eyes were open or closed. The smell coming from the bone pile reminded Eli of the dump behind Johnny's house back home, Johnny's dad the butcher, whose shop was on the riverbank where the carcasses had piled up for years. Slovin straightened himself in his chair and showed something like a smile. He tapped his fingers together. "I've seen him, yes. But God knows where he might have gone. Ulysses Pope — my, what a venerable name for a one-eared man."

"He sold to you?"

"He did. And I paid him handsomely, more than his shit was worth. What are bones, after all?"

"When?" Eli asked him.

The man yawned, coughed into his fist, then took a neatly pressed handkerchief from his pocket, shook it out, and wiped his mouth before saying, "Two mornings back, I believe it was. No, yesterday." He smiled. "I saw your father yesterday."

Eli wanted to knock the ugly grin from Slovin's face, throw him off his chair and kick him — for the handkerchief he used and for his pale skin, for the haughtiness in his voice. But Slovin stood abruptly. "I know somebody who might be able to help us," he said. "Why don't we go and see him."

He led them outside along the bone pile, then across a short dirt yard to the door of a tiny, unpainted house. "Here," he said, and ushered them inside.

It was a single room, lamplit, with a pair of upholstered chairs and a sofa with ornate carvings on the armrests. "Wing!" Slovin

271

called out, "where in damnation are you?" He walked to a door at the rear of the house and stuck his head outside. "There you are," he said, and stood aside to let the man enter — a Chinaman with a skinny mustache that drooped from both sides of his chin who was wearing a black skullcap. He looked at Eli and then Danny, and finally back at Slovin.

"Mr. Wing," Slovin said, by way of introduction.

"Yes," Wing said.

Slovin pointed at the floor. "Is Skinner here?"

"Yes," Wing said.

"We need to see him."

Wing nodded. Then he squinted at Danny and reached out his hand, pointing. "He okay? Don't look so good."

"He's only tired," Eli told him.

Wing retreated a couple of steps and crouched down on the floor. He grabbed hold of an inlaid handle and yanked on it, lifting a big trapdoor that revealed a stairway going down. A pungent odor rose up, sweet and flowery — but sharper than that, like something burning.

"Here we go," Slovin said, and led the way.

Eli followed the Chinaman, and Danny took up the rear, his hands on Eli's shoulders. The steps were narrow, and at the bottom everyone waited in dim light to get their bearings, the smell so strong now that Eli's eyes watered. Soon he could make out bunks against the walls, right and left, two pallets high, figures lying in each one, and a single bunk straight ahead. Five people in all, some on their backs, apparently dozing, some on their sides or half propped up. One of the men groaned — not out of pain but pleasure, as if inspired by the taste or sight of something heavenly. Wing pointed straight ahead and moved toward the bunk at the end of the room, the man lying thereon full-bearded and large. He was smiling sleepily and sucking on a straight, narrow pipe two feet long with a doorknob-shaped bowl affixed to its side. In front of him on a short table was a glass contraption that contained a tarry substance smoldering above a redhot coal. The man's eyes were open, but they looked as shiny as wet tin. Eli wondered if he could see anything.

"What's he doing?" Danny asked.

Slovin laughed. "Taking a well-deserved holiday, but I think I can rouse him." Slovin bent over and put his face right down close to the man. "Skinner," he said, "you have a pair of young visitors."

The man's eyes fluttered and his head

reclined to one side.

"Skinner, you piece of dung, pay attention here."

"Somebody's after me," Skinner said.

Slovin reached out and rapped him on the shoulder, telling him, "That's right, you're the man of the hour."

The man straightened up, moistened his lips with his tongue. "Are *you* the one?" he asked, pointing at Eli.

"Me and my brother. We're trying to find our dad. Ulysses Pope."

Skinner glanced all around, scowling, as if a trap had been laid for him. He pushed a hand back through his long, snarled hair and lifted his nose like a dog scenting the country ahead.

Slovin prompted him: "You came into town yesterday with another man, both of you with bones to sell. Remember?"

"Ain't seen the fellow since," Skinner said. "Not like we were friendly, or somehow related. But you know? This man, he had no ear on one side of his head. Right side — or it could have been the left."

"Did Pope tell you how long he planned to stay around? Do you know where he might be headed?"

Skinner lifted a hand, paused. Then he whistled a few notes — not a melody, as far

Eli could tell. It sounded more like a bird singing.

"You dreaming fat-ass," Slovin said, and threw up his hands. But Wing bent down close and slapped Skinner's face hard enough to make his head snap.

"These boys here," Wing said. "Their father. Okay?"

"Beautiful," Skinner said, rubbing his beard.

"Okay!" Wing said, and took a fierce grip of one of Skinner's earlobes with a thumb and index finger.

The man winced, blinked, and sighed. He said, "Run into him on that trail down to the Cheyenne reserve. Me on the comeback, filling my cart, him with an ox that give up the ghost. Plumb dead, it was. And shitfire! That high load of his almost tipping over."

Wing let go of the man's ear and stepped back.

"So you gave him a hand?" Slovin asked.

"Had me a pair of Percherons, yes, which I give him the use of one," Skinner said. "Piece of pure providence for him that he run into somebody like me."

Slovin chuckled. "At what cost to him?"

"My horses got the worst of the bargain, pulling twice what they should."

Wing put his face right in front of Skinner's. "Where was he going? This Pope?"

At which Skinner bolted up straight in his bunk, eyes clicking open. "You think I'm a goddamn fortune-teller?" he shouted. "Well I ain't. Now leave me the hell alone, I paid you good money." He'd set the pipe aside, but now he grabbed hold of it and clamped his teeth on its tip and drew in deeply, his eyes going back in his head then closing. He turned away toward the wall, and a tremble ran through him.

Slovin pointed a stubby finger at Eli. "I guess you heard him as well as I did."

"We saw the livery man, Church, this afternoon," Eli said, "and our father hasn't been around there, not since he rented the rig."

Slovin huffed. He said, "You think he's going to buy himself a dead ox? I don't think so. We're done here, let's go."

Yes, Eli thought. *Let's get out of this crazyhouse.*

They left by way of the backdoor into a fenced yard filled with sheep, the mist of their breath hanging in the air. A stiff wind had blown up out of the north, and the sky was quilted with stars, wide, gauzy patches of them. Eli took Danny by the hand and led him to the gate, the sheep scattering before them and butting each other. "We'll find him in the morning," Eli said, but his heart was dead in his chest, like a lump of meat. He filled his lungs with the cold air, trying to free up the choking tightness. Their father wasn't here, Eli felt sure of that. They'd missed him, probably by less than a day, and now Danny was going to be ill.

"I want Mother," Danny said.

"I know that — but I'm going to take good care of you. And as soon as you're better, we'll put you on the train for home, all right? Everything is going to be fine. I promise you."

Danny held on tight to Eli's coat as they walked, but his legs kept tangling up with each other. Eli stopped and bent down and hoisted him onto his back.

"I'm going home," Danny whispered into his ear. Then: "I'm cold."

By the time they reached the Drover House, Eli's hands ached and his eyes streamed from the cold. Danny's breath came in fast shivers. In the corner room upstairs they found Hornaday bent close over his desk, writing in a notebook. He was puffing on a fat cigar.

"Bitter out there, isn't it, boys," he said. "And you didn't find your father."

"No." Eli lowered his brother into a corner, spread a blanket for him, and rolled him up in it. Danny was inert, as loose as a sack of grain.

"What's wrong with him?"

"He gets headaches. Bad headaches."

"Just what we need, another sick one." Hornaday pointed to the corner, and as if on cue a deep moan issued from the bed there. The bedsprings squeaked and jounced. Hornaday took off his spectacles and rubbed his eyes with his knuckles.

"Sully?" Eli asked.

"Must have eaten something bad tonight, the catfish, maybe — or so I hope, because if Sully goes down, I'll have to find another hand. And all we have is one more day." Hornaday came over and crouched on the floor next to Danny. He lifted him up and studied his face. "Doesn't seem to be in any pain," he said.

"Not yet, no."

"How long do they last?"

"A day, two days — longer. Mother can make them go away sometimes."

"We'll fetch a doctor first thing in the morning," Hornaday said, tucking Danny back into the blanket. "And I'll speak to the sheriff about your father. That's the best I can do. Now get some sleep, it's late."

Across the room, Sully cried out in his bed: "Mother of God, my bowels!"

"Go outside and purge yourself, man," Hornaday said. "Give us a little peace, you hear me?"

The cowboy rolled out of bed and rushed from the room, apelike, one arm hanging, the other clutching his belly, a foul smell trailing behind him. When he came back five minutes later, he was ashen-faced and groaning. There was little sleep to be had, what with Sully suffering as he was, cursing and bawling, and every so often sitting up in his bed to shout "Bloody ballocks!" as if fighting God or the devil for a bit of relief. At one point Hornaday lit a lamp and tried calming him, but Sully rose to his knees and swung a roundhouse punch that Hornaday managed to slip, his head whipping so fast his spectacles went flying. After which Sully was quiet for a time and Eli finally went off to sleep, only to be stirred awake by his brother.

"You hear that?" Danny asked.

"What?"

"That."

In the faint light from the window, Danny's face was white and feverish, his wide eyes glossy, his lips chapped. He was propped on an elbow and pressing a finger into Eli's shoulder. "Listen," he whispered.

Eli heard only the ragged grunts of Sully

and, beneath them, Hornaday's breathing. "It's your dreams. You've got to sleep now."

"No, listen."

"Quiet." Eli laid a hand over his brother's mouth.

In the corner Sully whimpered, "No, no, no," then came a rustle of blankets, a jostle of bedsprings. Danny wriggled free of Eli's hand and got up on his knees. He tugged on Eli's sleeve, took hold of a fistful of cloth, and got to his feet. "Let's go out in the hall. Come on, I have to tell you something."

Reluctantly Eli allowed himself to be led toward the door, but Danny bumped into the wall and Eli had to guide him out of the room. The hallway was dark and empty, a single lamp burning at the end near the stairwell.

Danny's breathing was fast and light. "There's a boy, a little boy in my dream. And I heard him crying. I think he's hiding someplace."

"You heard Sully."

"No, his voice is high, and it's coming through the window. We need to go and find him. There, you hear it?" Danny lifted a hand to his ear. "There. He's in trouble."

"We're the ones in trouble," Eli said.

"We can't just leave him. We have to go outside and look." Danny's eyes glistened and blinked. He was taking air in fast gulps. Eli placed a hand on his brother's chest and felt his heart going like a squirrel's, way too fast.

"All right, relax. We'll go out and check."

Danny started off toward the stairs, arms half raised for balance, and Eli had to run to catch up with him. He took him by the shoulders and turned him around and told him to wait where he was, then returned to the room for their pants and shoes and coats, Danny's big, floppy hat. The north wind had let up some, but the cold had settled in beneath a clear sky. In front of the hotel a cowboy lay spread-eagled on the boardwalk. As Eli and Danny stepped past him, he lifted up and asked if they could spare two bits, then fell back again, his head banging the planks like a dropped pumpkin. They walked fifty paces north before Danny stopped and looked up at the smear of stars, his face sad and rapturous.

"Do you hear him?" Eli asked.

"Only a little. No, I can't tell where it's coming from — I think we're too late." He let go of Eli's arm and dropped his hands to his sides. His head fell forward on his neck. His body quaked. "We can't help him anymore," he said.

"Let's go back in then. It's cold."

For a moment Danny stood thinking, or possibly sleeping on his feet, Eli thought, but then he turned and set off for the saloon across the street, where light still leaked from the shuttered windows. He moved like an animal lame in one foot, listing to one side as he walked. Eli followed, half-heartedly. "We'll go ask if they've seen him," Danny said. "As long as we're out here."

Inside, men were gathered in twos and threes at half a dozen tables across the low-ceilinged room. Hanging lamps cast a sickly light on their drawn faces. Most were quiet, slouched in their chairs or half sprawled across their tables — though off in a corner a bald man told a story, his hands drawing pictures in the air. Something about a rainstorm and a mud hole. One of his listeners, coming awake, stood up and moved for the door, and as the roomful of men registered his passage, their dull eyes landed on the boys. Eli, wishing he were anywhere else, felt Danny's elbow in his side.

He cleared his throat, took a breath, and summoned the deepest pitch he could manage. "We were wondering," he said, "if any of you might have seen our father." Beside him, Danny nodded.

The men waited. The one heading for the door stopped to look at them. He wrinkled his nose and shook his head.

Eli offered their father's name and described what he looked like, explained that he'd just gotten back into town yesterday, having made a trip south for bones.

"I ain't seen a one-eared man," the bald one said. "Never have, thank God."

"Nor me," said the one standing, and he moved on past them and out the door, saying "Best of luck" before he slammed it behind him.

At one of the back tables a cowboy with a bony skull-face raised one finger. He said, "Well *I* seen him. I seen him sure as I see the pair of you right now."

Everybody turned to look. "Where?" the bald man asked him. "Can't you see these boys are dyin' here?"

"Might be it was down next to the river — yes, close by the pier. This morning, I believe it was."

"You believe?" asked the bald man.

"The ferryman, Williams, he owed me a dollar, and I was there to fetch it. And that's when I seen him. The bare side of his head is what you can't help but pay some mind to. Wondered at the time if he could hear anything."

"He can hear fine," Eli said.

"Now listen, boys," the bald man told

283

them. "I advise you to wait until morning. There is some folks down there you had best stay clear of, I mean down along the riverbank. You don't want to walk into anything."

"It's morning enough," Danny said, and he made a shuffling line to the door, Eli close behind. They were half a block from the saloon and heading west when the cowboy with the bony face came chasing after them.

"Maybe you'll want some help," he called.

"We'll be fine," Eli said, and kept walking, Danny at his side but fading now, his feet getting sloppy. He had one fist knotted into the side of Eli's coat.

"River's down that way." The man pointed out the obvious with a skinny finger. "Just stay on this here road and there is a pier where the ferry ties up. You'll see a few dugouts off to your left. The man that's got no ear — well, your old man — he was out squatting next to the second dugout from the pier. On your left. Actually tried renting my horse off me. Wanted to give me four dollars and the boots on his feet. Told me they would be the finest boots I'd ever wear. But look at this." The cowboy had caught up to them now, and he lifted one of his feet for the boys to see — a small foot, as it happened, tiny for a grown man, hardly bigger than Danny's. "Not much good those boots'd do me, right?"

"Did he look sick or anything?" Eli asked.

"Sick? No. A little wore out, you might say, in want of a good nap and some hearty victuals. But healthy enough."

They had walked well beyond the influence of the town's few lights, and the ground was beginning to drop toward the river when the cowboy suddenly pulled up short. "You boys are good from here — just keep your noses in the wind." He turned and headed back toward the saloon.

"Dad must need a horse pretty bad," Eli said. He was thinking of the pride their father had always taken in the boots he ordered from a shop in Minneapolis, from a bootsmith who used the finest bullhide and carved U.S.P. — for Ulysses Samuel Pope — into the tops of the uppers.

"I don't feel good," Danny said.

The pier was a broken-down concern, barely long enough for the ferryboat tied to its pilings, and just like the cowboy told them, there was a string of dugouts along the riverbank to the left. In fading starlight, the crude structures looked like arrangements of castoff junk — walls made of planks and crates and bricks, with pipes sticking up at odd angles from earthen roofs. From the second chimney, a stone's throw from where the boys stood on the pier, smoke rose in a thin trail that angled south with the breeze. Eli led his brother to the door, which appeared to have had a previous life as a tabletop, and knocked on it, using the rhythm their father had always used: *da-da, di-daa-da.* He was preparing himself for the worst. *There's another man here, not my father,* he thought, and he was ready to pick up Danny and run if that was necessary — back up the hill and straight into town.

But there was movement inside, and a voice called out: "Who is it?" A voice like none other: a low growl, but soft, too, like a big dog that would rather lick you than use its teeth.

Danny said "Dad" — just that, with utter conviction, as if peering at him through an open window in full sun.

Then the door swung open, and before them in lamplight was a man hunched beneath the low ceiling who might, Eli thought, be their father — if he would stand up straight, that is, and if his face were not hidden behind a filthy beard, and if his eyes weren't small and tight like those of a wary animal. And if he didn't carry the sour smell of a horse that's been run to froth and allowed to dry in its own sweat.

"Hi, boys," the man said.

17
THE ARM OF FLESH

He wanted to tell his sons that he'd lived for years in a shadow world, everything seemingly half real, the sky dim, the sun weak, the taste of his favorite foods — apples, fresh bread, fried eggs — dull and sad. That he had often felt invisible, surprised when men nodded to him in the street. That some nights, lying in the dark, wife beside him and boys in the loft above, he'd feared they were all part of an elaborate dream, gone at first light. He wanted to explain to them about his sins, about his hope of finding relief from God, and of course about his leaving — but he couldn't summon the words, not yet. Or at least there was no coming at things straight on, with Eli sitting there like a stranger, all the baby fat gone out of his face, and Danny curled on his side, moaning and twitching inside his pain, arms wrapped around his head.

"You can rest now, it's all right," he told Danny, and sponged his neck and back with a damp rag.

When Danny finally slept, Ulysses got up and went down to the river to get some air, Eli following after him, and there in the paling darkness he recounted to his son an older story, from another time, a story he was *able* to tell — about himself at ten, when he hitched his father's new stallion to the spring wagon, this against his father's orders, the stallion being young and wild. It bolted of course and ran off, careening down a hill and through a yard, where the wagon it pulled struck an old collie dog, the neighbor girl's favorite pet.

"Why are you telling me this?" Eli asked. "This isn't what I came to hear."

They were squatting side by side in the sand and watching the river go by, black and shimmering. A fish rolled to the surface and flipped its silver tail. Birds were calling already. Sandpipers with their high straight notes, and doves, too, low and soft. The sun was an hour yet from rising, the morning starting to lighten around them.

"I picked up that dog," he said. "It was crushed, dead, and I hauled it home and buried it behind the barn. I didn't want anybody knowing about it, especially my dad. Except I couldn't keep it to myself, either — I was too young for secrets back then. I ended up telling an old man who lived in a cabin down the road, a blind man with no teeth in his head. His well had gone dry, and I hauled water for him. He wasn't given much to conversation and generally only nodded when spoken to."

"And this blind man told your dad," Eli said.

"No, he didn't. He told me I should tell the girl, because she was the one who had been wronged, she was the one I'd hurt. But you see, I hadn't expected any advice — I was only getting it off my chest."

"*Did* you tell her?"

"I did. I had to work up the courage, though it took me a few days. And naturally she cried and made me take her back behind the barn to dig up her dog, which stank to high heaven, maggots all over it. Then she told her dad, who told mine, and that was the worst part of the whole thing, the whipping I got from him. And the fact he wouldn't let me forget what I had done."

"We saw Mrs. Powers in Bismarck," Eli said. "She'd sent you a letter that we read, me and Danny. We never showed it to Mom."

"I suppose you have it with you."

Eli withdrew it from his pocket, saying, "Mother is unsettled, hardly able to think straight. And she fears we might lose the house."

Nodding, hating himself, Ulysses took the letter and slipped it inside his coat next to the leather pouch. But he was not going to be pushed into changing course, not now, and he set his jaw against the idea, looking hard into his son's eyes. "I meant to send money, I did," he said, "but it's not been easy to come by. And your mother is stronger than you know. She will find a way to hang on."

"I didn't want to leave her," Eli said. "At least not by herself. I meant for Danny to stay behind."

"Yes, the boy has no business out here, he isn't strong enough."

"You're telling *me* that?" Eli snapped. "You can't tell me anything."

Ulysses felt a wash of shame across his face and looked away. "You're right, of course," he said, quietly. "And you have to know that I didn't want to leave her, either. I love your mother. It was the hardest thing — I miss her so much. And I didn't want to leave you and Danny."

"But you did leave us."

For a little while they sat without speak-

291

ing, Ulysses absorbing just how much he'd damaged those he loved most. And yet no less certain of what he was doing. "I need to work my way up to this," he said.

"Mrs. Powers told us that you served with Custer," Eli said.

"That's right. And what did she say about it?"

"Not a whole hell of a lot. That you and her husband were good friends."

"We were, yes." Ulysses nodded.

"Who *is* she, anyway?" Eli asked. "To you, I mean?"

"My dead friend's wife, Eli," Ulysses said. "Only that. Now run and check on your brother, will you? Make sure he's all right." Ulysses got to his feet, knees and hips burning after too long in a crouch, and watched his son go up the bank and duck inside. In less than a minute he was on his way back, coming fast — though he looked off-balance somehow, his gait uncertain.

Eli said, "He's still sleeping."

"We'll send him back as soon as he's better," Ulysses said. "Put him on the train for home."

Eli's face was closed, his brow squeezed tight, and Ulysses could feel the pressure of his eyes. "Fine, but you're not sending *me* home," the boy said. "I'm not going back, no matter what you say. I have a right to know what you're doing here. I'm not a stranger like you make me out, and I'm telling you now, I won't let you out of my sight till I know what's going on. Do you hear me? I'll never leave. I won't give you a moment of peace."

"All right, then." Ulysses led him to a tipped-over willow tree lying parallel to the water and sat down on its trunk. Eli sat, too. It was morning now, all the stars dissolved, and across the river a man poled out from the bank in a fishing skiff and let the current take him.

"About that dog," Eli said. "The person you should have told first was your father. Not the old blind man, and not the girl."

Ulysses nodded.

"Just start anywhere," Eli said.

And so he did, with the war, his first one, explaining that he wasn't young when it finally came to its end, twenty-five, lines in his face already, the world in his bones. He'd been in the Minnesota Ninth, marching up and down Missouri and Mississippi, Arkansas, Kansas. And Nashville, Tennessee, where he saw Landy Cooper, a boy he'd grown up with, lose his head to a cannonball. Afterward, back in St. Paul, he was plain worn out, lacking any notion of what to do with the rest of his life, of what he wanted or what might be required of him. After two years, he reenlisted. He took a train down to Fort Riley, Kansas, and joined up with the brand-new Seventh Cavalry.

"I don't see why you went back in," Eli said. "Why you left your family again."

Ulysses brought out his makings and began a pipe for himself, noting as he filled the bowl and tamped it down the way his son watched closely, eyeing the buckskin pouch. He struck a match and lit up.

"My parents were gone by this time. They died during the war — that was part of it. And though I lived with my sister and her husband, and they wanted me to stay on, there was something about St. Paul that I couldn't abide any longer. I woke up mornings wanting to pound the walls, kick my way out of that house. I had a decent job, working for a builder, learning that trade. But all the same, I thought I might do something terrible. I was afraid I might start screaming at somebody just to see fear in their eyes. I thought some morning on the way to work I might jump off the horse car, walk into one of those Summit Avenue mansions, and tell the man eating his breakfast I was there for my peace of mind and that he owed me a portion of his, whatever portion that might be, I didn't know."

Ulysses paused to rub the palm of his hand over his face. He drew on his pipe but it was cold and he had to relight it.

Eli waited.

"So when I heard the army was mustering up a new regiment to handle the Indian problem, I bought my ticket to Fort Riley. We were a ragtag crew, believe me. A few veterans of the war, like myself. A whole passel of men just off the boats who barely spoke the language. Dirt farmers looking for a free horse and the first chance to desert. A few young boys just trying to get out from under their old man. But don't you know, Custer managed to bring us all together — at the outset, anyway. Gave us a band and a marching song. He had that long yellow hair, you know, and fringes on his leather clothes. And put on a strut that made us think, *Here's a man that knows what he's about.* It's a strange thing, Eli, let me tell you. Men have a weakness that way, a need to find some king or preacher, a politician or a general, and then offer themselves up to him. It's a human trait that's come to make me ill. Respect where it's due, now that's one thing. But listen here — don't be quick to look up to a man who seems to take pleasure in your looking up to him."

"I don't."

"Good. You learned it early then."

"What sort of Indian problem?" Eli said.

"I'm getting there, damn it." His stomach flared in anger, and it was everything Ulysses could do not to turn his back and walk off. He raised a finger at his son. "You don't need to hear this," he said.

"I am *going* to hear it. I'm going to hear it now."

"You're a stubborn boy," Ulysses said, glaring at Eli, who glared back. *God protect him,* he thought.

"Just talk," Eli told him. "Just talk."

Of course talk was the terrible thing, and always had been. Talk seemed impossible — but more than that, foolish, like stepping off the peak of a barn into thin air. Nothing to hold you up. He looked hard into the eyes of his son and took a breath.

He said, "There was an endless parley in those days between the Indians and the government. Talks and treaties about the reservations and what their boundary lines should be and who belonged on which ones. How they should feed themselves with the game all hunted out. Things of that nature. The tribes, of course, couldn't control their young men, who wanted nothing to do with

296

any more deals, nothing to do with the reservations, or with the settlers coming in, or the railroads. Men who didn't have wives or children and could still afford to think about their honor. And others too, older ones who saw nothing to gain by giving in again. And so they were on the loose, raiding settlements and ranches, and generally making trouble. Drawing blood. They didn't want to stay home and raise vegetables on land too dry to grow anything. They didn't want to stay put inside the lines somebody drew on a map. Do you understand? They had nothing to lose. They'd already lost it all."

Eli nodded.

"So that was the situation after the war, and Custer was the man the generals thought could bring them to heel."

"Did you know him?"

"I knew him, sure, but he was no friend. He didn't consort with the likes of me. A high-handed fellow, the sort to hang portraits of himself on the walls of his house. A true fact, which I know from the people that cleaned for him. But yes, I was acquainted with him. The man was too proud for his own good, and a damn fool."

"Our teacher said he's a hero."

Ulysses allowed himself a quiet laugh. "He

would like that. He'd like it very much. But there are two or three hundred men whose wives and children have other names for him."

A stiff westerly breeze had come up with the sun, and Ulysses pulled his collar higher. Eli took out his felt hat and put it on. The ferry driver had arrived, and the first man he fetched from the north side ambled over to them, shading his eyes with a palm. He had no neck to speak of, and big rounded shoulders. He pointed uphill at the shack.

"Radish here?" he asked.

"He's not," Ulysses said. "I'm only watching the place for him, keeping squatters out. He should be along tomorrow or the day after."

"I'll come back then."

Ulysses said, "You've come from up north, I see. I'm heading that way myself. I was thinking I'd pull a wagon, collect bones. Will I find trails?"

The big man grimaced. Trails, yes, he explained, if you wanted to call them that — but no people to speak of, and too much bad ground, and brackish water in the streams. "You might think of striking out in a different direction, unless you have reason to head that way."

Reason enough, Ulysses thought. Then, as

he watched the man head uphill to town, he turned back to his son. He explained the way it was in the fall of 1868, chasing Indians all through the territories, never catching up, always a day or two behind, and how as winter came on, Custer — or it might have been Sheridan — conceived of a new plan. Instead of putting the campaign to rest until spring, this time they'd wait for the deep snows and terrible cold. Wait for the tribes to settle in, the men in camp with their women and children. And then hit them. It had never been done like that before.

As it happened, Black Kettle was the one they caught up with, a chief who'd sat down with the generals, a man of caution and compromise, trying the best he could to keep his young men close. A man of peace. None of which mattered to Custer. When reports came in from the scouts, the Seventh marched hard for Black Kettle's camp on the Washita, down in the Indian Territory. It was the end of November, behind a heavy storm, the air so cold it froze the hair in their nostrils, and Custer ordered a dawn attack.

"We went in at first light, Eli. No wind at all that morning, but cold, I'm telling you — it ached in my lungs. And still I was sweating, my shirt soaked through. I remember looking down from the scrub trees above their camp and seeing an old man come stooping out of his lodge and move through the snow. Slowly. When he reached an aspen tree, he took a piss. We all watched him, the thin stream of his urine steaming as it entered the snow, and him standing there, one arm stiff against the aspen, leaning on it. When he finished, the order came, the bugler blew the charge, and we jabbed our heels into the flanks of our mounts and rode down through the snow. I remember the breathing of our horses, and I remember the sound of the band behind us, if you can believe it — that damned Irish march Custer loved so much — the trumpets blaring and the snare drum rattling like a sack of bones. But I couldn't keep my eyes off that old man, who turned to watch us come, his mouth open, yelling something — warning the camp, I guess — though nobody would have heard him above the noise we were making. As I got close to him, his jaw flew off and he sat right down. But I was past him and shooting at somebody else, who'd jumped out of one of the lodges with a rifle. He went down too. And then we were like water swirling through that camp, men on horses and men on foot, all of us pumping shots into their tipis, and whole families spilling out, women with babies, boys and girls, old women — and a few men too, most everyone moving toward the trees and bushes down by the river, toward the cuts in the earth, ravines where they might find cover.

"I don't know how to tell you this next part, Eli — what happened then and what my life became, after. An act of forgetting is what it was, and then of hating myself, and then of hating people whose crimes were nothing compared to my own. Do you see? One thing grows into the only thing. That's how it works. I don't want you to be hearing this, I don't want to be telling it. A boy stepped from a tipi and drew down on me, both hands on this big Colt revolver, which jumped and boomed. I felt a blow on my head, right here, like someone had struck me with their fist."

"Your ear," Eli said.

"Yes. And my horse wheeled and reared, and I brought it back around. And then the boy was gone, back inside the tipi, or so I figured. I might have let him go — I like to think I would have — but my friend Jim Powers was there beside me, and he swung off his horse and went in after him. So I jumped down too, angry as the pain started in, blood all over my right side now, filling my right eye, and I followed him. I ran inside, and I saw two little boys, not one but two, the other one not more than three or four years old. And a young woman also, their mother. The boy who'd shot me was standing beside her, not trying to hide behind her either, but facing me straight on, the Colt hanging from his hand. He didn't lift it or point it at me. It must have been out of shells. He couldn't have been more than ten years old, Eli, smaller than your brother. And his face — there wasn't fear in it, only hate. I had every reason to walk away and let that boy live, but the pain in my head was screaming and the hate in that boy's face was burning in me, and I shot him, right here" — Ulysses touched his own chest — "and then Jim shot the other boy, I don't know why, and we ran out of there, my gun hand weighing more than the rest of me put together. A few minutes later we couldn't help going back. We went back for the mother, to get her out of there. But she was gone already, only the two dead boys were left. That's when I took the buckskin pouch, it was hanging from the lodge pole. Jim took a pair of beaded mocassins."

"You killed a boy," Eli said. He looked

pale and sick.

"Yes." Ulysses covered his face with a hand. "And that was not all. The mother, too, we killed her."

"You said you didn't kill her. You said she was gone when you went back."

"No, we killed her. We killed the whole family." He paused to breathe, his nostrils full of the blood smell, full of burning flesh, his stomach cramping from it. "Among the prisoners we took that day was an old woman who knew the beadwork of the pouch I had. She knew the maker of it — the mother of the boy I'd killed. She told me the mother survived the attack that morning. Avoided capture too. But instead of waiting to tell her husband what happened — he was out with a hunting party, as were many of the men that day — she drowned herself in the river. So her death, too, it's all mine."

Ulysses forced himself to look at his son, who sat with his knees against his chest, hands clasped in front of his mouth, gaze focused on a point in the distance. Eli didn't move a muscle — and though Ulysses wanted to reach out and put a hand on his shoulder, close the space between them, he couldn't bring himself to do it. He cleared his throat to go on, but Eli, coming back to himself, spoke first.

"We used to play with it, remember?" he asked, picking up the pouch, which lay between them on the willow branch. "And you always got mad at us." Eli weighed it in his hand, as if considering how far into the current he might be able to fling it, as if that might solve the whole problem.

Ulysses reached out for it, and Eli, handing it over, said, "What are you doing out here?"

"That's what I'm trying to tell you," Ulysses said. "Listen."

He tucked the pouch inside his coat then recalled for his son how afterward they gathered everyone up, all those who were still living, fifty-three women and children, and marched them back to Camp Supply. But first how they rounded up the horses, seven hundred animals, and shot them dead, each one. And burned the lodges and all the supplies of dried meat. Burned their stock of tobacco. And, later, how Custer claimed a great victory — a hundred and three warriors killed, a lie apparent to anyone who'd been there, the battlefield a carnage of women, children, and old men, some of them backshot, some trampled, some of the bodies burned inside their lodges.

"It's a terrible thing, Eli, but a man can live with blood on his hands. I've learned that. You pretend you had no other choice, tell yourself you did only what someone else would have had to do or that you were better than those you killed. Nighttime is the hardest, safe inside your house knowing that *your* family's under no threat of attack or death — and unable to understand how such a thing is possible, something that undeserved. Then at first light, all the petty cares come back, and along with them the certainty of knowing you're a good man after all, who takes care of his wife and his children."

He looked into his son's face, but Eli was gone beneath a mask, impossible to read.

"It went on like that till Reverend Pearl pushed my head beneath the surface of the Plainwater. You remember, don't you? I came up and looked around, and first thing I saw was you standing next to your mother, and Danny on the other side of her, the three of you, and though it's awful to say this — I've never to put it to words — you all had bloody holes in your chest, same as that boy I shot, and you looked at me the same way he looked at me, with hatred and anger. With no recognition at all for who I was. Since then I've come to see that I need to search out the ones I've wronged, that it's not God alone I have sinned against. If you steal ten dollars from a man, and God convicts you of your sin, it's not enough to make your confession, is it? No. You have to give that ten dollars back."

Beside him, Eli stirred on the willow trunk. He said, "You can't give back a life."

"No. But you can find the person you stole it from and tell him that you've been paying for it out of your own soul, that you'd give it back to him if you could. And in that way you might bring God into the place where He's needed."

"You believe that?" Eli asked.

"I do, yes."

"So you're looking for the man whose family you killed."

Ulysses described how the old woman had also given him the name of the dead boy's father: Magpie. He explained, too, about the story from the St. Paul paper, and how the writer had interviewed an Indian veteran of the Custer battle, a man Ulysses believed to be this selfsame Magpie.

"He was at the Little Bighorn too, all those years later?" Eli asked.

"Eight years. Yes he was, as far as I can tell."

"But you haven't found him."

"I'm getting closer."

"And what happens when you do?" Eli asked.

"I'm not certain."

Eli stifled an ugly laugh. There was scorn on his face, too, now, and Ulysses couldn't bear to look at him. And yet he couldn't help being angry with his son. He had no grounds for it, he knew that — but the boy should have stayed out of this. If only he had stayed home.

"Why didn't you say anything before you left?" Eli asked.

"Did you say anything to your mother before *you* left?" Ulysses said, ashamed as he spoke for making such a childish argument.

"You could have sent word to us, explaining where you were, telling us you were coming back."

"I'm sorry," Ulysses said.

"You ought to be. Can't you see? You're punishing us for the thing that you did?"

"Yes."

Ulysses wanted to say more, but his mind was blunted by his son's anger and by his own dumb response to it. He wanted to describe his old fear that Gretta and the boys, knowing the truth, wouldn't want him any longer. He wanted to explain that leaving, finally, had seemed like the only way possible to keep them. He wanted to say that every day he'd been gone had made returning home seem less possible, his wife and sons less his own, himself less deserving of them.

"So you're going to find Magpie," Eli said, "show yourself to him and give him the beaded pouch. He'll probably kill you."

"There are worse things than dying," Ulysses said. "Now let's get back. We need to look in on your brother."

"You just don't want to talk to me anymore."

"Come on, let's go," Ulysses said. He made no move, though, to rise from the willow trunk, glad for a moment of quiet with his son, the morning warming nicely, the clouds like puffs of milkweed in the sky. Finally, he got to his feet and stretched out his stiff bones. Then he offered Eli a hand up, and together they walked up the bank to the dugout.

18
THE HIGH DIVIDE

For all his bold talk of not letting his father out of sight, Eli had little choice, when Ulysses headed off to bargain with the liveryman, but to stay behind in the low-ceilinged shack and watch Danny ride out his storm, doing what little he could to make his brother comfortable. He wasn't sure how to live with what he'd just learned. Although he'd spent his life imagining the parts and pieces of war, nothing he had ever dreamed prepared him for this. The battles he had conjured, with their chaos of noise and stink and death, seemed like nothing now. Eli knew his father's dark broodings, and he knew his rage, too. Yet he'd always believed that for anything else he might be, Ulysses was a good man. A man who used his fury — or whatever it was — to good ends. Now he wasn't sure.

There was also the revelation, delivered only this morning, over coffee, that their

309

real name was Popovich, not Pope, and this tormented Eli as well. The name didn't sound right or match his notion of who their family was. It reminded him of the farmers back home by the name of Vorckovich whose field of potatoes flooded each year without fail — a family of eight boys, none of them healthy, their mother dead of typhus, their father given to taking long afternoon naps on their sagging front porch.

At noon Danny's fever spiked, and Eli hauled him out of the shack and down to the river and laid him in the shallows to cool off. Although it didn't bring him back from the place he'd gone to inside his head, it did seem to ease his pain, and by late afternoon when Ulysses returned with a bony workhorse in tow, Danny's fever had broken, and he was lying half asleep, breathing easy, a dim smile on his face.

"You pulled him through," Ulysses said.

"How did you finagle that?" Eli asked, pointing at the horse.

"Gave the man half my money. Which wasn't enough, so I told him I had a mind to sue him for leasing me a sick animal." He patted the front pocket of his pants. "Even got my watch back."

Ulysses prepared a supper of boiled potatoes and wild onions that Eli had to admit tasted as good as anything he'd eaten in days, and Danny was able to finish off a plateful himself. His face was still pale, but his eyes were clear again. They didn't have that dull, old-glass finish anymore.

"Your coming out here like you did is as brave a thing as I've seen," Ulysses told his younger son. "I'm proud of you, Danny. But tomorrow, after you've had a good night's rest, I'm sending you home. You need your mother. Riding straight on through, you'll be home in twenty-four hours."

Danny looked up, blinking, and for a moment Eli thought his little brother was going to stand up to their dad. His nostrils flared and he opened his mouth as if to speak — but then he gave a little nod.

"All right," he said.

The next morning was a clear fall day, their breath frosty in the air. They all three walked uphill to the depot, where Danny boarded an eastbound, Ulysses having spoken with the conductor, who promised to keep a close eye on the boy. Eli could see that Danny was relieved to be going back home, smiling for the first time in days — although at breakfast in the dugout he gripped his father's arm with one hand even as he spooned cold potatoes into his mouth.

"Tell your mother we're fine," Ulysses instructed him. "Tell her not to come looking, but to wait for us. We're going to make a couple more bone runs, until the weather turns." Ulysses paused a moment before taking a roll of dollar bills from his pocket and pressing it into Danny's hand. "And make sure you give her this, for next month's payment."

Not until the train pulled into the station did it occur to Eli how solitary this trip would have been without his brother, how daunting and lonely. More than that, without Danny they might well have missed their father altogether. In the Pullman car he set a fist on his brother's scrawny shoulder and said, "Don't talk to anyone but the conductor."

The boy was settled in his window seat, sunlight covering his face and sparkling in his long, sandy lashes. His hands were pressed together palm to palm and squeezed between his patched knees. His eyes were clearer than Eli remembered ever seeing them. He looked stronger, too, despite the pallor of his skin and the leftover pain wrinkles in his forehead and lips. The train jerked forward then and started moving, and they had to hurry to the end of the car and down the steps to jump free. On the

312

platform they waved at Danny but couldn't see him through his small window, which showed nothing but the sun's dazzle. They stood watching until the last car was out of sight, then started back through town.

As they walked past the Drover House, Eli ran up the steps for a look inside and spied Hornaday in a far corner of the lobby, holding court with a cluster of men surrounding him, several in cavalry blue, one draped in a filthy, ankle-length coat. The hunter, McNaney.

"Eli? Is that you?" Hornaday called out.

Eli waved.

Hornaday came up and shook hands with Eli first and then with Ulysses, who was taller than Hornaday by a head. "I have to say your son's a man to be reckoned with. I imagine he's told you, he got me out of an awkward pinch."

"He gave me the short version, yes."

"No doubt you've had other matters to discuss."

"We have."

"Where's your other boy?" Hornaday asked.

Ulysses looked down at the man, scowling, distracted. In fact he'd seemed preoccupied all morning. Even as they'd gotten Danny squared away at the depot and seen him off, Ulysses was only half present, eyes staring off in the distance. Eli knew that his father's mind was on what came next.

"We sent Danny back to his mother," Ulysses said.

"That's good, that's good. Your son tells me you're out here on a business venture. It's been fruitful, I hope."

"You've got a lot of questions."

"I apologize — it goes with my job. Tell me, Pope, do you have experience hunting big game?"

"Not to speak of, no. A few whitetail deer back in Minnesota, for venison."

"I'd like to offer you a job."

"I prefer working for myself," Ulysses said, but he took hold of his bottom lip with a thumb and forefinger and gave the man a careful look.

"I'm in need of a man who knows his way around guns and horses, and I can pay ten dollars a week. I would make it twelve for you, since you'd be coming aboard at last call. You won't find better wages out here."

"I can do better picking bones."

"Possibly. But there's always a risk for the businessman. I offer sure money and cover your board besides. Not only that, I'd hire your boy too and pay him half a wage."

"Why do you want *us*?"

Hornaday laughed, lifting his head and showing a knuckly adam's apple. Then he adjusted his spectacles on his nose and frowned. "You might say I'm desperate. My cowboy Sully is under the surgeon's knife as we speak, for what looks to be an over-ripe appendix. We have already waited an extra day on account of him, and now it's clear he won't be riding. I need someone in his place."

"My son tells me it's buff you're after," Ulysses said. "It seems a shame to take from the few still left out here."

"I couldn't agree with you more, Mr. Pope, and appreciate the sentiment. But those I'm after would be killed by others, if not by me — you can bet your last dollar on that. Eli may have told you where I work and where my interests lie."

"He did."

"Then I'm sure you can understand. Short of intervention from the government, it would be foolish of anyone to assume the species will survive the next decade. And in fact I am going to do everything in my power to see that it does. But meanwhile, I have little choice but to obtain whatever specimens are still available. For mount-ing."

"Maybe you're right. Maybe not." Ulysses

shook his head and gestured toward the north. "There's a lot of country up there, rugged country and hard to reach. What makes you think they won't find canyons and valleys to raise their young, start over again? That's what creatures do, isn't it? And the hunters, they've all gone back home."

"You're an optimist, Mr. Pope."

"No, I'm not."

"You sound like one."

"Tell me." Eli saw his father's eyes narrowing. He was tugging on his bottom lip again. "This expedition of yours. Where's it heading? Which direction from here?"

"North, northwest."

Ulysses waited, watching him.

"The rough country between the Yellowstone and Missouri rivers. The divide between those two watersheds. I scouted it this spring. It's full of rugged ground, like you say — coulees, buttes, and badlands, with a little dry-grass prairie thrown in. The High Divide, they call it. You've probably been up that way, bone hunting."

"No, I was south, along the Tongue. I went all the way to the Cheyenne Agency and back."

"There's a rancher by the name of Phillips, eighty miles or so northwest of here.

I've been in contact with him since spring. Two weeks ago his men reported a herd of some three dozen up around a creek called the Big Dry. Those are the ones I'm after."

Eli was aware that his father was holding his breath. A hint of a smile twitched at the corners of his mouth. He reached out and laid a hand on Hornaday's shoulder and spoke to the man quietly.

"I'll take the job," Ulysses said.

Hornaday tipped his head back and blinked at him, pushing the spectacles higher on his nose. "You will?" he asked.

"And my son will be coming too," Ulysses said. "When do we leave?"

19
A MAN'S BURDENS

The hand that shook her awake didn't belong to Agnes or Two Blood, and because of its urgency, its lack of regret at waking her, she knew whose hand it was, even before Danny spoke.

"It's me, I'm home, Dad sent me. What are you doing *here*?"

Gretta opened her right eye, the one not covered by the heavy robe, and though she couldn't see his face for the shadows, the shape of his head was the same as that of her own in a darkened mirror. She reached out and pulled him close. For several minutes she was unable to speak. She'd never seen her parents cry, not once, and hadn't cried herself in the presence of either of her sons, but she did so now.

"Don't make me ask," she said, finally.

"They're fine, both of them. But Mom, what are you *doing* here?"

She held on to him hard enough to know

for certain that he was back, but after a moment Danny pulled away and looked at her, the question still wrinkling his face.

"Fogarty," she said, by way of explanation. Then with little embellishment, and doing her best to hide her anxiety, she described what had happened since the boys left home, mentioning her trip to St. Paul — though not what she learned there — and Fogarty's seizure of their house. Danny seemed calm and mostly unconcerned. He was more interested in telling his own story, which he did now, talking for an hour straight, starting with the night he followed Eli to the depot and jumped into the moving boxcar. Gretta shivered out of fear for what could have happened to her boys. At almost any point and in nearly every way possible, they could have been harmed or killed. In the makeshift camp by the Red River. In the alley in Dickinson, faced with a knife-waving criminal. Or in what must have been an opium den in Miles City. And yet she said nothing. Even when it was clear that Danny was telling less than he knew, as when he slowed down and picked his words carefully, she kept her thoughts and questions to herself. Because she was certain he would say more if she didn't try to guide him. And so she held her breath when he told about the letter Eli intercepted from the mailman, and kept a straight face as he described their visit with the widow of Jim Powers in Bismarck, and bit her tongue as it became clear that he wasn't going to offer any explanation for why her husband had failed to send a telegram, why he'd left without so much as saying good-bye. When her son was finished, after he'd given her the money and laid himself down on her mat and gone straight off to sleep, she sat next to him with a hand on his back, listening to him breathe and considering her choices.

There were just two, as far as she could tell.

A few days had convinced her that she couldn't stay in Sloan's Crossing without her husband. Or at least without a man. The women she considered to be friends had turned against her, apparently willing to believe Fogarty's account of what happened between them. As for the men, in their eyes she was either invisible or fair game. There was no way forward in this town except through Fogarty, and though she despised herself for it, she had no choice but to give serious thought to his offer. She'd gone to visit him, of course, after the encounter with Herman Stroud, and though Fogarty was happy to boast of intercepting a telegram meant for the sheriff, he remained tight-lipped about her sons — saying only that he knew their whereabouts and could vouch for their safety and health.

"What about my husband?" she'd asked him.

To which Fogarty only shook his head and smiled. "You know what I need from you, Mrs. Pope. This doesn't have to be difficult."

And in fact it wouldn't have to be a permanent situation. Or at least that was what she'd been telling herself. She could move into his building, perform the cooking and cleaning — put up with the other requirements, too, such was the curse of women — and save every penny she earned until she was able to book passage to Denmark for Danny and herself. For Eli, too, if he came home. After all, she was still young enough to start over again, wasn't she?

The other choice, which was clearer in mind, especially now that she knew where her husband was and knew that he was alive, was almost more frightening, because it would force the questions she had been asking ever since Ulysses left in July. Questions she might not want answers to.

She covered Danny with the robe and left him there, sleeping. Outside she found Two Blood sitting by the front door, smoking his pipe. He nodded at the empty chair next to him, and she sat down. It was eight o'clock, and a weak sun peeked over the top of Two Blood's gun shop across the alley. The chill of last night's hard freeze hadn't burned away yet. Two Blood got up and went inside to fetch a blanket, which he draped over Gretta's shoulders.

"Thank you," she said.

He sat back down and took a long pull on the pipe, his eyes meeting hers only briefly before glancing away. They looked like pieces of sky with thin clouds drifting through.

"I was out front of my shop, first light," he said, "and Danny comes along, fresh from the train. Heading to your house." Two Blood pointed.

"Thank you," she said, again. The man had been so kind to her — his wife, too. But competing now with Gretta's sense of gratitude was the sudden anger she felt toward her husband. For the first time since Ulysses left home, she felt at liberty to hate him, and the cold rush in her lungs and belly made her almost dizzy. She closed her eyes and clenched her fists to gain control

322

of herself. After a minute, she said, "Danny knows where he is. They found him out in Miles City. Montana Territory."

Two Blood looked away. He blew out a long stream of smoke. The tobacco smell was sweet and sharp.

Gretta said, "He doesn't want me to come after him. That's what Danny told me. Danny says they're planning to come home in a month or so, he and Eli. And that I should wait here for them."

Two Blood nodded at this.

"But I don't think they're coming back, and I doubt if Danny does either."

Two Blood cleared his throat and spat.

Gretta said, "Ulysses doesn't know anything about what's happened here. To me. About the house, or about Fogarty."

"I suppose not."

"I don't know what to do. I don't know if I should go after him or not. I'm afraid he doesn't want to come home. I'm afraid he doesn't want me anymore. And the way it is right now, I don't know if I want him." She opened her hands close beneath her breasts, as if holding a baby there. "Look at what he's done," she said. "Look at what he's done."

"If you find him, you could give him what he's got coming," Two Blood said.

"I could?" she said. "No, I don't think so."
Two Blood didn't speak.

"I could stay here, you know. Not with you and Agnes, I don't mean that. But Fogarty's offered me a job at his place, and I could work for him. At least for now. That might not be such a terrible thing, right?"

Two Blood turned and looked at her straight on, his light blue eyes blazing now. He said, "As terrible things go, maybe not."

"Is that what you think? Do you think it would be an awful thing to do?"

The old man drew on his pipe and held the smoke in his lungs for longer than seemed possible. He cleared his throat then looked past her. "If it's traveling money you need, I could help," he said.

"No, no." She reached into the pocket of her skirt and took out the bills and held them up. "He sent this with Danny."

"Well, then," he said, and turned his pipe over and knocked it against the side of his house. He used an index finger to clean out its bowl then wiped the blackened finger on his pants before glancing at her once more, getting up from his chair, and walking back inside.

That afternoon he took them to the depot in his donkey cart, the one he drove each week out to Prairie Lake, where he liked to fish for northern pike and walleyes. He sat up on the plank seat, elbows on his knees, not acknowledging those they happened to pass in the street. Gretta, too, had learned to keep her eyes to herself and did so even as Danny greeted everyone he knew. At the station Gretta carried their satchel inside and bought two tickets for the westbound leaving at three.

Through the early hours of the afternoon they watched the country roll past, most of it flat prairie the color of weathered wood. Occasional small settlements appeared then faded away, unpainted ranch houses, struggling farms with chickens and pigs, one-street towns, people carrying on their ordinary lives. Gretta couldn't help the envy she felt — women darning and baking and collecting eggs.

Danny stared listlessly out their window. His face was flat, his expression saying, *I've seen this already, I've seen it all,* and it hurt Gretta, knowing her son's life would never be as carefree as it had been until now, something for which she felt responsible. If only she had been able to summon the strength to draw the poison out of Ulysses. If only she hadn't turned away when she saw the pain in his eyes. In truth, she knew early on that something was wrong, even if she didn't know what it was. But she had been raised to believe that a man's burdens were meant for him alone to carry.

When Gretta was thirteen or fourteen, late one night, long after bedtime, she'd overheard her parents speaking in hushed tones in the kitchen. She crept down the hallway to crouch at the corner where she could listen, not daring to peek but knowing what she would see if she did — her father leaning forward, hands clasped in front of him, his face downcast but peering up at his wife nonetheless, who would be sitting erect, chin level or slightly raised. Gretta heard her father say, "I don't know what to do," and her mother respond in the even, toneless voice Gretta despised: "Your complaining to me doesn't help anything, does it?" It wasn't long — a few months at the most — before he lost his store to the bank, and soon thereafter went to live with the woman in Nyhavn. Although he did return home the next year, he was never well again. Shortly, in fact, he died, the final sign of his fundamental weakness, according to Gretta's mother. As a girl Gretta was willing enough to accept this judgment. It explained their predicament, after all. But having someone to blame didn't save her mother from being a miserable person, more difficult than Gretta was willing to suffer. And so she made her escape to America, to the middle of the continent in St. Paul, where she imagined she would be free from the struggles she'd witnessed — although she still hadn't learned, any better than her mother, how to listen.

It was dusk before she finally got Danny to talk. She'd been avoiding the very thought of Jim Powers's widow but knew that she needed to prepare herself for seeing her, talking with her. She wanted to ask her son about the letter — whether it was a long one and what it said, what kind of paper it was on, what sort of penmanship the woman had. And how she'd signed it: *Sincerely, Mrs. Powers? Yours truly? Love, Laura?* She wanted to know why Eli had chosen not to bring it home to her but opened it himself instead. He must have been trying to protect her, she thought, though it seemed like a betrayal nonetheless. She wanted to ask Danny what the woman looked like, whether she was pretty or not, whether she had a pleasant voice. Whether she wore fashionable clothes. What, she wanted to ask him, had the woman said to them that might shed light on her motivations? Was she simply the wife of a friend? And if Jim Powers had been such a *good* friend, why hadn't Gretta heard of him until now?

Gretta remembered now the young woman from church who always stared at Ulysses during their first year in Sloan's Crossing, the one who sat on the far right side of the sanctuary with old Mrs. Wooten. Mrs. Wooten's grandniece. The girl ended up marrying and leaving town, and Gretta didn't even recall her name. But she had been so obvious in her interest that it had been all Gretta could do not to get up and walk over and tell her to keep her big eyes to herself. In truth, few other women had ever seemed to notice Ulysses. The missing ear, Gretta believed, tended to overshadow his jawline and good shoulders and sensitive mouth — this, a blessing for her, although she was ashamed to think so.

"What did she feed you the night you stayed there?" Gretta asked her son. A harmless enough question, something to get him started.

"What?"

"The widow, in Bismarck?"

"Oh. Chicken."

"Does she raise them?"

"Yup."

"She must have been surprised to see you. I mean, she couldn't have been expecting two boys at her front door."

Danny pointed out the window at a hawk on a telegraph pole.

"Danny?"

"Yeah, I guess so."

"What did she say about your father?" Gretta watched her son's face. He'd always seemed old beyond his years, but now there was a new calculation in his eyes, a cautious control she hadn't seen before. "Danny?"

"Only what I told you. About her husband and Dad in the service together. And Dad heading out to Montana, for bones." Danny glanced up, then he looked back out the window.

"Did you like her, Danny? Was she nice to you?"

"She was nice enough."

"But you didn't like her," Gretta said, unable to help herself.

"No."

"Why not?"

He thought for a moment, squinting. "Because of the way she looked at us. Her eyes. Like she was trying to see into our skulls. She made me nervous."

A satisfying heat burned in Gretta's stomach. She bent down for the jar of water from her bag and took a drink, but it was lukewarm and stale.

Danny moved closer and squeezed her arm, looked up at her. "It's going to be all right, don't worry so much," he said, smiling now, his eyes clear and guileless, very much her boy again.

■ ■ ■ ■ ■

II
CONFLUENCE

■ ■ ■ ■ ■

20
STORM GODS

They rode out that day at sun-up with a breeze behind them, the sky cloudless and light blue. Before crossing at the shallow ford north of town, they stopped to survey the country beyond the Yellowstone, rolling and dusty brown, buffalo grass as far as you could see, not a tree or bush in sight except for what grew along the riverbank and bluffs. No shade and nowhere to hide.

Eli turned in his saddle and looked over at his father next to him, sitting up straight on the big Appaloosa mare he'd chosen yesterday from the corral at Fort Keogh. When Ulysses glanced back and winked, Eli was reassured despite himself. Maybe this whole enterprise was going to turn out all right. Maybe his father would find the man he was looking for, and maybe the two of them would reach an understanding of some kind. Maybe it was a holy thing, after all, tracking down a man whose family you had killed. Maybe God was behind it, instead of plain craziness. Then again, probably not.

"Here we go," Hornaday said, and looked around at the party he'd put together, including an escort of four soldiers from the fort, led by Sergeant Bayliss with his large belly and fat mustache. There was also the celebrated buffalo hunter McNaney, and of course Ulysses and Eli themselves — everyone lined up at the river's edge, their animals nosing the water. Behind them, perched on the buckboard of a light wagon, was a butcher's apprentice from Miles City, a boy not much older than Eli by the name of Gumfield, hired to serve as Hornaday's assistant in matters concerning specimen collection. And finally a six-mule team pulling a month's provisions, including a ton of oats for the animals, driven by a white-bearded veteran of the Mexican War, McAnna, who had also been hired to cook. Yesterday in a light rain they'd all gathered at the fort to pick up their wagons and teams, load their commissary stores, and choose firearms and horses — everything courtesy of the United States War Department.

Hornaday called out to the men, his voice striking an odd pitch: "Sergeant Bayliss wants us to gather up on the other side. He has a few words."

Bayliss tipped a hand toward Hornaday as if to say *You first,* and Hornaday urged his black gelding into the water, which flowed shallow and quick here over polished gravel. Bayliss and his troopers followed after. Then at his father's nod Eli touched his heels to the buckskin mare he was on and splashed into the current, the water soon rising to the boy's knees, the cold catching the breath out of his lungs. He whipped the horse with his reins, and they surged up the bank to the top of the rise, where his father soon joined him.

"Will you look at that, Eli," Ulysses said. "They built a regular highway for us."

Winding north was a double-rutted trail that followed a dry creek marked by its alkaline bed, dull-green clutches of sage on either side. It rose, dipped, curved, and rose again, finally seeming to pass into the sky. Clumps of white bones were scattered everyplace.

"Sunday Creek Trail," Hornaday said.

Eli swung around to watch the mule team huffing through the ford, the air cold enough this morning to make small clouds of their breathing. In his belly and lungs he felt the days ahead, stirring. He also felt

Gumfield's eyes on him and, glancing back, made out the boy's sullen face from fifty yards off, calling to mind Herman Stroud somehow, the same short nose and slack mouth. Or maybe it was just the way he held his head up, like he was better than everybody else. In the corral at the fort yesterday, Gumfield had been quick to claim the sleek-boned Appaloosa mare. He barely got the saddle cinched, though, when Hornaday pulled him aside, whispered in his ear, and pointed to a light wagon, which an orderly was hitching to a cold-blooded gray. The boy's face loosened and his shoulders fell. When he threw the Appaloosa's reins on the ground, Hornaday said, "Pick those up," which Gumfield did just in time for Ulysses to come along and take them from his hand.

Now on the north bank of the Yellowstone, Sergeant Bayliss climbed into the bed of Gumfield's wagon as the expedition assembled around him. He took off his faded McClellan cap to reveal the gleaming pink dome of his head. Then he opened his long coat and rubbed his big stomach, grimacing. The set of his red-rimmed eyes was hard. "Something you all need to hear before we start out," he said, lifting a hand. "There's talk of Indians loose off the reservations and skulking around the country we're headed for." He aimed a fat thumb over his shoulder, north. "Crow, by my reckoning, or they could be Assiniboine for all we know, or Piegan — but out to make trouble, whoever they are. To cause what hell they can. The War Department has ordered a military escort for Doctor Hornaday, as you know, and I'm in charge of it. Are we clear on that?"

Saddles creaked, and Eli's mare tossed her head.

Bayliss turned to Hornaday. "Anything you want to toss in?"

"I'm happy for the escort," Hornaday said, "which the Secretary of War has offered as a precaution. But he assured me, in person, that there's no cause for worry."

"The Secretary's back in Washington, last I heard," Bayliss snapped.

Hornaday smiled. "You're right about that, Sergeant. And I'm not a doctor, by the way."

"My error. Now like I was saying, these reports are coming from up in the breaks and coulees, and all along the Divide. Renegades doing who knows what, and nobody can say how many there might be. I have it from Ned Phillips at the Cross Bar Ranch that one of his range hands is unaccounted for. The man was supposed to come in last week and never showed. Not to mention cattle losses steady as the wind. So I'm telling you right now, all of you — stick close till we make our permanent camp. That clear?"

Eli looked around at the men, none of them looking surprised, though in fact he'd heard no talk until now about Indian troubles. He wondered if Hornaday had been playing it down. He glanced at his father, whose eyes were scanning the hills ahead.

"And no running off and chasing after meat," Bayliss added. "If you see the buff you're after, well then, my boys go with you. Understand? Otherwise, why the hell have you got us along on this chase? Which, by the way, is a waste of grain and good animals, if you ask me. The herds have been gone from this country since eighty-four."

Hornaday laughed, but his eyes glittered hard behind his spectacles. "Respectfully, Sergeant, your man, Ned Phillips? It's on his word we're heading to the Big Dry. He's the one who spotted the animals. Or I should say, his men did."

"Spotted them back in June, sir. A small herd is what they saw, a dozen at most. Tell me, do you think our red friends didn't get wind of that? Of course they did. You think they haven't had themselves a good hunt? Course they have."

Hornaday smiled. "I guess we'll find out."

"That's it, then," Bayliss said, and put his hat back on, squeezing it tight over the crown of his bald skull and yanking the small brim down for shade. "Any questions?"

"What makes you think Crow?" Ulysses asked him.

Bayliss looked up, his small eyes widening. "Does it matter?"

"Why not Cheyenne?"

"Indian expert, are you?"

"Enough to know the Crow stay home mostly, and have for a long time. Enough to know the Assiniboine are pretty well under control, with that big fort up there. But the Cheyenne —" Ulysses shook his head. "They've still got a taste for meat, and they've figured out the government shipments aren't something you can set your clocks to. What are they supposed to do — sit around and wait, like a bunch of old women?"

Eli, recalling the day his father stood up in church and pointed at the elders sitting red-faced in the pews beside their wives, reached over and touched his elbow, took hold of it and gave it a squeeze.

"But my son here is telling me to shut up," Ulysses said.

"Maybe the boy's got more sense than you have."

"We can hope so."

Bayliss nearly smiled. He looked around at the group, kneading his belly as if it were hurting him. He squinted his little eyes. "Let's move out, then. Unless you're all wanting to stay here and debate the state of the world."

For a good share of the morning Eli and Ulysses rode at the front next to Hornaday, the two men carrying on a lively talk, both certain of their own ideas and therefore butting heads on occasion. The curator had cowboy clothes on, sheepskin chaps and a wide-brimmed hat in place of the bowler he'd worn earlier. With a thick cigar clenched in his teeth, he held forth like a politician, going on at length about the bison, its fitness for the climate and resistance to disease, its ability to move great distances with no water at all. Ulysses for his part told stories of the great herds still roaming the territories during the Indian wars, entire landscapes covered in black and moving like a single creature, clouds of their dust filling the sky.

"It's awful hard to describe. If you never

saw it, there's no possible way you could understand. No matter how much you've read or studied. It was like fish in the ocean. Great schools of them. Uncountable."

"Of course I understand," Hornaday said, indignant. "Only human beings could have accomplished their demise."

"The railroads. Commercial hunters."

"And the Indians too," Hornaday added.

"Are you lucid, man?" Ulysses made a full circle in the air with his arm. His voice dropped to a near whisper, as if to make Hornaday listen harder to what he said. "You mean to tell me the Indians could have hunted out the herds on their own? I don't believe it. Not in a thousand years."

Eli didn't stick around for the argument, but turned his mare and trotted back past Bayliss and McNaney, past Gumfield on his buckboard who gave him a dark stare, past the last two troopers and, finally, the big, six-mule wagon, on top of which old McAnna sat cockeyed, half-grinning inside his beard and eyes closed, drifting through some reverie. Eli let the clank and squeak of the train recede ahead of him and sat his mare for a time, looking off in the direction from which they'd come, south, the ground receding in rolling hills toward the Yellowstone, which was long out of sight. He didn't know what to make of the argument between his father and Mr. Hornaday, but after seeing Slovin's pile in Miles City and now the litter of bones out here, he wished he'd had the chance to see this country years ago, before the slaughter.

He was about to turn back when he spotted something moving against the grayish brown of the buffalo grass. It was down in the dry streambed a hundred yards off, and his first thought was *Indians.* He tried to make out the figure of a man or horse, but instead the slender shape of an antelope firmed up around its white face, and Eli without deliberating dismounted and drew from his scabbard the rifle he was issued at Fort Keogh, a .50-caliber Spencer, same as the one he gave Two Blood as part of the payment for the Smoot's. He chambered a round, flattened himself against the ground, and put the open sights on the front shoulder of the antelope, which as if to offer itself up, had turned to one side. He squeezed off a careful shot, the sound filling up the whole dome of the sky, making it seem for an instant like a space contained and finite. Then silence again, followed in turn by the high shouts of men barking like prairie dogs.

"What in the hell?"

It was Bayliss, shouting over the sound of

hoofbeats. He was coming straight on, as if to run Eli into the ground, but then pulled up short and swung himself free and clear to his feet. He stood spraddle-legged on the ocher dirt, one hand on the butt of his holstered Colt. "What in the living tarnation are you shootin' at, boy?"

Eli, still lying flat, pointed south, but there was nothing there to see. The antelope had sprung away at the blast, and by the time the barrel came to rest, Eli saw only its tail and springing rear legs disappearing into sagebrush.

"You take a shot at Sitting Bull?"

Eli pushed up and got to his feet. The whole party had turned and was advancing on him now, posthaste. He couldn't help but see the smirk on Gumfield's face. His father's head was cocked as he waited for an explanation. Same for Hornaday. Eli went to his mare and threw himself on its back and dug in his heels. Before pulling the trigger, he'd marked the spot, just like his father taught him — in this case a little alkaline triangle beside a tuft of olive sage. He rode straight to it and jumped to the ground and bent to look for blood, which he found straight off, a spot the size of his thumbnail on the gray-white soil. Then another, two paces west of the first, this one elongated, a stripe as long as a table knife. He remounted and rode up out of the dry creekbed, then reined in to scan the country. When he dismounted again, whispering into the mare's ear, it was because of the tracks he found, clear prints in the dirt, and the trail of blood. The animal itself was lying in a slight depression, in what looked like a sleeping groove, its eyes glazing already in the sun, no movement at the rib cage, dead as dead.

Within minutes Eli had bled it and gutted it and tied its legs to a picket rope, and was pulling it back north toward the cluster of men, off their horses now and standing about on the side of a hill. He imagined their faces bright at the prospect of fresh meat for lunch, but riding up he found himself looking into the small, unhappy eyes of Bayliss. His arms were crossed in front of his chest. The others had drawn away from him, all except for Ulysses, who was crouched within arm's reach of the man and chewing on a strand of grass. From the buckboard of the light wagon Gumfield looked on.

"Didn't you hear what I said this morning?" Bayliss asked.

Eli cleared his throat. "I heard you."

"I said, stay close."

344

"I was at the rear, *behind* everybody else. And I didn't go far." Eli turned and pointed down the streambed. "It didn't run more than a hundred yards."

"Out of sight, though, yes?"

"Yes."

"And didn't I say no chasing after meat?"

Eli's instinct was to argue with the man, though he knew that was a bad idea. He glanced at his father, whose face was blank, eyes dark. *What the hell,* Eli thought, and he said, "This is a hunting party, isn't it?"

"If and when we find something to shoot at, yes. Until then — until we make permanent camp, like I said — we'll exercise caution. We don't want to draw undue attention to ourselves, which is prudent, considering."

Still in his crouch, the strand of grass clenched in his teeth, Ulysses said, "It could be you're overstating the general threat."

Bayliss turned. "The general threat, as you put it, happens to rest on my shoulders and not yours, Mr. Pope. I have rank here."

Ulysses stood up. Eli could tell he was angry by the steady gaze of his eyes and the way his lips were flattened and drawn tight, like a line of fencing wire. His hands were loose at his sides. Bayliss took a step back. Ulysses said, "I mustered out in sixty-nine.

That's a long time ago, and I don't give a rat's ass about rank."

Hornaday came forward and put himself between the two men, who both towered over him. He took the stub of cigar from his mouth and blew a pair of perfect smoke rings in the still air. He said, "I respect your sense of duty, Sergeant, though I have to remind you that Mr. Pope is in my employ. And Mr. Pope, I want you to hear this. Until we reach the hunting grounds and establish our camp there, it's your obligation to defer to Bayliss in all matters regarding security. As we all must. Which means, Eli" — Hornaday turned — "that next time you have an antelope in your sights, you better ask before you squeeze your finger."

"Yes, sir," Eli said.

"Mr. Hornaday, if he had asked first, we'd be nooning up meatless," Ulysses said, nodding at the two privates who had already skinned the animal and were cutting strips of flesh from the carcass. McAnna in the meantime had built a fire, which was popping and smoking on green willow branches.

Hornaday looked from Ulysses to Bayliss and back again. He said, "We need to have an understanding here."

"We have an understanding," Ulysses said, though his gaze remained steady on Bayliss, who didn't speak.

"All right then?" Hornaday asked.

"All right," Bayliss muttered, and he walked off toward a small outcrop of rocks, kicking up dust with his boots.

Toward evening a bank of purple clouds massed in the west, swallowing the red sun. By McAnna's estimate they'd gone eighteen miles, easily the farthest Eli had ever ridden a horse in a single day, and he could feel every mile in his back and legs and ass. He was not at all sure he'd be able to climb back on in the morning but was looking forward to it all the same. As the men made their first camp, glancing up now and then to watch the thunderheads build, McNaney, who'd been scouting ahead, came riding back at full gallop.

"Indians," he said. "Two of them, mounted. Up there a mile or so." He pointed northwest, toward an elevation topped with a small crown of rock.

"Moving which way? What are they doing?" Bayliss asked.

"Just settin' their horses is all. Watching us, carbines on their lap."

"They make any sign?"

"Nope."

"Just two of them?"

"That's all I saw."

347

"We better go have a little parley then. You" — Bayliss pointed at Ulysses — "Come with me."

As the two rode off together, Eli got started on the fire for supper, the job he'd been assigned by Hornaday. All afternoon he'd been collecting deadfall — willow, dogwood, the occasional stunted juniper, anything burnable — and tossing it up into the wagons. Now as the old cook mixed up corn biscuits, beans, and antelope stew, Eli lit the kindling and built a steady flame. There was enough flow in the creek for the horses now, and they'd been turned loose to water themselves before being rubbed down, fed from the store of oats, and picketed.

By the time Ulysses and Bayliss rode back into camp an hour later, all the tents were pitched and everybody was sitting around the fire, their plates empty, drinking coffee brewed with creekwater too brackish to boil clean.

"Lost them," Bayliss said. "But found nothing to say there's more than just the two. Scavengers, likely. We'll have to keep an eye out."

"See any buff?" Hornaday asked.

"Don't you think we'd tell you?" Bayliss handed off his horse to one of the troopers and accepted a plate of food.

That night clouds moved in like giants with bulbous heads and massive shoulders, like the Danish gods in the stories his mother used to tell him. Storm gods, she called them. Eli watched through the front of the tent as they changed shape, growing into beasts with terrible noses, eyes swirling as they searched for a place to spend their fury.

"We're going to have a gully washer," Ulysses said.

But the storm passed on by, saving itself for the buttes to the east. Unable to sleep, Eli crawled out of the tent he shared with his father and watched the exhibition of lightning, each flash beginning at the center of heaven and following a complex geometry to earth, again and again, the booms jarring the ground before they arrived as thunder in the air. Later, Eli dreamed of home and his father standing in the yard, smoking, his mother at the kitchen window saying, *Where is he, I don't see him,* though in fact he wasn't twenty feet away in full sight. When Eli pointed him out to her, she gripped the neck of her dress with both fists and ripped it open. And in that moment, at the sound of cloth tearing, he woke up, aware of his father leaving the tent, brushing past the canvas flaps. Eli checked his impulse to call out and instead grabbed in the dark for his pants and boots, shirt and coat, and moved quickly toward the horses, picketed a hundred paces or so to the south. He could just make out his father's long shape and also that of the horses against the darkness.

"What are you doing?" he whispered.

"Just a little scouting trip."

Eli ran quietly back to the tent for his bridle, and when he came back Ulysses was waiting for him.

"You're going after them, aren't you."

"No need to come along," his father said.

"I'm coming. But we should bring our rifles."

"No," Ulysses said.

They led their animals north for a quarter of a mile, then mounted up and rode bareback at a fast walk, hunched in their coats against the cold air, down through a dry coulee and then up along a narrow divide that angled northwest. They stopped at the top of a hill, from which they could see, beneath a break in the clouds, a declining landscape of canyons and gullies and hoodoos. It looked like a place where the skin of the earth had come loose, torn away by some coarse hand to expose another world, the close edge of it marked by a stone spire.

"They're down in there?" Eli asked.

"Bayliss and I came this far but couldn't tell if they went straight on or broke off to the north on high ground. As we turned around to leave, though, I caught sight of a smoke line. Down there, yes." Ulysses pointed ahead. "Bayliss didn't see it."

The ground changed beneath them now, the iron shoes of their horses crunching and grinding on loose rock, and Eli sensed the mare's hesitation as she picked her steps carefully, rolling her neck this way and that, lifting her nose to smell the air. They came around the side of a rock face and then down another decline, this one steeper, Eli leaning back but sliding forward onto the mare's thick mane, nothing to do about it. And then he smelled something, camp smoke, and his father swung off the Appaloosa and crouched on one knee. He lifted something close to his face.

"It's cold, they've been gone awhile," he said.

"Do we go after them?"

"It's too late. And it's going to storm again. There'll be another chance."

As Ulysses spoke, the clouds filled in above them and the world closed down. Eli's mare trembled as if struck by a cold wind, and from the west came a quiet rumble, like a man clearing his throat in the next room.

"Let's go, come on," Ulysses said, mounting up. "It's going to get slick in a hurry down here."

They swung around and headed back, Eli in front this time — though every minute or so he pulled up to make sure his father was still there, saying, "You coming?"

"Just let her go, Eli. She'll take you."

The climb was steep, though, and it was no easy thing staying on, saddleless, especially when the icy rain came, which it did. Eli flattened himself on the horse's wide back, one fist twisted into her mane, the other gripping the reins, as the mare scrambled for purchase in the loose rock. Then a flash of brilliant light poured through a rip in the sky and all was momentarily visible, including the spire of rock Eli remembered from before, the monument marking the edge of this broken ground. Beneath him the mare, as if jarred into some new understanding of her purpose, began running hard, all out, the earth flattening here, the ground stable again, and Eli hanging tight like a monkey on a circus horse.

Side by side with Ulysses in the raucous storm, Eli was aware again of his anger. What did his father think he was doing, chasing after this man? How did he imagine it was going to turn out? What did he expect, a clap on the shoulder? A clean conscience? And what would he tell the man if he ever found him? *I'm the one who shot your son — your whole family is dead because of me.* It was hard to imagine it moving toward anything but calamity. His father might as well be some figure out of the Bible, one of the mad prophets — except none of those men, touched as they were, would have been so foolish as to offer himself up to those he had wronged.

The rain was steady as they rode along a ridge between two creeks, dry before but flowing now, and when Ulysses eased close and tapped him on the shoulder, Eli refused to look over at him.

"Hold up, something's wrong," his father said, and slid down off the mare. Eli reined in and turned to watch him lift the Appaloosa's left rear leg.

"What?"

"Busted a shoe back there. Split the hoof, too." With his picket pin he pried off the broken shoe and tossed it away. "We'll have to walk," he said.

"*You* will," Eli told him.

The rain was modest but steady, and most of the lightning stayed off to the south, punishing the country down around the Yellowstone, line after crooked line, sometimes four or five strikes in the same instant, as if there were no end to what the sky could give or the earth receive, as if all the light in heaven were being channeled through a few small punctures in the clouds.

By the time they got back to camp the storm had passed, the eastern hills just visible beneath pinking clouds. The men were up but silent, shaking out wet blankets and packs, rubbing down their horses. There was a fire crackling and smoking, the damp wood hissing like a pile of snakes. Bayliss and Hornaday stood next to it, watching Ulysses and Eli come on.

"She ran off when the noise started, yanked her pin and lit out," Ulysses said, nodding toward the Appaloosa. "Chased her three, four miles, at least. And then she threw a shoe on the way back, in loose rocks."

"Thought it was *you* that run off on us," Bayliss said.

"And what would I do that for?"

Bayliss said, "You got to admit they're nice horses. Top quality." He aimed his stubbled chin at Ulysses, looking down along his weatherworn nose like a judge and rubbing his fat belly.

Ulysses looked right at him. "I never stole a thing in my life, and I'm too old to start up now."

Hornaday blew into his hands. "We got a little anxious, that's all," he said. His cowboy hat, which looked new yesterday, was dented and stained and pulled down low on his ears against the damp cold.

"Anxious, shit." Bayliss turned and stalked off.

"The man's in a foul mood," Hornaday said.

The storm gave way to full sun, and by eight o'clock, after a breakfast of corn mush and bacon from the fort, they were moving again, Ulysses on one of the extra saddle horses, a roan gelding this time, the Appaloosa mare tied off behind the mule team at the rear of the column. For an hour or so the night's rain rose as steam from the ground, and when it finally burned off, the day started warming. Eli was aware of Gumfield on the light wagon and the way he kept looking over, a sneer on his face. About noon Eli rode up alongside him.

"Have you got some kind of a problem?" he asked.

"Huh?"

"I was thinking you must have something to say, the way you keeping craning your

355

neck at me. And of course being stuck on this wagon, and probably too shy to call out."

"I call out when I want to call out," Gumfield said.

"What's on your mind? I'm tired of your eyes."

Ahead, Ulysses sat the roan gelding, waiting for Eli to catch up.

"Go on ahead," Eli called to him.

Ulysses glanced from his son to the other boy and then clicked his tongue and went on. There was only one rider behind Eli, one of the privates from Fort Keogh, keeping pace with McAnna and the six-mule team, a good hundred yards back.

"What is it?" Eli asked. "You got a corncob stuck up your backside?"

"You think you're clever, don't you. The both of you."

"Clever?"

"Trying to make off with the horses like that. Your animals didn't run off like you say. I woke up before the storm hit, and seen you leaving."

"You've got eyes like an owl, then, seeing in the pitch dark."

"Well I seen *somebody* down by the horses. And then you're gone this morning."

"You saw somebody, but didn't get your-self up out of your bedroll and go check? That tells me you're either lazy or a chick-enshit. One of the two."

The young man glowered at him from his seat on the buckboard, his blunt nose, hang-ing mouth, and sharp teeth giving him the look of a rodent. Eli knew he might feel sorry for Gumfield except for the anger still burning in his stomach against his father and the entire mess.

"You're telling me you think we tried to steal those horses?" he asked.

"I'm looking out for Mr. Hornaday. He hired me to be his assistant, and that's what I'm doing. We can't be losing our animals."

"You think we tried to steal them."

"Setting out in the night like you did? Yes, I saw you."

"Did you tell Hornaday what you think you saw?"

"No, but I mean to. He should know what you're in it for."

"Get down off your wagon, Gumfield."

"I don't have to do nothing you tell me." The young man gave the gray pull-horse a slap with the reins to speed it along.

Eli rode up close alongside and grabbed hold of the hame and brought the wagon to a stop. He jumped off the buckskin mare and stood in place, holding both horses. "Get down off there, right now," he said.

"Why?"

"Because I want you to say it to my face. Unless you didn't mean it."

"I meant it."

"Are you getting down, or do I have to come up?"

Gumfield set the hand brake. Then he stepped down, stumbling as he came, the toe of his boot catching on the toolbox.

When he was back on his feet, Eli told him, "Say it again."

The boy turned to watch the six-mule team come on, white showing on all sides of his green irises. "What are you, deaf?" he asked.

"Pretty much, yes," Eli said. "Come on, let's hear it."

Looking down at his feet, Gumfield uttered the words quietly and without resolve: "You and your old man meant to steal them horses."

Eli hadn't forgotten the promise he made to his mother — no more fights — and he knew that hurting the boy was going to leave him with the same hollow, sick feeling he always got from eating too much brown sugar at Goldman's store. All the same he put a fist in Gumfield's stomach, hit him hard, and when the boy doubled over, slammed his right hand against Gumfield's left ear, sending him like a maul-struck beef to the ground, where he curled up tight, his breath coming fast and hard. The big wagon was rolling by now, and Eli nodded at old McAnna, who glanced down at Gumfield quivering in the grass and then looked away.

Eli waited until the boy peeked up from the crook of an elbow. Then he said, "Tell me what you think now. You still believe we tried making off with those horses?"

Gumfield shook his head. He hadn't managed to catch his breath yet.

"You don't know the first thing about my father, and if you did, you'd stay as far away from him as you could. Do you hear me? You'd never look at him again. Now listen — if I see you talking to Mr. Hornaday, I'm coming after you. And next time I'll hurt you."

The boy rolled over and sat up. He nodded, rubbing his face with both hands.

"Say something," Eli told him.

"I won't talk to him," Gumfield said. "I promise you."

"All right then." He left him there on the ground next to the wagon and swung back up on the buckskin mare and touched her with his heels.

■ ■ ■ ■

Eli couldn't look forward into the next span of days to see what they would bring. He couldn't know there would be no further sightings of Indians, and no buffalo-spottings either — not soon anyway. On the second evening out of Miles City, McNaney would take a mule deer that made the mistake of standing too long on a rise three hundred yards west of camp. On the third day out, they would pass beneath the red buttes, one pointed and the other squared off, before entering the valley of the Little Dry, which flowed north to the Big, which in turn emptied into the Missouri. On the fourth day they'd swing west and follow the Big Dry's broken course toward its beginnings in the high country, where the Phillips men had reported seeing the herd of some two dozen. From the night of the storm until the fifth day, when they'd make permanent camp on Calf Creek, not an hour would go by that Eli didn't catch some movement at the edge of his sight, some shadow or scrub tree, some piece of rock that made him think, *There they are.* By that point he would have given up all hope of his father coming to his senses, and yet for reasons unclear to him, after having given Gumfield the what-for, Eli would begin to see his father's obsessions as his own — the prospect of finding Magpie no longer a frightening thing, but instead a desire that brought purpose to his days.

21
BIRD IN FLIGHT

For Gretta, morning brought rain-speckled windows and a brand-new landscape, the occasional hump of jutting rock offering the promise of harder country to come.

Although she hadn't been able to relax in the night, not even to close her eyes, Danny had slept well, his warm head propped against her shoulder, and then on her lap, and then against the armrest. Finally, needing to stretch out, he'd sprawled on the floor, where his feet stuck into the aisle as a hazard for nightwalkers. Now, though, as the train slowed at the depot in Bismarck, its brakes gasping, wheels shrieking against steel, Danny was awake.

"Do you know the address?" she asked him, dismayed at not having thought of this earlier. *Keep your head on, Gretta* — that's what her father had always told her, and she whispered it to herself now: "Keep your head on." There was so much at stake. *God help me.*

"What?" Danny asked.

"Her address — Mrs. Powers's address. Do you know it?"

"I think so."

"You're not sure?"

"I know it, yes," he said.

She managed with the porter's help to hire a boy to drive them in his surrey. The day was cool beneath a bright sun, a storm having passed mostly to the north, and it was pleasant to have shade for their eyes. They'd been riding for only minutes, the houses getting larger and finer as they went, when she turned to Danny and said, "Does this look *right* to you?" She hadn't imagined a neighborhood like this one, so settled and well appointed, flower boxes and clean fences and large brick chimneys. It didn't help that the young man driving was an apparent deaf-mute who kept his eyes trained relentlessly on the street ahead, not even glancing over when spoken to.

"I'm not sure anymore," Danny answered. But then the driver made a sound that came out like *wup,* and the wagon slowed and came to rest.

It was more than she'd expected, the house he was pointing at, two-storied and handsome — gabled, shuttered, and sur-

363

rounded by a board fence covered in the same shade of creamy white as the clapboard siding on the house. Gretta was aware of feeling small, diminished, on top of the itching jealousy she was already suffering with. As she paid the boy and collected their satchel, her mind rushed forward to evening. Where would she and Danny spend the night? It was still morning, but already she knew this visit was going to go badly, that Mrs. Powers would be of no help at all, and that she and her son would soon be on their way, having wasted their time here.

She went up to the door and knocked, thinking, *Please God, don't let her be home.* "We shouldn't have come," she said.

"Why not?" Danny asked.

She was turning to leave, having grabbed Danny's hand, when a woman came around the side of the house and stopped short, grunting as if struck in the belly. She was older than Gretta, though not by much, and her face was pretty, if you didn't count the nose, which anyone would judge to be a bit too long. Her body was hard to read in the shapeless smock she wore. With both hands she clutched a small pile of chicken eggs in her apron.

"Excuse us," Gretta said.

"I'm sorry. You frightened me."

"Hi," Danny said.

"Danny," she answered. But she was looking at Gretta, her expression difficult to make out. It might have been disgust, but it was more like astonishment, her jaw thrust forward and down, as if looking at the last person she wanted to see.

Gretta let out a breath. "I'm Gretta Pope," she said, surprised at the satisfaction it gave her to say it.

"Yes." The woman was still for a moment, caught, it seemed, by a thought requiring all her concentration. Then she smiled. "And I'm Laura Powers, please come in," and she led them to the door.

Inside, she lifted her apron to the kitchen counter and allowed the eggs to roll free on it, catching one as it careened toward the edge. She took a bowl from the cupboard and set them in it one by one, all six. "I had an idea to boil an egg for myself," she said, and turned back to Gretta and Danny. They hadn't moved from just inside the door, Gretta taking everything in, telling herself to pay attention.

"Come in, sit down. You can set your bag right there," and she pointed to a little alcove off the kitchen, where the coats hung. "I'll get you some water. You must be thirsty." She filled two glasses at the counter pump and set them on the table, then excused herself.

Five minutes later she was back, wearing a crisp pale-green dress and a pair of polished lace-up shoes. Her auburn hair was caught up at the back of her head in a way that showed off the shape of her face.

"I haven't had lunch yet," Mrs. Powers said. "Would you care to join me? I'll fry some potatoes too."

Gretta glanced down at Danny, who was nodding. "My son would love that, thank you," she said. "But if you don't mind, I'll just sit here with you — I'm not very hungry."

The eggs and potatoes were ready in minutes, and as Mrs. Powers and Danny began eating, Gretta made anxious attempts at small talk — about the weather, about the floral-patterned curtains on the windows, about their night on the train. She wasn't prepared yet to confront the woman — she didn't know if she could keep a rein on herself, but also because Danny was here. Soon, though, it grew obvious that Mrs. Powers felt the same way, and Gretta was able to relax a bit. She sat back in her chair and let her shoulders drop, the long sleepless night catching up with her. She started to yawn. Her eyelids felt swollen, heavy. And when Mrs. Powers suggested that she lie down for a while, Gretta found herself nodding.

"For just a little while," she said.

How she made it to the second-floor, Gretta didn't know, but when she woke in the soft feather bed, hands and feet buzzing from sleep, the light was low, the afternoon all but gone. Downstairs, she found Danny smiling from the floor of the sitting room where he was sprawled, reading his Buffalo Bill novel yet again. In the kitchen Mrs. Powers was sliding a pan of biscuits into the oven. There was chicken and gravy boiling on the stove.

"You must have needed that," the woman said, a twist in her nose. "You look like someone else entirely."

There was nothing worse, Gretta thought, than the calculated savagery of women. The cruelty of men, by comparison, seemed plain and glandular.

Supper was an awkward affair, with Mrs. Powers shuttling between the table and stove and making a great show of her hospitality, bringing out at the end a plum pie she'd baked while Gretta slept upstairs. Afterward, though, in the parlor, their war of caution and courtesy began slipping away.

"My Jim knew your husband's family in

St. Paul," Mrs. Powers said, "before they ever served together. Jim grew up there too, I don't know if you were aware of that. Well, apparently you weren't aware of *Jim*. Or at least your boys weren't."

Gretta shrugged one shoulder and looked over at Danny, slouched catlike in his chair now, sleepily, though his eyes were bright and piercing.

"Jim was older than Ulysses by a few years. Closer in age, probably, to your husband's sister. What was her name again?"

"Florence — but she's almost twenty years older," Gretta said, recalling to mind her sister-in-law, bent over and leaning on her cane, and the weak voice drifting from the upstairs bedroom.

"Florence, of course. I never met her. Actually, Jim was fifty when he died." A flicker passed through the woman's eyes, and she said, "Florence Popovich, wasn't it? Yes, Jim was fond of the whole family, and spoke of them often."

"No, her name is Littlefield." Gretta shook her head, glancing at Danny. "She married Charlie Littlefield. They're still in St. Paul, same house."

"Ah." Mrs. Powers nodded, her eyes as hard as iron now.

"In fact I saw them last week." Gretta

imagined herself getting up from the soft, upholstered chair with its high, winged back, walking over to Mrs. Powers, and slapping the arrogance from her face.

"And it seems you didn't know anything about the Seventh, either, did you," Mrs. Powers said.

"I didn't, no."

Danny in his chair listened silently, head turning from his mother to Mrs. Powers and back again, not missing a thing. *How much does he know?* Gretta wondered. *How well does he understand what she's doing?*

"Well, I didn't meet your husband until this summer, though I certainly felt as if I had, because of Jim's stories. All those stories. So when he showed up in July, I knew him right off. I opened the door and his name jumped straight into my head." She smiled, pleased with herself, warming to her subject.

"Excuse me," Gretta said, and got up and went into the kitchen for a drink of water. For Danny's sake, and her own, too, she needed to slow this down a little. Being here, finally, and knowing Ulysses had been here ahead of her, she could see how unprepared she was to reconcile the life she thought she'd had with the life she'd been living. For a week and a half now, ever since her visit with Florence, she'd felt like a stranger in her own body, the very shape of her limbs and breasts and hips unfamiliar to her. Every time she looked in a mirror she half expected to see another woman's reflection — sometimes a woman far lovelier than herself, with perfect skin and hair, at other times a woman careless in appearance, fat and scornful.

Back in the parlor it was clear that Danny was exhausted, his face tipped to the side. Mrs. Powers suggested that Gretta take him upstairs and put him to bed, which Gretta did — and while she waited there for him to fall asleep, sitting on the edge of the feather bed, she tried to justify to herself why she ought to have any hope of keeping hold of what she'd had up until now — or thought she had: a man worthy of her trust.

A memory came back of a night in St. Paul when she was nineteen and living with her aunt and uncle, a memory she and Ulysses often spoke of in their early years, but which she had since forgotten. It was a cold night in January, well below zero, and Gretta lay restless beneath a pile of quilts, unable to sleep on account of the choice she faced between a boy she knew from the Lutheran church to which she belonged, and an older man — the horse-car driver —

whose intentions were impossible to read. That very day the boy whose name was Frederick had proposed marriage in the presence of her aunt and uncle, who'd been pleased and proud, since Frederick's parents were prominent in the neighborhood, the father a prosperous grocer. They'd also been stunned by Gretta's response.

"I'll have to think about it," she'd told Frederick.

It wasn't that she hadn't liked the boy. She'd liked him very much. Moreover, she trusted him, believed in his potential as a husband and father, and in his future as a businessman. What held her back was something she couldn't have divulged to anyone. It had to do with a sensation she experienced every time she saw the horse-car driver, Ulysses, whom she had come to know on her twenty-minute rides to and from the Summit Avenue mansion where she cleaned and cooked. Despite the scarring on the side of his head and neck, and despite the way his pale eyes could penetrate or dismiss her, whenever she saw him, a pleasant warmth flowed through her stomach and prickled in her breasts. This embarrassed her, and she feared that her blushing face might give her away, though if it did, he never let on. He simply drove the car, reins in one hand and gesturing with the other as he pointed out sites of interest on their route, or described his plan to move west, to some young town, and make a life there for himself, building houses. Often he was silent for long minutes, sometimes for the whole ride, every now and then letting his eyes come to rest on her and not looking away until she did. She had no good reason to believe he had intentions — and yet in his presence she often heard a voice inside her, saying, *He loves you, Gretta*. And so it was Ulysses who filled her mind as Frederick made his awkward proposal.

At ten that night someone had knocked at the front door, and Gretta heard her uncle scrambling in the adjacent room and then grumble as he padded across the floor to see who'd come to trouble them at so late an hour. She heard a low voice she didn't allow herself to hope she recognized, and then her uncle was at her bedroom door. "Get up at once," he said, his tone nervous and high-pitched.

Ulysses, it turned out, had spoken to the grocer that afternoon and learned from the man about his son's intentions. "Before you give Frederick his answer," he instructed Gretta, who was dressed in her cotton robe, hair pulled into a sleeping bun, "I believe

you and I should get to know each another."
And there in the small, cold parlor, with her
aunt and uncle sitting nearby in matching
rocking chairs, Gretta had agreed to this
request.

After Danny had fallen asleep, she went
back downstairs and settled into the chair
across from Mrs. Powers, who put her
needles and yarn aside. For a time they sat
without speaking, neither quite sure of
where to look. The anniversary clock on the
giant secretary clanged in Gretta's ears.
"Danny told me you said Ulysses was on
his way west, to gather bones," Gretta finally
said.

"Yes."

"That's more than he told me. For all I
knew he'd drowned in the river that runs
through town, or met up with some other
misfortune."

"That must have been difficult for you.
I'm sorry."

"Thank you."

"I know what it is to lose a husband. Mine
died last year."

Gretta said, "Do you have children?"

"Three. Well, two. A married daughter in
Denver whom I don't see often, a son in
Seattle, and another son who's gone. They
weren't Jim's, though. I had them by my

first husband, very early. It's a terrible thing, their living so far away. You never think of that when they're young."

For a time they made small talk, avoiding each other's eyes, Mrs. Powers clearly tired now, stifling yawn after yawn, her chin propped on her hand. Gretta sensed an opportunity had passed and was disappointed. And yet relieved, too. But then Mrs. Powers perked up, rising from her chair. "Let's go sit in the kitchen," she said. "It's getting cool in here. I'll put a little fire in the stove."

As Gretta sipped a cup of the strongest coffee she'd ever had, she studied the tintype that Mrs. Powers slid across the table — a pair of soldiers posing in uniform, staring out from beneath their campaign hats, rifles propped on their shoulders, fists holding the steel barrels, the wooden stocks pointing up behind them toward a façade of Roman columns. The man on the left was Ulysses, looking much younger than when she first met him. Well shaven. Two ears clearly visible. Curly, dark hair.

Gretta pointed at the other one, blond and stocky, his eyes magnified by thick lenses. He looked like a young scholar. "Your husband?" she asked.

"Yes. Taken at Fort Dodge, I believe."

"Kansas?"

374

"Yes, where the Seventh was encamped in the fall of sixty-eight. They were charged with punishing the Indians down there. The Cheyennes, Arapaho, and Comanches who were raiding the settlers."

In the tintype, Ulysses looked strangely calm and boyish. Not like himself at all. Gretta recalled his story of losing an ear at the Battle of Nashville in sixty-five, not long before Grant and Lee met at Appomatox to end the war.

"Do you have any idea why your husband never said anything?" Mrs. Powers asked.

Gretta pushed the picture to the middle of the table, planted her shoes on the floor and pushed backward. The legs of her chair scraped against the wood. In the lamplight Mrs. Powers looked beautiful and frightening, and Gretta's impulse was to run upstairs and grab her son, escape this place. But where would they go? The only way ahead was *through* this woman, smiling there across the table. Or not smiling — it was hard to be sure.

"No," Gretta said, "but I believe you're going to tell me."

"I don't think that's my obligation."

"It would be cruel not to, wouldn't it? Knowing as you do what I'm facing."

"Isn't it up to *him* to decide what he wants

you to know?"

"Put yourself in my place," Gretta said.

"I'm not sure, in your place, that I'd want another woman interposing herself between my husband and myself."

"You've already done that."

Mrs. Powers shook her head. "I didn't ask him to come here. He arrived at my door uninvited."

"How long did he stay?"

The woman looked down at the floor, her face rigid, and Gretta was reminded of a porcelain doll she was given as a child that she had kept on the dresser next to her bed, its face strangely assymetrical, one side of its smile turning up too far, giving the doll a devilish look that frightened Gretta at night.

"He stayed for a couple of days, looking through the odds and ends of Jim's possessions, what he left behind," Mrs. Powers said.

"Looking for what?"

Mrs. Powers didn't answer.

"You must think that knowing things about my husband — things I don't know — gives you some claim to him."

"Mrs. Pope, I didn't bring this on myself."

"Tell me."

"Can't you see? Telling a man's wife what

he can't tell her himself?" She laughed without smiling. "That's a terrible betrayal."

"You can't betray someone to whom you owe nothing. Someone who owes you nothing. What do you owe *him*?"

Mrs. Powers looked up for a moment into Gretta's face before sighing and turning away.

"Did he tell you to keep quiet?"

"Of course not. He had no idea you'd be coming here. But he did say this. He said he'd always meant to talk to you, that he wanted to — but you never liked to hear anything *upsetting.* His word. He said you'd had enough in your life that was troublesome, and he didn't blame you for not wanting any more of it."

Gretta sat back, chastised.

Mrs. Powers rose from the table and went to the stove for the coffeepot, which she brought back to refill their cups. "You grew up where?" she asked, as if she'd been told but couldn't seem to remember.

"Denmark."

"You probably drink more tea than coffee."

"I drink both." She lifted her cup from its saucer. It was made of delicate china, with a rose pattern painted on its side and gold around the rim.

"My husband purchased them from a salesman who claimed to have brought them back from Scandinavia," Mrs. Powers said. "From Sweden, I believe. He's a pompous man, this drummer, with an accent that changes, year to year. By his own account he's lived in Paris and Rome and London." She smiled to herself, looking away. "Jim was susceptible to that sort of persuasion. He liked to think of himself as a man of taste and good breeding. He liked to tell about his uncle, a professor of sorts, back in England — though of course Jim had no education himself. Once a year we took the train to Fargo, where he would buy a suit of clothes for himself and a new dress for me. He wanted to be seen as a man of the world. It was a weakness of his — but we all have weaknesses, don't you think? A weakness of mine is how much I miss him, and how alone I feel in this place."

"What sort of work did he do?"

"He was a land surveyor. He also delivered coal. We saved our pennies."

"Did you lie with with my husband?" Gretta asked.

Mrs. Powers winced, then looked up through narrowed eyes, her lips pursed.

"I have to know," Gretta said.

"Of course you do. But it doesn't matter

what I say, how I answer you. Can't you see? Because you're not interested in the right *thing*. It's like you're going to someone's grand house, but you've stumbled into the back door, or into the servants' quarters, and you're thinking, *This is it?*"

"I have no idea what you're talking about," Gretta said.

Mrs. Powers laughed. "What am I going to tell you, Mrs. Pope? Think about it. I'm going to say, *Of course not. How could you accuse me of such a thing? What do you think I am?* And you won't believe me. You're sure that you know what's important, what matters, but in fact you don't. And if you asked me the right question, and I answered it, you wouldn't want to hear that either."

"You don't know me."

"Maybe I don't. But your husband does, and he's out there somewhere, afraid of damaging you."

"Give me a chance, for God's sake. Who do you think you are? My judge?"

Mrs. Powers sipped her coffee. She'd turned to the side, staring into the darkened parlor, her eyes cold and bitter. From upstairs Danny called out in his sleep, something that sounded like *Here I am — let's eat.*

"Is he all right?" Mrs. Powers asked. "Do

you need to check on him?"

They both listened for a minute, but Danny didn't call out again. Outside, the wind had kicked up, and Gretta could hear it groaning in the trees that overhung the house. Through the kitchen window a thin smear of clouds was visible, half concealing the stars.

Mrs. Powers said, "Finish your coffee, there's something I have to show you," and she got up from the table and lit a hurricane lamp that hung by the door. She handed Gretta a heavy woolen shawl. There was nothing to do but stand up and put it on.

The grass behind the house was ankle high and stiff with frost. After a dozen steps Gretta could feel the dampness through her stockings. She followed the woman onto a plank walkway through the chicken yard, all mud and shit to the henhouse, the lantern throwing yellow light against the walls whose shelves were covered with broodhens, clucking and blinking. A rooster flapped down from a corner perch and high-stepped in a circle about the floor like some kind of untested soldier trying to convince himself of his own courage. His eyes in the lantern light were bloody pearls, and Gretta couldn't help but think of the rooster Ulysses got rid of on the day he left home.

Mrs. Powers moved to the far wall, empty except for a hanging quilt, and raised her lantern to it. The green and yellow design made Gretta think of the Great Pyramids of Egypt.

"I made this for Jim, for our tenth wedding anniversary. For batting I used his wool blanket-coat, the one they issued him for the winter campaigns. See the pyramids? I made those out of the robe I had when we married."

"It's lovely."

"And do you wonder why it's hanging out here with the fowl?"

Gretta found herself holding her breath, shifting her weight from her heels to her toes. Mrs. Powers stepped forward and lifted the quilt from the hooks that held it, bunched it up and grasped it close to herself.

"It used to smell like him," she said. "Not anymore. But look here." She lifted the lantern close to the wall where the quilt was hanging. The wood was stained dark in a rushing pattern, like a bird in flight, a crow, its wings spread and legs trailing like strands of twine beneath it.

"What do you see?" Mrs. Powers asked.

"A bird?" Gretta said.

Mrs. Powers stood back and took a long

look, as if trying to see it through Gretta's eyes. Her face was concentrated and dark. "No," she said. "It's two eyes, staring. And a toothless mouth. And those long streams of tears. See them? He came out here on the most beautiful night of the spring. We'd had a rain, and then it cleared off. I was starting to think he'd put it all behind him. He was sleeping better, eating more, enjoying the food I made him. Gaining weight too. These were the things I saw. The people who knew him — they thought he was happy. When I heard it, though, I knew. I knew. It was about this time of night, and you can imagine the hens and how they were screaming. I had to come out here alone, with this lantern. Believe me when I say it would have been better for me if he'd gone off somewhere, without telling me, and done what he needed to do in order to put things right for himself. Please don't expect my sympathy, Mrs. Pope."

The woman shook out the quilt, causing a stir among the hens, and then rehung it, covering up the stains. As much as Gretta would have liked to say something to ease Mrs. Powers's pain, no words formed in her mind.

Back inside, sitting in the parlor again, Mrs. Powers said, "There was no one your husband could talk to, not that talking would have been enough. But when he got here, at least he could do that. I didn't stop him. And if I gave him any comfort by listening, you have my permission to hold that against me." She reached her fingers into the *V* at the top of her blouse and with a quick motion flipped out a round tag about the size of a dime, threaded on a gold chain. It was made of tin, a tobacco tag from a plug issued — Gretta knew — by the P. Lorillard Tobacco company, and stamped with a green turtle against a yellow background.

"That's my husband's!" Gretta said. "He wears it all the time. On a brass chain he got from his grandmother."

"So he said."

"He gave it to you? No, I don't believe that."

"Of course you don't."

"I don't understand — is he coming back *here*? Is that what he said? To you?"

"I believe he is. Yes."

The woman sat there, half smiling, rubbing the green turtle between her thumb and forefinger. Gretta couldn't speak. So much was happening, so fast, that she couldn't keep hold of it all, the pressure inside her head like a fist squeezing down on her brain. She thought of her wedding night with Ulysses, and the green turtle dipping and dipping on its chain, each time touching her briefly on the soft skin of her breastbone, each time just the lightest, coolest touch. She didn't know what questions to ask anymore but understood at least that she was a damn fool for not knowing.

"What exactly could you tell me about the Seventh Cavalry?" Mrs. Powers asked, tucking the turtle back inside her blouse.

Gretta closed her eyes. She took a breath, trying to compose herself. She shook her head. She said, "The Little Big Horn, of course. And Custer."

"But you must also know, if Danny talked to you, that our husbands mustered out long before that debacle. Thank God for small blessings." She rose from her chair, knelt in front of the big secretary, and with a key she opened its long bottom drawer. Over her shoulder she said, "Have you ever heard of the Washita?"

"No," Gretta told her.

"It's the bone that's caught in your husband's throat," she said, and turned. She was holding a pair of small, beaded moccasins and an envelope. She put the envelope on the arm of her chair, sat back down and leaned into Gretta, the moccasins rest-

384

ing on her upturned palms. They were child-sized, and the familiar pattern of beads across the toes turned Gretta's stomach cold: a blue mountain beneath a yellow sun, same as the pattern on the buckskin pouch Ulysses had kept in his lockbox all these years.

"You don't want to hold them?"

Gretta made fists of her hands.

Mrs. Powers set the moccasins on the floor, removed a letter from the old envelope and handed it to Gretta. It was written on United States Cavalry stationery and dated February 12, 1869, a single paragraph commending Lieutenant James Powers "for bravery in a theatre of war, at the Battle of the Washita," and signed by Lieutenant Colonel George Armstrong Custer.

"I didn't show it to your sons. I didn't show them the moccasins either."

"Thank you," Gretta said.

"It might have helped if he hadn't been lauded for what he did. It might have made the difference. That's what I think sometimes. But I'm always one to imagine how things might have turned out differently. Anyway, I'll tell you now — if you still want to hear it — what Jim told me, and your husband kept to himself. And truth be told, it'll be a relief for me to give you a piece of it to carry." She sighed and laughed, a dreadful smile on her face. "You see, I'm jealous of you for not knowing, not having to bear it like I have. And for thinking your husband loved you too much to let you hear it."

"Please," Gretta said. "Just get it over with."

They stayed where they were, in the parlor, Mrs. Powers staring out the window as she talked, Gretta looking down at her own hands, accepting the story like the punishment she deserved, and when she finally went upstairs to bed, her body was numb, her mind dulled enough to achieve a fitful sleep. By morning she could see it was pointless to pursue her husband any further. She could go on to Miles City, of course, and implore him to come back home with her to Sloan's Crossing where they could make an effort to take up their old lives again. Or she could suggest they move somewhere else and start fresh. She wanted nothing more than to press her face into his chest, explain that what he'd done could not be helped, that he was a good man, that she loved him — except she wasn't sure about any of those things, not sure at all. His actions, damning as they'd been, were made even worse by his inability to speak of them. He hadn't been honest with her, not for a single day of their lives together, and the very idea of seeing him again frightened her. What else had he done that he hadn't told her about?

However she sorted out her feelings, though, and despite anything she did or didn't want, Gretta knew it was too late anyway. She'd managed to prove, over seventeen years, that she was not the woman Ulysses needed. Mrs. Powers, evidently, in just a night or two, had proved that she *was* — by means of her willingness to understand him in ways Gretta could not.

At breakfast an awkward formality disguised the strain. Gretta kept herself in check for Danny's sake while Mrs. Powers bustled about the kitchen. When Gretta and Danny took their leave, the woman stood at her door, wearing again the yellow dress that declared her shape, full and slim in all the places that counted. A curl of rich, auburn hair had fallen into her eyes, and long loops of it reached to her shoulders. Her lips were painted a shade of red intended to send a message: *You can't compete with me.*

Gretta had no intention of trying.

They walked to the depot on streets icy from an overnight rain, some of the puddles so wide that mallards and bluebills were landing, breaking the panes of ice. Danny was quiet but lively, his eyes clear. He had eaten two platefuls of food at breakfast and now moved fast along the street, keeping ahead of his mother and describing as he went the dream he had before waking — his father and brother high on a mountain and trying to climb down, the pitch steep and the rocks wet and slick as they descended, both of them slipping at times and having to catch the other, while Danny watched from below, helpless to do them any good.

"What happened?" Gretta asked.

Danny shrugged. "I woke up."

"Did they make it down?"

"I don't know."

"Are you feeling all right?" she asked, her neck and shoulders already tensing with fear.

"I'm fine," he answered.

"No pain?"

"No," he said.

At the depot she watched him for signs, but he wasn't squinting against the light, and his gait wasn't clumsy, and he wasn't clinging to her dress or shifting inside his clothes like he did when a headache was coming on. His jaw was set hard in a way that made him look older, stronger. She went to the ticket window and asked about the next eastbound.

"There's one in half an hour, Ma'am. Where you heading?"

"Minnesota, Sloan's Crossing, third stop inside the state line."

"For both you and your boy?"

"Yes, please."

Danny pulled away and looked up at her. He said, *"Home?"*

She nodded.

"No, we're going to Miles City — that's why we're out here, remember? That's where we have to be."

"I've changed my mind, Danny. We'll let them come home to us, like your father said we should do. He had his own reasons for leaving, and he'll come home when he's ready."

"Ma'am?" the ticket agent asked.

A blush rose in Danny's cheeks and bloomed in his ears. "No," he said, and he backed up a few steps then turned and ran across the gleaming wood floor of the depot and out the side door. Gretta dropped her bag and took after him into the cold brightness of the morning, though she hadn't gone a dozen steps before she tangled in her skirt and fell on the wet cobblestone, regaining her feet in time to see Danny bound over a frozen puddle, cut to his right, and disappear between the hardware and barber shop. Gathering her skirt in her fists, Gretta went after him.

"Danny, you get back here," she yelled. "Right now!"

In the alley behind the hardware she stopped short, with no idea which way her son had gone. She looked right and then left, not a soul in view.

A sharp rapping sound, like a woodpecker on a healthy tree, drew her eyes up and straight ahead, where a woman gestured from a second-floor window. She pointed west. Gretta waved a thank-you and moved down the alley at a half run, more careful now, knees stinging, hands bleeding, grains of sand wedged into her palms. In the gaps between buildings she stopped and looked both ways, but Danny may as well have flown off into the sky. He was gone. At the next street she had the choice of going right, toward the city's main thoroughfare, or left toward the tracks, but instead continued straight down the alley. She was halfway through the second block when a spot of yellow-gold caught her eye: a sign, or part of one, painted high on the brick wall of a building whose front faced the tracks. It was an advertising sign for flour — a field of ripening wheat with a man in a blue shirt and pants standing in the middle of it. And just beneath this, scuttling up a long ladder, was Danny. As Gretta ran toward him, he climbed faster, then stepped from the ladder onto a wide plank of scaffolding. He rotated himself up there and pressed his back against the brick wall — three stories up — and stared down at her, chin against his chest.

"Don't move," she told him, trying to keep her voice steady. "Don't move. I'll come and get you."

Danny shook his head. "I'm staying up here."

At the base of the ladder, scattered on the ground, was an assortment of paint cans and brushes. She looked around for the painter — or anybody, for that matter — but she and Danny were alone, the only person in sight three blocks away, next to the tracks, a porter pushing a luggage cart across the boardwalk there.

"I'm not coming down till you say we're going to Miles City." Danny lifted one foot and aimed a toe at the top of the ladder to his left. "I'll kick it over," he said.

"Stop that!" She grabbed hold of a ladder rung at eye level and began to climb.

Above her, though, Danny braced the sole

391

of his shoe against the top rung. "I mean it," he yelled. "Don't!"

She was already four rungs up, but now retreated. As her feet hit the ground, Danny gave the ladder a hard sideways shove with his foot, and it slid along the scaffold plank and fell, hitting the dirt with a *whomp*. She ran over and tried to lift it back up, but it was too heavy.

Blood pulsed in a hot line above Gretta's brow. "What's gotten into you?" she asked.

"I'm not going back."

"Oh yes you are. And you're getting a good spanking to boot."

"No, I'm not — he's my father," Danny said, and the strength of his voice took her by surprise, made her notice the shrillness in her own. He'd always been such a mild boy, dependent and pliable, but now as he stood up there, flattened against the brick wall, his head a foot or so beneath the head of the painted farmer in his yellow field, Gretta couldn't help the surge of respect for him that coursed through her, causing her throat to thicken. She had to swallow it down. For the first time ever, she could see what kind of man he was going to be.

"Isn't that paint wet?" she asked.

He wiggled his shoulders against the wall. He nodded.

"How are we going to get you down?" she asked.

"We're not going home," Danny said.

"All right."

"You mean it?"

"We'll sit down and talk. We'll figure out what to do, you and I together," she said, proud of his strength and his will, even if she had no intention of letting him blackmail her.

"I don't think so," he said.

"How're you doing up there? How does your head feel?"

From below, his face looked pale to her, and his fists were clenched at his sides.

"I said, how's your head, Danny?"

"I'm good," he said. "We're going to Miles City."

Something gave way inside Gretta, dissolved, as if her body were telling her she'd eaten something bad. She had to get him down. She said, "Danny, I'm going for help. Please don't move. I'll be right back. Now just stay put."

She ran out into the street and down to the first corner, where she tried to hail a man passing in a horse and buggy. He was going at a good clip and didn't turn his head. Another man, on a big bay, nodded and waved as he cantered by. Gretta went after him, but then stopped short when a voice addressed her from behind.

"That your boy?"

She turned. The man was smaller than she and wore a paint-splotched tunic that covered him up, neck to shins. The skin of his face was smooth and tight, like linen stretched over a round of cheese. His mouth was turned up in a big smile. She couldn't tell how old he was.

"Yes," she said.

"Well he doesn't appear much enamored with his place in the world," the man said. "Let's go and get him down."

Gretta rushed past him toward her son, but the man overtook her easily and, reaching the ladder, hoisted it up with seemingly no effort. He planted one end on the ground, walked it up to ninety degrees, then turned it toward the building and allowed the ladder's top to fall lightly against the scaffold plank, not a yard from Danny's feet. "Up we go," he said, and started to climb, chattering as he went, moving as fast as a boy on a stairs. Danny made no effort to resist him, allowing himself to be taken by the arm and eased onto the top rung. Then they began their descent, Danny above, the little man below, steadying him with one hand. They were two stories in the air, Gretta holding her breath, when Danny slipped — leg jutting out, body twisting. And then he was hanging there at the painter's side, clutched like a bag of feed as the small man came down on the run, nearly in freefall, boots rattling against the rungs. He leaped the last few feet for a perfect landing, Danny flopping like an overgrown fish in his arms.

Gretta came forward, but Danny — on his feet now — put out a hand to keep her away.

"What are you doing?" the painter asked him, standing with his hands on his waist, his face perplexed.

Danny's lips flirted with a smile but then flipped over in a frown. "Looking for my father," he said.

The little man glanced over at Gretta, who could only shake her head, embarrassed. Then he looked at Danny again. "Did you *see* him from up there?" he asked.

"I think I saw him, yes."

Gretta took her son by the shoulder and started to lead him back toward the depot, but then turned, realizing she hadn't even thanked the man. He was standing there watching them, scratching his skull and chuckling. She started to speak, but he shook his head.

"Go on," he said, shooing them off with his fingers. "Go find him now. Just go and find him."

22
REAL MEAT

Eli woke fully alert, certain he'd heard gunshots, something, anyway — but there was nothing. The night was still. Easing open the flap of the tent, he stuck his head outside and looked around. Nothing was moving in the camp. There was no one about. Even the horses, picketed along Calf Creek, were silent. He listened for as long as he could, until sleep took him again, and when he woke at first light McAnna was frying the greasy side-pork from the fort's commissary and flipping pancakes. The men were up and moving, most of them, Sergeant Bayliss down on one knee by the creek, shaving, McNaney sitting off at the edge of camp on a little tumble of limestone, having his morning smoke. Two of the troopers were hunched at the fire with McAnna, drinking coffee. Gumfield, who kept mostly to himself, hadn't emerged yet from the tent he shared with Bayliss and the soldiers. So far the weather had been good, with hard frosts at night and warming afternoons. They'd been in permanent camp on Calf Creek for a couple of days now, up on a good plateau that was flanked on the north by the Big Dry and on the south by the Little Dry — the highest country there was between the watersheds of the Yellowstone and Missouri. Promising hunting grounds, according to McNaney and his rancher friends, with ready access to rugged canyons and badlands, dry coulees, deep ravines, hiding places of all kinds.

So far, though, no sightings at all.

Ulysses sat cross-legged on an empty keg in front of the tent, Bible on his lap, while Hornaday crouched next to him, going through his plan for the day. Eli wasn't sure why his father was the man Hornaday had chosen to trust and confide in, though it could be that he enjoyed the stimulation of a contrary opinion, which Ulysses could be counted on to offer.

"McNaney spoke last night with a couple of hands from the Cross Bar, who told him they came across a fresh trail south of here six, seven miles, at the head of the Calf. As many as eight animals, they said."

"They're sure it was buff?"

"I don't know what they know, only what

McNaney said they claim to know. Guess they were headed southwest, toward that rocky tit down there. Remember? We scouted that country. A lot of nice grassy land once you get past the butte. Smooth and rolling."

"Did you say 'rocky tit,' Professor?"

"McNaney's word for it." Hornaday blushed. "Anyway, I got this story late — you heard him ride in. Ten-thirty, eleven. I say we head down there, all of us, and try to cover that whole area at the head of the Calf. Must be seven or eight miles up and down, maybe four across. What do you think?"

"I don't think so." Ulysses clasped his hands behind his head and made a big fan of his elbows. He stared up at the sky, a dull blue color now, more gray than blue, the last few stars blinking in the west, little pinholes there.

"Why not?" Hornaday tugged on his mustache. "We haven't seen a thing, and now we have a spotting — well, a possible spotting."

Ulysses reached out and broke off the top of a few strands of grass, rubbed them between his palms and tossed the seeds in the air. They drifted down in a westerly direction, pushed by a breeze from the east.

"That's why," he said. "And look over there." He pointed south and west, where a band of darkening clouds showed behind the buttes. "Rain by ten, I believe. Or sleet. They'll be staying down in the draws. Probably down along the Porcupine. They were headed that way if the man was reading his signs right. Let's do a couple of parties, one coming into the Porcupine from the top, from the north, the other from down along the east side, going in from the Cross Bar, or thereabouts, and heading upstream. We cover that whole creekbed, ride up the little washes and gullies and coulees that feed it, and meet someplace in the middle."

Hornaday frowned. "Can't say it smells much like rain to me."

Ulysses stood from the keg and gestured toward the fire, where the men were plating up and filling their cups with McAnna's coffee. He said, "If I'm going to hunt today, I need some of that mud." As Eli followed his father to the fire for breakfast, Hornaday ambled down to join McNaney on his rock, in search of another opinion.

Twenty minutes later eight men, all but McAnna and Gumfield, were mounted and ready to ride, their horses blowing steam and cropping the frosted grass.

"We're splitting up," Hornaday announced. "East wind, and rain's coming. Make sure you've got your ponchos."

Eli rode with his father and Hornaday and one of the troopers from Fort Keogh, a young private with bushy side-whiskers and a habit of blinking in a flutter whenever he spoke. His name was Moffit. The other group was made up of McNaney, Sergeant Bayliss, and the other two privates. Eli's party rode straight down across the high plateau and into the broken ground, the badlands, where the horses had to step with care and at times be led by the reins, their riders on foot in front of them. By the time the sun was a hand's width above the horizon, they'd dropped into the valley of the Porcupine, moving toward a rendezvous with the others. They saw antelope, hares the size of small coyotes, and a longhorn steer badly lost, with the Cross Bar branded on its rump. But no buffalo — and Hornaday voiced his fear that reports he'd gotten had been trumped up.

"Could have moved on west," Ulysses said. "More likely, taken by the cowboys. It's hard to resist a chance at the old king, now that he's all but gone."

By noon they'd ridden some seven miles, according to Hornaday's calculations, two to reach the Porcupine and another five along its channel, sometimes following a dry ravine or coulee for half a mile or so, up to higher ground, for a chance to glass the distance. No signs of anything worth shooting at. It had been raining ice for an hour, and the horses were slick and blowing, the riders wet clear through, despite their ponchos.

After a cold lunch of beans and biscuits in an old growth of wild chokecherry trees, they headed south again and finally at three o'clock met up with the party of Bayliss and McNaney, the lot of them in a state of high excitement. The sleet had tailed off and the skies were starting to clear.

"Nine, we saw nine, and drove them this way." It was McNaney talking. "Ain't you seen anything at all?"

Hornaday urged his big mare up the bank of the ravine and across a short flatland to a high, broad hill topped with rock, with McNaney, Ulysses, and Eli following after and then the rest of them, all dismounting finally and climbing the last stretch to a tumble of limestone piled up like an ancient cabin fallen in on itself. Hornaday glassed the entire country, 360 degrees, moving clockwise and humming a tune Eli had heard before, a march that brought to mind the traveling circus with its brass band that came to Sloan's Crossing when he was small. Hornaday swiveled the other way now, counterclockwise, a methodical sweep, stopping every few seconds and backing up, before moving again, humming all the while.

From below, McNaney called out, "What do you see, damn it."

Hornaday had stopped moving, stopped humming. He'd found something off to the north and watched hard, his face like stone. Eli heard him suck in his breath, as though he'd been hit by a smell and was trying to place it.

"What?" Ulysses said.

Hornaday lowered the glasses and looked around, a smile broadening his face before he caught himself and put the mask back on — the scientist and curator, the man of purpose. "The cowboys were right," he said, and he held up an open hand, all five fingers, clenched them into a fist and then showed four. Nine animals. He handed the glasses to McNaney, who stepped up onto the rock table in Hornaday's place, for a look. Then Ulysses. When it was Eli's turn, he found with his father's help the gentle swale at the head of a small ravine — and the nine animals lying there regal and shaggy in the dusty green sage.

"We must've been riding too close to the

valley floor, and missed them," Ulysses said. "There's no high perch to make a stand, not that I can see. But I believe we can get up on them through the ravine." He turned to McNaney. "What do you think?"

McNaney nodded.

They climbed down off the rocks and made their plan, which wasn't complicated: Retrace the main channel of the Porcupine to the mouth of the ravine, follow it southwest, single file, to its head, then make a full-on charge, with any luck surprising the beasts.

Eli rode toward the rear of the file, with two of the troopers from Fort Keogh behind him — privates Moffit and Williams — and everybody else ahead. The Spencer he left in its scabbard, a round in its chamber. He wondered how this would go, trying to shoot from the saddle. He'd fired the gun only three times, twice at the fort when it was issued to him, and then again on the first day, when he shot the antelope. He knew the recoil was strong enough to throw him off balance, but trying to hold the barrel steady while mounted on a galloping horse besides — it didn't seem possible.

They'd gone a mile or so when the crack of a gunshot caused Eli to rein up and spin around in his saddle. One of the privates,

Moffit, was lowering his gun, smoke trailing from its barrel. He shrugged, *Oh well,* and managed a weak smile as he shoved the rifle back in its boot. The other trooper, Williams, was urging his horse to the top of the ravine, in the direction of Moffit's shot. Ahead, Hornaday and Bayliss had wheeled around and were heading back at a full gallop, flying past Eli and reining up on either side of Moffit, whose smile had fled. The trooper's eyes were all aflutter.

"Are you dimwitted, man?" Hornaday asked. "You think we're on some kind of a turkey shoot here? What's wrong with you?"

"A redskin, I think I saw one. On the ridge." He pointed to the right, due west, toward the red willow at the top of the ravine. Williams was up there now, off his horse and holding the front brim of his hat with both hands, scanning the distance.

"You *think*?" Bayliss said.

"I think so, yes. Sitting his horse up there."

"And so you fired on him," Hornaday said.

"I couldn't tell what he might do, sir."

Ulysses rode up, his brow knotted, and listened as Hornaday filled him in. "I thought the wars were over," he said.

Hornaday aimed a finger at Bayliss. "Tell your man to ride on back. I don't want him along today."

"He's just watching out for us. And he's only a kid." Bayliss rubbed his belly and turned to Private Williams, who was back down off the ridge and reining in his big white horse. "What've you got?" he asked him.

"Saw a bunch of antelopes skedaddling." He glanced at his friend Moffitt with a pained, flat smile. "That's it."

"All right then." Sergeant Bayliss turned to Moffit and waved a hand to the north. "You're done for the day. Go on, get."

"Yes, sir." Moffitt kicked his horse, which turned its head and swiped at the soldier's knee before starting off at a trot in the direction of camp.

The ravine widened, rising into grass and sage, and by the time all seven riders emerged from the cut, the small herd was on the move, drifting in a southwesterly direction across the rolling tableland. Mc-Naney, Ulysses, and Hornaday unbooted their rifles and galloped after them, Eli and the rest following behind. When the gap had closed to forty or fifty yards, the buffaloes started running in earnest, no longer nine of them but only eight, their bodies surprisingly narrow as viewed from behind, slicing this way and that, moving as one being, their heads tucked low, shoulders thrusting.

The roar of hooves against the earth and the motion of their surging bodies, and also the smell of them — a mix of rank cow and dead grass — was nearly enough to unhorse a man. Eli couldn't bring himself to unboot his rifle, let alone free both hands to take a shot. Up ahead, though, a gun boomed, and a small yellow cow broke from the herd in a stuttering, stumbling run, one of the riders pulling up and swerving to stay with it. Below him, Eli's mare hesitated. There was a break in its cadence, a tremor, and he snapped the reins like a whip, afraid of losing ground. "Come on!" he yelled. And then in front of him a horse went down, its rider tossed in the air, the animal tumbling and rolling, and Eli's mare pivoted and leaped sideways, nearly going down itself. He hauled back on the reins and managed to turn the mare, the world quieting as the chase moved on without him. Eli saw for the first time the pocked ground they were on, holes everywhere, and there was his father, lying on his back, the lathered gelding on its knees beside him.

Ulysses rolled over and sat up. He examined himself, rocked his head to one side then the other. "Will you look at this," he said. "Damn prairie dogs."

"Didn't seem to slow the buff down much." Eli was off his mare now and he gave his father a hand up. "You still in one piece?"

"I'm not the one that put my foot in a hole." Ulysses bent to run his hands over the legs of the big gelding, which jerked to its feet, snorting and blowing. "I think he came through it," Ulysses said.

Off to the south the hunt had disappeared over the rise, only Hornaday and McNaney having stayed with it. But here, scattered over two hundred yards, Eli saw two riders off their mounts and walking, picking their steps through the prairie dog town. A quarter-mile west and north, yet another man, still mounted — it looked like Bayliss — lifted his rifle and drew down on a yellow cow that stood facing him. The barrel jumped. Then a brief silence before the report reached them.

"Is that the sergeant?" Ulysses asked. "We better go and see what he's got."

They all converged on Bayliss and the little cow, which was bleeding out in the grass. Bayliss was having trouble with his horse — it reared and shrieked, eyeballs rolling in its head.

"Some don't like the blood smell." This from the young private, Williams.

"Or the smell of buff," Ulysses said.

Bayliss got the skittish roan back on all four legs and walked it off twenty paces to picket it. Then he came back and joined the circle that had formed around the little cow, a yearling from the look of it, maybe three hundred pounds, wet.

"You try for smallest one you could find?" Ulysses asked him.

"Go hang yourself. Least I stayed on my damn horse. You, now, I'd say you've become a danger to the government's animals."

Williams was sent to the main channel of the Porcupine to intercept Gumfield and his wagon for transport of the cow back to camp. Ulysses and Eli gutted and skinned the animal, careful to keep the head on, according to Hornaday's directions. Eli tried to imagine how the creature would look after being stuffed and mounted and put on display in Washington. Not impressive, he thought, not after he'd ridden alongside that running herd. The animal was bony, clumsily shaped, ugly, and Eli saw in his mind the people in their clean, pressed clothes walking right past it, not giving it a second look.

When they'd finished their work, they rode for camp, leaving Bayliss and the other private, Jensen, to wait for Gumfield. Late as the hour was, the decision was made to let McNaney and Hornaday return on their own time, and to send out a wagon for their kill in the morning, if necessary.

That night the men — back in their permanent camp at Calf Creek — ate their fill of roasted backstrap and sampled the tender tongue, which McAnna boiled in salted water. Around the fire they speculated on the whereabouts of Hornaday and McNaney, wondering if they'd chased the herd clear down to the Yellowstone. The air was cooling fast, no wind to signal a change, and it was only after they'd decided the hunters must be spending the night out there, might as well turn in, that a man's voice — or two men, singing — pricked at their ears, one voice low and terribly off key, the other higher and almost sweet-sounding:

My Bonnie lies over the ocean, my Bonnie lies over the sea,
My Bonnie lies over the ocean, oh bring back my Bonnie to me.

A few minutes later two faces appeared at the edge of the firelight, their mouths moving around the words of the song. McNaney, it turned out, was the one who could

410

actually sing. Moffit was dispatched to tend their horses and McAnna loaded up plates for them as everyone waited for the story. Eli had never seen Hornaday so relaxed, his eyes sparkling like quartz. He might have been drunk, except he was steady as a post. McNaney for his part was all smiles as he took his food and burrowed into it, but Hornaday was more interested in talking than eating.

They had stayed with the herd for a good six miles, he explained, shooting a couple of cows on the run, when one of the bulls, the largest, broke off from the rest and headed for a coulee. "This was the one I had my eye on the whole time, a regular monster, and I could hear him breathing like a leaky bellows. But my horse was getting rugged too, and I figured I better get a shot off while I could."

So he'd reined in, jumped down, thrown his rifle over the top of the saddle to steady himself, and popped off a shot, then popped off one more, the old bull running almost straight away from him. The animal didn't flinch, not right off — but after a dozen or so strides it turned fast like a deer, stumbled, turned back again, then stopped short and stood there. After a minute or two, maybe longer, the old bull went down to his knees, gracefully, then gave up and laid himself out on the ground.

"I stepped it off. A hundred and twenty paces. Shot the old boy on a dead run. Bullet entered the vent, and I figure it took out his lungs or heart, possibly both on the way through. And you should see the horns on him — like scythes. I'm telling you, he'll go two thousand pounds, and five and a half feet at the shoulder. And he's got the longest beard you've ever seen. He's the one I came out here for, boys. After this, everything's gravy."

The men sat quiet for a moment. The lenses of Hornaday's spectacles flashed and glimmered in the firelight. Then Bayliss rose from across the fire, circled around and extended his hand. Hornaday stood up and took it.

"Congratulations, Professor. I wasn't altogether sure you had it in you."

Hornaday grinned at that and stayed on his feet to shake hands with the rest of them, Eli included, then retreated to the canvas supply shelter and came back with a small cask, gallon-size, and hoisted it above his head. "Toss out your coffee, men," he said, provoking a low cheer. Or more like a collective sigh. Some threw their coffee hissing into the fire, while others spilled it on the ground between their feet. Bayliss tossed his over his shoulder. Eli wasn't sure what to do, whether this moment included him at all — he'd never tasted whiskey. But his father nodded at him, and so he emptied his cup in the grass.

Everyone waited until the last man had been served, until Hornaday raised his own cup in a toast: "To all of you," he said. "And to the American bison, may it live forever."

At first it was just the buzzing heat that burned all the way down to Eli's stomach, seeping into his chest and arms, and tingling into his fingers. But after a few more swallows there was something different about the men around him — they were quieter, duller somehow — and about his own place among them, as if he'd been removed from the fire and hovered nearby, just outside the circle of light. By the time Hornaday came around with his cask a second time, Eli was watching and listening from a place so far outside himself he wondered whether any of the others could even see him any longer. Ulysses waved Hornaday on by. "Enough," he said, and took the cup from Eli's hand and filled it with the dark mash from the bottom of the coffee pot.

"Drink that down, you'll feel better."

Eli sat for the rest of the evening amused

but removed from the talk around him, and later remembered only a general low noise and the image of Hornaday loping around on all fours, disappearing into the darkness then galloping back into sight, spectacles askew on his face, rear-end higher than his shoulders, cavorting like some creature from the jungle. And next thing he knew it was morning, and he was being shaken awake by his father.

"Wake up, come on. We've got to go after Hornaday's bull."

It required Eli's focused concentration to throw off the blanket, get to his feet, and marshall the energy to put on his clothes and boots and coat. By the time he'd saddled the mare, though, the dense matter was lifting and clearing from his brain.

"How you feeling there?" his father asked.

"Good, I think."

"Glad to hear it. I feel like the devil got inside my head and kicked his way out. Last time I drink any of that man's whiskey."

With Gumfield following in his wagon, they rode south across the high, frost-covered plateau, not following the course of the Porcupine this time but going as the crow flies, over the rolling tableland, through the prairie dog town, and then past a few high buttes on their right, Hornaday

414

riding up front with Ulysses, Eli following after, Bayliss and Williams at the rear. By midmorning Eli rode asleep, one hand planted behind him on the mare's wide back. Then, before he realized what was happening, Hornaday was off his horse and running on foot toward a blackened mound ahead of them. The man took off his hat and dropped it next to his feet. He folded his hands on top of his balding head.

Eli and the others swung off their mounts.

"Damnation. Sons of bitches." Tears stood out in Hornaday's eyes. The bull he'd killed had been skinned and its carcass ransacked at the hump and back for the best cuts of meat. The head was intact, but the horns were broken off, and heavy stripes of red and yellow paint were smeared across the nose and forehead. Tied to the base of one of the broken horns was a piece of red flannel. Hornaday pointed at it.

"What is that supposed to mean?" he asked.

"A message," Ulysses said: " 'Leave us alone.' "

"Savages," Hornaday said. "They don't know what they're doing."

"Oh, they know what they're doing. You can be sure they've been following the same herd."

Hornaday raised a fist. "I'd hunt them down if I could," he said.

"They've been hunted down for less."

His face crooked, Hornaday stared up at Ulysses. "Whose side are you on?" he asked.

"They want us to leave, that's all. Can you blame them?"

"By God I'll blame them if I want to, it's my right." He picked up his hat and slapped it back on his head. "And look what they got for it. A couple day's worth of meat."

"They got your attention, Professor."

Hornaday drew himself to full height, which brought him up to the tip of Ulysses's nose. Eli saw the man's chin ticking, his lips tightening against his teeth, his eyes hardening behind the heavy lenses. "You can stop calling me that," he said.

"Professor?"

"If you don't respect me, that's your business," Hornaday said, voice shaking. "But remember, you are still working for me."

"My apologies."

Hornaday breathed in and out, blowing hard, as if trying to bring something up from his lungs. Then he turned and walked back to his horse. Mounted, he pointed at Gumfield still sitting on his buckboard. "Quarter it out and haul it back," he said. "I'll have Williams stay and help. Make sure

416

you don't damage any of the bones."

"Mr. Hornaday," Ulysses said. "Can I have your permission to leave and try to parley with the Indians?"

"What for?"

"Doesn't make much sense, does it, everybody chasing after the same animals? I could try to explain what we're doing."

"They wouldn't understand. They're not capable."

"I might be able to strike a bargain."

Hornaday seemed unsure, lifting a hand and crooking an index finger under his nose. He shook his head.

"I've had dealings with the Cheyenne. Give me a chance."

"Do you speak their language?"

"Enough to get by."

"Fine, then." He hauled around on the reins and headed back toward camp, his big black horse picking its way over loose ground.

Ulysses swung up on his saddle and turned the gelding in the other direction toward a high butte that widened at the top, like an anvil. Eli headed after him on the buckskin mare. When they were out of earshot of Gumfield and Williams, he asked, "How are we going to track them over this ground?"

His father pulled up and pointed ahead. "See that?"

"The butte?"

"No, closer. That scrub line. See how it runs down into the coulee?"

A hundred and fifty or two hundred yards off, a faint line of green darkened as it fell away into a cut.

"We get down into that ravine, down along the stream, and I think we'll find their tracks. If we surprised them this morning, and I'll bet that's what happened, they had to find the closest place to disappear."

The grass was longer in the coulee, the ground softer, and they crisscrossed the width of it three times, angling downstream on foot, leading their horses as they searched for signs. Eli had been praying for this chance ever since the night of the storm. Not that he was looking forward to the confrontation, or the meeting, or whatever it was going to be — if, in fact, they found their man at all. In truth he was afraid, but he wanted to have it over with. He wanted to see what would happen. He wanted his father to be satisfied. As a little boy, when he ate too many of the rich cookies his mother made with butter, or stuffed himself with the ice cream his father made in the wintertime, he always suffered for his pleasure, his stomach doing a slow, terrible turn. His practice, in those moments, had been to get up at the first trace of discomfort, go outside in the backyard, and stick a finger down his throat. He was never one to wait it out, in the hope he might be spared — because he knew better. Just like he knew now from the look in his father's eyes that Ulysses was getting no rest from the need that drove him.

From down beneath a stunted cottonwood, Ulysses called out, "Here," and motioned for Eli to join him. "What do you think?" he asked.

Eli saw hoofprints in the gray-brown soil, several of them, not as large as the prints of their own animals. Indian ponies. Moving ahead they found more, and by the time they reached damp ground nearer the stream, the tracks were plentiful and clear. Three ponies, as best they could tell, moving farther into the draw, northwest, at a fast walk or easy trot. The cut narrowed and deepened as they went, filling with scrub cedar and greasewood, the stream flowing faster now, more than just a trickle.

"This is a tributary of Taylor Creek, or I think it is. We're angling more to the west now, and Taylor dumps into the Missouri."

"What if this gets us killed?" Eli said.

Ulysses reined in the gelding. He said, "We don't even know it's him."

"Then what are we doing?"

His father looked over, showing a flash of tooth. "You're right."

Eli said, "You don't care if you die, do you?"

His father looked at him for a long moment. "Eli, it's time you ride on back. You have nothing more to prove."

"You think I'm trying to prove something? It's not about proving. We're not enough for you — Mom, Danny, me." And hearing it come off his own tongue like that, it sounded like the truth.

Ulysses urged the gelding ahead but then reconsidered and reined in, letting Eli ride up alongside him again. "That's what I kept telling myself — what you just said. I kept thinking, 'Look at what you've got — a wife you love, and two sons. Nothing else matters.' But you know what? I was wrong. Because no matter what he has, there are things a man can't leave behind, things beyond him. There's right and wrong, Eli, and I think what I'm doing is right — I don't know how else to say it. God help me."

"What about me?"

"God help you, too."

"That's not what I mean."

"Look, son, that first night down by the Yellowstone I did my best to explain it all. I didn't mislead you. I told you what I was doing, and you know how it stands. You're a man now, or you had better be, and I'm not going to tell you what to do anymore. You'll have to make a choice. Just you."

"I already have."

"Then live with it." Ulysses turned away and nudged the gelding with his heels.

They rode on, descending, the cedars getting fuller and taller as they went, though not by much, the stream wider, the tracks easy enough to follow. There wasn't any use, Eli knew, in wishing his father were different than what he was, no use in wishing that he himself hadn't joined this party.

"What do you know about him?" Eli asked.

"Magpie? What I told you already — how he lost his family at the Washita, then fought at the Little Bighorn eight years later. He spent a year with Buffalo Bill's Wild West show, too, touring all through the states. Still, nobody I've talked to out here admits to knowing him, or even knowing *about* him, except for the old woman. I was starting to wonder if he was real."

"He might have given the newspaperman

a false name," Eli suggested.

"He could have, yes."

"Do you think he knows you're looking for him?"

"Wouldn't surprise me at all."

They followed the trail until dusk, until the stream emptied into a larger creek that flowed northwest toward the Missouri. Soon, however, the horse tracks disappeared into the gravel bottom of the creek-bed and didn't come out again.

"They might have doubled back and climbed up out of here," Ulysses said. "Maybe they're up on top and making time."

"But we would've seen tracks coming out, wouldn't we?"

His father pulled up on his reins. "Damn it. We've been on this side of the creek for what, a mile now? We haven't kept track of the other side."

They turned their horses and headed back toward the place they lost the trail, but now the sun was low, the light failing badly, and there was little point searching in the dark when they weren't sure which way to go — upstream, downstream, or out of the valley entirely.

"We'll have to sleep on it," Ulysses said. "Figure things out in the morning."

The night was cloudless, and from the high country above them the cold came down hard, as if poured from a pitcher. At least there was no threat of rain in the air. Or sleet. Or snow. For supper they ate biscuits and cold bacon, and afterward they wrapped up in their bedrolls, spreading on top of themselves a buffalo robe Hornaday had brought from Fort Keogh.

"You smell that?" Ulysses asked, once they'd settled in. He sat up halfway, propping himself on his elbows. He turned his face downstream, the direction from which a breeze was blowing in.

Eli didn't want to move and sacrifice any warmth, but he lifted his nose free of the robe and took a breath. Woodsmoke was what he got, just a hint of it — but then something else, too, that pricked his jaw and made his mouth water. Roasting meat.

"About a mile away, maybe two," Ulysses said. He laughed. "They're feasting on Hornaday's old bull. "You know what they say. Once you've had real meat, beef never tastes quite the same again."

They got up out of their bedrolls, dressed, and led their horses downstream half a mile at least, the smell of roasting meat growing stronger as they walked. It was full dark now, and cold. Eli knew his father had come too far and lived through too many bad nights and bloody dreams to chance losing the man now, and as they picked their way along the creek, his stomach turned over on itself.

"We're not going in there *tonight,* are we?" Eli whispered. He was ashamed of his voice, which sounded thin and frightened.

"No," his father said.

Eli had the sensation of a giant hand hovering over him, malign or friendly, he couldn't tell which, and his impulse was to turn around and go back, put an end to this craziness.

They picketed their horses well short of the camp and moved ahead on foot. It was situated some hundred paces above the stream on a flat rise, with a rock wall to the west and a few scraggly cedars to the north. A lean-to of cedar branches opened to the creekside. Near the water's edge their horses were hobbled and grazing. From downwind, hunched inside a tight clutch of willows, Eli and his father saw three men at the fire.

"You think he's there?" Eli whispered. "You think it's him?"

"I don't know. But we don't want to surprise anybody tonight, that's for sure. We'll go back upstream a little ways and sleep near the horses. Then come back in the morning, first thing."

"And just walk right up? Say hello?"

"That's exactly what we do," his father said. "No circus tricks, nothing clever. Now what do you say we try to get some rest."

23
A Woman's Charge

Back behind the Drover House, a long line of sheets flapped in the crisp morning wind, snapping and breaking like the sails on the boat her grandfather kept in the canal and recalling to Gretta's memory her childhood weekends on the water. Sometimes they sailed as far north as the coastal village of Skodsborg, where one of his old navy friends ran an alehouse, the only place beyond the city that Gretta experienced before she left for America at eighteen. Now, looking back from twice that age, she couldn't help but see that her grandfather, in dying when she was young, had established the pattern for all the men in her life.

"So you're telling me you won't take him back?" May asked, lifting a damp sheet from the basket. She shook it out then pinned it to the line, going way up on the toes of her square-toed boots to do it.

"You don't approve?"

"It's not for me to approve or disapprove," May said.

"I'm asking you, though."

May shook her head, lifting another sheet from the basket.

"You have to agree my prospects are limited," Gretta said.

"No woman can expect her prospects, as you call them, to be anything but capricious. All the more reason that her *judgment* had better be sound."

When Gretta and Danny had arrived in Miles City a week ago, Gretta had struck an agreement with May to work off their room and board until the expedition returned. From her contacts at Fort Keogh, May knew it could be another week or two, even a month, depending on the hunt, and of course on the weather, which this time of year — the second half of October — could swing from Indian summer to full-scale blizzard in twenty-four hours. So far there had been no word at all from Hornaday or Bayliss.

"What will you do, then?" May asked. "Cook and clean for that lizard Fogarty?"

"I've taken his money before, like I said. It probably wouldn't kill me to take it again. At least for a little while."

"He'll be giving you more than his money, dear."

"I wasn't born yesterday," Gretta said.

"Just don't want to see you fooling yourself."

"You seem so sure about things," Gretta said. In fact she'd never met a woman quite like May, so independent in everything — from the way she spoke her mind, straight out, to the way she dressed.

"When it comes to men, I am. I can read them like a book. And you'll notice I'm on my own here."

"Have you ever been married?"

May shook her head. "After the father I had, it would have been daft of me to sign up for more. You could say that he cured me of the sort of wanting that comes naturally to most women. On the other hand I've known men, a few of them, who are worthy of trust. More than a few. And if I were of a different mind concerning their gender, which I am not" — she laughed — "I wouldn't be too quick about giving up on a good one."

"You're assuming he's a good one."

"Yes, I suppose I am."

"And do you think that's what I'm doing? Giving up?"

"I don't know. But you better be damn

sure it's not."

Gretta bridled at the woman's tone. "Don't pretend like you know him better than I do," she snapped.

Without speaking, May picked up her empty basket and walked off into the back of the hotel. In a couple of minutes she returned with another wet pile of linens. Tablecloths and napkins and towels and bedclothes. "Forgive me," she said quietly, "I don't mean to give advice. But you might not know him as well as you think you do."

"I know," Gretta said. She had already explained to May about her husband's secrets — his years out west with the Seventh, the disaster at the Washita. She'd also described the widow's patent claims on her husband's love.

"What I meant was, knowing what you know now, maybe you need to think harder about *why* he did what he did. In not telling you, I mean."

Gretta bent down and plucked up a damp pillowcase. She glanced over at Danny, who was out of earshot and struggling to wield a sledgehammer half his size against the crumbling stone squatter's cabin that May wanted razed. It was a task well beyond her poor son's strengths, Gretta feared.

"Also," May said, "what you don't know

might work to your husband's favor. Have you thought of that?"

"What I've learned doesn't favor him, that's for certain."

"Tell me this," May said. "If at some point, say, ten years ago, he'd come to you and explained it all — what he did and why he never told you — would you have let it come between the two of you?"

"It might have taken some time, but no, I like to think I wouldn't have," Gretta said. "I like to think I would have come to accept it."

"Why?"

"Because at least he would have loved me enough to put himself in my hands."

"And now, knowing how he must have suffered for what he did, is it possible to forgive him for leaving you, and then for letting you sit home with your boys and wonder what might have happened to him?"

"I'm not sure," Gretta said. "That was so cruel. But it might be possible to forgive him. In time."

"You could forgive your husband for killing a young boy, destroying a family, and keeping that from you. On top of that, you could forgive him for leaving you. Is that right?"

"I'm saying it might be possible."

"How long have you been married to him?" May asked.

"Nearly seventeen years."

"Has he been faithful?"

"Until now, you mean? Until Mrs. Powers? Yes, I believe he has. But of course I can't be sure."

"As far as you know, he was faithful all those years. And yet you're willing to take this woman's word at face value, a woman you've never met before, who has nothing to lose and much to gain by saying what she said. I don't understand."

"The green turtle," Gretta said. She'd described to May how Ulysses wore the tag on the brass chain of his grandmother's. And how he tended to be sentimental in that way, keeping small objects of no practical value — the watch she'd given him that hadn't worked for years, the agate from Eli. The beaded pouch. What Gretta had not explained was the little tag's meaning for her, the way seeing it on her husband's chest always brought to mind their first night together, and the bond of love she believed they had shared.

May sighed. "It's a tobacco tag, for heaven's sake, a scrap of tin, not a locket with your picture in it. Do you hear me? Those little tags are everyplace, in case you haven't noticed. All the men have got them. Has it occurred to you that *her* husband might have had that one, too?"

Gretta didn't have a chance to answer, because Danny came up, complaining he was hungry, and May took him inside. But in fact Gretta had thought of this already — she'd tried to convince herself of it. What were the odds, though, that Jim Powers would have saved that same tag, out of the dozens of tobacco brands men could choose from? And there was something else May didn't see. She didn't see that Mrs. Powers was exempt from the dilemma Gretta had been facing for years: how to hold on to a man you were afraid of knowing. Yes, Gretta may have been able to forgive Ulysses if he had come to her, explaining and asking. But the truth was, she hadn't wanted him to do anything of the sort. And she knew something else about herself, too — she would *not* be the second woman in his life. She was thirty-six years old and figured if she could cross the ocean at eighteen, alone, and then stake her future in a prairie town with a man she barely knew, she was certainly able find her way back to Denmark and start again. Of course she needed to think of her boys also. She'd have to convince Ulysses to let her have Danny — and, if it came to that, learn from Mrs. Powers how she felt about mothering a son who was not her own, although Eli was mostly past the point of mothering.

Suddenly Gretta felt overwhelmed, her legs weak and prickly as if they'd fallen asleep, and she grabbed hold of the clothesline for balance. She lowered herself to the ground and sat on the cold, dead grass, trying to empty her mind.

Keep your head on, she told herself. *Don't be a fool.*

Later, as she peeled a sack of red potatoes from the root cellar, she tried to decide if there was anything in May's warning that she ought to heed. It was no easy thing, pushing her mind in that direction. Ever since the night in Bismarck with the widow, she had forbidden herself any warm memory of her husband, suppressing every tender thought that might sway her. She'd done this sort of thing before. After leaving her mother's house, she learned it was possible to lay down a veneer of new impressions on top of the old. During her first year in St. Paul she'd covered up her Copenhagen life so thoroughly with sensations of her new river town that every time someone asked her about Denmark, she had to stop and hunt for Danish words that should have been tripping from her tongue. And yet even now, long after that first life had disappeared like an old foundation buried in the woods, the simplest dream could cause her, on waking, to believe no time had passed at all, that in the kitchen she'd find a plate of steaming eggs, her mother and father at their respective ends of the table, looking up at her.

No, she must not listen to May. It was time to start her third life, which she was already planning, with Fogarty as her stepping-stone and Danny her companion. This week she'd begun telling stories to her son about the city where she grew up, with its cheese and pastry shops, smoky-colored buildings and dark canals, and the flat, green country around it. The pastures full of brown-and-white cows. The dazzling blue of the sky, which above the old city, though, was too often marred by dirty clouds.

She needed to prepare him — carefully, over time — so that when the day arrived, he would be ready.

After dinner she tried explaining this to May, justifying herself. It seemed important right now that someone listen to her and understand. But May would have none of it, shaking her head and making a face. It was midafternoon and they were standing at the big washtub in the kitchen, May scrubbing and Gretta drying.

"One question," May said. She lifted her stubby, red hands from the soapy water and pushed the sleeves of her coarse shirt up past her elbows. "Why didn't you want to know what your husband was hiding?"

Gretta didn't answer.

"Did you think it was another woman?"

Gretta thought for a moment. She wanted to be honest, but it was impossible sometimes to know your own mind. She said, "No, I don't think so."

May's eyes stayed on her. She waited.

"It's not a woman's charge, is it, to take care of a man that way?" Gretta asked.

"What way?"

"Well — to prop him up like that." Gretta was aware of sounding like her mother, but she wasn't able to keep the words inside her head. "To indulge his concerns and his worries. To *coddle* him."

"I don't know." May looked up at the ceiling, then down at the dishwater. She looked over and smiled at Gretta. "I'm not the woman who could tell you."

"That's how it seems to me, at least. No, that's how it *is.*"

"Men are that much different from us?" May's smile wasn't quite straight on her face anymore.

"They have to be," Gretta said. She swallowed to check the indignance she felt at being judged like this, questioned by a woman who had never even been married.

May started scrubbing on a big pot. After a time, she asked, "Weren't there any hints at all about those two years he spent out west? Or about the name change?"

Gretta shook her head — too quickly, she realized. "No, he never said a thing. And he kept me away from his sister and brother-in-law, who knew, of course. Or knew more than I did. Before leaving St. Paul we saw them all of three or four times."

"I just can't help but wonder," May said, after a minute or two.

"Wonder what?"

"Whether you're afraid of your husband leaving you for the widow, or coming back to you. I'm wondering if you *want* him coming back."

Gretta laughed, but without humor. "If I knew the answer to that, it wouldn't be so hard," she said.

May handed over a dripping pot. "Foolish question. I apologize."

"No need."

What appeared in Gretta's mind now, vivid, like a waking dream, was Mrs. Powers's face, the expression on it when she pulled the little green turtle from inside her blouse, a look of pity and disbelief that said, *You have no idea who he is, do you?*

Putting a hand on May's hard shoulder, Gretta said, "I only wish you could understand. I need someone to understand."

May nodded. She scratched her nose with a wet finger. She was still smiling, but her eyes were solemn and glossy. "I understand why you're tempted. I do. And do you know what else? I believe you'll make the right choice."

"Do you mean it?" Gretta asked.

"I do," said May.

In Gretta's belly a cool ache began to pulse, a welcome pain. "I hope you're right," she said.

24
ON MORIAH

They'd spent a restless night on hard ground, Ulysses afflicted by competing doubts, pressure building in his chest, while next to him Eli struggled through dreams. As the sky paled in the east, they threw off the big robe, dressed, and approached the camp once more, on foot and leading their horses. There was no morning fire, though, no movement at all. No sounds. "They're still asleep," Eli whispered, but Ulysses shook his head and pointed downstream at the grassy flat where the men had hobbled their ponies the night before. The ponies were gone. Moving cautiously through the camp, they found bedrolls, a cache of food, and a big meat-pile wrapped in green hide and strung up in a cedar tree, hot embers in the fire.

"Do we go after them?" Eli asked.

"Nope, we wait here. They'll come back."

Upstream they found a small grove of

crooked plum trees where they spent the day, Ulysses going out every hour to check, and finally, when the sun was three fingers above the western buttes, the men returned.

Ulysses pulled his rifle from its boot.

"We're taking our guns?" Eli asked.

"We'd look like damn fools without them, wouldn't we?"

By the time they walked up the creek bank, a small fire was burning, a narrow smoke trail rising straight up, no wind at all this afternoon. Ulysses looked at his son and nodded. They moved to within fifty paces of the camp before he lifted a hand for Eli to hold up. In a normal speaking voice he said, "Haaa-he."

"You *do* know the language," Eli whispered.

Ulysses shook his head. "Just to say hello."

Beneath the shelter of cedar branches a man straightened up and leaned forward in a crouch, his elbows on his knees, fire glimmering in his face. Two other figures showed themselves as well, one next to the fire and the other just outside the shelter, to the north.

"We're coming up," Ulysses called, and he touched his son's elbow.

They walked right into camp, side by side, the three men watching as they came. A watery pot of something had been set to boil on the fire, and it smelled like pine needles. The crouching man had long braids wrapped in weasel fur and wore a cavalry coat with herringbone piping on the chest. He had small, hooded eyes, a sharp nose. He was alert but indifferent, his faded campaign hat lying next to him on the ground, the corner of his mouth twisting just enough to let Ulysses know the recognition was mutual.

"You're not alone this time," the man said. His English, as before, was practiced and careful. The bone-handled Colt was stuck in the waistband of his pants, and his Henry repeater leaned upon a length of firewood an arm's length away. His eyes glanced over at Eli and then came back again.

Ulysses nodded.

On the other side of the fire sat the small man with the tree-bark face and narrow body. Outside the lean-to, propped against the cedar tree, was the third one, his shoulders as wide as a door, revolver still hanging from a cord around his neck. Long, graying hair. After a long moment of silence, the man in the cavalry jacket stood from his crouch and moved to his left, stepping over the Henry to seat himself on a chunk of limestone next to the fire.

"Did you come to bring us more of the United States dollar coins?" he asked.

"No," Ulysses said.

"So we're not that lucky."

"No."

"Before, you were gathering bones. Now you're on a big hunt." He gestured northeast, toward the permanent camp on Calf Creek.

"We've been riding with them, yes. But we're not interested in shooting buffalo. That's not why we're here."

Eli, breathing light and fast, leaned close and whispered, "You *know* him?"

"We ran into each other a few days back, down along the Tongue."

The man said, "I see the bluecoats riding along. What are you afraid of?"

"There's talk among the ranchers of horse stealers and cattle poachers. Crow, they're saying, or maybe Piegan."

The man laughed at this. "If they were Cheyenne, then there might be cause for fear."

Ulysses reached into his coat, slowly. "I brought this for you," he said.

Instead of the beaded pouch, he pulled out a little sack filled with tobacco, a string tied around its top, something he'd bought in Miles City from an old woman who'd fashioned it from the scrotum of a buffalo calf. He gave it to the man, who opened it, lifted it to his nose, then retied the bag and tucked it into the pocket of his jacket.

"Are you here to parley for the buffalo hunters?" he asked.

"No, I'm looking for Magpie. As you might remember."

The words had no effect on him. "What name do you go by?" he asked.

"Ulysses Pope. And this is Eli, my son."

"Does your son also have matters to discuss with Magpie? Or maybe he's looking for a watch."

Ulysses only smiled.

The man looked around at his two friends and spoke for a few moments in their own tongue. It sounded sharp and smooth, rushing and hard at once, like fast water over rocks. The men got up and moved off, the small one with tree-bark skin going down toward the horses, the big one uphill to a table of limestone, where he began to clean his rifle with a rag.

"You must be hungry." The man ducked out from under the lean-to and walked over to the hide-wrapped meat pile hanging in the cedar tree. He opened it and carved off several big strips then came back and fixed the meat on skewers at the edge of the fire.

It started sizzling. He motioned for Ulysses and Eli to join him, and soon they were all three chewing the tough, juicy meat and washing it down with dark tea that tasted like licorice.

"You don't seem to mind eating from the old bull. Your friend with the beard, he might be unhappy. Does he come from the east?"

"Yes," Ulysses said, "from Washington."

"I've been there, I didn't like it much. Why does he wait to come shoot them now, after they're all gone?"

"He's trying to save their memory."

The man frowned, waited.

"You've probably seen how dead animals can be made to look as if they're still living," Ulysses said. "There are men who know how to take out their insides and fill them up with sawdust and make them look real again. That's what he plans to do with the animals he shoots."

The man reached out with his foot and pushed an ember toward the center of the fire pit, where it flamed up. "Your people seem to think it's necessary to remake the world of their fathers into something all their own. I've noticed this. Your children will do the same. And theirs will, too — and then they will wonder who you were, and how you lived. It's a sad thing. But the buffalo, it wasn't yours to begin with."

Ulysses couldn't find a suitable answer. He asked a question instead. "Are you Magpie?"

"I might tell you that if you tell *me* something first."

"All right."

"Was your brother with Custer at the Greasy Grass, the way you explained to me on the Tongue?"

"No," Ulysses said.

"I didn't think he was."

"Why not?"

"You don't look angry enough."

Ulysses wondered if he was being toyed with. It occured to him that it wasn't too late to get up and leave, take his son away from here — although very soon that possibility would have run out. He said, "No? What do I look like, then?"

"Like you've been watching over your shoulder too long. Like you're trying to understand what you believe."

"I've answered your question," Ulysses said.

"So you have. And you know the answer to yours." With long, blunt-tipped fingers he fiddled with the collar of his coat, unbuttoning it. The lapel flopped down, and then he buttoned it again. "Why have you come out here?" he asked. "And this time please tell the truth."

"To finish something I started," Ulysses said.

"Something you started with Magpie?"

"You could say that, yes."

"How did you find me? Who did you speak to?"

Ulysses described his search among the reservation Cheyenne and then his evening with the old woman in the cabin on the Tongue, the antelope shank she was roasting on her woodstove. "By that point I started to wonder if you were a ghost," he said. "No one else knew anything, or so they claimed."

Magpie laughed. "*She* should know. She is my mother."

Ulysses stroked his beard. A picture came to mind of her old face, upside down against the morning sky, staring at him as he lay in the bed of his wagon, her eyes fixed on the beaded pouch. "So you knew I'd be coming," he said.

"She sent word, yes, but didn't tell me what you were looking for."

The big man above them on the rock had finished cleaning his rifle and started ambling toward them. Magpie waved him off.

"I have something else for you," Ulysses said, and now he could feel his lungs rising into his throat. In order to get enough air, he had to focus his mind on the act of breathing.

"Before you let me see it," Magpie said, "tell me something else. Tell me if your god sent you here. The one who allowed the men to kill him. The god you killed."

Ulysses breathed. He was aware of a sudden lightness, as if the crown of his head were lifting away. He placed the heels of his hands against his temples and squeezed, forcing himself to think. *Let me say this right.* "God doesn't speak to me in a way I can be sure of" was how it came out.

"You don't hear him?"

"Not in the way I'd like to."

For a long moment Magpie was silent. It was impossible to read his eyes, narrowed as they were, shiny slits. He said, "Well, then," and elevated his chin, squared his shoulders, and sat up straight. He looked like a man preparing himself for his own execution, though his hands were quiet on the ground beside him.

Ulysses glanced over at Eli, whose expression showed nothing. He would have liked to reassure his son, tell him all was going to be fine. Instead he reached for the beaded pouch that hung inside his coat, below his left arm. He pulled it out and lifted the strap from around his neck and held it on his lap where the last of the sun was caught in the blue and yellow beadwork.

Magpie sat still, his eyes holding fast to the bag. He leaned to his right and took hold of the Henry and rose to his feet, all in a single movement. Then he crooked the rifle loosely in his right elbow, barrel pointing at the sky. He stared hard at Ulysses, who was aware of his own rifle propped beside him on the ground. No one moved. Then Magpie leaned over and plucked up the pouch from Ulysses and walked uphill and out of sight beyond a heap of limestone. Ulysses looked around to see where the others had gone but there was only the smaller man out in the middle of the creek, his chest bare, his arms wet and glistening and extended out on the surface of the water.

"Where did he go, what's he doing?" Eli whispered.

Ulysses shook his head.

"What, we just sit here? Let's go, leave while we can."

"No."

Ulysses saw himself at the center of a storm. He imagined himself waiting through the final moments before a battle, when you know your lot has been decided, your future beyond any control. Turning, he looked into his son's face, where he saw fear and defiance both. He put an arm around Eli's shoulder, but Eli shrugged it off. It may have been a quarter of an hour that Magpie was gone, or twice that, but when he came back down the hill, tobacco pouch slung across his shoulder, the Henry balanced in his elbow, he wasn't alone. Behind him walked the man with the barrel chest and graying hair, his eyes shining like two black stars.

"This is Bull Bear, my brother," Magpie said, and the two men sat.

In Magpie's face Ulysses saw something new, the kind of distance he'd often seen in Danny's eyes when a headache was coming on. Bull Bear set his rifle on the ground and picked up a stick and began to jab at chunks of burning wood. A pulsing blue vein stood out on his forehead.

Magpie cradled the Henry on his lap. He touched the buckskin pouch, which rested at the center of his chest. "Where did you get this?" he asked.

"At the Washita."

"You rode with Squaw Killer then?"

"I did."

"Do you know who made this pouch?"

"Yes."

"How could you know?"

Ulysses explained about the old woman he'd met at Camp Supply during the week following the massacre, one of fifty-three hostages Custer had taken that day. And how she had recognized the beading pattern of the pouch and identified its maker.

"My wife's aunt," Magpie said. "She lived. My wife also survived the attack that morning, so I was told. She made her way safely across the river. Did her aunt tell you that too?"

"Yes."

"That's how it was. She was in the lodge with our son and our nephew, her sister's son. The soldiers killed both boys, but my wife escaped and swam across the icy channel. To no purpose. Later that day she lost her courage and drowned herself. It was that or tell me about my son. Her old aunt told me this."

Magpie cleared his throat, and for a while there was no talking. Ulysses sat looking at his hands, thinking, *I asked for this, I asked for this,* while opening in his mind was the smallest peephole into that day, a view more than adequate for the purpose. Next to him, he could feel Eli holding his breath. Absurdly, a pair of ducks began to scold each other in the creek below.

"How old was your son?" Ulysses asked, finally.

"You want to know if you killed him. But no. You tell *me.* You tell *me* what happened. Tell me what you did."

Ulysses looked across at Magpie sitting there rigid and grave, his skin taut, fists gripping the lapels of his faded blue coat. It was impossible to account for the co-incidences and for the years of grief that had led to this moment, preposterous to hope that a minute from now the two of them would still be alive and sitting here across from each other. And yet there was nothing to do but go on, to speak, which Ulysses did, half convinced his words would choke him, catch in his throat like dry stones.

He wasted no time on details that would be all too familiar, but moved right to the moment in front of the lodge, and the boy with the Colt revolver. "He shot me here," he said, laying a hand to the right side of his head, where his ear was gone. "He was nine or ten years old. He shot me and then ran into the lodge, and my friend went after him. I went in too. There was a woman there and another boy, younger than the first. Three years old, or four. The one who shot me wasn't trying to hide. He didn't seem afraid. He was looking up at me, fierce, as if he wanted to kill me." Ulysses paused and touched his own chest. "I shot him here," he said, his voice catching, "I can't tell you why — out of anger, I suppose. My friend shot the other boy, and then we ran out, leaving the woman there. Your wife. Not long after, we went back for her, trying to gather up everyone who was still alive. But she was gone. The lodge was empty except for the two boys we had killed." Ulysses paused to breathe. "I'm sorry," he said. "I'm here to tell you that I'm sorry."

Magpie hadn't blinked or looked away. The Henry still rested in the crook of his elbow. His hands were loose on his knees now, but there was a tremble in his fingers. He turned to Bull Bear and spoke for a while, his chin raised almost formally, then lifted a hand when his brother took a grip on the pistol that hung from his neck. Magpie turned to Ulysses again. "Yes, that was my son," he said, his face stricken and pale. "And your friend killed his cousin, my nephew. They were good boys. Their grandmother and grandfather also died that morning. Several aunts and one of their uncles. Many cousins. The boys were found in the tipi, of course, their bodies charred.

My wife was floating at the edge of the river. She'd told her aunt what she meant to do. You may as well have killed her."

Magpie sat for a time, the shadows in his face so deep the shape of his skull was plainly visible — the eye sockets and cheekbones, the abrupt angle of his jaw. "You have a son," Magpie said, gesturing toward Eli. "And I think you have a wife too, at home?"

Ulysses nodded.

"If Bull Bear and Leather Top went there, and one of them put a bullet through her heart or crushed her head with a club, it would be the same as if I had done it. There is no difference."

"There is no difference," Ulysses said.

"Are you prepared to die?" Magpie asked. "Is that why you came? Do you want us to kill you? Because I am ready."

Ulysses said nothing. All down the center of himself, from the bottom of his throat to his groin, he felt an icy coldness. He had come here for this moment, and it belonged to Magpie, who would do with it as he liked. There was no other way it could be. Ulysses turned to his son, whose mouth was set hard, his eyes full of distance.

"Spare him," Ulysses said.

Magpie didn't respond. In the cedar tree

nearby a pair of crows had come to light upon the hanging meat pile, and now they began to pick and jab at it.

Bull Bear leaned over and spoke into Magpie's ear, his gaze fixed on Ulysses. Magpie shook his head. He said, "My brother forgets how much time has passed, how many things have changed. He wants to know if you see yourself as a good man for coming here and saying these things. He wants to know if you think your god will love you again now. He wants to know if that's why you came here."

"I was taught to believe that God loves us all, no matter what we do," Ulysses said. "No, I'm not a good man. But I had hoped to give my sons a father again, and my wife a husband. And I had to tell you I am sorry."

"You're here to please yourself then," Magpie said. "It would have been better if you had stayed home. You think because your god suffered, you don't have to suffer. That all has been made smooth, the world is yours to take. You think if there is pain, there must be a way to be rid of it, like a buffalo sheds his winter coat by rubbing on a rock. And that I'm your rock." Magpie shook his head. "You took a boy's life, but you're not worthy to carry his spirit."

Ulysses couldn't defend himself. He

didn't try. There wasn't a thing the man could say that he hadn't said to himself. Next to him, Eli began to speak, but Ulysses glanced over, frowning, to silence him. Then Bull Bear leaned over and whispered into Magpie's ear again, his eyes fastened on Ulysses.

"My brother tells me your words are like a rifle without shells. That if you mean what you say, you should load it, put a round in the chamber."

"How? Tell me," Ulysses said.

Magpie looked up at the darkening sky. He lifted the pouch in his hand and examined it. He said, "I've lived all these years without a son. At one time I thought if I could kill those soldiers who did it, I would want to make children again, a son to take hunting with me. But then Long Hair came to the big camp we had on the Greasy Grass, hoping to drive us back to the reservations. We rubbed him out. I took many lives that day. Bull Bear and I, we killed your friends, and our women cut them up into pieces and took their clothing and their guns and their money. And their watches. What we did was good and what we had to do — but it didn't change things." Magpie laid a palm across his chest. "Not for me. I could see that even if I did have a

454

son, I would have no world for him."

Ulysses could feel a buzzing inside his ribs, like a large insect was caught there.

"But here is what you can do, if you mean to settle this wrong you have done me." Magpie turned his face toward Eli. "You can give me *your* son. He is close to being a man but still boy enough to learn. Give him to me, and then I will know that you have heard your god. I'll know that your heart is as good as you think it is."

"I didn't say I thought my heart is good."

"But you want it to be good. That's why you're here."

"Yes."

Magpie grabbed hold of the beaded leather pouch that his wife had made and lifted the strap over his head. He lowered it to his lap and clutched it in both hands. "If you won't do this," he said, "you can take your trinkets back home with you. They have no meaning by themselves."

Ulysses looked straight ahead. He felt ill suddenly, damp all over his back and neck, yet cold at the same time.

"Your son, he wants a father he can be proud of, a man with honor," Magpie said.

Next to Ulysses, Eli cleared his throat. He said, "My father *is* honorable."

Across the fire, Bull Bear's broad face was

hard with anger. Magpie's was open, waiting. Ulysses got up on one knee, an action that brought pain to his joints, then he stood and said to Eli, "Hand me my gun," which Eli did. "Get up," he told his son. Eli rose to his feet. Ulysses went around the fire and reached an open hand down to Magpie. "All right then, give it to me," he said.

Magpie seemed unable to move at first, still holding the beaded pouch on his lap. Then he shot air through his nose and handed it over. Next to him, Bull Bear twisted around to snatch his rifle from the ground, but Magpie extended an arm in front of his brother, a palm flat against the man's thick chest.

Ulysses turned and took his son by the elbow and led him down the bank past Leathertop, snoring in the lee of a stunted juniper, and all the way to the creek's edge, careful not to hurry. Upstream, their horses whickered at their coming. He and Eli mounted up and headed northeast for Calf Creek on the High Divide, riding until well past dark, drawing up finally in a stand of little pines, a good enough place to sleep, Ulysses all this while uttering just four words to his son — "What could I do?"

To which Eli had no response.

25
SAWDUST

By the height of the quarter moon it must have been three or four in the morning. There was no light in the east, and though his father was finally sleeping, Eli couldn't keep his eyes closed. As quietly as possible, he unwound himself from his blankets, slipped his pants and boots and coat on, and crept over to the horses, which were cropping the rimy grass in a willow-rimmed swale. He pulled the picket pin, bridled the mare, and led her away, his escape all but silent, his father's gelding snorting just once.

He waited until out of earshot before swinging up on the mare's back and easing her into a fast walk. Beneath a clear sky, the way back wasn't difficult to find, the moon casting faint shadows behind the grease-wood trees and skunkbrush, behind the occasional stunted pine or outcropping of rock. Although Eli had been frightened yesterday — terrified, certain he was going to be killed — he wasn't frightened now. Nor did he examine, as he would in later years, the reasons compelling him to leave. It seemed like a simple thing. He'd left home to help his father, and now there was no other way to do it. This had to be finished. The moment seemed inevitable, his decision less a choice than a reflexive act, and he was calm, almost joyful, as he covered the miles, glancing time and again over his shoulder for the first sign of morning. He kept thinking, *Don't let him wake up yet.* And, *Don't let them break camp too early.*

He arrived with nearly an hour to spare.

All was still as he sat the buckskin mare at the edge of the creek below their camp. No wind down here in this shallow valley, and no sound except for water flowing over pebbles. At the first sign of movement on the table rock and the flaring up of the fire in the lean-to, Eli picketed the mare and walked up the bank, no one speaking as he came on, none of the three pausing in their morning routines, Magpie stitching a broken seam in his moccasin, Bull Bear carving at the meat pile, Leather Top feeding the fire. Magpie nodded at the cedar stump next to him, and soon they were all four chewing on strips of the roasted meat, which tasted even better this morning, and drinking from the pot of bittersweet tea.

"I didn't expect he would send you back," Magpie said.

"He didn't send me back," Eli told him.

Bull Bear handed Eli another piece of meat and spoke a few words to Magpie. Leather Top leaned his head back and laughed, his face squeezing into a furrowed map.

"My brother wants to know if you brought your war paint. He says he was your age when he took his first scalp."

Eli said nothing.

"He likes making jokes," Magpie said, then he nodded toward the Spencer carbine resting on Eli's knees. "Did your father teach you how to use it?"

"Not this one, no. It's from the fort."

"That one isn't much better than the rifle they used in Custer's troop. Those shot a single bullet then had to be reloaded. And once the barrel heated up, the cartridges stuck in the chamber. Not that some of those boys knew how to use them anyway. Farm boys. And poor men working for money. Toward the end there were those who threw down their guns and lay on the ground, waiting for death, staring up at the sky. Others shot themselves or shot each other. I almost felt sorry for them."

"You could have let them live," Eli said.

"Can I see it?" Magpie asked, gesturing toward the Spencer.

Eli handed it to him, and Magpie got up and walked over to the jut of rock against which the lean-to was built. He gripped the end of the rifle's barrel, spun himself around and struck the weapon against the rock, splintering the wooden stock and separating barrel from breech. He tossed it away.

"Piece of shit," he said. "Here" — he signaled to Leather Top, who came over with his own rifle, which Magpie offered in turn to Eli, a Winchester lever-action, similar to one of the guns Two Blood had in his shop. He motioned for Eli to follow him down to the creek. There he tossed cedar sticks for Eli to fire at as the current floated them away, urging him to shoot as fast as he could, levering in round after round, the sticks exploding and leaping in the water, until the magazine was empty and the hammer made a hollow click against the firing pin. The weapon was warm in his hand, the stink of gunpowder sharp in the air. Eli liked how the Winchester felt in his hands, he liked the smooth quickness of the action.

"That big soldier horse you're riding," Magpie said. "Is she a battle horse or a plow puller?"

He told Eli to mount up and ride hard along the creek, full gallop, and fire a shot down into the water. Eli had never ridden no-hands. He held the reins tightly in his left, the rifle in his right, kicked his mare into a gallop and then at the last instant looped the reins around his wrist, raised the rifle to his shoulder, and got off a quick shot without aiming. The mare veered right at the sound, away from the blast, and Eli pitched left and landed at the creek's edge, managing at least to keep hold of the rifle. The men laughed and hooted, pointing, then watched him as he got up and chased down the mare, remounted and came trotting back.

"Try one of our ponies," Magpie said.

Eli swung off the mare and Magpie walked over, looking him up and down. He ran a hand over the arm and shoulder Eli had landed on, his fingers squeezing to the bone, and then brushed the dirt from Eli's coat. "Nothing broken," he said.

It was a dark pony, a stallion with a white face and a white tornado shape along one side that started by the withers and ended at the hip. A small animal, compared to the buckskin mare Eli had been riding, only thirteen or fourteen hands, but big-boned, wide, with sturdy legs and a straight back, its eyes large and vigilant, as if watching to see whether Eli knew what he was doing. Magpie demonstrated how to grab its mane and leap onto its back — not a hard thing for Eli to do, as it turned out, and the pony didn't seem to mind, only tossed its head and took a little jump-step to the side. The bridle was a single length of soft leather rope that ran through the mouth, tied beneath the jaw, the two ends coming back along the pony's neck as reins. There was no saddle at all.

"Hold on with your knees and use them to turn him — he knows what to do. And this little boy, he likes the crack of your rifle. You'll see."

Magpie was right. The little stallion stayed on a line, running fast and smooth, without swerving at the boom of the rifle, while Eli held tight with his knees, getting off three shots into the creek. They broke camp and followed a dry ravine that led them out of the valley and up to the tableland above, where they rode west toward a line of buttes that looked like the silhouettes of three people, their heads and shoulders unmistakable against the sky, two parents on the outside, with a small child between them.

Pointing, Eli asked if they had a name.

"Walking with the sun," Magpie said, and

though Eli wondered if he meant sun or son, he didn't ask.

They moved at a brisk trot through the cool day, their breath steaming in the air, Eli's buckskin mare packing the meat pile and tied on a lead behind them. Midmorning they stopped to water their ponies at a fast-running stream. The three buttes were closer now, the middle one a distinctive coppery color, the larger, flanking ones gray-black. In the shade of a cottonwood the men chewed on cold meat. Upstream from the horses they filled their hide bladders. Then Leather Top rode to the top of the next ridge, jumped off his pony and stood there eyeing the country before remounting and riding back down to rejoin them. He gestured, talking fast.

"We're close," Magpie said. "Yesterday he tracked the herd your friends were chasing, and we should be on them soon."

Within the hour they'd ridden to the top of a rise from which they could see below them a stream that widened into a green pool and next to it twenty or so animals grazing, among them a black-maned bull that every so often rose up and looked around. As they watched, he put his shaggy head down and plowed forward, twisting a horn into the soft earth near the water, then lifting up and swinging his head, throwing a torrent of mud. He finally went down to his knees, fell to his side, and rolled in the muddy wallow.

Magpie sketched out his plan, using a stick in the dirt and gesturing to Bull Bear and Leather Top. He pointed at himself and Eli, and then to the ridge on which they sat, which extended in a hogback toward the stream. The place where it fell in a hard decline toward the water marked the southern edge of the grazing animals. Magpie spoke briefly to the men, and then turned to Eli and explained. Bull Bear and Leather Top would go first and drive the herd south, squeezing it between the water and the hogback, down from which Magpie and Eli would ride to fire on them as they tried to escape along the water.

"This will happen fast," Magpie said. "We'll take cows for their meat and let the bulls run."

Leather Top and Bull Bear jumped on their ponies and rode straight downhill at a full gallop, calling out in high, shrill yips. The buffaloes lifted their heads and poked up their tails and started to move, slowly at first, the whole mass of them together, but then with gathering speed. By then Eli and Magpie were running their ponies along the hogback, side by side. The surface of the ground was dotted with stones the size of hammerheads, but Eli's pony ran without hindrance, as if racing on a dirt track, Eli hanging onto the reins, his knees gripping the animal's wide back so hard that his groin burned with pain. Magpie glanced over, a smile widening his face, his teeth shining, one hand on his rifle, the other wrapped in the pony's mane, the reins tied off and flapping. He might have been caught up in holy zeal, or a man returning from a far-off place and just now catching sight of home. He lifted his rifle in the air and pumped his arm.

They were on the downhill now and closing with the herd, at the front of which was the black-maned bull, running as if to kill itself — the ground thundering like a storm beneath them and the men singing, their bright voices high above the shuddering noise of the herd. Then Magpie's pony surged ahead as if flung by a giant sling and moved up next to the bull. Magpie leaned over, way over, horizontal in the air, and he took a grip on the bull's curly, mud-caked mane with his fist and gave it a shake, just as neat as that, before letting go and allowing the animal to pound away with the herd. He rode back alongside Eli and pointed out a big, hard-running cow and shouted, "Go and put her down," his face glistening.

"For my son — now!"

Eli kicked his pony but didn't need to. The animal was already going flat out, galloping straight for the big cow, which huffed and blew, white foam spraying in clots and jets from its shovel-size nose. Eli let go of the reins, the pony knowing this sport and edging close enough for Eli to put the barrel of the Winchester almost smack up against the monster's heaving ribs. Before he got off a shot, though, the big cow cut away and the pony followed in a hard pivot, leaving Eli to grab at the flying mane for balance, ashamed of his hesitation and clumsiness. But there was almost no break in rhythm, no slowing the chase at all — and there was no other place to be but here, fixed by the violent, bloodshot glare of the cow's left eye. Eli heard himself yelling in a voice he didn't know he had, high-pitched, ecstatic, and this time he got off a shot, missing wide. He jacked the lever of the Winchester and shot again, barrel jumping, and a small puff of hair leaped from the very top of the cow's humped shoulder. The animal stumbled, recovered, and charged on. Eli's third shot, though, was true, entering behind the shoulder and staggering the animal, which pulled hard to the left. Eli's pony cut fast in a sort of rabbit hop to stay clear of it.

Magpie came up alongside him, and together he and Eli watched the big cow go round in a steep curve until it was coming back at them, seeming to gain strength as it came, head lowered and wagging its black horns. Abruptly it fell to its knees. Blood poured from its mouth into the brown grass. A quarter of a mile ahead another cow fell out of the herd, and Bull Bear reined up as the rest of the buffaloes rumbled away, dust hanging over them like a rain cloud.

A couple of hundred yards back, Eli saw two other cows down, close together, Leather Top already at work over one of them. His own, meanwhile, had tipped over dead. It lay on its side, lifeless eye staring dully at the sun, which stood just past noon. From head to tail the cow was eight feet long, and its girth at the shoulders brought it just past Eli's waist. The curved, black horns, if straightened, would have equaled the length of a man's forearm. Magpie pried open the mouth and deftly carved out the tongue, which he set aside. Then he made a deep cut all around the neck before slicing straight down to the vent and around the tail.

"If we want to get at the best parts, we open up the back," Magpie said. "But we want to save the robe, so we do it like this."

They removed the entrails and organs first — the grass-engorged stomach almost large enough to crawl inside of, the twisting mass of purple intestines, and then the flaccid liver and steaming red heart, both of which they put off to the side, along with the tongue. The smell was rank and lush, but Eli had gutted enough whitetail deer that he wasn't bothered by it. Magpie sliced off a piece of the hot liver and handed it to Eli, then cut some off for himself and took a bite of it, the blood dripping from the corners of his mouth. Eli did so, too, the taste metallic and strong, something like the blood sausage his father used to buy from the butcher in Sloan's Crossing — though this was spongier, tougher, harder to chew and swallow. "Now you'll do some work," Magpie said, and while he scraped and nipped with his skinning knife, separating hide from fascia, Eli pulled and yanked on the slippery skin to expose the top side of the fatty yellow carcass. Together they pulled away the entire half-skin and drew it back on the grass. With the help of Magpie's pony, they turned the animal over, the stiffening legs swinging up in the air then whacking down on the other side, and before long, the entire bloody hide was free, the hulking carcass naked and white.

"The good eating," Magpie said, and he cut away the marbled hump as big as a man's head, then stripped off the heavy backstraps, two feet long, from both sides of the spine.

They skinned and butchered the four cows, a pack of skulking coyotes watching from the hills above, and by the time the sun was low they'd built a travois of cedar poles to carry the hide-wrapped meat piles. Leather Top rode ahead to scout the herd, while Magpie, Bull Bear, and Eli headed back toward Taylor Creek. On the way, they rode to the top of a high round bluff that offered a long view in all directions and above which hung a blue-tinged cloud. On the highest point of the bluff Magpie laid out the best of the four robes — the one taken from Eli's cow — and spread it out on a table of limestone and set rocks all around its edge to hold it in place.

They left it there and rode on.

At the camp above the stream, they rubbed down their ponies and hobbled them by the water. They built up a good fire, then feasted on hump roast and tenderloin, on boss ribs and boiled tongue, as they watched the lavender sky darken and the stars emerge by ones and twos, threes and fours, and finally by the dozens. Magpie took out tobacco and filled the redstone bowl of his wooden-stemmed pipe. He lit it, and they passed the pipe among the three of them, Magpie and Bull Bear laughing each time Eli tried to fill his lungs but coughed.

"Don't keep your lips closed that way," Magpie told him. "When you draw in the smoke, open your mouth and take in some air along with it." He nodded for Eli to try again. "Yes, like that, good," he said.

They were silent as the night deepened. Finally, Magpie said, "I remember my first hunt. It was a small herd like the one today, and I was using a heavy, one-shot gun that burned the black powder and threw iron balls as big as this" — he held up a fist and wiggled the tip of his thumb. "It had a kick, too. It was my father's. I rode my pony up next to this fat cow, running hard, and when I shot *this* way" — Magpie rotated to his left and pretended to fire a rifle — "I fell off my horse *that* way," and he jerked a thumb over his right shoulder. "My father had to ride through that running herd and pick me up."

"Did you kill the cow?" Eli asked.

Magpie nodded, handing the pipe back to Eli. He said, "But you didn't fall off your pony."

"And I wasn't shooting a black-powder rifle," Eli said.

They all lay back and looked up at the sky, the constellations beginning to show themselves. Eli thought of his own father and wondered where he was, whether he was back at the permanent camp with Hornaday or out here somewhere, searching — or even watching. As the outermost star of the Big Dipper's handle twinkled into view, Eli couldn't help but wish his father had been there today to see him take down the cow. But it didn't matter, because he knew that Ulysses understood: to answer for a son, a son was required.

"Some say the buffalo have gone north across the medicine line," Magpie said, "a herd of five thousand. That they're finding others there and getting fat in those mountain meadows, increasing themselves for the day when they can return to this country. Others, from down in the territories, they talk about a hidden cave in the great grasslands of the Staked Plains. A cave where the herds first came from. And how the mouth of that cave has been stopped up so the buffalo can't get out anymore. I talked to a man at the agency. He was a chief from the southern tribes, and he said he knows where this cave is. I would like to believe him. I would like to believe the story about the big herds north of the line. But I can't. My son, if he had lived, would have spent the rest of his life eating the skinny longhorns and the spotted weaklings they want us to raise on the agency land. He would have had to raise vegetables in that dry soil. And wait for shipments of food that never came."

They'd finished smoking now, and all three were lying next to the spit and plucking at the tenderloin with their fingers when Leather Top came riding into camp. Bull Bear got up and took his pony for him, and Leather Top sat down directly and set himself to the task of eating. It wasn't until he was satisfied, belching and wiping his hands on his deerskin pants, that he gave his report, gesturing and pointing and nodding, his face in the firelight like an ancient pumpkin, all creases and shadows.

"He followed the herd until they found a place to graze," Magpie explained. "They're in a box canyon just beyond that little butte, the red one between the two big ones."

"The butte you call the son?" Eli asked.

"Yes, that one."

"What's a box canyon?"

"A canyon with just one way out. Leather Top says there is good grazing inside, and a good pool of water, too. They'll be staying a little while."

Eli was exhausted, his head so full of the day it was blurry inside, and he couldn't seem to focus his thoughts. His belly was distended, but he couldn't stop feeding himself. Even after he'd laid out his bedroll and climbed inside of it, he got up for another try at the backstraps, charred now.

"Tell me," Magpie said. "Is it only the memory of the buffalo that your friend from Washington believes he can save? Or does he think he can save its spirit too by stuffing its dead skin to make it look real?"

"I don't know." Eli shook his head. With the smell of blood in his nose, and with the grease that coated his lips and hands, and with the power of the running herd still moving inside his bones, he couldn't be sure of anything.

"What do they use to fill up their dried skins?" Magpie asked.

"I'm not sure. Sawdust, maybe, as my father said. Cloth and wood. Something, anyway, to take the place of their muscles and bones and guts. Something to give them some shape, make them look like they might still be alive."

Magpie was quiet, thinking. Then he said, "Once the buffaloes are all gone, I'm afraid we'll be following after them. Will they skin us too and fill us up with sawdust and put us inside a building for people to come and look at?" He turned to his brother and spoke for a few moments in their own tongue.

Bull Bear uttered a quick retort. Then he lifted a finger, cocked an ear, and ripped a fart that echoed like a piece of canvas being torn in half.

"My brother," Magpie said, "wants you to know that's for the man who tries to stuff *him* after he's dead."

Eli rocked forward to a sitting position, then fell back on the robe again and closed his eyes. He was too tired to laugh and too old to cry. For weeks now he'd been living his father's life, living inside his father's dream. He knew he was close to reaching the end of his strength, close to waking into some other world entirely in which he was no longer the person he had been, his father's son, mother's son, his brother's brother. A world in which he might no longer recognize himself. He felt like he'd died and come back again, the life ahead of him no longer his own — although he wasn't sure whose it might be. Not his father's, certainly, and not Magpie's either. God's, maybe. Whatever that could mean. He lifted a hand to push the hair out of his face, and his fingers encountered stiff snarls caked with blood and grime from the afternoon of skinning and butchering. He tasted the blood on his fingers, not an unwelcome flavor, earthy and sour. Not unwelcome at all. Then he moved onto his side and made himself comfortable, turning his face toward the heat of the fire.

26
FROM DREAM TO DREAM

He hadn't been sleeping much since they got here, but not because he was nervous or afraid or feeling poorly. The truth was, Danny wasn't tired. He felt as if he had new iron in his bones, sharp little spurs in his blood, and there was a swelling pressure in his muscles that made him want to lift things — heavy things like wagons and tables — just to celebrate his strength. Even better, inside his brain was a clarity and vividness that made him wonder that he'd ever been sick, that his head had ever caused him pain. It was nine o'clock in the evening, but he'd been lying here in bed since eight, sent by his mother who refused to let him stay up any later, despite his begging. She was downstairs in the hotel lobby, talking with May, and would no doubt come up to bed within the hour.

But he couldn't stand it anymore, and he got up and put on his pants and shoes and went over to the window, the one with the fire-ladder. The stars were bright, there was a quarter moon, and below him in the alley was the work he'd been doing for May. He opened the sash and crawled out on the sill, manuevered himself around backward and located a rung with his foot, descended. From the bottom rung, six feet or so above the ground, he dropped.

On their second day in Miles City, Danny had overheard May telling her bookkeeper that she needed to hire someone to fill in the old cistern behind the hotel and demolish the crumbling squatter's cabin next to it. "The cistern's a danger," she'd said, "and that hut is a miserable eyesore."

The next morning Danny had told May *he* wanted to do the work. Although his mother insisted that he lacked the constitution, not to mention the necessary physical strength, May provided the sledgehammer, shovel, and wheelbarrow, and Danny set himself to it, breaking up the stones that formed the tiny cabin's four walls and dumping them load by load into the cistern hole. Ten days later his blisters had turned to calluses, his frail arms and shoulders had thickened, and the aching in his muscles had given way to a quiet, humming vibration. It was as if they were unwilling to be granted even a moment's rest.

Beneath the starlight, Danny inspected his achievement, the old cabin down to its last row of stones now, and the cistern nearly full of busted rock and chunks of mortar. He took a deep breath, filling his chest with the freezing air. He stood up tall. He was proud to be grown up now, or nearly so, proud and happy that he was no longer the sickly boy he'd been, the boy his brother needed to protect and his mother had to cater to, the boy who lived from dream to dream. He walked back to the ladder, jumped to grab its second rung, chinned himself on it, and then did so again — and again and again, his arms burning, until he was ready, finally, to climb up and go back to bed.

27
CALF CREEK

By the time he'd finally ridden into camp, they were all inside their tents and long settled in their bedrolls. It was well past midnight, clear and cold, rime coating every surface. Ulysses rubbed down his horse, staked it out by the creek, and sat down outside his tent with a cup of icy coffee and a few biscuits from McAnna's wagon. He was exhausted, spent, but there was too much to think about even to consider sleeping. He'd been in no mood to give an accounting of himself, either, and when Hornaday approached, the orange glow of his cigar shining in the lens of his spectacles, Ulysses put up a flat hand, told him they would talk in the morning.

"I'll give you the full report," he'd said. "But not now."

"Where's your boy?"

Ulysses waved the man back to his tent. "He's fine."

"What about the Indians?"

"We'll talk after we've had some sleep. Go to bed. Please."

Hornaday spat. "All right then, first thing in the morning," he'd said, and reluctantly walked off.

The day before, when Ulysses had woken at first light to find Eli gone, he hadn't panicked, because he knew what his son was doing, and why. He was frightened, though, shaken, and he punished the gelding cruelly, riding it hard back to the camp by Taylor Creek and then following their trail west toward a line of three buttes.

After Magpie, everything had looked different to him. Whereas before, he'd convinced himself that his instincts were founded in good intentions, as he had ridden that morning for Taylor Creek, he had had nothing but questions. Had he been a coward for not telling Gretta about the Washita? Had she needed to know about it, even if she didn't want to be told? Had he been a fool for thinking he could help a man by putting a face on the worst wrong he'd ever suffered? Ulysses thought of the verse in Luke he had claimed for his own: "And when they bring you unto the synagogues, and unto magistrates, and powers, take ye no thought how or what thing ye shall answer, or what ye shall say: For the Holy Ghost shall teach you in the same hour what ye ought to say." In truth, no words had come when he needed them. Still, Ulysses had no regrets about stepping into the glare of judgment. And if his confession had brought no relief to Magpie — if it was the act of selfishness Magpie said it was, there was nothing to be done about that. He was lighter and freer for having offered it. If only Eli had stayed put, though. And if only Jim Powers had waited longer, another year, before giving up.

His last long climb had given him a view of the hunt unfolding below, his son astride the mottled pony, riding with unbelievable confidence and with so much grace Ulysses knew it was right, this thing he was doing, knew it as surely as he'd known anything — although it wasn't entirely pleasing for all that, making Ulysses feel slight and corruptible. And yet fortunate, too, like an undeserving heir. He waited until the sound of his son's shots came rippling back through the day — one, two, three of them — until the cow had fallen. And then he'd swung around and started back toward Hornaday's camp, in no hurry now, taking his time and letting the worn-out gelding set its own pace, grazing where it chose in the shaded swales and picking its careful way through the rocky, broken places. He felt strangely at ease about his son, not sure just how things would go from here or what might happen, but he was nevertheless at peace. Through the long afternoon and evening, Ulysses's thoughts turned often to Gretta, wondering if she would ever have him back, wondering how she'd find the largeness of heart to forgive him. In his mind he saw her standing in full sun, hair shining, and though he tried to read her lovely face, she was always looking off into some distance, her head tipped back and trying to see.

Ulysses thought, too, about Jim Powers. He remembered their skittery way with each other after the battle, and then the evening at Fort Dodge, a month or so later, drinking with the old priest there late into the night, and how it all came out then, the whole story. When everything had been said, and they were all three sitting silent at the table, more or less drunk and hardly knowing where to look, Ulysses surprised himself by asking the old man for Communion. "I'm no Catholic," he'd said, or something to that effect. "I'm hardly anything, but I think I could use it, I think it might help me." The priest thought long and hard, slumped in his chair and scratching at his white skull, his hooded eyes drooping. Finally he shook his head and told Ulysses he wasn't permitted to offer sacraments to somebody outside of the Church. But then he reached down into his bag and pulled out two twists of tobacco, right from the store, uncut, and he pushed them across the table. "We'll do it like this instead," he told the two soldiers. "Cut off a piece and have a go at it, both of you. And give me a piece too." Which is just what they did. And it was the tin tag on that plug of tobacco that for years seemed to help Ulysses — at least help him some — in warding off the guilt.

There was no way of knowing how Jim sorted out his life with God, or failed to — although Ulysses had tried to learn what he could from Jim's widow. They'd talked at length, sitting in her front room, and then again that night in his bed, she having come to him unbidden, crawling in close against him and drawing out the pain of his secrets, taking hold of the tin turtle on his chest and insisting that Ulysses start his life over again, with her, insisting that she understood him in a way his wife could not. That she would be good to him. The toughest part had been turning down the soft warmth of her, which she offered freely.

Now, at dawn, as the first specks of light appeared in the ceiling of his tent, Ulysses got up and went straight to Hornaday, having decided to tell the man only as much of the truth as he asked for and only those untruths that were necessary. Hornaday listened keenly, puffing away, as Ulysses explained how he'd sent Eli back to Miles City, where he would catch a train home to his mother. That the boy had been gone from home long enough.

"He knows his way down there?"

"We rode south a long distance yesterday. Not much farther and he'll hit the Yellowstone. It's downriver from there." Ulysses winced, uncomfortable with the lie. "Don't worry, he'll turn in the mare and the rifle at Keogh. And no need to pay him, since he cut out early."

Hornaday waved a hand, dismissing this. "Did you find them?" he asked.

"The Indians, yes. Caught up to them the night before last, by Taylor Creek. Feasting on your bull."

The man uncrossed his legs and leaned forward, elbows on knees. He took a deep pull on his cigar. "Well, let's hear it," he said.

"There were three of them. Cheyenne. And one speaks English just fine. I explained what you're trying to do, about the museum, everything, but I can't say how they thought about it or what they'll do next. Mostly, they're just hungry. My guess is, they'll be heading south, back to the reservation."

"You see anything more of that herd?" Hornaday asked.

"No," Ulysses told him.

"Well, it doesn't matter anyway." Hornaday leaned over and stubbed out his cigar on the ground. He sighed. "I had McNaney scouting the country to the north and west the last two days, all through the breaks up there. He talked to the ranchers, and to their hands too. There's nothing up that way. Nothing at all. And this afternoon a couple of Phillips's cowboys stopped over. They're on fall roundup, riding the tributaries of both the Big and Little Dry, which cover the best grazing between the Missouri and the Yellowstone. And of course you've been south and west. I think that herd we saw, if you want to call eight animals a herd — and that's before we took three of them — I think that's all there is left in this part of the world. As you know, my resources are limited. We're going to break camp tomorrow."

"Maybe we should give it another couple of days."

"And then there's McAnna," Hornaday said. "He's worried about the weather. Wind shifted east this morning, and his bad hip's got him convinced the pressure's falling, a storm on the way. Look, the season's getting late. We don't need an early blizzard catching us out here. It's too dangerous."

Hornaday looked up suddenly, his eyes scanning to the southwest. Ulysses looked, too. He could feel riders in the ground beneath him.

There were two of them coming over the nearest rise, and a third horse trailing. They were heading straight in, right toward camp. Ulysses stood up, watching them come on. It was Eli — *Thank God* — and Magpie. Soon the others were taking notice. Bayliss emerged from his tent, rifle in hand, and behind him Gumfield ducked out, too, squinting. Two of the troopers scrambled up from the creek, shaving soap on their faces. McNaney sat on a rock by McAnna's wagon. Still mounted, Magpie and Eli walked their ponies right up to the fire, the buckskin mare following on a lead rope behind them. Eli's hat was gone, and his hair was matted on his forehead. His coat and pants were black with dried blood and viscera. His face was dark and old, a different face entirely.

"Here's your son," Magpie said. "Do you have my pouch?"

Ulysses laid a hand on the place inside his coat where he kept it.

"We'll trade, then," Magpie said.

In the corner of his eye Ulysses saw movement and turned — Bayliss, coming forward — and he gave the man a look. Bayliss backed away. Ulysses loosened his coat and lifted out the beaded pouch, removed its strap from around his neck. Magpie's hands were steady as he reached for it, though an unmistakable pulse beat in his jaw. He looped the strap over his head and the pouch fell against the front of his chest where the blue and yellow beads winked and glimmered in the new sun. He looked over at Eli.

"Is your belly full?" he asked.

Eli laughed. Then he jumped down and handed the reins of his pony to Magpie and freed the mare from its lead.

"Remember what to tell your father," Magpie said before clucking his tongue and leaning his pony around. The animal gave a little hop then started out in a slow canter that gave way to a gallop at the edge of camp.

"I'm going to get these clothes off and clean myself up," Eli said, and together the two of them walked past Bayliss, who was scowling and rubbing his big stomach, and then Hornaday, who watched them hard through his spectacles, hands on his hips, unlit cigar jutting from his mouth. The others were retiring, Gumfield back into his tent, McNaney and the troopers to McAnna's wagon and breakfast.

They staked the mare with the other horses then walked down to a bend in the creek where the water pooled deep, and there on a spit of sand Eli removed his boots and stripped off his clothes — coat, shirt, pants — the cloth so stiff with dirt and dried gore that you could have propped them up and used them for hat stands. Ulysses stripped off his own clothes, too; it had been weeks since he'd bathed. In the presence of his son's supple strength, he was aware of the stringiness of his own body, sinewy where it used to be full, and bones showing through everywhere, at the shoulders and ribs and elbows and knees. He was aware of the ugliness of a missing ear. He was an old man now, and had never seen it coming.

They waded in up to their knees and waited for a minute, then up to their thighs and waited a bit longer, then finally and painfully to their groins, the water so cold it cut them in half. They slid forward and swam to the middle of the current, splashing and shouting from the discomfort of it, and stood for a time on the smooth pebbles, water to their armpits. The cold made the day seem brighter and bluer than before. Eli dove and sputtered, dove again and stood there, working his fingers into his hair, raking out the blood and the snarls, his face shining.

Ulysses smiled at him. "What is it you're supposed to tell me?" he asked.

"They're heading back to the agency," Eli said. "They're finished hunting for the year."

"Is that all?"

His voice shaking from the cold, Eli explained about the herd Leather Top followed to the box canyon, down beneath the smallest of the three buttes, a herd of more than a dozen animals, including one large, curly-haired bull. And how the grazing there was so good it would keep them for days.

They stayed in the river as long as they were able to stand it, up to their chests in water too numbingly cold to believe, Ulysses reluctant to lose this moment with his son, and entertaining a strange illusion he had — brought on by the cold, no doubt — that if he allowed himself to slip beneath the surface, submerge completely, he would come up again whole. Contented. Ageless.

He gathered all the air his lungs could hold and let the water have him.

28
THE COMING STORM

Late October and the wait had gotten long, though with every day that passed, Gretta was more able at least to imagine life without him, and stronger in her conviction that all was going to be well.

She and Danny had finished the noon-meal dishes when May asked if they wouldn't mind doing one more job before they started preparing supper. The garden, of course, had been harvested weeks ago — more than a month — but all the vines and dead stalks were still there, browning and rotting. Would they please pull them up and haul them over to the compost heap? "If we don't do it today, it might be too late," May said. "You smelled snow in the air this morning, didn't you? I know I did."

Outside, Gretta began with the cucumber vines, yanking them one by one from the tough gray soil, then moving to the ropy tangle left by the melons. She made a large pile at the edge of the garden as Danny moved up and down the rows of beans and peas. The tomato plants were sprawled dark and twisting on crossed wooden stakes, which had been driven into the earth at an angle and then tied together where they intersected, a couple dozen of these set down in rows that reminded Gretta of the fish-drying racks along Denmark's coast. She tore the stalks from the frames then ripped out the roots, which made a quiet gasp coming free. The crossed stakes too had to come up. They were fixed hard in the soil, and Gretta's hands kept slipping on the wood. She wasn't careful where she grabbed, and when she sliced her palm on a splinter, she cried out.

"You all right?" Danny called. He was standing at the compost pile, hands on his hips. She couldn't help noticing the color in his cheeks and the way he'd been filling out from the work he'd done for May. His pants, which had always hung on him like rags on a scarecrow, rippling and flapping as he moved, were almost snug now. He hadn't complained about headaches since leaving Sloan's Crossing, and though she knew it was too soon to hope, she couldn't recall the last time he'd been well for this long.

She said, "Maybe you could go ask May if she has a pair of gloves I could wear."

Gretta's hand was bleeding, but the cut was shallow, a flap of topskin lying open against the pad of her palm. As Danny ran inside, she bent to pull up the next stake. Straightening, she sensed a presence, a darkness against the sky.

He didn't look as tired or bent or as filthy as she'd expected he would. Thinner, yes, but hard and strong, with no extra flesh beneath his chin. His hair was cut short and he was shaved clean, his lips familiar, the bottom one fuller than the top. His pale eyes were clear.

What he said was "You're beautiful," his words causing her to feel the sweat on her face and think of the stains on her work-dress. He didn't smile, but the strength in his eyes made her step back and grab hold of a tomato stake for balance.

He walked right up and stood so close that his white breath dissipated in the air around her. His lungs seemed to be working hard, as if he'd been out chopping wood. He took her hand, the one that was bleeding, and lifted it to have a look, but she pulled away, saying, "No, it's all right." Wasting no time, she opened his coat, unbuttoned his wool shirt, and spread the top of his union suit.

493

His grandmother's brass chain glowed dully against his white skin and the gray, wiry hairs on his chest. She set her jaw and pulled on the chain, yanking it hard enough to break it from his neck — except it didn't break, and he resisted the snap of it, his eyes following hers to the dancing tin turtle that swung out then rocked to a stillness. She leaned in, making sure of the green color against the yellow background, and the telltale nick on one side, before tucking it back in against his chest and allowing him to wrap his arms around her.

"Do you need some help finishing up out here?" he asked.

But she was trying to find her way through all of the campfires and long rides, all the greasy meat, through all the gunpowder and sweat to his old smell. And when she finally got a hint of it, she said, "Yes," her voice the smallest breath against the skin of his neck.

He was holding her like that, his fingers gripping her head, when glancing up he saw Danny at the back door of the hotel, pausing there, older now and strangely sure of himself, and then Eli, too, kneeling at the edge of the garden, Ulysses unaware of the picture he and his wife made, unaware that his elder son, in seeing them together like that, was overwhelmed with a mix of joy and sadness, the strength going out of him and the ground rising to meet his elbows.

And so it came to this, Eli behind the Drover House in Miles City, Montana, lying on his back against the cool ground, every muscle and fiber relaxed, his arms and legs spread wide. Then a shadow fell, and his brother occupied briefly the space above him, smiling before he disappeared.

Danny? You're that big now?

The first snowflakes arrived, one stinging his cheek, just beneath his right eye, another his chin, a third his forehead, the sky suddenly full of them, Eli searching for the point from which the swirl originated, the effect so dizzying that he closed his eyes. And now he saw the snow falling thick in the high country, Magpie and Bull Bear and Leather Top well camped near a running stream, a roof of cedars above them, an orange fire blazing, real meat sizzling and crackling on spits, the men wrapped in winter robes and telling stories of their hunt. And laughing. He saw, too, the herd that Hornaday had found in the box canyon, the gathering of twenty or more from which a bull had been taken, large and curly-haired, and he watched as the rest of them — brown cows, yellow calves, and a young black bull — moved sure-footed into a coulee down inside the breaks, a place to wait out the storm.

ACKNOWLEDGMENTS

Thanks first to my wife, Kathy, for being with me in this from the very beginning, and thanks to the next generation — Hope, Nick, Jesse — for all the joy. Thanks to PJ Mark for believing. Thanks to Kathy Pories for making this a better book, and to everyone else at Algonquin for their good work on its behalf. Thanks to my parents and grandparents for granting me a look at the old times. And thanks to God for allowing me to be here. Still.

AUTHOR'S NOTE

The Hornaday expedition of 1886 and the Washita incident are historical events, and I have tried to remain true to the spirit of both, even as I invented for the sake of my narrative. The novel's characters are all products of my imagination, including these few — William T. Hornaday, Magpie of the Southern Cheyennes, the hunter Jim Mc-Naney, the camp cook McAnna, and the expedition sergeant, Bayliss — who are inspired by real people. Of the many books I read while preparing to write this novel, the following were especially helpful:

The Extermination of the American Bison, by William Temple Hornaday
Forty Miles a Day on Beans and Hay, by Don Rickey, Jr.
The Horse Soldier, Volume II, by Randy Steffen
Life in Custer's Cavalry: Diaries and Letters of

Albert and Jennie Barnitz, 1867–1868,
edited by Robert M. Utley
Mr. Hornaday's War, by Stefan Bechtel
Neither Wolf nor Dog, by Kent Nerburn
The Time of the Buffalo, by Tom McHugh
*Washita Memories: Eyewitness Views of
Custer's Attack on Black Kettle's Village,* by
Richard G. Hardorff
The Ways of my Grandmothers, by Beverly
Hungry Wolf